ALEX

PIERRE LEMAITRE

ALEX

TRANSLATED FROM THE FRENCH
BY FRANK WYNNE

MacLehose Press
New York • London

MacLehose Press
An imprint of Quercus
New York • London

© 2011 by Éditions Albin Michel, Paris
English translation © 2013 by Frank Wynne
First published in the United States by Quercus in 2013

ISBN 978-1-62365-124-4

Library of Congress Control Number: 2013937737

Manufactured in the United States

10 9 8 7 6 5 4 3

www.quercus.com

For Pascaline

To Gérald, for our friendship

1

Alex is in seventh heaven. She has been trying on wigs and hair extensions for more than an hour now, hesitating, leaving, coming back, trying them on again. She could spend all afternoon here.

She stumbled on this little shop on the boulevard de Strasbourg by pure chance three or four years ago. She wasn't really looking, but out of curiosity she went inside and was so astonished seeing herself as a redhead, seeing herself completely transformed, that she bought the wig on the spot.

Alex can wear pretty much anything because she is truly stunning. It wasn't always that way; it happened in her teens. Before that she had been a scrawny, rather ugly little girl. But when she finally blossomed, it was like a tidal wave, like a computer morphing program on fast forward; in a few short months Alex became a devastating young woman. Perhaps because by then everyone—particularly Alex—had given up hope that she would ever be beautiful, she has never really thought of herself as beautiful. Even now.

For example, it had never occurred to her that she could wear a red wig. It had been a revelation. She couldn't believe how different she looked. Wigs seemed so superficial, and yet the moment she first put one on, she felt her whole life had changed.

In the end she hardly ever wore it, that first wig. As soon as she got it home she realized that it looked tawdry, cheap. She tossed it. Not into the garbage, but into the bottom drawer of her dresser. Every now and again she would take it out, try it on, gaze at herself in the mirror. Though it was indeed hideous, the sort of thing that screamed "tacky nylon fright-wig," what Alex saw when she looked in the mirror kindled a hope in which she wanted to believe. And so she went back to the shop on the boulevard de Strasbourg and lingered over elegant, high-quality wigs that were a little beyond the means of an agency nurse. But they looked astonishingly real. And she took the plunge.

At first it wasn't easy; it still isn't—it takes nerve. For a shy, inse-cure girl like Alex, just getting up the nerve could take half a day. Putting on the right makeup, finding the perfect outfit, the match-ing shoes and handbag (well, rummaging through the closet to find something that might match, since she can't afford to buy a new outfit every time . . .). But then comes the moment when you step out into the street, and you're someone else. Not entirely, but almost. And though it's hardly earth-shattering, it passes the time, especially when you're not expecting much from life.

Alex prefers wigs that make a statement, wigs that say *I know what you're thinking*, or *I'm not just a pretty face, I'm a math genius too*. The wig she's wearing today says *You won't find me on Facebook*.

As she picks up a wig called "Urban Shock" she glances out through the shop window, and she sees the man. He is standing on the far side of the street pretending to be waiting for someone or something. This is the third time in two hours she has seen him. He is following her. She now realizes that he must be. Her first thought is "Why me?," as though she could understand why a man might follow any other girl, but not her. As though she didn't forever have men looking at her, on the bus, in the street. In shops. Alex attracts attention from men of all ages. It's one of the benefits of being thirty.

And yet every time it happens, she feels surprised. *There are much prettier girls out there than me.* Alex is chronically insecure, crippled by self-doubt. She has been since she was a child. Until her teens, she had a terrible stammer. Even now she stammers when she's nervous.

She doesn't recognize the man; she has never seen him before—with a body like that, she would remember. What's more, it seems strange, a guy of fifty following a girl of thirty . . . It's not that she's ageist—far from it—she's just surprised.

Alex looks down at the wigs, pretends to hesitate, then wanders over to the other side of the shop, from where she has a good view of the street. From the cut of his clothes you can tell he was once an athlete of some sort, a heavyweight. Stroking a platinum-blonde wig, she tries to work out when she first noticed him. She remembers seeing him in the *métro*; their eyes met for a moment—though long enough for her to notice the smile intended for her, a smile clearly meant to be warm and winning. What troubles her about him is the obsessiveness in his eyes. And his lips, so thin as to be almost non-existent. She felt instinctively suspicious, as though somehow all thin-lipped people are hiding something, some unspeakable secret, some terrible vice. And his high, domed forehead. Unfortunately, she didn't really have time to study his eyes. The eyes never lie, Alex believes, and it is by their eyes that she judges people. Obviously, in the *métro*, with a guy like that, she hadn't wanted to linger.

Discreetly, almost imperceptibly, she turned so that her back was to him, rummaging in her bag for her iPod. She put on "Nobody's Child," and as she did she wondered if she hadn't seen him hanging around outside her building the day before, maybe two days ago. It's vague—she can't be sure; the memory might be clearer if she turned to look again, but she doesn't want to lead him on. What she does know is that two hours after seeing him in the *métro*, she spotted him as she turned again onto the boulevard de Strasbourg. On a whim she had decided to go back to the shop and try on the midlength auburn wig with bangs, and as she turned around, she spotted him a little way away, saw him stop dead and pretend to look at something in the window . . . of a women's dress shop. It was pointless for him to pretend . . .

Alex sets down the wig. For no reason her hands are trembling. She's being ridiculous. The guy fancies her; he's following her, thinks he's in with a chance—he's hardly going to attack her in the street. Alex shakes her head as though trying to make up her mind, and when she looks out at the street again, the man has disappeared. She leans first one way, then the other, but there's no one; he has gone. The relief she feels seems somehow disproportionate. I'm just being silly, she thinks again, as her breathing begins to return to normal. In the doorway of the shop, she can't help but stop and check the street again. It almost feels as though it's his absence now that worries her.

Alex checks her watch, looks up at the sky. The weather is mild, and there's at least an hour of daylight still. She doesn't feel like heading home. She needs to stop off and buy food. She tries to remember what she's got in the fridge. She's always been a bit lax about grocery shopping. She tends to focus all her energy on her work, her comfort (Alex is a little obsessive-compulsive), and—though she's reluctant to admit it—on clothes and shoes. Plus handbags. And wigs. She wishes her love life had worked out differently; it's something of a touchy subject. Her love life is a disaster area. She hoped, she waited, and eventually she gave up. These days, she thinks about it as little as possible. But she is careful not to allow regret to turn into takeout and nights in front of the television, careful not to put on weight, not to let herself go. Though she's single, she rarely feels alone. She has lots of projects that are important to her, and they keep her busy. Her love life might be a train wreck, but that's life. And it's easier now that she's resigned herself to being alone. In spite of her loneliness, Alex tries to live a normal life, to enjoy her little pleasures. It consoles her to think that she can indulge herself, that like everyone else, she has the *right* to indulge herself. Tonight, for example, she's decided to treat herself to dinner at Mont-Tonnerre on the rue de Vaugirard.

She arrives a little early. It's her second time. The first was a week ago, and the staff obviously remember the attractive redhead who was dining alone. Tonight they greet her like a regular, the waiters jostling to serve her, flirting awkwardly with the pretty customer. She smiles at them, effortlessly charms them. She asks for the same table, her back to the terrace, facing into the room; she orders the same half bottle of Alsatian ice wine. She sighs. Alex loves food, so much so that she has to be careful. Her weight keeps fluctuating, but she has learned to control it. Sometimes she will put on twenty or thirty pounds, become virtually unrecognizable, but two months later she's back to her original weight. It's something she won't be able to get away with a few years from now.

She takes out her book and asks for an extra fork to prop it open with while she's eating. Sitting facing her is the guy with light-brown hair she saw here last week. He's having dinner with friends. For the moment there are only two of them, but it's clear from their talk that they are expecting others to turn up soon. He spotted her the moment she stepped into the restaurant. She pretends not to notice him staring at her intently. He will stare at her all night, even when the rest of his friends show up, and they launch into their endless banter about work, about girls, about women, taking turns telling stories that make them sound good. All the while, he will be glancing at her. He's not bad looking—forty, forty-five maybe—and he was clearly handsome as a young man; he drinks a little too much, which explains his tragic face. A face that stirs something in Alex.

She drinks her coffee, and—her one concession—as she leaves, she gives him a look; she does it expertly. A fleeting glance, the sort of look Alex does perfectly. Seeing the longing in his eyes, for a split second she feels a twinge of pain in the pit of her stomach, an intimation of sadness. At moments like this Alex never articulates what she is feeling, certainly not to herself. Her life is a series of frozen images, a spool of film that has snapped in the projector—it is impossible for her to rewind, to refashion her story, to find new words. The next time she has dinner here, she might stay a little later, and he might be waiting for her outside when she leaves—who knows? Alex knows. Alex knows all too well how these things go. It's always the same story. Her fleeting encounters with men never become love stories; this is a part of the film she's seen many times, a part she remembers. That's just the way it is.

It is completely dark now and the night is warm. A bus has just pulled up. She quickens her step, the driver sees her in the rearview mirror and waits. She runs for the bus but, just as she's about to get on, changes her mind, decides to walk a little way. She signals to the driver, who gives a regretful shrug, as if to say *Oh well, such is life.* He opens the bus door anyway.

"There won't be another bus after me. I'm the last one tonight..."

Alex smiles, thanks him with a wave. It doesn't matter. She'll walk the rest of the way. She'll take the rue Falguière and then the rue Labrouste.

She's been living near the Porte de Vanves for three months now. She moves around a lot. Before this, she lived near Porte de Clignancourt and before that on the rue du Commerce. Most people hate moving, but for Alex it's a need. She enjoys it. Maybe because, as with the wigs, it feels like she's changing her life. It's a recurring theme. One day she'll change her life.

A little way in front of her, a white van pulls onto the pavement to park. To get by, Alex has to squeeze between the van and the building. She senses a presence, a man; she has no time to turn. A fist slams between her shoulder blades, leaving her breathless. She loses her balance, topples forward, her forehead banging violently against the van with a dull clang; she drops everything she's carrying, her hands flailing desperately to find something to catch hold of— they find nothing. The man grabs her hair, but the wig comes off in his hand. He curses, a word she can't quite make out, then viciously yanks her real hair with one hand, and with the other punches her in the stomach hard enough to stun a bull. Alex doesn't have time to scream; she doubles over and vomits. The man has to be very powerful, because he manages to flip her like a piece of paper so that she is facing him. His arm slides around her waist, pulling her against him while he stuffs a wad of tissue paper into her mouth and down her throat. It's him: the man she saw in the *métro*, in the street, outside the shop. It's him. For a fraction of a second they look each other in the eye. She tries to struggle, but he's got her arms in a tight grip; there's nothing she can do, he's too strong; he pushes her down, her knees give way, and she falls onto the floor of the van. He lashes out, a vicious kick to the small of the back, sending Alex sprawling into the van, the floor grazing her cheek. He climbs in behind her, forcibly turns her over and punches her in the face. He hits her so hard . . . This guy really wants to hurt her, he wants to kill her—this is what's going through Alex's mind as she feels the punch. Her skull slams against the floor of the van and bounces, and she feels a shooting pain in the back of her head—the occiput, that's what it's called, Alex thinks, the occiput. But apart from this word, the only thing she can think is I don't want to die, not like this, not now. Huddled in a fetal position, mouth full of vomit, she feels her arms wrenched hard behind her back and tightly bound, then her ankles. I don't want to die now, Alex thinks. The door of the van slams shut, the engine roars into life, the van pulls away from the pavement with a screech. I don't want to die now.

Alex is dazed, but aware of what is happening to her. She is crying, choking on her tears. Why me? Why me?

I don't want to die. Not now.

2

When he called, Divisionnaire Le Guen gave him no choice.

"I don't give a shit about your scruples, Camille, you're seriously pissing me off. I haven't got anyone else, and I mean anyone, so I'm sending a car for you, and you're fucking going!"

He paused a beat, then, for good measure, he added: "And stop being such a pain in the ass."

Then he hung up. This is Le Guen's style. Impulsive. Usually Camille takes no notice of him. Usually he knows how to handle the divisionnaire.

The difference this time is that it's a kidnapping.

And Camille wants nothing to do with it. He's made his position clear: there aren't many cases he won't handle, but kidnapping is top of the list. Not since Irène died. His wife had collapsed in the street, eight months pregnant, and been rushed to the hospital; then she'd been kidnapped. She was never seen alive again. It destroyed Camille. *Distraught* doesn't begin to describe it; he was traumatized. He had spent whole days paralyzed, hallucinating. When he became delusional, he had had to be institutionalized.

He was shunted from psychiatric clinics to convalescent homes. It was a miracle he was alive. No one expected it. In the months he spent on sick leave from the *brigade criminelle*, everyone had wondered whether he would ever show his face again. And when finally he came back, the strange thing was that he was exactly the same as before Irène's death, just a little older. Since then, he's only taken on minor cases: crimes of passion, brawls between colleagues, murder between neighbors. Cases where the deaths are behind you, not in front. No kidnappings. Camille wants his dead well and truly dead, corpses with no comeback.

"Give me a break," Le Guen has told him more than once—he's doing the best he can for Camille. "You can't exactly avoid the living; there's no future in it. Might as well be an undertaker."

"But . . . ," Camille said, "that's exactly what we are!"

They have known each other for twenty years, and they like each other. Le Guen is a Camille who gave up on the streets. Camille is a Le Guen who gave up on power. The obvious differences between them are two pay grades and 140 pounds. That, and about eleven inches. Put like that it sounds preposterous, and it's true that when they're together they look like cartoon characters. Le Guen is not very tall, but Camille is positively stunted. He sees the world from the viewpoint of a thirteen-year-old. This is something he gets from his mother, the artist Maud Verhœven. Her paintings are in the collections of a dozen museums abroad. She was an inspired artist and an incorrigible smoker who lived in a cloud of cigarette smoke, a permanent halo; it is impossible to imagine her without that blue haze. It is to her that Camille owes his two distinguishing traits. The artist left him with an exceptional talent for drawing; the inveterate smoker left him with fetal hypotrophy, which meant he never grew taller than four foot eleven.

He has rarely met anyone he could look down on; he has spent his life looking up at people. His height goes beyond a mere handicap. At the age of twenty it's an appalling humiliation, at thirty it's a curse, but from the outset it's clearly a destiny. The sort of handicap that makes a person resort to using long words.

With Irène, Camille's height became a strength. Irène had made him taller on the inside. Camille had never felt so . . . he gropes for a word. Without Irène, he's lost for words.

Le Guen on the other hand qualifies as colossal. No one knows how much he weighs; he refuses to discuss it. Some people claim he's at least 260 pounds, others say 290, and there are some people who think it's more. It doesn't matter: Le Guen is gargantuan, an elephantine man with hamster cheeks, but because he has bright eyes brimming with intelligence—no one can explain this, men are reluctant to admit it, but most women are agreed—the division-naire is a very attractive man. Go figure.

Camille is accustomed to Le Guen's tantrums; he's not impressed by histrionics. They've known each other too long. Calmly he picks up the telephone and calls the divisionnaire back.

"Listen up, Jean: I'll go . . . I'll take on this kidnapping of yours. But the fucking second Morel gets back, you're putting him on it, because . . ." he takes a breath, then hammers home every syl-lable with a calmness that is filled with menace, "I'm not taking the case!"

Camille Verhœven never shouts. Or very rarely. He is a man of authority. He may be short, bald, and scrawny, but this is something that everyone knows. Camille is a razor blade. And Le Guen is care-ful not to say anything. Malicious gossip has it that Camille wears the trousers in their relationship. It's not something they joke about. Camille hangs up.

"Fuck!"

This is all he needs. It's not as if they get kidnapping cases every day; this isn't Mexico City. Why couldn't it have happened some other day, when he was on another case, on leave, somewhere, any-where! Camille slams his fist on the table. But he does so slowly, because he's a reasonable man. He doesn't like outbursts, even in other people.

Time is short. He gets to his feet, grabs his coat and hat, and takes the stairs two at a time. Camille walks with a heavy tread. Before Irène died, he walked with a spring in his step. His wife used

to say, "You hop like a bird. I always think you're about to take off."
It has been four years since Irène died.

The car pulls up in front of him. Camille clambers inside.

"What's your name again?"

"Alexandre, bos—"

The driver bites his tongue. Everyone knows Camille hates to be
called "boss." Says it sounds like a TV police show. This is Camille's
style: he is very cut-and-dried, a pacifist with a brutal streak. Sometimes he gets carried away. He was always a bit of an oddball, but
age and widowhood have made him touchy and irritable. Deep
down, he's angry. Irène used to say, "Darling, why are you always so
angry?" Drawing himself up to his four foot eleven, and laying the
irony on thick, Camille would say, "You're right. I mean, what have
I got to be angry about?" Hothead and stoic, thug and tactician,
people rarely get the measure of Camille on first meeting. Rarely
appreciate him. This might also be because he's not exactly cheerful.
Camille doesn't like himself very much.

Since going back to work three years ago, Camille has taken
responsibility for all the rookies, a blessing for the duty sergeants,
who don't want to be bothered with them. What Camille wants,
since his own imploded, is to rebuild a loyal team.

He glances at Alexandre. Whatever he looks like, it's not an
Alexandre, but he's alexandrine enough to be four heads taller
than Camille, which isn't much of a feat, and he set off without
waiting for Camille to give the order, which at least shows he's got
some balls.

Alexandre drives like a maniac; he loves driving, and it shows.
The GPS system seems to be having trouble catching up with him.
Alexandre wants to show the commandant he's a good driver—the
siren wails; the car speeds assertively through streets, intersections,
boulevards; Camille's feet dangle eight inches off the floor, his right
hand gripping his seat belt. In less than fifteen minutes they're at
the crime scene. It is 9:50 p.m. Though it's not particularly late,
Paris already seems peaceful, half-asleep, not the sort of city where
people are kidnapped. "A woman," according to the witness who

called the police, clearly in a state of shock, "kidnapped, before my very eyes." The man couldn't believe it. Then again, it's not exactly a common occurrence.

"You can drop me here," Camille says.

Camille gets out of the car, straightens his cap; the driver leaves. They're at the end of the street, about fifty yards from the police tape. Camille walks the rest of the way. When there's time, he always likes to view the problem from a distance—that's how he likes to work. The first view is crucial, so it's best to take in the whole crime scene; before you know it you're caught up in countless facts, in details, and there's no way back. This is the official reason he gives for getting out a hundred yards from where a crowd is standing waiting for him. The other reason, the real reason, is that he doesn't want to be here.

As he walks toward the police cars, their lights strobing the buildings, he tries to work out exactly what he is feeling.

His heart is hammering.

He feels like shit. He'd give ten years of his life to be somewhere else.

But however slowly and reluctantly he walks, he's here now.

This is more or less how it happened four years ago. On the street where he lived, which looks a little like this one. Irène wasn't there. She was due to give birth to a little boy in a few days. She should have been at the maternity unit. Camille raced around like a madman, searched everywhere for her, did everything he could that night to find her . . . but none of it changed a thing. When they found her, she was dead.

Camille's nightmare had begun in a moment just like this one. This is why his heart is pounding fit to burst, why his ears are ringing. His guilt, the guilt he thought was dormant, has awakened. He feels physically sick. A voice inside him screams *Get away*; another voice says *Stay and face it*; his chest feels tight. Camille is afraid he might pass out. Instead, he moves one of the barriers and steps into the taped-off area. From a distance, the duty officer acknowledges him with a wave. Even those who don't know Commandant Verhœven personally know him by sight. It's hardly surprising. Even if he wasn't some sort of living legend, they know about his height. And his past.

"Oh, it's you."

"You sound disappointed."

Flustered, Louis starts to panic.

"No, no, not at all."

Camille smiles. He's always had a knack for winding Louis up. Louis Mariani has been his assistant for a very long time, and he knows him as well as if he'd knitted the man himself.

At first, after Irène was murdered, after Camille's breakdown, Louis used to visit him at the clinic. Camille hadn't talked much. Sketching, which until then had been a hobby, suddenly became his chief, in fact his only, activity. Pictures, drawings, and sketches lay in heaps around a room that Camille had otherwise left institutionally spartan. Louis would make a place for himself, and they would sit, one staring out at the trees, the other down at his feet. They said many things in that silence, but it was no match for conversation. They simply couldn't find the words. Then one day, without warning, Camille said he would rather be left alone, that he didn't want to drag Louis into his grief. "A miserable policeman isn't exactly riveting company," he said. It was tough on both of them, being separated. But time passed. By the time things had improved, it was too late. After grief, all that remains is barren.

They haven't seen a lot of each other for a long time now; they run into each other at meetings, briefings, that kind of thing. Louis hasn't changed much. If he lives to be a hundred, he'll die young—some people are like that. And he's as dapper as ever. Camille once said to him, "If I was dressed for a wedding, I'd still look like a tramp next to you." Louis, it has to be said, is rich: filthy rich. His personal fortune is like Le Guen's weight: nobody knows what it amounts to, but everyone knows it's fat and getting fatter. Louis could live off his private income for four or five generations. Instead, he works as a policeman for the *brigade criminelle*. He completed an assortment of degrees he didn't need and has such a breadth of knowledge that Camille has never caught him out. There's no denying Louis is a queer fish.

He smiles. It's weird, Camille just showing up like this without warning.

"It's over there," he says, nodding toward the police tape.

Camille hurries after the younger man. Though he's not so young anymore.

"How old are you, Louis?"

Louis turns.

"Thirty-four. Why?"

"No reason. Just curious."

Camille realizes they're a stone's throw from the Bourdelle Museum. He can clearly remember the face of *Hercules the Archer*, the hero triumphing over monsters. Camille has never sculpted—he never had the physique for it—and he hasn't painted for a long time now, but he still sketches. Even after his long bout of depression, he can't stop. It's part of who he is; he has always got a pencil in his hand—it's his way of looking at the world.

"You ever seen *Hercules the Archer* at the Musée Bourdelle?"

"Yeah," Louis says and looks confused. "You sure it's not in the Musée d'Orsay?"

"Still an irritating smart-ass, then."

Louis smiles. Coming from Camille, this kind of quip means *You know I care about you*. It means *Jesus, time flies, how long have we known each other?* Mostly, it means *We haven't seen a lot of each other since I killed Irène, have we?* So it's weird the two of them being at the same crime scene. Camille suddenly feels the need to explain:

"I'm filling in for Morel. Le Guen didn't have anyone else, so he put me on the case as a temporary measure."

Louis gives a shrug to say he understands, but he has his doubts. The idea of Commandant Verhœven "filling in" on a case is improbable.

"Call Le Guen," Camille goes on. "I need forensics down here now. Given how late it is, we're not going to get much done, but we have to try."

Louis nods and fishes out his cell phone. He agrees with Camille. You can look at a crime like this two ways: from the kidnapper's point of view, or from the victim's. The kidnapper's presumably long gone, but the victim may have lived in the area, might have been snatched near home, and it's not just what happened to Irène that makes both men think this; it's the statistics.

Rue Falguière. They're surrounded by sculptors tonight. They move slowly, walking down the middle of the street, which has been taped off at both ends. Camille glances up at the buildings. All the lights are on; they are tonight's reality TV show.

"We've got a witness, just the one," says Louis, turning off his cell. "And we know the position of the vehicle used in the kidnapping. The forensics boys from *l'identité judiciaire* will be here any minute."

And here they come. The barriers are pushed back, and Louis indicates the gap on the pavement between two cars. Four forensics officers, laden with equipment, pile out of the van.

"Where is he?" Camille says. The commandant is edgy. It's obvious he doesn't want to be here. His cell phone vibrates—it's the procureur.

"No, sir, by the time the call came through to the squad from the fifteenth arrondissement, it was far too late to start setting up road blocks."

It's a curt, almost insolent tone to take with a procureur. Louis discreetly moves away. He can understand Camille's frustration. If the victim had been a minor, there would already have been an amber alert, but the victim is an adult woman. They'll have to manage on their own.

"I'm afraid what you're asking will be difficult, sir," says Camille. His voice has dropped almost an octave, and he's speaking too slowly. Anyone who knows Camille would recognize the sign.

"You have to understand, sir, that as I'm talking to you there are . . ." He looks up. ". . . I'd say a hundred rubberneckers staring out of their windows. The teams manning the police tape will have to inform another two or three hundred. But, obviously, if you've got any ideas about how to stop news getting out, I'm all ears."

Louis smiles to himself. Classic Verhœven. Louis is overjoyed because it means Camille hasn't changed. He's aged a lot in four years, but he's still completely up front. And a public menace as far as his superiors are concerned.

"Of course, *monsieur le procureur*."

From his tone, Camille obviously has no intention of keeping the promise he's just made. He hangs up. The conversation has clearly done nothing to improve his mood.

"And where the fuck is *your partner Morel*? Why isn't he here?"

Louis is surprised. "Your partner Morel." Camille is being unfair, but Louis understands. Giving a case like this to a man like Verhœven, who already has a certain propensity for grief . . .

"He's in Lyons," Louis says calmly, "for the European seminar. He's back the day after tomorrow."

They walk on toward the witness, who is being guarded by a uniformed officer.

"Jesus fucking Christ!" Camille says.

Louis says nothing. Camille stops.

"I'm sorry, Louis."

But he doesn't look at him as he says it; he looks down at his feet, then back up at the windows, at the heads all craning in the same direction, like a train setting off for war. Louis wants to say something, but he doesn't know what to say, and besides, there's no point. Camille makes a decision. Finally, he turns back to Louis:

"Why don't we just act like . . ."

Louis pushes back his bangs. With his right hand. It's like a whole language, this thing of pushing his hair back. Right now, using his right hand, it means *Sure, okay, why not, let's just get on with it.* Louis nods to a figure standing behind Camille.

He's a man of about forty. He was out walking his dog, a creature currently sitting at his feet and looking like something that God cobbled together on an off-day. Camille and the dog stare at each other. The mutual loathing is instant. The dog growls, then scurries to its master's feet, whimpering. But of the two of them, it is the dog's owner who seems most surprised to find Camille standing in front of him. He glances at Louis, astonished that a dwarf like this could be a police commandant.

"Commandant Verhœven," Camille says. "You want to see my I.D., or are you going to take my word for it?"

Louis is lapping this up. He knows what's coming next. The witness will say:

"No, no, it's fine . . . It's just—"

"Just what?" Camille will interrupt.

The witness will dig himself deeper.

"I wasn't expecting, you know . . . It's just . . ."

At that point, there are two possible scenarios. Either Camille keeps up the pressure, forces the guy to keep digging until at last he begs for mercy—he can be ruthless. Or he gives up. This time, Camille gives up. They're dealing with a kidnapping. This is serious.

So: the witness was out walking his dog, and he saw a woman kidnapped. Right before his eyes.

"Nine o'clock exactly," Camille says. "You're sure about the time?"

The witness is like most people—when he talks about something, he's really just talking about himself.

"Certain. I have to be home at half past to watch the car crashes on '*No Limit*'. So I always take the dog out just before."

They start with a physical description of the perpetrator.

"Thing is, I saw him only in profile. But he was a big guy, a big lunk, you know."

He clearly thinks he's being helpful. Camille stares at him, already exhausted. Louis takes over the questioning. Hair? Age? Clothes? Didn't really see, hard to say, ordinary.

"Okay. What about the vehicle?" Louis does his best to sound encouraging.

"A white van. The sort a tradesman would drive, you know—"

"What kind of tradesman?" Camille interrupts.

"Um . . . I don't know what kind—a tradesman, you know."

"What makes you say that?"

It's obvious Camille is trying to catch him out. The guy stands there, his mouth hanging open.

"Well they do, don't they, tradesmen," he mumbles. "They've all got white vans."

"Yes, they do," Camille says. "In fact, they tend to paint their name, address, and phone number on the side. Free advertising. So what did he have painted on the side of his van, this tradesman of yours?"

"Well, that's the strange thing: there was nothing on the side of the van. At least I didn't see anything."

Camille takes out his notebook.

"Let me get this down. So, we're saying an unknown woman kidnapped by an unknown tradesman in a vehicle with no distinguishing marks—am I missing anything?"

The dog owner panics. His lip is quivering. He turns toward Louis as if to say *Come on, help me out here, please.*

Camille snaps his notebook shut and turns away. Louis takes over. Their sole witness statement doesn't amount to much, but they'll have to make do. Camille overhears the rest of the interrogation. Make of the vehicle? ("A Ford maybe . . . I don't know much about cars. I haven't owned one for years.") But the victim was definitely a woman? ("Absolutely, positively.") The description of the aggressor remains vague. ("He was alone, I know that; I didn't see anyone else.") All that's left is the MO.

"She screamed, she was struggling . . . so he thumped her in the stomach. He didn't pull his punches. In fact, that's when I screamed. I was trying to scare him, you know."

Every detail is like a knife in Camille's heart, as though every word is directed at him. A shopkeeper had seen Irène the day she was snatched: it was exactly the same—he had nothing to say; he hadn't seen anything, or hardly anything. Same deal. We'll see. He comes back.

"Where were you standing exactly?"

"Over there."

Louis looks at the ground. The guy points.

"Show me."

Louis closes his eyes. He knows what Verhœven is thinking; it's something he wouldn't do. Flanked by the two policemen, the witness drags his dog along the pavement, then stops.

"About here . . ."

He thinks, turns one way, then the other, pulls a face. Yeah, about here. Camille wants confirmation.

"Here? Not farther back?"

"No, no," the witness says triumphantly.

Louis comes to the same conclusion as Camille.

"He kicked her, too," the man says.

"I can see everything," Camille says. "So, you were standing here, about . . . what?" He glances at the witness. "Forty yards away?"

Yeah, the guy's happy with the estimate.

"You see a woman being beaten up and yelled at forty yards away, and you have the balls to . . . scream."

He looks up at the witness, who is blinking rapidly as though overcome with emotion.

Without a word, Camille sighs and walks off, giving a last parting glare at the mutt who looks about as courageous as his master. It's obvious that he'd like to put a bullet in them both.

He feels—he gropes for the word—a sort of distress, a sort of . . . electric feeling. Because of Irène. He turns, looks at the deserted street. And, finally, he feels the shock. He understands. Until now, he has done his job, technically, methodically, in an organized manner, taking the initiatives expected of him. But only now, for the first time since he got here, does he realize that on this very spot, less than an hour ago, a woman screamed, was beaten, bundled into a van; that right now she is being held somewhere, terror stricken, possibly being tortured; that every second matters, and here he is working on autopilot because he's trying to remain detached, to protect himself, because he doesn't want to do his job, this job he chose to do. The job he chose to continue doing after Irène died. You could have done something else, he thinks, but you didn't. You're here right now, and there is exactly one reason for you to be here: to find the woman who's just been kidnapped.

Camille feels a wave of dizziness. He puts a hand out and steadies himself against a car; with the other hand he loosens his tie. Being in this situation is probably not the best idea for a man so easily crushed by disaster. Louis has just come over to him. Anyone else would ask, "Are you okay?" Not Louis. He stands beside Camille, stares into the distance as though patiently, feelingly, anxiously awaiting a verdict.

Camille shrugs off the dizziness and turns to the forensics officers working about three yards away.

"What have we got?"

He walks over to them, clears his throat. The problem with a crime scene in the middle of the street is that you have to collect everything and then try to figure out which bits are connected to your case.

One of the officers, the taller of the two, looks up:

"Couple of cigarette butts, a coin . . ." He peers at the plastic evidence bag lying on his briefcase. "Foreign. A *métro* ticket and, if we move a bit farther away, I can offer you a used Kleenex and a plastic ballpoint cap."

Camille picks up the plastic envelope with the *métro* ticket, holds it up to the light.

"And he obviously knocked her around a bit," the officer continues.

There are traces of vomit in the gutter, which his colleague is collecting using a sterile spoon.

There's a commotion at the barriers. A group of uniformed officers has just turned up. Camille does a head count. Le Guen's sent him five officers.

Louis knows what he has to do. Three teams. He'll fill them in on the preliminary details; they need to cover the area—not that they'll get much at this time of night—and get the word out; it's textbook with Camille. One of the officers will stay behind with Louis to interrogate the residents, get the curtain twitchers nearest to the crime scene to come down.

Just before 11:00 p.m., Louis the Charmer has found the only building in the street that still has a concierge living on the ground floor—a rarity in Paris these days. Seduced by Louis's elegance, she allows them to use her apartment as temporary headquarters. Just one look at the commandant's height, and the aging concierge feels a twinge of compassion. The man's handicap is like an abandoned animal; it touches her. She covers her mouth with her fist—*my God, my God, my God*. The very sight moves her to pity, her legs give way, she feels faint, *makes you sick just to think of it*. She glances surreptitiously at the commandant, screwing up her eyes, as though he has an open wound and she can feel his pain.

In a stage whisper, she asks Louis:

"You want me to get a little chair for your boss there?"

It's as though Camille is suddenly shrinking, as though something has to be done.

"No, thanks," Louis the Dutiful says, closing his eyes. "We'll be fine as we are, but thank you so much, madame."

Louis flashes her a dazzling smile. So she brews up a big pot of coffee for everyone.

She adds a spoonful of mocha to Camille's cup.

The teams all hard at work, Camille sips his coffee under the compassionate eye of the concierge. Louis is thinking. That's his thing: Louis is an intellectual; he thinks all the time. Tries to understand.

"Money?" he ventures carefully.

"Sex," Camille says, "madness . . ."

They could reel off the whole litany of human passions: the urge to destroy, to possess, to rebel, to dominate. They have seen a lot in their time, these men. Now here they are standing in this concierge's apartment. Standing idle.

They've combed the area, brought down the neighbors, checked witness statements, hearsay, various opinions; they've rung doorbells on the strength of hunches that proved to be unfounded: it's taken most of the night.

And so far: nothing. The kidnapped woman obviously doesn't live in the area, or at least not in the immediate vicinity of the kidnapping. No one seems to know her around here. They have three descriptions of women who might fit the bill: women who are away on vacation, on business . . .

Camille doesn't like the sound of any of this.

3

She is awakened by the cold. And the bruises, because it was a long journey, and, being tied up, she couldn't stop herself from rolling around and slamming into the sides of the van. Then, when the van eventually came to a halt, the man opened the door, bundled her into a sort of white plastic tarp, tied it, then slung her over his shoulder. It's terrifying being reduced to a piece of cargo and terrifying, too, to realize you're at the mercy of a man who can sling you over his shoulder. It's not hard to imagine what he might be capable of.

He took out her gag, but he took no care putting her on the ground or dragging the tarp down the stone stairs. Her ribs banged against every step, and it was impossible to protect her head. Alex screamed, but the man just kept moving. When she hit the back of her head a second time, she passed out.

Impossible to know how long ago that was.

Now there's no sound, but she feels an acute cold in her shoulders, in her arms. Her feet are frozen. The packing tape is wound so tight it's cutting off her circulation. She opens her eyes. Or tries to open them, since her left eye is stuck shut. And she can't open her mouth. A thick strip of duct tape. She doesn't remember that. Must have happened while she was unconscious.

Alex is lying on the ground on her side, arms tied behind her back, feet lashed together. The hip bearing all her weight is painful. She regains consciousness slowly, like a coma patient; her whole body aches as though she's been in a car crash. She tries to work out where she is, rocks her hips, and manages to turn over onto her back. Her shoulders hurt. Her left eye finally comes unstuck, but it registers nothing. I'm blind in one eye, Alex thinks, panicked. But after a few seconds, the half-open eye sends a blurred image that seems to come from a planet light years away.

She sniffles, empties her mind, tries to think rationally. It's a warehouse or a storeroom. A large, empty space, diffuse light pouring in from above. The ground is hard, damp; there is a stench of dirty pools of rainwater. This is why she feels so cold: the place is sodden.

The first thing she remembers is a man pressing himself against her. A strong, pungent smell, the smell of animal sweat. At terrible moments, the things you remember are often trivial: he tore out my hair; this is the first thing she thinks. She pictures her skull with a large bald patch, a whole fistful of hair yanked out, and she starts to cry. In fact, it's not really this thought that makes her cry, but everything that has happened, the exhaustion, the pain. And the fear. She cries, and it's hard to cry with the packing tape over her mouth. She chokes, starts to cough, but finding it difficult to cough, she starts to suffocate; her eyes fill with tears. She retches, feels her stomach heave. It's impossible to throw up. Her mouth is filled with a sort of bile that she is forced to swallow. It takes forever. It makes her feel nauseous.

Alex struggles to breathe, to understand, to make sense of things. Despite the desperate situation, she tries to calm herself a little. Calm is not always enough, but without it, you're doomed. Alex tries to relax her body, slow her heartbeat. Tries to understand what is happening to her, what she's doing here, why she is here.

Think. She is in pain, but something else is bothering her; her bladder is full and compressed. She's never been very good at holding on when it comes to peeing. It takes less than twenty seconds to decide: she lets go and pisses herself for a long time. This loss of control is not defeat, because she made the choice. If she hadn't, she would have gone on suffering, squirming and writhing maybe for hours, and in the end it would come to this. And given the circumstances, she has greater things to fear: the need to piss is an unnecessary hindrance. Except that a few minutes later, she is even colder, and this is something she hadn't thought of. Alex is shivering, and she no longer knows whether it is from cold or from fear. Two images come to mind: the man in the *métro*, at the far end of the carriage, smiling at her; and his face as he holds her pressed against him, just before he shoves her into the van. She was badly hurt when she bounced onto the floor.

Suddenly, some way off, a metal door clangs and echoes. Alex immediately stops crying, alert, frantic, about to crack up. Then she manages to heave herself back onto her side and closes her eyes, steeling herself for the first blow, because she knows he will beat her; that is why he abducted her. Alex has stopped breathing. In the distance she hears the man approaching, the footsteps heavy and deliberate. Finally he stops in front of her. Through her eyelashes she can see his shoes, sturdy, well-polished shoes. The man says nothing. He towers over her, silent, stands there for a long moment as though watching her sleep. At last, she makes a decision, opens her good eye wide and looks up at him. His hands are behind his back, his face bent toward her. It is impossible to make out what he's thinking, and he simply bends over her as he might bend over a *thing*. From below, his head is impressive, his thick black eyebrows casting shadows that partly hide his eyes, but mostly it is his forehead, bigger than the rest of his face; it seems out of proportion. It makes him look retarded, primitive. Pigheaded. She racks her brains for the word. Doesn't find it.

Alex wants to say something. The tape makes it impossible. In any case, the only words that would come out would be "Please, I'm begging you . . ." She tries to think what she might say to him if he unties her, to come up with something that does not make it sound as if she is pleading, but she can think of nothing: no questions, no demands, nothing but this entreaty. The words won't come; Alex's brain is frozen. And the baffled thought: he's abducted her, tied her up, dumped her here—what is he going to do to her?

Alex cries; she can't help herself. The man walks away without a word. He goes to the far corner of the room. With a sweeping gesture, he pulls away a tarp; it's impossible to tell what it was covering. And that magical incantation begins again: please don't let him kill me.

His back to her, bent double, the man staggers backwards, both hands dragging something heavy—a crate?—that screeches against the concrete floor. He's wearing dark-gray cotton trousers and a striped sweater, large and baggy, which looks as if he's had it for years.

After moving backwards for several yards he stops, looks up at the ceiling as though calculating something, then stands, hands on his hips, as though wondering how best to proceed. Finally he turns and looks at her. He comes over, crouches down, his knee close to her face, reaches out, and suddenly slashes the tape binding her ankles. Then his fat hand grips the tape at the corner of her mouth and rips it savagely away. Alex howls in pain. He manages to haul her to her feet with one hand. Not that Alex weighs much, but even so, one hand. A wave of dizziness courses through her—standing sends blood rushing to her head, and she falters again. She barely comes up to the man's chest. He grips her shoulder hard and turns her around. She doesn't have time to say anything before he cuts the tape around her wrists.

Alex summons all her courage; she doesn't think, she simply says the first words that come to her.

"Please, I'm b— b— begging you . . ."

She barely recognizes her own voice. And she's stammering, like a child, like a teenager.

They're standing face-to-face. This is the moment of truth. Alex is so terrified at the thought of what he might do to her that suddenly she wants to die, right here, wants him to kill her right now. What she fears most is this waiting, which her imagination fills with images of what he might do to her. She closes her eyes and sees her body, pictures it as though it is no longer a part of her, a body lying as she was a moment earlier: it is mutilated, bleeding profusely, in excruciating pain; somehow it is not her, but it is her. She sees herself lying dead.

The cold, the stink of piss, the shame, the fear—what's going to happen, don't let him kill me, please don't let him kill me.

"Strip," the man says.

His voice is deep, calm. The order is deep, calm. Alex opens her mouth, but she does not have time to utter a word before he slaps her so hard she spins around, losing her balance. Another slap and she crumples on the floor, her head smashing into the ground. The man comes toward her slowly, grabs her by the hair. The pain is vicious. He pulls her up. Alex feels as though her hair is going to be ripped out of her scalp; she grips his fist in both hands, tries to hang on, in spite of herself, she feels strength returning to her legs, and she stands up again. When he slaps her a third time, he's still gripping her by her hair, so her body just gives a jolt, her head whips around a quarter turn. The sound is so loud. She is in so much pain she can barely feel anything.

"I said strip," the man says again. "Everything."

And he lets her go. Alex takes a step, dazed. She tries to stay standing, collapses onto her knees, stifles a whimper of pain. The man comes over, bends down. Lowering over her, his fat face, his large head with its oversized skull, his gray eyes . . .

"Do you understand?"

As he waits for an answer, he raises his hand, the fingers splayed. Alex panics. "Yes," she says over and over, "yes, yes, yes." She immediately gets to her feet, prepared to do whatever he wants so he doesn't hit her again. Quickly, so he will realize that she is prepared to do whatever he says, she peels off her T-shirt, rips off her bra, fumbles hurriedly with the buttons of her jeans as though her clothes had suddenly caught fire—she wants to be naked as quickly as possible so he won't hit her again. Alex wriggles and squirms, takes off everything she's wearing, every last stitch, quickly, then stands up, arms against her body, and it's only then that she realizes what she has lost and can never get back. Her defeat is absolute—by undressing so quickly she has accepted everything, said yes to everything. In a sense, Alex has just died. She dimly feels something, though it is very far away. As though she is outside her own body. Perhaps this is how she finds the courage to ask:

"Wh— what do you want?"

His lips are so thin they're almost invisible. Even when he smiles, you can tell it's anything but a smile. Right now, it's a question.

"What have you got to offer, you filthy whore?"

He tries to make it sound lascivious, as though actually attempting to seduce her. To Alex, the words make sense. They would make sense to any woman. She swallows hard. She thinks: he's not going to kill me. Her mind coils around this thought, knotting itself tightly against all contradiction. Something inside tells her he'll kill her anyway, later . . . but the knot in her mind is tight, tight, tight.

"You can f— f— fuck me," she says.

No, that's not right, she can tell, that's not the right way . . .

"You can r— rape me," she says, "You can do wh— whatever you want."

The man's smile freezes. He takes a step back so he can look at her. From head to foot. Alex spreads her arms wide; she wants him to know she is offering herself, surrendering herself—she wants to show him she has relinquished her free will, that she is putting herself in his hands, that she is his, so she can buy some time, just a little time. In these circumstances, time means life.

The man studies her steadily; his eyes move slowly down her body, finally coming to rest over her genitals. She doesn't move. He leans toward her slightly, questioningly. Alex feels ashamed of what she is, exposing herself like this. What if he's not attracted to her? If what little she has to offer is not enough, what will he do then? He shakes his head as though disappointed, no, not good enough. And to make her understand he reaches out, grips Alex's right nipple between thumb and forefinger and twists it so hard, so fast, that the young woman immediately doubles up and screams.

He lets go, and Alex holds her breast, eyes bulging, gasping for breath, hopping from one foot to the other, blind with pain. The tears come in spite of herself as she says:

"Wh— wh— what are you going to do?"

The man smiles as though simply stating an obvious fact.

"Me? I'm going to watch you die, you filthy whore."

Then he steps to one side, like an actor.

And she sees. Behind him. On the floor, an electric drill lying next to a small wooden crate. About the size of a human body.

4

Camille pores over a map of Paris. Outside the concierge's apartment, a uniformed officer assigned by the local station spends his time telling the rubberneckers and the neighbors that they've no business being there unless they have vital information about the kidnapping. A kidnapping! It's entertainment, almost like being in a movie. Granted the star is missing, but that doesn't matter—just being on the set is magical. As the night wears on, the news spreads like wildfire, like village gossip. People can't believe it, *Who is it, who is it, who is it, I told you I don't know, some woman is what I heard, but do we know her, tell me do we know her?* News travels fast—even kids who should be in bed by now are coming down to check out what's going on; the whole neighborhood is thrilled by this unexpected situation. Somebody asks whether they're going to be on TV. Over and over, people ask the duty officer the same questions. They hang around waiting for no one knows what, just so they can be there in case something finally happens, but nothing happens, and gradually the whispering dies away, interest fades, it's getting late; a few hours later and as the night draws on, excitement becomes irritation, the first shouts of protest come from the windows: *Can you keep it down? There are people here trying to sleep.*

"Maybe they should call the police," Camille says.

Louis, as always, is more stoical.

On his map, he has marked out the main roads leading away from the scene of the abduction. There are four possible routes the woman could have taken before being kidnapped. Place Falguière, boulevard Pasteur, or rue Vigée-Lebrun, or, from the other direction, rue du Cotentin. She might have taken a bus—either the 88 or the 95. The nearest *métro* stations are quite some distance from the scene but can't be discounted: Pernety, Plaisance, Volontaires, Vaugirard . . .

If they don't find anything, tomorrow they'll have to widen the search area, comb farther afield in search of some scrap of information, and for that, they'll have to wait for people to get up, to wait for tomorrow, as if they've got time.

Kidnapping is a singular crime: unlike murder, the victim is not present; you have to imagine them. This is what Camille is trying to do. With a pencil he sketches the figure of a woman walking down the street. He looks at it critically: too elegant, a society woman. Maybe Camille is getting too old to draw women like that. He puts a line through it and starts again, making telephone calls as he sketches. Why does he imagine she is young? Do people kidnap old women? For the first time he thinks of her not as a woman but as a girl. "A girl" has been kidnapped on rue Falguière. He goes back to the drawing. Jeans, short hair, handbag slung over her shoulder. No. Another sketch: in this one she has a pencil skirt, a big bust. Exasperated, he crosses it out. He pictures her young, but actually he can't picture her at all. When he pictures her, he sees Irène.

There was never any other woman in his life. On the rare occasion the opportunity has presented itself to a man of his height, his sex drive has been complicated by too many factors—a feeling of guilt, a touch of self-loathing, and the fear of resuming normal relations with women—so things never worked out. That's not quite true: there was one exception. A colleague who'd got herself into a jam, a girl he'd helped out of a tight spot. Turned a blind eye. What he saw on her face at the time was relief, nothing more. Later he had run into her by chance near his apartment. They went for a drink on the terrace at La Marine, then on to dinner, and—one thing leads to another—you go upstairs for a nightcap and then . . . In normal circumstances, it's not the sort of behavior a decent, upstanding officer should allow. But she was sweet, a free spirit, and seemed genuinely eager to show her gratitude. Or at least this is what Camille told himself later to allay his guilt. It had been more than two years since he'd touched a woman—that was one reason, but it wasn't reason enough. What he had done had been unethical. That casual, tender evening, they hadn't felt it necessary to think about feelings. She knew his story—it's one everyone in the *brigade criminelle* knows: Verhœven's wife was murdered. She had said things, simple everyday things; she had undressed in the next room and immediately climbed on top of him with no foreplay; they looked into each other's eyes. Camille had closed his at the end—he couldn't help himself. They run into each other from time to time; she lives close by. Forty-something, maybe. And six inches taller than him. Anne. Tactful, too: she hadn't spent the night, had told him she had to get home. It was the right thing to do; it spared Camille pain. When they run into each other, she acts as if nothing happened. The last time, there was a crowd of people, and she even shook hands with him. Why is he thinking about her now? Is she the kind of woman a man might want to abduct?

Camille turns his thoughts to the kidnapper. It's possible to kill in many ways, for many reasons, but all abductions are alike. And one thing is certain: kidnapping someone requires planning. Obviously it's possible to do it on impulse, in a sudden fit of anger, but it's pretty rare and doomed to failure. In most cases, the perpetrator organizes, plans, meticulously prepares. The stats are not good: the first few hours are critical; the chances of the victim being found alive soon plummet. A hostage is a liability—you want to get rid of them quickly.

Louis is the first to get a lead. He's been telephoning every bus driver who worked the route between 7:00 and 9:30 p.m. Dragging them out of bed one by one.

"The driver of the last 88 tonight," he says, cupping his hand over the receiver, "about nine o'clock. Remembers a girl who ran to catch the bus, then changed her mind."

Camille puts down his pencil, looks up.

"Which stop?"

"Institut Pasteur."

A shiver runs down his back.

"Why does he remember her?"

Louis repeats the question into the phone.

"Pretty," says Louis, putting his hand over the receiver again. "Very pretty."

"Ah . . ."

"And he's sure about the time. He waved to her, she gave him a little smile, he told her his was the last bus that night, but she headed off on foot down rue Falguière."

"Which side?"

"Right-hand as you go down."

The right direction.

"Description?"

Louis asks the caller for details but doesn't get very far.

"Vague. Very vague."

This is the problem with very pretty girls: they take your breath away; you don't think to notice the details. You remember her eyes, her lips, her ass, maybe even all three, but you have no idea what she was wearing . . . This is the problem with male witnesses; women are more precise.

Camille spends much of the night brooding about such things.

By 2:30 a.m. everything that can be done has been done. Now all they can do is wait and hope something happens in a hurry, something that gives them a solid lead. Receiving a ransom demand that opens up a new line of investigation. Discovering a corpse that shuts down all other lines. Some clue, anything to work on.

The most urgent task is to identify the victim. For the moment, police headquarters has said there have been no reports of a missing woman that might correspond.

Nothing in the area where the abduction took place.

It has been six hours.

5

It's a simple wooden crate. The slats are spaced about four inches apart, making it easy to see what's inside. For the moment, there's nothing; the crate is empty.

Grabbing Alex viciously by the shoulder, he drags her as far as the crate, then turns away as though she is not there anymore. The drill turns out to be an electric screwdriver. He unscrews a plank from the top of the crate, and then another. He has his back to her, bent over. His thick neck is flushed red and beaded with sweat . . . *Neanderthal*: this is the word that Alex thinks.

She is standing directly behind him, a little to one side, naked, an arm covering her breasts, a hand cupped over her genitals because she feels ashamed—even in these circumstances, which is madness when you think about it. Shivering from head to foot from the cold, she waits, utterly passive. She could try something. Hurl herself at him, hit him, run. The warehouse is vast and empty. About fifteen yards in front of them is an opening, a large breach in the wall; the big sliding doors that once sealed the warehouse are missing. While the man unscrews the slats, Alex tries to get her brain back into gear again. Run? Lash out? Try to grab the drill? What is he planning to do after he's unscrewed the crate? Watch her die, he said, but what does he mean? How is he planning to kill her? She realizes that in a few short hours she has moved all the way from *I don't want to die* to *please make it quick*. As she is thinking this, two things happen. First, a simple, dogged, stubborn thought occurs to her: don't let yourself be pushed around; resist, fight back. Second: the man turns, sets the screwdriver down next to her and reaches out to grab her shoulder. In that moment a decision mysteriously pops in her brain, like a bubble, and she starts running for the gap in the wall at the far end of the storeroom. In a matter of nanoseconds, she has vaulted the crate and is running, barefoot, as fast as she can. Surprised by this burst of speed, the man has no time to react. There is no cold, no fear now; every fiber of her being urges her to run, to get out of here. The floor is cold, hard, slippery from the damp; the concrete is rough and uneven, but she feels nothing—she is swept along in a wild dash. The ground is wet where rain has come through the roof, and Alex's feet splash through puddles of stagnant water. She doesn't turn back, urging herself on: *run, run, run*, she doesn't know whether the man is chasing her. You're faster than he is. You know you are. He's old and overweight, you're young and slim. You're alive.

Alex makes it through the gap in the wall and slows just long enough to notice, on her left, that at the far end of this room is another opening like the one she has just come through. All the rooms are the same. Which way is out? The thought that she will be running out of the building stark naked, bursting out into the street like this, has not even registered. Her heart is hammering fit to explode. Alex is desperate to look around, to see how far ahead of him she is, but even more desperate to get out of here. A third room. This time Alex stops, gasping for breath, and almost collapses. She can't believe it. She starts running again, but already she can feel tears welling—she's reached the other end of the building, come to the door that must surely lead to the outside world.

It is bricked up.

From between the large red bricks oozes still-wet mortar that has not been smoothed, simply thrown on in slapdash fashion to seal the doorway. Alex feels the bricks, which are also damp. Trapped. The cold suddenly hits her again. She pounds on the bricks with her fists, she screams—maybe someone on the other side will hear her. She screams; she can't find words. *Let me out of here. Please.* Alex pounds harder, but already she's tiring; she presses herself against the wall as she might a tree, as though trying to become one with it. She stops screaming, has no voice left, only a plea that is lodged in her throat. Sobbing quietly she stands, plastered against the wall like a billboard poster. Then suddenly she falls silent because she senses the man behind her. He did not chase her; he simply walked to where she is standing. She listens to the approaching footsteps. She doesn't move; the footsteps stop. She thinks she hears him breathing, but what she hears is her own fear.

The man does not say a word, he simply seizes her by the hair—this is how he does things—grabs a fistful of hair and tugs violently, jerking Alex toward him so that she falls heavily onto her back, stifling a scream. For a moment she is convinced she is paralyzed; she whimpers, but the man is not prepared to leave it at that. He gives her a vicious kick in the ribs and when she fails to move quickly enough, gives a second, even more brutal kick. "Slut!"

Alex howls—she knows this is not going to stop so, mustering all her strength, she curls into a ball. Bad move. As long as she refuses to obey him, he will keep beating her. He lashes out again, this time driving the toe of his boot into her kidneys. Alex howls in pain, struggles up onto one elbow, raises a hand in surrender, a gesture that clearly says *Stop, I'll do whatever you want.* The man doesn't move; he is waiting. Alex is on her feet now— she staggers, tries to get her bearings, sways, almost falls, moves in zigzag fashion. She is not moving quickly enough, so he kicks her from behind, sending her sprawling, but she gets to her feet again, knees streaming blood, and keeps moving, more quickly now. It's over; he has no other demands of her. Alex surrenders. She walks back toward the first room, goes through the gap; she is ready now. Utterly exhausted. When she comes to the huge crate she glances at him. Her arms dangling, she has given up every last shred of modesty. He does not move either. What was it he said? What were his last words? "I'm going to watch you die, you filthy whore."

He looks at the crate. Alex looks at it, too. This is the point of no return. What she is about to do, what she is about to accept, is irreversible. Irrevocable. She can never go back. Will he rape her? Kill her? Kill her before, after? Will he make her suffer endlessly? What does he want, this mute executioner? In a few minutes she will have the answers to these questions. Only one mystery remains.

"P— please . . ." Alex begs. She is whispering, as though asking him to confess a secret. "Why? Why me?"

The man frowns like someone who does not speak her language trying to guess what her question might mean. Reflexively, Alex reaches behind her, her fingertips brushing against the rough wood of the crate.

"Why me?"

The man smiles slowly. Those invisible lips . . .

"Because you're the one I want to watch die, you filthy whore."

He says it as though stating the obvious. He seems satisfied he has answered her question.

Alex squeezes her eyes shut. Tears trickle down. She wants her life to flash before her, but nothing comes. It is no longer simply her fingertips touching the wooden crate; her whole hand grips it to stop herself collapsing.

"Go on," he says, impatient, and nods toward the crate.

When she turns back, Alex is no longer herself; it is not she who steps into the box—there is not a shred of her in this body that curls up inside it. She squats, feet apart to balance on the slats, arms wrapped around her knees as though this crate is her sanctuary and not her coffin.

The man approaches, gazes at the image of the naked girl curled up at the bottom of this crate. Eyes wide with delight, like an entomologist studying some rare species. He looks jubilant.

6

The concierge left them to it and went to bed. She snored like a pile driver all night. They left her some money for the coffee, and Louis left a note to say thank you.

It is 3:00 a.m. The various teams have all left now. It has been six hours since the abduction, and the evidence they have collected so far would fit in a matchbox.

Camille and Louis are out on the street, each heading home to take a quick shower before meeting up again.

"You go ahead," Camille says.

They've arrived at the taxi stand. Camille isn't taking a cab.

"Don't mind me, I'll walk part of the way."

They go their separate ways.

Camille has sketched her over and over, this girl, as he pictures her, walking down the street, waving to the bus driver; constantly starting again because there was always some trace of Irène about her. Even the thought makes Camille feel sick. He walks faster. This girl is a different person. This is what he needs to remember.

Especially the one terrible difference: this girl is alive.

The street is deserted; cars go by every now and then.

He tries to think logically. Logic is what has been worrying him from the start. People don't kidnap at random; more often than not they abduct someone they know. Maybe not very well, but well enough to have a motive. So the kidnapper must know where she lives. This thought has been running through Camille's mind for the past hour. He quickens his pace. And if he didn't snatch her from home or from outside her house, it has to be because it was impossible. He can't think why, but it must have been impossible; otherwise he wouldn't have snatched her here in the street, with all the risks that that entails. Yet that's precisely what he did.

Camille speeds up, and his thoughts keep time.

Two possibilities: either the guy is following her, or he's waiting for her. Could he have followed her in the van? No. She didn't take the bus, and the idea of her walking down the street with him driving behind in slow motion waiting for the right moment to pounce is completely preposterous.

So he must have been waiting.

He knows her, knows the route she takes; he needs a place where he can wait, somewhere he'll be able to see her coming . . . and be able to rush out and snatch her. And that somewhere has to be before the spot where he actually abducted her, since this is a one-way street. He sees her, she walks past, he catches up, snatches her.

"That's the way I see it."

It's not unusual for Camille to talk to himself out loud. He hasn't been widowed long, but it doesn't take long for the habits of the single man to set in again. This is why he didn't ask Louis to walk with him. He's no longer used to being part of a team—he's spent too much time alone, too much time brooding and hence thinking only of himself. They would only have ended up arguing. Camille doesn't much like the man he has become.

He walks for a few minutes mulling over these thoughts. He's looking for something. Camille is one of those people who seem stubbornly wrongheaded until the evidence proves they were right all along. It's an irritating weakness in a friend, but an important strength in a policeman. He walks past one street, and then another, but it triggers nothing. Then, suddenly, a lightbulb flickers on in his head.

Rue Legrandin.

A cul-de-sac that can't be more than thirty yards long but is wide enough for cars to park on both sides. If he were the kidnapper, this is where he would have parked. Camille walks on a little, then turns to look at the street.

At the intersection there's a building with a pharmacy on the ground floor.

He looks up.

Two closed-circuit TV cameras are trained on the shop front.

It doesn't take long for them to find the footage of the white van on the tape. M. Bertignac is deferential to the point of syco-phancy, the sort of man who revels in the thought of "helping the police with their inquiries." The sort of person Camille finds vaguely irritating. They are in the dispensary at the back of the shop. M. Bertignac is sitting in front of a huge computer moni-tor. He doesn't look much like a pharmacist, but he certainly has the character traits. Camille is quick to spot this, since his father was a pharmacist. Even after he retired, he behaved like a retired pharmacist. He died just over a year ago. Camille can't help but think that, even in death, there's something of the pharmacist about his father.

M. Bertignac is eager to help the police, and so was more than happy to get out of bed at 3:30 a.m. and open the door to Comman-dant Verhœven.

Nor is Bertignac a man who bears grudges, even though the Pharmacie Bertignac has been robbed five times. With the rise in drug dealers targeting pharmacies, he turned to technology. After every break-in, he bought a new camera. There are five now: two outside covering the pavement, the other three inside.

The tapes are kept for twenty-four hours; after that, they're automatically erased. And M. Bertignac loves his gadgets. He didn't need the police to get a warrant before showing off his equipment; he was only too happy to oblige. It took only a few minutes to bring up the section of the tape covering the cul-de-sac. There's not much to see: just the wheels and the lower part of the vehicles parked against the sidewalk. The white van arrives and parks at 9:04 p.m., inching forward so the driver has a sidelong view of the rue Falguière. For Camille, it is not enough to have his theory confirmed (though he is happy about that—he loves to be proved right); he would have liked a better view of the vehicle, because in M. Bertignac's freeze-frame all that is visible are the front wheels and the lower section of the body. He now knows more about the MO and about the timing of the abduction, but not about the kidnapper. Nothing happens on the tape. Absolutely nothing. They rewind.

Camille can't quite bring himself to leave. Because it's infuriating to have the kidnapper right there while the camera is focused on some trivial unimportant detail. At 9:27, the van pulls out of the cul-de-sac. And it's at that moment it happens.

"There!"

M. Bertignac bravely plays the studio engineer. Spools back the tape. There. They peer at the screen; Camille asks if it's possible to enlarge. M. Bertignac twiddles various knobs. Just as the van pulls out of the parking spot, it's obvious from the lower part of the body that it has been repainted by hand, leaving part of the lettering still visible. It's impossible to read what it says. The characters are barely legible, and besides, they're cut off along the top edge of the screen, out of shot of the closed-circuit TV camera. Camille asks for a printout, and the pharmacist obligingly gives him a USB flash drive onto which he's copied the whole sequence. At maximum contrast, the pattern looks something like:

It is like Morse code.

The van has clearly scraped against something, and there are small traces of green paint.

More work for forensics.

Camille finally makes for home.

The evening has shaken him somewhat. He takes the stairs. He lives on the fourth floor and on principle never takes the elevator.

They've done what they can. What comes next is the worst part. The waiting. Waiting for someone to report a woman missing. It could take a day, two days, maybe more. In the meantime . . . When Irène was kidnapped, she had been found dead within ten hours. Half that time has already elapsed. If forensics had found anything useful, he would know by now. Camille is all too familiar with the sad, slow melody of cross-checking evidence, this war of attrition that takes ages and leaves your nerves shot.

He broods over this endless night. He's exhausted. He barely has time to take a shower and knock back a couple of coffees.

Camille sold the apartment he once shared with Irène; he couldn't bear to live there—it was too difficult seeing her everywhere he looked. To stay on would have required a strength of will better expended elsewhere. He wondered whether to go on living after Irène's death was a matter of courage, a matter of will. How was it possible to carry on alone when everything around you had crumbled? He needed to check his own fall. He knew that this apartment was dragging him down, but he couldn't bear to give it up. He asked his father (who could always be relied on to give a straight answer) and then Louis, who had said: "To hold on, you have to let go." It's from the Tao, apparently. Camille wasn't sure he understood what it meant.

"It's like 'The Oak and the Reed,' if you prefer."

Camille preferred.

So he sold the place. For three years now he's been living here on the Quai de Valmy.

He steps into his apartment, and Doudouche immediately comes to greet him. Ah, that's something else. Doudouche, a little tabby cat.

"A middle-aged widower with a cat," was Camille's reaction. "It's a bit of a cliché, don't you think? Or am I being over the top?"

"I suspect it depends on the cat, doesn't it?" Louis said.

And that's the whole problem. Out of love, or a desire to fit in, through unconscious mimicry or a sense of propriety—who knows?—Doudouche has remained incredibly small for her age. She has a sweet little face, bandy legs like a cowboy, and she's tiny. It's a mystery so profound even Louis had no theory to propose.

"You think maybe she's a little over the top, too?" Camille asked.

The vet was embarrassed when Camille brought the cat in to ask about its size.

No matter what time he gets in, Doudouche wakes up and comes to greet him. Tonight—this morning—Camille just gives her a quick scratch on the back. He doesn't really feel like opening up. The day has been somewhat overwhelming.

First, the woman being kidnapped.

Then, meeting up with Louis again, especially in these circumstances. It's as though Le Guen deliberately engineered things . . .

Camille freezes.

"The bastard!"

7

Alex climbs into the crate, bows her head, huddles up.

The man puts the lid back on, screws it into place, and then steps back to admire his handiwork.

Alex is bruised from head to foot, her whole body shaken by spasms and tremors. Though it feels utterly absurd, she cannot deny the fact that inside the crate she feels somehow more at ease. As though sheltered. She has spent the past few hours constantly picturing what he might do to her, but aside from the brutality of the abduction itself, aside from the beating . . . It's hardly nothing—Alex's head is still throbbing from the force of the blows—but now here she is, in the crate, in one piece. He hasn't raped her. He hasn't tortured her. He hasn't killed her. Not yet, says a little voice, but Alex doesn't want to listen; as far as she is concerned, each second gained is a second gained, every second yet to come is yet to come. She tries to take deep breaths. The man is still standing, frozen—she can see his heavy work boots, the bottoms of his trousers. He is staring at her. "I want to watch you die . . ." This is what he said; it's almost the only thing he has said. Is that it? He wants to kill her? He wants to watch her die? How is he planning to kill her? Alex is no longer wondering why, but how? When?

Why does he hate women so much? What is this guy's story that he could set this whole thing up? Could beat her so brutally? The cold is not too bitter, but what with the exhaustion, the beatings, the fear, the darkness, Alex feels frozen stiff. She tries to shift her position. It's not easy. She is sitting hunched up, head resting on the arms hugging her knees. As she lifts herself to try and turn around, she lets out a scream. She's just managed to drive a long splinter into her arm, high up near the shoulder, and has to use her teeth to pull it out. There's no room. The wooden crate is rough, makeshift. What can she do to turn around? Rest her weight on her hands? Swivel her pelvis? First she will try to move her feet. She feels terror well up in her belly. She starts to scream, shifts this way and that; she's terrified of injuring herself on the rough-hewn planks, but she needs to move; it's enough to drive her mad. She thrashes about but succeeds only in gaining a few inches. Panic grips her.

The man's large head suddenly appears in her field of vision.

So suddenly, she jerks back and bangs her head. He has crouched down to look at her. He smiles broadly with his missing lips. A grim, joyless smile that would be ridiculous if it were not so threatening. From his throat comes a sort of bleating sound. Still no words. He nods as though to say *Do you get it now?*

"You . . . ," Alex begins, but she cannot think what she wants to say to him, to ask him.

He goes on nodding his head, smiling that moronic smile. *He's insane,* thinks Alex.

"You're c— crazy . . ."

But she doesn't have time to say more; he has just backed away, he is walking away—she can't see him anymore, so she trembles even more. As soon as he disappears, she panics. What is he doing? She cranes her neck; she can hear noises coming from a little way off—everything reverberates in the vast, empty room. Except now, she's moving. Imperceptibly the crate has begun to swing. The wood makes a creaking sound. Out of the corner of her eye, if she swivels her body as much as possible, she can see the rope above her. It is attached somehow to the crate. Alex twists her body so as to slide her hand up over her head and between the slats: there is a steel ring to which is attached a thick rope; she grips the huge, tight knot.

The rope shudders and tenses, the crate seems to shriek as it rises, lifts off the floor, and begins to rock, to spin slowly. The man appears in her field of vision again, some seven or eight yards away, standing near the wall where, with sweeping movements, he tugs on the rope connected by two pulleys. The crate rises very slowly, and for a moment it seems as though it might topple. Alex doesn't move; the man stares at her. When the crate is about five feet off the ground, he stops, ties off the rope, then goes and rummages in a pile of things next to the gap in the far wall and comes back.

Face-to-face, at the same height, they can look each other in the eye. He takes out his cell phone. To take a photograph of her. He looks for the right angle, shifts to one side, steps back, chicks the shutter once, twice, three times . . . then checks the images, deletes those he's not happy with. Then he goes back over to the wall, and the crate rises again; it's now six feet from the floor.

The rope now tied off, the man is visibly pleased with himself.

He slips on his jacket, pats his pockets to make sure he's forgotten nothing. It's as though Alex doesn't exist anymore—he hardly glances at the crate as he leaves. Satisfied with his handiwork. As though leaving his apartment to go to work.

He's gone.

Silence.

The crate swings heavily at the end of the rope. A blast of cold air whirls around her, lapping against Alex's body, which is already frozen to the marrow.

She is alone. Naked. Trapped.

Only now does she understand.

This is not a crate.

It's a cage.

8

"You fucking bastard . . ."

Over the years, Divisionnaire Le Guen has tried nearly everything with Camille: "Mind your language." "I'll thank you to remember I'm your superior officer." "What would you have done in my shoes?" "You should improve your vocabulary, your bad language is getting tedious." These days, rather than rehashing old arguments, he no longer responds. This rather cuts the ground out from under Camille, who now simply storms into his office without knocking and stands glowering at his boss. At best, the divisionnaire gives him a philosophical shrug; at worst, he looks down, pretending to be contrite. Not a word is spoken; they're like an old married couple, which is something of a no-win situation for two men pushing fifty, both of whom are single. Or rather, neither of whom has a wife. Camille is a widower. Le Guen racked up his fourth divorce last year.

"It's strange how you keep marrying the same woman," Camille said at Le Guen's last wedding.

"What can you do?" Le Guen quipped. "Old habits die hard. I mean I always have the same witness at my weddings—you!" Then tetchily he said, "Besides, if I have to have a new wife, I might as well marry the same one," proving that when it comes to fatalism, he's a match for anyone.

The fact that they no longer need to say anything to understand what the other is thinking is the primary reason Camille does not tear a strip off Le Guen this morning. He brushes aside the petty manipulations of the divisionnaire, who could obviously have put someone else on the case but pretended there was no one. It dawns on Camille that he should have realized straight off, but he completely missed it. This is strange; in fact, it is rather worrying. The other reason is that he hasn't had a wink of sleep, he's exhausted, and he doesn't have the energy to waste because he has a long day ahead of him before Morel takes over.

It's 7:00 a.m. Dead-tired officers move from office to office yelling to one another, doors slam, people shout, dazed citizens wait in corridors; for the station, this is the fag end of a sleepless night like any other.

Louis shows up. He hasn't slept either. Camille looks him up and down. Brooks Brothers suit, Louis Vuitton tie, a pair of Finsbury loafers; sober as always. Camille can't comment on the socks yet, and besides he knows nothing about socks. Louis looks elegant, but though he's perfectly shaven, he looks awful.

They shake hands as if this is just an ordinary morning, as if they had never stopped working together. Since meeting up for the first time again last night, they haven't really talked. Haven't even referred to the four-year break. Not that it's a big secret—no, this is about embarrassment, about grief—besides, what is there to say about loss? Louis and Irène were fond of each other. Camille thinks that, like him, Louis felt responsible for her death. Louis did not lay claim to the same grief as Camille, but he grieved just the same. Grief that was beyond words. Deep down both men were devastated by the same tragedy, and it left them speechless. Of course, everyone had been shaken, but these two should have found a way to talk. They never did, and gradually, though they still thought about each other, they stopped seeing each other.

The preliminary report from forensics is not encouraging. Camille flicks swiftly through it, passing the pages to Louis as he reads. The rubber from the tire tracks is the most common of all kinds and would be found on five million vehicles. The van, too, is the most common make. As for the victim's last meal: mixed salad, beef, green beans, white wine . . . It's not promising.

They set themselves up next to the big map of Paris pinned to Camille's office wall. The telephone rings.

"Hey, Jean," Camille says, "perfect timing."

"Yeah, and good morning to you too," Le Guen says.

"I need fifteen officers."

"No chance."

"Mostly female officers, if possible." Camille thinks for a moment. "I'll need them for at least two days. Three, if we haven't found the girl by then. Oh, and one more vehicle. No, make that two."

"Listen—"

"And I want Armand assigned to me."

"Okay, well, that I can do. I'll send him over now."

"Thanks for everything, Jean." Camille hangs up.

He turns back to the map.

"So, what are we likely to get?" Louis says.

"Half of everything I asked for. Plus Armand."

Camille keeps his eyes fixed on the map. With an arm at full stretch he could just about touch the sixth arrondissement. To reach the nineteenth, he would need to stand on a chair. Or use a pointer. But a pointer would make him look like a priggish schoolteacher. Over the years, he's considered a number of solutions. Pinning the map lower down on the wall, spreading it on the floor of the office, cutting it into various sectors and pinning them side by side . . . He's never actually implemented any of them, since any solution that compensated for his height would simply make things difficult for everyone else. Besides, just as he has at home or at the mortuary, Camille has a battery of equipment here in the office. When it comes to stools, steps, ladders, Camille is a connoisseur. For files, archives, stationery, and technical documentation, he uses a small, narrow aluminum stepladder; for the map of Paris, a library step stool, one of the models with wheels that lock when you step on it. Camille rolls it to the wall and stands on it. He studies the main roads that converge on the site of the abduction. Teams will be dispatched to do a detailed search of the whole area; the question is where to fix the boundaries of the search area. He points to an area, suddenly looks down at his feet, thinks for a moment, then turns to Louis and says: "I look like some douchebag general, don't I?"

"I'm guessing 'douchebag general' is a tautology in your book?"

They banter back and forth, but neither is really listening. Each is pursuing his own line of thought.

"But still . . . ," Louis says broodingly, "there's been no van reported stolen in the past few days. Unless he's been planning this for months. I mean, abducting a girl using your own van is taking a hell of a risk."

"Or maybe the guy's dumb as a box of rocks."

Camille and Louis turn around. It's Armand.

"If the guy's dumb, he'll be unpredictable," Camille says, smiling. "That's going to make things more difficult."

They all shake hands. Armand has worked with Camille for more than ten years, nine and a half under his command. He is a terrifyingly gaunt man with a sad face who suffers from a pathological tight-fistedness that has blighted his whole life. Every second of Armand's life is geared toward saving money. Camille's theory is that he's scared of death. Louis, who's studied just about every subject possible, confirmed that this is a valid psychoanalytical theory. Camille felt proud to be an able theorist in a subject he knows nothing about. Professionally, Armand is a tireless worker ant. Give him a telephone directory for any city, come back a year later, and he'll have checked every number.

Armand has always felt an unalloyed admiration for Camille. Early on in their careers, when Armand discovered Camille's mother was a famous painter, that admiration became a fervor. He collects press cuttings about her. On his computer, he has images of every painting of hers available on the Internet. When he learned that Camille's short stature was due to his mother's inveterate smoking, Armand felt conflicted. He tried to reconcile his admiration for a painter whose work he doesn't understand, but whose fame impresses him, and his resentment for a woman who could be so selfish. He never quite resolved these incompatible feelings; he seems to struggle with them still. But he can't help it: the moment there's a mention of Maud Verhœven or one of her paintings on the news, Armand is ecstatic.

"Maybe she should have been *your* mother," Camille said one day, peering up at him.

"That's low," Armand muttered. For all his faults, he has a sense of humor.

When Camille was forced to take sick leave, Armand visited him at the clinic. He'd wait until he could find someone driving that way so he didn't have to pay to get there, and he invariably turned up empty-handed, always with a different excuse, but at least he visited. He was devastated by what had happened to Camille. His anguish was genuine. You work side by side with someone for years only to find out you don't really know them. All it takes is an accident, a tragedy, an illness, a death for you to realize how much of what you know about them is simply random information. Armand can be generous, though that may sound bizarre. Obviously, he's not generous with money, or with anything that costs money, but he has a generosity of spirit. Not that anyone in the squad would believe it; mention it, and anyone he's ever hit for money—meaning everyone—would crack up laughing.

When he came to the clinic, Camille would give him money to get a newspaper, a couple of coffees from the machine, and a magazine. Armand always kept the change. And at the end of the visit, as he leaned out of the window, Camille would see Armand wandering around the car park talking to people leaving the clinic, trying to find someone who could drop him close enough to his place that he could walk the rest of the way.

It's painful, finding themselves together again after four years. The only person missing from the old team is Maleval. He was kicked off the force. Spent a couple of months on remand. What's become of him? Camille suspects Louis and Armand still see him from time to time. He couldn't bring himself to.

The three of them are standing in front of the huge map of Paris, not saying anything, and when the silence starts to feel like a furtive prayer, Camille snorts. He points to the map.

"Okay Louis, as we discussed, you take the teams up to the crime scene. Get them to comb the area."

He turns to Armand.

"You, Armand: we've got a standard-issue white van, a set of generic tires, the victim's run-of-the-mill meal, a *métro* ticket . . . An embarrassment of options."

Armand nods.

Camille picks up his keys.

All he has to do is get through today, and then Morel will be back.

9

The first time the man comes back, Alex's heart heaves into her throat. She can hear him, but she cannot turn to see him. The footsteps are slow, heavy; they echo like a threat. Alex has spent every single hour anticipating his return, has imagined herself being raped, beaten, killed. She has seen the cage being lowered, felt the man grab her by the shoulder, drag her from the cage, slap her, twist her, force her, rape her, make her scream, kill her. Just as he promised. "I'm going to watch you die, you filthy whore." When you call a woman a filthy whore, it means you want to kill her, doesn't it?

It hasn't happened yet. He hasn't touched her yet; perhaps he's getting off on the waiting. Putting her in a cage is designed to turn her into an animal, to degrade her, break her, to show her he is the master. This is why he beat her so savagely. These thoughts and a thousand others more terrible still prey on her mind. Dying is no picnic. But waiting for death . . .

Alex resolves to make a mental note of when he comes, but all sense of time quickly becomes blurred. Morning, daytime, evening, night are all part of a continuum in which her mind finds it increasingly difficult to navigate.

Every time he comes he stands in front of the cage, hands in his pockets, and stares at her for a long time; then he puts his leather jacket on the floor, winches the crate down to eye level, pulls out his cell phone and takes a photograph, then walks the short distance to the place where he has dumped everything else—a dozen bottles of water, plastic bags, Alex's clothes strewn on the floor: it's hard for her, seeing these things almost within reach. He sits down. For a while he does nothing, he simply watches her. He looks as though he's waiting for something, but he doesn't say what.

And then, something, she doesn't know what, something prompts him to leave; he gets up without warning, slaps his thighs as though to spur himself on, winches the crate up again and, with a final glance, he leaves.

He never says a word. Alex has tried asking questions—not too many because she doesn't want to make him angry—but he only ever answered once; the rest of the time he says nothing, seems to think nothing. He simply stares at her. As he said: "I'm going to watch you die."

Alex's position is—literally—unendurable.

It's impossible for her to stand; the cage is not high enough. Impossible to lie down, since it's not long enough. To sit, since the top is too low. She lives curled up on herself, almost into a ball. The pain soon became unbearable. Her muscles have begun to permanently cramp, her joints to seize up; everything is numb, everything is rigid, to say nothing of the cold. Her whole body is stiff, and, as she is unable to move, her circulation has slowed, which adds to the pain of the muscle contractions she must endure. She remembers images, diagrams from her nursing training of atrophied muscles; stiff, sclerotic joints. Sometimes it feels as though she is observing her own body wasting away, as though she is a radiologist, as though this body is not hers, and she realizes that her mind is beginning to divide into a person who is here and another who is not, who lives elsewhere, the beginnings of a madness that lies ahead, which is the inexorable result of this insufferable, inhuman position.

She cried for a long time, but then she found she had no more tears. She sleeps little, never for very long, since she is continuously awakened by muscle spasms. She experienced the first really painful cramps last night, waking up screaming, her whole leg wracked by a terrible spasm. In an attempt to relieve the pressure, she pounded her foot against the planks as hard as she could, as though trying to smash the cage to pieces. Gradually the cramp passed, but she knows that it had nothing to do with her efforts. The spasm will come back just as it went away. She has succeeded only in rocking the cage. When it starts to swing, it takes a long time to come to a standstill again. After a while it makes her stomach heave. Alex spent hours dreading that the spasm would come back. She monitors every part of her body, but the more she thinks about it, the more painful it becomes.

In the rare moments when she sleeps, she dreams of prison, of being buried alive, or drowned; when it's not the cramps, the cold, or the fear, it is the nightmares that wake her. Now, having moved only a few inches in the space of twenty or thirty hours, she is experiencing convulsions, as though her muscles are trying to move. These are reflex spasms over which she has no control; her limbs slam against the planks; she howls.

She would sell her soul to be able to stretch out, to be able to lie down for an hour.

On one of his first visits, using another rope, he hoisted a wicker basket up to the cage, where it swung for a long time before finally coming to a halt. Though it was very close, Alex had to summon all her reserves of willpower, had to rip her hands pushing them between the slats just to grab part of the contents: a bottle of water and some dry dog food. Or maybe cat food. Alex didn't stop to think; she wolfed it down. Only later did she wonder whether he had spiked it with something. She has started trembling again, but it's impossible to know whether she is trembling from cold, from exhaustion, from thirst, from fear . . . The dog food doesn't fill her up, it simply makes her thirstier. She eats it only when the hunger gnaws at her. And then there's the fact that she has to piss and everything else . . . At first, she felt ashamed, but what could she do? It splatters beneath the cage like the droppings of some giant bird. The shame quickly passed; it's nothing compared with the pain, nothing compared with the dread of having to live like this for days on end, unable to move, to change her position, not knowing how long he is planning to keep her captive, not knowing whether he really intends to let her die in this crate.

How long would it take to die like this?

The first few times he came, she pleaded with him, she begged for forgiveness, she doesn't know why, and once—it just slipped out—she even begged him to kill her. She had not slept for hours, the thirst was excruciating, and though she had chewed it for a long time, she had puked up the dog food; she stank of piss and vomit; being unable to move was driving her insane; and in that instant, death had seemed preferable to carrying on. She immediately regretted her words, because she does not want to die, not now—this is not how she imagined her life would end. She still has so much she wants to do. But it doesn't matter what she says, what she asks: the man never replies.

Except once.

Alex was crying hard, she was exhausted, she could feel her mind starting to wander, her brain becoming a free electron, with no self-control, no ties, no bearings. He had lowered the crate to take a photograph. For perhaps the thousandth time, Alex said: "Why me?" The man looked up, as though the question had never occurred to him. He leaned over. Their faces a few inches apart, separated only by the slats.

"Because . . . because you're you."

For Alex this was a bolt out of the blue. It was as though everything stopped, as though God had flicked a switch; all at once she felt nothing, not cramp, nor thirst, the ache in her belly, not her bones, frozen to the marrow, her mind was so focused on what he was about to say.

"Who are you?"

The man smiled. Maybe he's not accustomed to saying much. Maybe those few words exhausted him. Rapidly he hoisted the cage, grabbed his jacket, and left without looking back—in fact he seemed angry. He had obviously said more than he intended.

That time, she hadn't touched the dog food—he had added more to what was left over—but she took the bottle of water and is saving it. She wanted to think about what he had said, but when you are in such pain it's impossible to think about anything else.

She spends hours with her arms tensed above her head, her hand gripping, stroking the huge knot in the rope holding up the cage. A knot as big as her fist, incredibly tight.

Over the course of the next night, Alex slipped into a sort of coma. Her mind could not focus on anything. She felt as though her muscle mass had wasted away, that she was nothing but bone, a singular contraction, a vast spasm from head to foot. Up until then, she had been able to stick to a regimen of infinitesimal exercises she repeated every hour or so. Wiggling her toes, moving her feet, then her ankles, turning them three times one way then three times the other, moving up, tensing one calf and relaxing it, tensing it again, then the other calf, stretching her right leg as far as it will go, drawing it back, and again, three times, etc.

But now she no longer knows whether she dreamed the exercises or whether she actually did them. What has awakened her is her moaning. At first it sounded as if it were someone else, some voice outside her. Little groaning sounds from deep in her belly, sounds she has never heard before.

And though now wide awake, she cannot stop these moans, which come in time to the rhythm of her breathing.

Alex realizes something. She has started to die.

10

Four days. Four days the investigation has been going nowhere. Forensics have turned up nothing; the witness statements have led nowhere. Somewhere someone had spotted the white van; somewhere else the van was blue. Somewhere else again, someone reported a woman, their neighbor, missing; they phone her—she's at work. Another woman being investigated is already on her way home from her sister's; her husband didn't even know she had a sister . . . It's a nightmare.

The procureur has appointed an investigating magistrate: a young, dynamic guy from a generation that likes things hot and heavy. The media have scarcely published the story—it was mentioned in the news in brief and immediately submerged by the daily wave of rolling news. All in all, they're no closer to identifying the kidnapper, and they still don't know the name of the victim. Every reported missing person has been checked, and none could be the woman on the rue Falguière. Louis has widened the search area to include the whole of Paris, checked into missing persons reports filed several days earlier, then several weeks, finally several months, but nothing—nothing that tallies with the description of a young, pretty girl whose route might have taken her along the rue Falguière in the fifteenth arrondissement.

"So we're saying no one knows this girl? She hasn't been seen for four days, and no one out there is worried?"

It's almost 10:00 p.m.

The three of them are sitting on a bench, staring at the canal, a neat little row of officers. Camille has left the rookie to man the office and taken Armand and Louis out to dinner. When it comes to restaurants, he has no imagination and no memory; trying to remember an address is like pulling teeth. There's no point asking Armand—he hasn't been to a restaurant since the last time someone else offered to pay, which means the place has probably been closed for a long time. As for Louis, anything he might recommend is well beyond Camille's budget. For dinner, his idea of a simple little restaurant is Taillevent or Ledoyen. So Camille takes the decision. La Marine on the Quai de Valmy, more or less next door to his building.

Time was, they had a lot to talk about. When they worked together, they quite often had dinner after clocking off. The rule was that Camille always paid. By his reckoning, letting Louis pay would be humiliating to the others, reminding them that though he works as a police officer, he's not short of money. No one would even think to ask Armand: if you invite Armand to dinner, you've already offered to pay. As for Maleval, he always had money problems, and everyone knows how that turned out.

Tonight, Camille was glad to pick up the tab. Though he doesn't say as much, he's happy to have his boys back. It's unexpected. It's something he couldn't have imagined three days ago.

"I don't get it . . . ," he says.

Dinner is over; they've crossed the street, and they're walking along the canal, looking at the barges.

"Nobody's missed her at work? No husband, no fiancé, no boyfriend, girlfriend, no one? No family? Though I suppose in a city this size, the way things are these days, the fact that no one's looking for her . . ."

The conversation tonight is just like all the conversations they've ever had, punctuated by long silences. They each have their own: pensive, introspective, or focused.

"I suppose you used to check in on your father every day?" Armand asks.

No, obviously, not even twice a week—his father could have dropped dead at home and lain there for a week before . . . He had a girlfriend he saw a lot of—she was the one who found him, who let him know. Camille met her for the first time two days before the funeral. His father had mentioned her in passing as though she were a mere acquaintance. It had taken three car trips to ferry everything she had at his place back to hers. A small woman, fresh faced and rosy cheeked as an apple with wrinkles that looked new minted. She smelled of lavender. For Camille, the idea that this woman had taken his mother's place in his father's bed was, in the literal sense, unimaginable. Two women who were polar opposites. It was a different world, maybe a different planet; he sometimes wondered what his parents had had in common—nothing, on the face of it. Maud, an artist, had married a pharmacist—go figure. He'd asked himself the question a thousand times. The little apple seemed to him a more natural fit. Whichever way you think about it, what goes on between our parents often remains a mystery, he thought. That said, some weeks later, Camille discovered that over a few short months the little wrinkled apple had siphoned off a large chunk of the pharmacist's assets. Camille had a good laugh about it. He never saw her afterwards, which was a pity; she was obviously a character.

"It was different for me," Armand went on. "My father was in a home. But when someone's living on their own, what can you do? They die, and for the body to be found right away . . . it would be sheer chance."

This thought puzzles Camille. He starts telling a story he read somewhere. Some guy called Georges. A combination of circumstances meant that no one was surprised not to hear from him for more than five years. Officially, he disappeared without anyone asking questions; his water and his electricity were cut off. His concierge believed he'd been in the hospital since 1996, but he had come home without her realizing. His corpse was finally found in his apartment in 2001.

"I read that in . . ."

He can't think of the title.

"It was by Edgar Morin, a title like *Thoughts on. . .* something."

"*Toward a Politics of Civilization*," Louis supplies gravely. He pushes his hair back with his left hand. Translation: *sorry . . .*

Camille smiles.

"Good, isn't it, having the old team back together?" says Camille.

"This case makes me think of Alice," Armand says.

This is hardly surprising. Alice Hedges, a girl from Arkansas, found dead in a dumpster on the banks of the Canal de l'Ourcq, whose body had not been identified for three years. When all's said and done, disappearing without a trace is not as rare as people think. But still you can't help wondering. You sit here staring at the greenish waters of the Canal Saint-Martin, and you know that a couple of days from now the case will be closed; you tell yourself the disappearance of this unknown woman will have touched no one. Her life will have been barely a ripple on the water.

No one mentions the fact that Camille is still working on a case that he wanted nothing whatever to do with. The day before yesterday, Le Guen called to tell him Morel was back from leave.

"Don't fucking talk to me about Morel," Camille said.

As he said it, Camille realized something he had known from the start: that provisionally taking on a case like this meant seeing it through to the end. He's not sure whether he should be grateful to Le Guen for dropping him in it. As far as his superiors are concerned, the case isn't even a priority any more. An unidentified kidnapper has abducted an unknown woman, and apart from a single witness who's been interviewed over and over again, there's no proof that the kidnapping even took place. There's the pool of vomit in the gutter, the squeal of tires heard by several people, the neighbor parking his car who remembers seeing a white van pull up onto the pavement. But it doesn't exactly amount to much; it's not like having an actual body, a bona fide corpse. As a result Camille has had to sweat blood to keep Louis and Armand on the case with him. But deep down, Le Guen, like everyone else, is happy to see Verhœven's old squad back together. It can't last long—a couple of days at the most—but for the moment, he's prepared to turn a blind eye. As far as Le Guen's concerned, even if the case is never solved, it's an investment.

The three men walked for a while after dinner, then found this bench where they're sitting watching people stroll along the canal: lovers mostly, people walking their dogs. You'd think you were in the provinces.

It's a hell of an odd team, though, Camille thinks. *On the one hand you've got a kid who's rich as Croesus, on the other a miser worthy of Scrooge McDuck. Maybe I've got issues with money?* He smiles as he thinks this. A few days ago, he received an information pack from the auctioneers about the sale of his mother's paintings, but he cannot bring himself to open the envelope.

"Okay," Armand says. "That just means you don't want to sell them. I think it's better that way."

"Oh sure, if it were up to you, he'd hang on to everything."

Particularly Maud's paintings—that's something that sticks in Armand's craw.

"No. Not everything. But, I mean, his mother's paintings . . ."

"You're talking like it's the crown jewels!"

"Well, we're talking about the family jewels, aren't we?"

Louis doesn't say anything. The minute things get personal, he clams up.

Camille goes back to the abduction.

"Where are you at on tracking down the van owner?" he asks Armand.

"Barely scratched the surface . . ."

The only lead they've got for the moment is the image of the vehicle. From the closed-circuit TV footage taken outside Bertignac's pharmacy, they've identified the make and model. There are tens of thousands of them on the road. Forensics have analyzed the lettering that was painted over and sent through a list of names that could correspond. From "Abadjian" to "Zerdoun." Three hundred and thirty-four names. Armand and Louis are working their way through the list. When they come across the name of someone who has ever owned or rented the same make of van, they check, find out who it was sold to down the line, whether it matches the one they're looking for, then send an officer out to look at the vehicle.

"It's a pain in the ass, especially if it's out in the sticks somewhere."

To make things worse, vans like this are constantly bought and sold—it's an endless cycle, tracking down every person and questioning them . . . The more people there are and the more difficult the search, the happier Armand is. Though "happy" is perhaps not the best word to describe him. This morning Camille watched him work, in his ancient, threadbare sweater, a sheaf of recycled paper in front of him and a ballpoint pen emblazoned with a logo for *Saint-André Dry Cleaners*.

"It's going to take weeks at this rate," Camille commented.

Not really.

His cell phone vibrates.

It's the rookie, spluttering and stammering, so excited he's forgotten Camille's instructions.

"Boss? The kidnapper's name is Trarieux—we've just tracked him down. The divisionnaire says you're to come in right now."

11

Alex hardly eats at all. She is terribly weak, but most importantly, her mind is in bad shape. The cage constrains the body and catapults the brain into the stratosphere. An hour in this position is enough to have you in tears. A day, and you think you'll die. Two days, and you start to lose it. Three days, you go mad. Now she doesn't even know how long she's been caged and hanging here. Days. Days.

She is no longer aware of the constant groans of pain coming from the pit of her stomach. She whimpers. She no longer has the strength to cry. She bangs her head against the slats again and again and again, and the moan becomes a wail—her forehead is streaming blood, her head is a howling madness; she wants to die as quickly as possible because it is living that has become intolerable.

Only when the man is here does she not moan. When he is here, Alex talks and talks; she asks questions not so that he will answer (he never speaks), but because when he leaves she feels terrifyingly alone. She understands now how hostages feel. She could beg him to stay, so great is her fear of being alone, of dying alone. He is her executioner, but it is as though while he is present she cannot die.

Of course, the reverse is true.

She is hurting herself.

Deliberately.

She is trying to kill herself because no help will come. She no longer has control of this broken, paralyzed body; she pisses herself, she is shaken by spasms, stiff from head to foot. In despair, she scrapes her legs against the rough edge of the plank; it burns at first, but Alex keeps on scraping, keeps on because she hates this body that is making her suffer—she wants to kill it. She rubs her leg with all her strength, and the burn becomes an open sore. She stares at a fixed point. A splinter pierces her calf. Alex rubs again and again waiting for the wound to bleed. She is hoping, longing to let herself bleed to death.

She is alone in the world. No one will come to rescue her.

How long will it take her to die? And how much longer before her body is found? Will he make her disappear, bury her? Where? She has nightmares, sees her body wrapped in a tarp, a shapeless lump, darkness, a forest, hands tossing the bundle into a pit—it makes a disturbing, desolate sound—she sees herself lying dead. She might as well be dead already.

An eternity ago, when she still knew what day it was, Alex thought of her brother. For all the good it will do her, thinking of her brother. He despises her; she knows that. He's seven years older, always known more about everything, been able to get away with anything. From the beginning, he was always the strong one. The one to teach her a lesson. Last time she saw him and he noticed her taking out a bottle of pills to help her sleep, he snatched it from her and shouted, "What the hell is this shit?"

Behaving as though he's her father, her conscience, her boss, as though he controls her life. That's how he's always been.

"Well, what the fuck is this shit?"

His eyes were bulging. He's always had a vicious temper. On this occasion, Alex reached out and ran her fingers slowly through his hair to calm him, but her ring snagged on a lock of hair as she pulled her hand away too quickly. He cried out and slapped her—just like that, in front of everyone. It doesn't take much to make him angry.

If Alex disappeared he . . . He'd be happy to have a bit of peace. It would be two or three weeks before he even started to wonder.

She thought about her mother, too. They don't talk much; they can go for months without telephoning. And her mother is never the one to call.

And her father . . . At times like this it must be good to have a father. To think he might come and save you, to believe, to hope, it must be soothing, but it would also drive you to despair. Alex doesn't know what it must be like to have a father. Mostly, she doesn't think about it.

But these were things she thought at the beginning of her incarceration. Now she would scarcely be able to string two rational ideas together; her mind simply cannot do it—it can only register the pain her body is inflicting on her. In the beginning, Alex even thought about her work. She works as a temp, and when the man abducted her, she'd just finished a contract. She was planning to sort out the various things she had going on, sort out her life. She has a little money put aside, enough to survive for two or three months at least—her needs are few—so she hadn't asked for a new assignment. No one is going to turn up asking for her. Sometimes, when she's working, a colleague will call, but right now, she's between contracts.

She has no boyfriend, no husband, no lover. This is what she has: nobody.

Maybe people will begin to worry about her months after she dies here, exhausted and insane.

Even if her mind still worked, Alex would not know which question to ask: how many days before I die? What will the pain of death be like? How does a corpse rot suspended between earth and heaven?

For now, he's waiting for me to die; those were his words: "watch you die." And she is dying.

Suddenly the "why" that has been nagging at her all this time bursts like a bubble, and Alex's eyes grow wide. The germ of an idea she has been brooding on unconsciously has inadvertently sprouted like a tenacious weed. It has triggered something in her mind—who knows how?—a revelation like a jolt of electricity.

She knows.

He's Pascal Trarieux's father.

Not that the two men look much alike, not at all, in fact—they're so dissimilar, it's hard to imagine that they would know each other. There's something about the nose, maybe; it should have dawned on her before. But there's no doubt it's him, and this is bad news for Alex because now she knows he was telling the truth: he brought her here to watch her die.

He wants her dead.

Until now, she has refused to believe that. Now the knowledge rushes through her mind—suddenly lucid as in those first moments—locking every door, extinguishing every last flicker of hope.

"So that's it . . ."

To her horror she realizes she did not hear him arrive. She cranes her neck trying to catch a glimpse of him, but before she has time, the crate begins to sway slightly, then to turn. And suddenly he appears in her line of sight. He is standing next to the wall winching the cage down. When she is at the right height, he ties off the rope and comes over. Alex frowns because there is something different about him this time. He is not looking at her; it's as if he's looking *through* her, and he's moving slowly, as though afraid of stepping on a land mine. Now that she can see him close-up, she can make out a slight resemblance to his son, that same willful face.

He has stopped two yards from the cage. He is not moving. She watches him take out his cell phone; she hears a rustling sound above her head. She tries to turn, but she can't; she's already tried a thousand times—it's impossible.

Alex feels desperate.

The man holds the phone at arm's length, smiles. It's a rictus Alex has seen before, and she knows it is an ominous sign. Again, she hears the rustle above her head, then the click of the camera. He nods, giving his approval to who knows what, then goes back to the corner of the room and hoists the cage again.

Alex's eyes are suddenly drawn to the wicker basket of dog food next to her, jerking and twitching as though it's alive.

Suddenly, she realizes. What's inside is not dog food or cat food.

She realizes as she sees the snout of a large rat appear over the side of the basket. Above her, on the lid of the cage, she can just make out two dark shapes scuttling, and she can hear the rustle of claws she heard earlier. The two shapes stop and poke their heads between the slats just above her head. Two rats with black, glittering eyes, both bigger than the first one.

Alex cannot help herself; she shrieks hard enough to tear her lungs.

Because this is why he has been leaving the dog food. Not to feed her. To attract them.

He is not going to kill her.

The rats are.

12

A former outpatient clinic, completely surrounded by walls near the Porte de Clichy. A huge, derelict nineteenth-century building that has long since been condemned, the area now served by a new teaching hospital at the other end of the suburb.

The place has been standing empty for two years; it's an industrial wasteland. The company redeveloping the site employs a security guard to keep out the squatters, the homeless, the illegal immigrants. Intruders and undesirables. The security guard has a small apartment on the ground floor and is paid to keep an eye on the place until building work starts some four months from now.

Jean-Pierre Trarieux, fifty-three, formerly a member of the clinic's cleaning staff. Divorced. No criminal record.

It is Armand who tracked down his van from a name on the list provided by forensics: Lagrange, a freelance contractor specializing in the installation of PVC windows who had retired two years earlier and sold off all his equipment. Trarieux had bought his van and had simply spray-painted over Lagrange's signage. Armand had e-mailed the image of the lower section of the vehicle to the local police station, who sent an officer out to check. Sergeant Simonet swung by as he was clocking off shift since it was on his way home and for the first time in his life regretted having always refused to buy a cell phone. Instead of going home, he rushed back to the station to report that the green paint mark on Trarieux's van—which was parked in front of the derelict clinic—is identical to the one in the closed-circuit TV footage. Camille, however, wanted to be absolutely sure. You don't launch the Siege of Troy without taking a few basic precautions. He sent an officer to discreetly scale the perimeter wall. It was too dark to take photographs, but there was no sign of any van there anyway. In all likelihood, Trarieux was not at home. There were no lights on in the apartment, no sign of life.

The trap is set, everything is ready; they're waiting for him to get back so they can take him in for questioning. Plainclothes officers hole up and wait. Everything is going according to plan until the *juge d'instruction*—the investigating judge—turns up, accompanied by Le Guen.

The meeting takes place in one of the unmarked police cars parked several hundred yards from the main gate.

The *juge d'instruction* is a guy of about thirty by the name of Vidard, the same name as Giscard d'Estaing's *secrétaire d'État*—or maybe Mitterrand's—who is probably his grandfather. He is a thin, gruff man who wears a pinstriped suit, gold cuff links, and loafers. Details like this speak volumes. The fellow looks as if he was born in a suit and tie. Try as you might to focus on what he is saying, you can't help imagining him naked. He's a straight arrow with the good looks of a playboy and a thick mane of hair parted at the side—he looks like an insurance salesman who dreams of going into politics. He's a future aging Lothario.

When she saw men like this, Irène used to laugh and say to Camille: "My God, he's handsome! Why can't I have a husband as handsome as that?"

Moreover, he seems rather stupid. *Probably runs in the family*, Camille thinks. Vidard is a man in a hurry; he wants to storm the place. There must be a three-star general somewhere in his family tree, too, because he wants to launch an offensive on Trarieux as soon as possible.

"We can't do that, it's ridiculous."

Camille could have chosen his words more judiciously, could have respected the proprieties, but this asshole is planning to risk the life of a woman who's been held hostage for five days. Le Guen steps in:

"As you'll see, *monsieur le juge*, Commandant Verhœven can be a little . . . abrupt at times. He's simply trying to say that perhaps it would be more prudent to wait for Trarieux to make his appearance."

Commandant Verhœven's abruptness doesn't faze the magistrate one little bit. In fact, he's determined to prove he's fearless, a man of decision. Better still, a strategist.

"I suggest we surround the building, free the hostage, and wait for the kidnapper inside."

Then faced with the stunned silence that greets this brilliant suggestion: "We'll have him trapped."

The team is flabbergasted. A silence Vidard evidently reads as admiration.

"And how exactly do you know the hostage is inside?" Camille is the first to react.

"Are you even sure he's definitely the man?" Vidard counters.

"We're sure that his van was at the scene at the time the woman was kidnapped."

"Which means it must be him."

Le Guen tries to think of a way to defuse the situation, but the magistrate gets there first.

"I understand your position, gentlemen, but you see, things have changed . . ."

"I'm all ears," Camille says.

"Forgive me for putting it so bluntly, but as a society we are no longer focused on criminals; we focus on the victims."

He looks from one to the other before concluding grandiloquently: "Tracking down criminals is entirely laudable; indeed it is our duty. But our greatest concern must be for the victims. They are the reason we are here."

Camille opens his mouth, but he has no time to say anything before the magistrate opens the car door and gets out. Cell phone in hand, he turns back, leans through the car window, and glares at Le Guen.

"I'm calling in RAID right now."

Camille to Le Guen: "This guy's a complete dick."

The magistrate is still standing next to the car but pretends not to hear. Genetics.

Le Guen rolls his eyes, and he, too, takes out his cell phone. They'll need backup to cover the perimeter in case Trarieux reappears just as they storm the building.

In less than an hour, everything is in place.

It's 1:30 a.m.

Sets of keys for the building have been urgently dispatched so all doors can be opened. Camille doesn't know Commissaire Norbert from the RAID squad. With a surname like that, no one ever asked his first name: shaved head, sure-footed as a cat. Camille feels he's seen the type a hundred times.

Having studied the maps and the satellite photos, the RAID officers are dispatched to four key points: one unit to the roof, one to the main entrance and two units covering the windows. The *brigade criminelle* is tasked with manning the perimeter. Camille has put units in unmarked cars at each of the three entrances. A fourth unit has been discreetly posted to cover the storm drain, the only other possible exit should the suspect try to make a run for it.

Camille has a bad feeling about the whole operation.

Commissaire Norbert is being careful. Caught in this standoff between a divisionnaire, a colleague, and a *juge d'instruction*, he sensibly limits his remarks to his area of expertise. When asked by the magistrate, "Can you storm the building and free the woman being held in there?" Norbert studied the maps, checked out the building, and in under eight minutes came back with the response: yes, they could storm the building. The advisability and appropriateness of such an action are a different matter, on which he has no authority to pronounce. But from his silence, his opinion is deafeningly clear. Camille likes the guy.

Of course it's frustrating to have to wait for Trarieux to come back when you know that inside is a woman who has been held in conditions you hardly dare imagine, but, he feels, it is the best course of action.

Norbert takes a step back; the investigating judge takes a step forward.

"What does it cost us to wait?" Camille says.

"Time," Vidard says.

"And what does it cost us to play it safe?"

"A life, maybe."

Even Le Guen is reluctant to intervene. Camille suddenly finds himself in a minority of one. The RAID team will storm the building.

Camille takes aside the officer who scaled the perimeter wall.

"Tell me again what it's like in there."

The officer doesn't quite know what to say.

"I mean," Camille is getting a little irritated, "what did you see in there?"

"I dunno, not much: construction machinery, a dumpster, a storage shed, some demolition equipment. Well, one excavator anyway . . ."

The mention of an excavator makes Camille think.

Norbert and his units are all in place and give the signal. Le Guen is following behind. Camille decides to stay within the grounds of the building.

He notes the precise time Norbert launches the operation: 1:57 a.m. From here and there in the deserted buildings lights flash on; there is the sound of running.

Camille thinks. Construction machinery. Some demolition equipment.

"There's been a lot of coming and going here," he says to Louis.

Louis gives a quizzical look, waiting for Camille to explain.

"Construction workers, engineers, I don't know what all, people delivering tools and materials before the building work starts, maybe even conducting meetings about the development project. Accordingly . . ."

"He's not going to be holding her here."

Camille doesn't have time to respond because just at that moment, Trarieux's white van appears around the corner, slows, and then takes off.

From this point, things move very quickly. Camille jumps into the car Louis is driving, radios the four units manning the perimeter wall, and then they give chase. Camille juggles with the car radio, providing running commentary of the exact location of the suspect's van heading for the suburbs. It's not very fast, and it's belching smoke—it's an old, worn-out model, so even if he floors the accelerator, Trarieux's got no hope of getting more than forty-five miles an hour out of this rust bucket. And it's not like the guy's a Formula One driver. He hesitates and wastes precious seconds making ridiculous maneuvers, allowing Camille to close the net. Louis has no problem staying right up his ass, lights flashing, siren wailing. Before long the police cars will have got the van boxed in; it's only a matter of seconds now. Camille continues to give their position, Louis drives up behind the van, headlights on full to freak the guy out, make him panic; two more cars appear, one from the left, one from the right; the fourth car has taken a parallel route, crossed the Périphérique and is coming back the other way. The die is cast.

Le Guen telephones Camille, who's hanging on tight to his safety belt.

"You got him?"

"Nearly," Camille shouts. "Anything your end?"

"You can't afford to fucking lose this guy, because the girl isn't here."

"I know."

"What?"

"Nothing."

"I said we've drawn a blank, do you copy?" Le Guen roars. "There's no one here."

As Camille is about to find out, this is to be a night of key images. The first, the opening scene in a way, is the overpass across the Périphérique, where Trarieux's van skids sideways and screeches to a halt. Two police cars behind him, a third in front blocking his escape route. The officers pile out, take cover behind the car doors and train their weapons on the van. Camille gets out, too—he's pulled his gun and is about to shout the standard warnings when he sees the man jump down from the van and lumber across to the railing, where, unbelievably, he sits facing them, as though goading them to come closer.

Everyone immediately knows what's coming next. One look at him is all it takes as he sits on the railing, his back to the traffic below, his legs dangling, staring at the line of police moving slowly toward him, weapons trained on him. This first image is the one that will stick: a man staring at the advancing officers.

He flings his arms wide, as though about to make some momentous statement.

Then he raises his legs high.

And topples over the edge.

Before they even reach the railing, they hear the body smash on the freeway below, the sound of the truck hitting him, the shriek of brakes, the car horns, the screech of metal of cars unable to stop in time.

Camille looks down. Below is a tangle of cars, a blaze of headlights and hazard warning lights. He turns, runs across the overpass and leans over the opposite railing. Trarieux has gone under the wheels of an articulated truck. Camille can see half the body, the shattered skull, blood spreading across the asphalt.

For Camille, the second image comes about twenty minutes later. The Périphérique is completely taped off, the whole area is an eerie scene of flashing lights and sirens, horns, paramedics, firefighters,

police, drivers and gawkers. They're on the overpass, in the car.
Louis is taking notes as Armand reels off the information they've
got on Trarieux. Next to him, Camille has snapped on latex gloves;
he's holding the suspect's cell phone, which somehow escaped the
wheels of the articulated truck.

Photographs, six of them, of a sort of wooden crate, the slats
regularly spaced, suspended above the ground. Inside, imprisoned,
a woman, young, maybe thirty, her hair lank, greasy, dirty, completely naked, huddled in a space clearly much too small for her. In
each picture she is looking at the photographer. Her eyes are frantic, ringed by dark circles. But her features are delicate, her dark
eyes are striking; she is in a terrible state, but this cannot hide the
fact that in ordinary circumstances she must be quite pretty. But
right now all the images tell the same story: pretty or not, this caged
woman is dying.

"A *fillette*," Louis says.

"A what? What are you talking about?"

"The cage. It's a *fillette*."

And seeing that Camille is still puzzled: "A cage that makes it
impossible to stand or sit."

Louis stops. He doesn't like to flaunt his cleverness; he knows
what Camille's like. But this time Camille gives an exasperated
nod—*come on, get on with it.*

"It's an instrument of torture created under Louis XI for the
bishop of Verdun. He was kept in it for ten years. It's a passive but
very effective torture. The joints fuse, the muscles atrophy . . . and it
drives the victim insane."

They can see the girl's hands frantically gripping the wooden
slats. It's enough to turn your stomach. The last photograph shows
only part of her face and three large rats scuttling across the top of
the cage.

"Fucking hell . . ."

Camille tosses the phone to Louis as though afraid of burning
his fingers.

"Check the date and time of the images."

Camille's not much use when it comes to technology. It takes Louis precisely four seconds.

"The last photograph was taken three hours ago."

"What about calls? The calls!"

"Last call was ten days ago."

Not a single call since he abducted the girl.

Silence.

No one knows who this girl is or where he's been keeping her. The one person who did know has just been hit by an articulated truck.

Camille picks two images from Trarieux's cell phone, including the one with the huge rats. He types a text to the magistrate, copying the message to Le Guen:

Now that the "criminal" is dead, how do you suggest we focus on the victim?

13

When Alex opened her eyes, the rat was staring at her inches from her face, so close it seemed three or four times its actual size.

She screamed, and it scurried back to the basket, then darted up the rope, where it hung for a long time, whiskers twitching, uncertain of its next course of action, gauging the level of the threat. And the potential benefits of the situation. She screamed and swore, but the rat ignored her efforts, clinging to the rope, head down, staring at her. The pinkish nose, the glittering eyes, the glossy coat, the long white whiskers, and that tail that seems to go on forever. Alex is numb with terror, unable to catch her breath. She shouted herself hoarse, but, being very weak now, eventually she had to stop, and the two stared at each other for a long time.

Motionless, the rat dangles about sixteen inches above her, then, cautiously, climbs down into the basket and starts eating the kibble, shooting frequent looks at Alex. From time to time, suddenly panicked, it scampers away to take cover, only to quickly return. It seems to realize she is no threat. It is hungry. It's an adult rat, about twelve inches long. Alex crouches down in her cage, as far away as possible. She stares at the rat with a fury all the more absurd since it is intended to keep the animal at bay. It's eaten the dog food now, but it doesn't scamper back up the rope. Instead it moves toward her. This time Alex doesn't scream, she squeezes her eyes shut and cries. When she opens them again, the rat is gone.

Pascal Trarieux's father. How did he find her? If her brain weren't so slow, she might be able to think of an answer, but her thoughts now are frozen images, like photographs: nothing is moving. Besides, what does it matter how he found her? She has to negotiate; it's her only option. She has to come up with a story, something credible, anything that will persuade him to let her out of this crate—after that, she'll think of something. Alex gathers all the information she can, but her thought process goes no further. A second rat has just appeared.

A bigger rat.

The king rat, maybe. Its coat is much darker.

This one did not crawl down the rope to the basket, no, it darted down the rope supporting the cage and appeared just above Alex's head. And unlike the previous rat, it didn't scurry away when she screamed and swore at it, simply moving in short, fitful bursts until it could rest its forepaws on the top of the crate. Alex can smell the acrid stench of it; it is a fat, sleek rat with long white whiskers and deep black eyes. Its tail is so long that it dangles between the slats and touches Alex's shoulder.

She screams. The rat turns unhurriedly to look at her, then paces up and down the slat three or four times, stopping from time to time to stare at her as though taking measurements. Alex follows it with her eyes, her whole body tensed, her breathing ragged, her heart beating fit to burst.

That's what I smell like, she thinks. *I smell of shit and piss and vomit. It smells carrion.*

The rat rears up on his hind paws, sniffing.

Alex's eyes move up along the rope.

Two other rats have just begun their descent toward the cage.

14

The building site at the old clinic looks as if it's been overrun by a film crew. The RAID team has left, forensics have laid dozens of yards of cable, and the courtyard is flooded by the glare of spotlights. It's the middle of the night, but there's not an inch of shadow anywhere. Sterile walkways have been created, marked off with red-and-white police tape, making it possible to walk around without contaminating the scene. The forensics crew are collecting evidence.

What they need to find out is whether Trarieux brought the girl here at any point after the abduction.

Armand likes to have people milling around. As far as he's concerned, a crowd is first and foremost a ready supply of cigarettes. He glides easily past those he's already scrounged off too often before they get a chance to warn newcomers; he's already stocked up enough to last him four days.

Standing in the courtyard, he finishes a cigarette whose stub has begun to burn his fingers and gazes perplexedly over all this activity.

"Well?" Camille says. "I'm guessing the magistrate didn't hang around?"

Armand thinks about saying something, but he's philosophical; he's learned the virtue of patience.

"It's not as if he came out to the crime scene on the Périphérique either," Camille goes on. "Pity, because it's not every day you get to see a criminal apprehended by an articulated truck. Still . . ."

Camille deliberately checks his watch. Armand, unflappable, stares at his shoelaces. Louis seems to be mesmerized by the outline of an excavator.

"Still, at three in the morning, he's probably getting some sleep. I mean, coming out with that level of bullshit all day long must take it out of a man."

Armand drops the microscopic remnant of the cigarette butt and sighs.

"What? What did I say?" Camille says.

"Nothing," Armand says, "nothing. So are we going to do some fucking work or what?"

He's right. Camille and Louis elbow their way through to Trarieux's apartment, which is also crawling with techs from *l'identité judiciaire*, and since the place isn't exactly roomy, everyone tries to be accommodating.

Verhœven takes a general overview. It's a smallish apartment, rooms tidy, dishes tidied away, tools set out like a hardware shop window, and an impressive stockpile of beer. Enough to get all of Nicaragua shit-faced. Apart from that, no papers, no books, not even a notepad: an illiterate's apartment.

There is one curious thing about the scene: a teenager's bedroom.

"The son, Pascal," Louis says, checking his notes.

Unlike the rest of the apartment, this room obviously hasn't been cleaned in ages; it smells musty and damp, like moldy laundry. There's an old Xbox with a wireless controller caked with dust. Only the huge screen of the state-of-the-art computer looks as though it's been recently cleaned, probably a quick wipe with the back of a sleeve. A crime scene investigator is already checking the contents of the hard drive before it's taken away for a thorough analysis.

"Games, games, more games," the tech reports, "Internet connection . . ."

Camille goes on listening as he checks out the contents of a closet being photographed by another officer.

"Porn sites," says the guy checking out the computer. "Video games and porn. My kid's just the same."

"Thirty-six."

Everyone turns to look at Louis.

"Trarieux's son is thirty-six," Louis says.

"Okay," the tech says. "Well, that obviously puts things in a different light."

In the closet, Camille itemizes Trarieux's arsenal. The building site security manager plainly took his job very seriously: baseball bat, blackjack, brass knuckles—he went on his rounds fully equipped. Surprising not to find a pit bull.

"The pit bull here is Trarieux," Camille says to Louis, who had made the observation. Then, to the officer checking the computer: "Anything else?"

"E-mails, only a couple. Then again, given the guy's spelling . . ."

"Your kid's just the same?"

This time the officer looks irked. It's different when he says it.

Camille peers at the monitor. The guy's got a point. From what he can see the messages are inoffensive, the spelling almost phonetic.

Camille snaps on the latex gloves proffered by Louis and picks up a photograph someone has found in a chest of drawers. A snapshot clearly taken a couple of months ago since it shows the son with his father on the building site; you can see the site and the bulldozer through the window. Not exactly a handsome lad, tall and lanky with the face of a spoiled brat, a long nose. He thinks of the images of the girl in the cage. Distraught but still pretty. Not exactly a matching pair.

"Looks thick as pigshit," Camille mutters.

15

She's remembered something, something she heard somewhere. Whenever you see a rat, there are nine others nearby. So far she's seen seven. They've fought over the rope, but especially over the kibble. Strangely, the biggest rats don't seem to be the most voracious. They seem to be strategists. Two in particular. Utterly oblivious to Alex's screams, her insults, they spend most of their time on the top of the cage. The thing she finds most terrifying is when they sit up on their hind paws and sniff the air. They're huge, monstrous. Over time, some of the rats become more insistent, as though they've worked out that she does not represent a threat. They become bolder. Earlier this evening a medium-sized rat, trying to scrabble over the others, fell through the slats and landed on her back. Nauseated by the physical contact, she let out a scream—there was a brief uncertainty among the other rats, but the disturbance didn't last long. A few minutes later, they were back in their serried ranks. One of the rats—a young one, Alex suspects—is particularly persistent, particularly greedy; it creeps right up and sniffs her, she inches away, but it just keeps coming—it retreats only when she screams at the top of her lungs and spits at it.

Trarieux hasn't been for a long time now, a day at least, maybe two. Now another day drags on. If only she could know what day it is, what time it is . . . She's surprised he hasn't been by to see her, surprised he's missed three or four visits in a row. What worries her is that she might run out of water. She tries to save as much as she can and, fortunately, managed to drink very little yesterday. She has almost half a bottle left, but she was relying on him to bring more. And the rats are less skittish when they've got dog food; when there's none, they become irritable and impatient.

Ironically, what panics Alex is the thought of Trarieux abandoning her. Of him leaving her in this cage to die of starvation, of thirst, watched by the beady eyes of rats that will surely become more daring before long. The larger rats are already looking at her in a worrying way; she can't help but ascribe intentions to their behavior.

Since she saw the first rat, there's never been a period of more than twenty minutes when one or another of them didn't scuttle across the top of the cage or scrabble down the rope to check for kibble.

Some of them swing in the wicker basket, staring at her.

16

7:00 a.m.

The divisionnaire has taken Camille to one side.

"Listen, this case—I need you to play it straight, okay?"

Camille doesn't promise anything.

"Well, that's a good start . . . ," Le Guen says.

And he's right. From the moment Vidard shows up, Camille can't help throwing the door open, gesturing to the photographs of the young woman that are pinned to the wall and announcing: "Since you're so focused on the victim, *monsieur le juge*, this should make your day. She seems perfect."

The pictures plastering the wall have been enlarged so that they look like S&M porn. They truly turn your stomach. In one shot, all that is visible of the girl's haunted face is a horizontal strip framed by two slats; her body, curled into a fetal position, looks broken, the head tilted, pressed against the top of the cage. In another, a close-up of her hands, the fingernails bleeding, probably from clawing at the wood. Another shot of her hands, clutching a bottle of water clearly too big to fit between the slats.

You can picture the prisoner having to drink out of the palm of her hand like a castaway. Clearly she's not been allowed out of the cage because she's been forced to relieve herself as she squats there and her legs are spattered with filth. Dirty, bruised, she's been beaten, probably raped. But the pictures are all the more disturbing because she is still alive. It's impossible to imagine what lies in store for her.

But faced with this spectacle, and in spite of Camille's taunting, the magistrate remains calm, studies the photographs one by one.

Everyone falls silent. Everyone meaning Armand, Louis, and the six detectives Le Guen has assigned to the case. Coming up with a team like that at a moment's notice took some doing.

The magistrate, his face solemn and pensive, moves slowly along the line of photographs. Like a junior minister opening an exhibition. *He may be a stupid little fool and a bastard, but he's not a coward*, Camille thinks, as the man turns to face him.

"Commandant Verhœven," he says, "I know you disagree with my decision to storm Trarieux's residence; for my part, I disagree with the way you have been running this investigation from the beginning."

Seeing Camille open his mouth, the magistrate raises a hand, palm out, to cut him off.

"What we have is a difference of opinion, one that I propose we settle later. It seems to me that, whatever you might think, the most pressing matter now is to quickly locate this . . . victim."

He may be a bastard, but he's undeniably a cunning bastard. Le Guen lets two or three seconds of silence pass then coughs. But the magistrate quickly turns to the team and continues.

"If I may, divisionnaire, I'd like to congratulate your men on having tracked Trarieux down so quickly with such scant evidence. Remarkable work."

This really is too much.

"Are you running for election?" Camille says. "Or is this a particular approach you've patented?"

Le Guen coughs again. Another silence. Louis purses his lips delightedly. Armand smiles down at his shoes. Everyone else wonders what the hell is going on.

"Commandant," the magistrate says, "I'm well aware of your service record. I'm also aware of those details of your personal history intimately related to your work."

This time, the smiles of Louis and Armand freeze. Camille and Le Guen go into high-alert mode. The magistrate has stepped forward, though not close enough to seem as though he is eyeing the commandant scornfully.

"If you should feel that this case—how shall I put it?—might have too great an impact on your personal life, I would of course understand."

The warning is clear, the threat only thinly disguised.

"I'm sure that Divisionnaire Le Guen could bring in someone less conflicted to run the case. But, but, but . . . ," he spreads his hands wide now, as though holding back the clouds, "but I leave that to your commanding officer. I have every confidence."

As far as Camille is concerned, this settles the matter: the guy is a grade-A asshole.

Camille has long understood how those murderers feel, the ones who kill without meaning to, in a fit of blind rage; he's arrested dozens of them. Husbands who strangled their wives, wives who stabbed their husbands, sons who pushed their fathers out of windows, friends who shot friends, neighbors who ran over their neighbor's son—now he racks his brains trying to remember a case where a police commandant drew his service revolver and put a bullet through the forehead of a magistrate. But Camille says nothing, merely nods. It takes every ounce of strength to say nothing in spite of the magistrate's dismissive reference to Irène. In fact it is the reason he finds the strength to hold his tongue: because a woman has been abducted, and he has sworn to himself that he will find her alive. The magistrate knows this. He understands and clearly decides to take advantage of Camille's self-imposed silence.

"Very good," he says with evident satisfaction. "Now that ego has deferred to the spirit of public service, I think you can all get back to work."

Camille is going to kill him. He knows this. It will take as long as it takes, but he will kill him. With his bare hands.

"Divisionnaire." The magistrate turns to Le Guen and, making good his exit, says in measured tones, "It goes without saying I expect to be kept closely informed."

"We have two key priorities," Camille says to his team. "First, work up a profile of this Trarieux guy, get to know everything about his life. Somewhere in there we'll find a link to our girl and maybe her identity. Because our main problem is that we still don't know anything about her, we don't know who she is, so obviously we don't know why he abducted her. This leads me to the second priority: our only lead on Trarieux is the list of contacts in his cell phone and the one on his son's computer—which Trarieux obviously used. The list is not up-to-date, a couple of weeks old to judge from the call log, but it's all we've got."

It's not much. The only facts they have right now are alarming. No one can say what Trarieux intended when he locked the girl in that suspended cage, but now that he's dead, they all know she hasn't got long to live. None of them puts the danger into words—dehydration, starvation—they all know such a death is slow and painful. Not to mention the rats. Marsan is the first to speak. He'll be acting as liaison between Verhœven's squad and the forensics teams working on the case.

"Even if we do find her alive," he says, "dehydration can have irreversible neurological consequences. By the time we get to her, she might be a vegetable."

He doesn't pull his punches. And he's right, Camille thinks. *I don't dare because I'm scared, but we're not going to find this girl by being scared.* He shakes himself.

"What do we have on the van?" he says.

"Forensics went over it with a fine-tooth comb last night," Marsan says, checking his notes. "Found hair and blood, so we've got DNA for the victim, but since she's not on file, we still don't know who she is."

"What about the E-FIT?"

Trarieux was carrying a picture of his son in his inside pocket. It was taken at an amusement park and showed the son with a girl whose arm was draped around his neck, but the photograph was soaked in blood, and, besides, it was taken from some distance away. The girl looks quite fat, and there's no guarantee it's the same person. The photographs on the cell phone are more promising.

"We should end up with something good," Marsan says. "It's a cheap phone, but we've got several shots of the face from different angles, pretty much everything we need. You'll have it this afternoon."

Analyzing the location will be crucial. The problem is that all the shots were taken in close-up or tight close-up; there's very little of the location where the girl is being held. Digital forensics have been over them, making measurements, analyses, projections . . .

"We still don't know what kind of building it is. Given the date on the photographs and the available light in the pictures, we know the room faces northeast. That's pretty common. There's no perspective in the pictures, no depth of field, so it's impossible to calculate the dimensions of the room. The light is coming from above, so we estimate the ceilings are at least fourteen feet high. Maybe more . . . we can't be sure. The floor is concrete, and there seems to be a leak from somewhere. All the photographs were taken in natural light, so there might not be any electricity supply. As for the materials used by the kidnapper, from what little we can tell, there's nothing out of the ordinary. The crate is made of planks of untreated timber you can get anywhere, it's screwed together, the steel ring it's suspended from is standard issue, and there's nothing on the rope either—it's standard hemp rope. From what we can tell, the rats aren't specially bred. So we're probably looking at an abandoned, disused building."

"The dates on the photographs prove Trarieux visited at least twice a day," Camille says. "So it has to be somewhere in the Paris suburbs."

Everyone around him nods in agreement. Camille can tell they knew this already. Fleetingly he imagines himself at home with Doudouche. He doesn't want to be here anymore; he should have handed the case over when Morel got back. He closes his eyes. Pulls himself together.

Louis suggests Armand take charge of making a short description of the place based on the limited information they have and urgently circulate it to stations all over the Île-de-France. "Yeah, of course," Camille agrees. They're under no illusions. Their information is so generic, it applies to three out of five buildings, and, according to the figures Armand has collated from other police stations, there are sixty-four sites in the Paris area classified as "industrial wasteland," not to mention hundreds of buildings and warehouses standing empty.

"Anything in the media?" Camille asks Le Guen.

"You kidding?"

Louis heads down the corridor toward the exit, then turns and hurries back.

"I was thinking . . ." he says to Camille. "It's all a bit sophisticated, don't you think? Building a *fillette*? Maybe a bit too clever for someone like Trarieux?"

"No, Louis, I don't. I think *you're* too clever for Trarieux. He didn't build a *fillette*; that's *your* word, a nice, obscure word that shows everyone how cultivated you are. But he didn't build a *fillette*: he built a cage. And it's too small."

Slumped in his chair, Le Guen listens to Camille. His eyes are closed; he looks as if he's asleep. This is how he concentrates.

"Jean-Pierre Trarieux," Camille begins. "Fifty-three years old, born October 11, 1953. A qualified metalworker with twenty-seven years' experience in aeronautical workshops—starting out at Sud Aviation in 1970. Laid off in 1997, two years on unemployment; he ends up getting a maintenance job at René-Pontibiau Hospital, laid off again two years later, unemployed again; in 2002 he gets a job working security on the building site. He gives up his apartment and goes to live on the site."

"Violent?"

"Brutal. His personnel record is full of scraps and fights; the guy's got a hair-trigger temper. At least that's what his wife thinks. Roseline. Married her in 1970. One son, Pascal, born the same year. Now that's where things get interesting, but I'll get back to the son."

"No," Le Guen interrupts him. "Tell me now."

"He was reported missing. July last year."

"Go on."

"I'm waiting on further information but, roughly speaking, Pascal fucked up pretty much everything: school, vocational college, apprenticeship, job. As failures go, he's got the full set. He does unskilled labor—removal man, that kind of thing. Emotionally unstable. The father manages to get him a job in the hospital where he works—this is in 2000. They're coworkers. The following year they're both made redundant—that's working-class solidarity—and wind up on unemployment at the same time. When the father gets the security job in 2002, the son comes to live with him. Let me remind you, Pascal is thirty-six! We've been through his room in his father's apartment. Video game console, soccer posters, and a broadband connection for looking at porn sites. If it weren't for the six-packs of beer under the bed, you'd think he was a teenager. In books, when they're afraid it might not be clear, people say an 'overgrown teenager.' Then—bang—July 2006, the father reports the son missing."

"Any investigation?"

"Of sorts. The father's worried, but given the circumstances, the police couldn't do much. The son ran off with some girl, took his clothes, his personal effects and the contents of his father's bank account—623 euros—you get the picture. Anyway, the father is sent off to the *préfecture*'s missing persons division. They put the word out locally: nothing. In March, the search was widened to include the whole country. Still nothing. Trarieux's screaming blue murder; he wants this thing solved. So early August, a year after the son disappeared, he gets the standard form letter: 'All attempts to locate the person have been unsuccessful.' According to the latest information, the son is still missing. I'm guessing that when he gets wind of his father's death, he'll show up."

"What about the mother?"

"Trarieux divorced in 1984. Well, actually, his wife divorced him: spousal abuse, brutality, alcoholism. The son stayed with the father. Peas in a pod, those two. At least until Pascal decided to fuck off. The mother remarried, lives in Orléans. Madame . . ." Camille checks his notes, can't find the name. "Doesn't matter, I've sent someone to pick her up and bring her back here."

"Anything else?"

"Yeah, Trarieux's cell phone was a company phone; his employer wanted to be able to get in touch with him wherever he was on the site. The call log shows he barely used it; most of the calls are to his boss or fall under the category 'work related,' as they say. Then, suddenly, he starts using it. Not much, but it's something he hasn't done before. A dozen different numbers suddenly show up in the logs, people he calls once, twice, three times . . ."

"So?"

"So, this sudden urge to get chatty starts two weeks after he receives the letter saying the search for his son has been 'unsuccessful,' and they stop three weeks before the girl's abduction."

Le Guen frowns.

Camille offers his conclusions:

"Trarieux thinks the police are doing fuck all so he starts up his own little investigation."

"You think the girl in the cage is the one the son ran off with?"

"I think so, yeah."

"I thought you said the girl in the photograph was fat? The one in the cage isn't fat."

"Depends what you mean by fat. Maybe she lost weight; how do I know? All I'm saying is, I think it's the same girl. But as for where this Pascal guy is, search me."

17

Since the beginning, Alex has been suffering from the cold, despite the fact that it's been particularly mild for September. She can't move, and she's suffering from malnutrition. Now things have deteriorated, because suddenly, in a few short hours, the weather has taken a turn for the worse. Previously the cold she felt was a symptom of her exhaustion, but now the temperature has actually dropped several degrees. The weather is overcast, so the level of light from the skylights has also gone down. Then Alex hears the first gusts of wind whipping through the warehouse; it whistles and howls painfully, sounding like the moans of someone in despair.

The rats, too, have pricked up their ears, whiskers quivering. A sudden downpour lashes the building, which rumbles and creaks like a ship about to founder. Before Alex has realized what is going on, all the rats are scurrying along the walls in search of the rain-water now streaming across the floor. She counts nine of them this time. She can't be sure that they're the same rats. The large piebald rat that arrived recently, which the other rats are afraid of—she watched it wallowing in a puddle, it had a puddle to itself—this rat is the first to come back. The first to scramble up the rope. It is a single-minded creature.

A wet rat is even more terrifying than a dry one: the fur looks dirtier, the eyes beadier, seemingly more vicious. When wet, the long tail looks slimy, as though it is a different animal, a snake.

After the rain comes the storm; after the humidity, the cold. Alex is scared stiff—she can't move, she can feel herself shiver all over; but these are not shivers, they are convulsions. Her teeth start to chatter. The wind blasts through the rooms so fiercely that the cage begins to spin.

The piebald rat on the rope scuttles up and down the top of the cage, rears up on its hind paws. It's obviously given a rallying signal, because seconds later all the rats are scampering up the rope—there are rats everywhere, on the lid, in the wicker basket swinging next to her.

A lightning flash illuminates the room, and the rats rear up as one, snouts pointed toward the heavens as though electrified, then scamper off in different directions. Not that they're afraid of the storm; it's like a sort of dance. They're galvanized.

Only the black-and-ginger piebald is left, on the plank nearest to Alex. He pokes his head toward her, his eyes widen, then he sits up on his hind paws, his ginger belly swollen, enormous. He starts to squeal, waving his forepaws about wildly. His paws are pink, but Alex can see only the claws.

These rats are clever. They've realized that to her hunger, the thirst, the exhaustion, they need only add fear. In chorus they begin to shriek and screech, trying to scare her. Alex feels the icy rain carried by the gusts of wind. She's not crying; she's shivering. She had thought death would be a deliverance, but the prospect of being gnawed by rats, the idea of being eaten alive . . .

How many days' food does a human body represent to a dozen rats?

Petrified, Alex lets out a wail.

But for the first time, no sound comes from her throat.

She passes out from exhaustion.

18

Le Guen sits up, gets to his feet, and paces around his office as Camille continues with his progress report, then he comes back and resumes his position, a brooding potbellied sphinx. As he takes his seat, Camille notices the divisionnaire trying to conceal what looks like a satisfied smile. He is probably satisfied that he's got his daily exercise routine out of the way. Twice or three times a day he does this, gets up, paces as far as the door and back. Sometimes four times. A training regime that demands iron discipline.

"Seven or eight people in Trarieux's contact list proved interesting," Camille picks up again. "He called each of them, some of them several times. The questions were always the same. He was trying to find out about his son's disappearance. When he went to see them, he'd show them the photograph of his son at the amusement park with the girl."

Camille interviewed only two witnesses personally; Louis and Armand talked to the others. He's come to Le Guen's office to keep him up to date, but the divisionnaire isn't the reason he's back in the headquarters of the *brigade criminelle*. He's here to see the former

Mme. Trarieux, who has just arrived from Orléans. The local police arranged the transport.

"Trarieux probably got their contact details from his son's e-mails. They're a pretty mixed bunch."

Camille checks his notes.

"Valérie Touquet, thirty-five, a former schoolmate Pascal Trarieux spent fifteen years desperately trying to get into bed."

"At least he's consistent."

"The father called her a number of times to ask if she knew where his kid was. According to her, the guy's a complete oddball. 'A weirdo.' And if you say nothing for a minute, she says, 'He was a total loser. Always trying to impress girls with his stupid stories.' All in all, a bit of a halfwit. But nice with it. Anyway, she has no idea what happened to him."

"Anyone else?"

"Patrick Jupien, a delivery driver for a laundry company, a friend of Pascal's from the racetrack. Hasn't heard a peep out of Trarieux either. Doesn't recognize the girl in the picture. There's another schoolmate, Thomas Vasseur, a sales rep., and an old workmate, Didier Cottard, a warehouseman Pascal worked with at a mail-order company—but it's the same shit with all of them: the father telephones, drops by to visit, pisses everyone off. And obviously none of them have heard from Pascal in ages. The ones who know anything know there's a girl mixed up in the whole business. This was big news, apparently, Pascal Trarieux having a girlfriend. His pal Vasseur cracked up when he mentioned the girlfriend as if to say *For once in his life*. His friend the laundry driver confirmed that he spent weeks going on about some Nathalie, but as for Nathalie's surname, no one knows. And none of them ever got to meet her."

"That's interesting . . ."

"No, it's not really surprising. He met this girl sometime in mid-June and ran off with her about a month later. He didn't exactly have much time to introduce her to his friends."

The two men sit, thinking. Camille, frowning, flicks through his notes, glances toward the window from time to time as though looking for the answer to some question, then buries his face in his notebook again. Le Guen knows him all too well. He gives it a moment, then says:

"Go on, spit it out."

Camille is embarrassed, which is rare for him.

"Well, if you want the truth . . . This girl, there's something not right about her."

He quickly brings his hands up as though to protect his face.

"I know, I know, Jean! She's the *victim*. Victims are sacrosanct. But you asked what I thought, and I'm telling you."

Le Guen sits up in his chair, both elbows planted on the desk.

"That's pathetic, Camille."

"I know."

"For the past week this woman's been locked up like a bird in a cage hanging six feet off the ground—"

"I know, Jean."

"You only have to look at the photographs to know she's dying."

"Yeah."

"The guy who abducted her is a violent, illiterate, alcoholic scumbag . . ."

Camille just sighs.

"Who's locked her in a cage and left her to the rats . . ."

Camille opts for a pained nod of the head.

"And threw himself off the Périphérique overpass rather than tell us where she is!"

Camille closes his eyes like someone who doesn't want to witness the extent of the damage he's caused.

"But you think there's 'something not right about her'!? Have you told anyone else about your hunch, or did you save the scoop for me?"

But when Camille does not protest, when he remains silent, worse still, when he does not defend himself, Le Guen knows there's something else. Some anomaly. Silence, then:

"I just don't get it," Camille says slowly. "Why has no one reported this woman missing?"

"For Christ's sake, thousands of women—"

"Go missing. I know, Jean, thousands of people no one ever comes looking for. But . . . this guy, Trarieux, he's a moron, agreed?"

"Agreed."

"Not exactly sophisticated."

"You've made your point."

"Then tell me this: What was it about this girl that made him so enraged? And why go about it the way he did?"

Le Guen rolls his eyes; he doesn't understand.

"Because, let's look at the facts: here's this guy plodding along investigating his son's disappearance, then he goes and buys timber, builds a cage, finds a place where he'll be able to keep the girl for days on end; then he kidnaps her, locks her up and leaves her to die slowly and painfully, and comes back and takes pictures to make sure she's on her way . . . And you're telling me this was just some spur-of-the-moment stunt?"

"I never said that, Camille."

"Of course you said it, or you might as well have. He just came up with the idea. This sheet metal worker suddenly thinks to himself *Hey, why don't I track down the girl my son ran off with and shut her in a wooden crate?* And by pure coincidence, this girl turns out to be someone we can't identify. But this guy, who's a certifiable dumbass, has no trouble tracking her down, which is more than we've been able to do."

19

She barely sleeps now. She's too scared. Inside her cage, Alex squirms and writhes more than ever, suffers more than ever. From the moment of her abduction, she hasn't eaten properly, hasn't slept properly, hasn't been able to stretch her legs or her arms, to rest even for a moment, and now, the rats . . . Her mind is failing her: for hours at a time, everything she sees is misty, blurred; every sound she hears is muffled, like the echo of distant noises. She hears herself whimper and moan, hears low-pitched howls that come from deep in her belly. She is steadily growing weaker.

She keeps nodding off and jolting awake. Some time ago she blacked out from sheer exhaustion, half-mad with tiredness, with pain, her mind wandering, seeing rats everywhere.

Then all of a sudden—she doesn't know how—she knows that Trarieux is never coming back, that he's abandoned her here. If he comes back, she'll tell him everything—she says this to herself over and over as though it is a spell: Just let him come back, and I'll tell him everything, anything he wants, anything he wants. I just want this to be over. Let him kill her quickly—she can accept that—anything but the rats.

In the early hours, they scramble down the rope in single file, squeaking and screeching. They know she is theirs now.

They won't wait for her to die. They're too excited. Since this morning they've been fighting among themselves more than ever. They come closer and closer to sniff her. They're waiting until she's totally exhausted, but they are agitated, feverish. How will they know the sign? When will they decide to attack?

She shakes herself out of her stupor and has a moment of blinding clarity.

When he said, "I'm going to watch you die," what he meant was "I'm going to see you dead." He won't come back now; he won't come back until she's dead.

Above her, the largest of the rats, the black-and-ginger piebald, is sitting on its hind paws making high-pitched squeaks. It bares its teeth.

There's only one thing to do. Her feverish hand feels about for the splintered edge of the slat beneath her, the one she's been trying to avoid for hours because it's so jagged she cuts herself every time she touches it. Little by little, she digs her fingernails into the crevice; the wood parts slightly, she gains ground, she concentrates, applies as much force as she can. It takes some time and several attempts, but finally it snaps. Alex finds herself clutching a sliver of wood about six inches long. Razor-sharp. She peers up between the slats of the cage top, near the ring, near the rope holding the cage. Then, swiftly, she slips her hand between the planks and, with the pointed end, pushes the rat into the void. It tries to cling on, scrabbling desperately at the edge of the crate, gives a fierce shriek, and drops the six feet to the floor. Without waiting an instant, Alex stabs the splinter of wood into her hand and twists it like a knife, howling in pain.

Immediately blood starts to flow.

20

Roseline Bruneau has no desire to talk about her ex-husband; what she wants is news of her son. He has been missing for over a year.

"July fourteenth," she says anxiously, as though disappearing on Bastille Day might have some sort of symbolic weight.

Camille has come from behind his desk and is sitting next to her.

He used to have two chairs in his office, one with the seat deliberately raised, the other deliberately lowered. The psychological effect was very different. Depending on the circumstances, he would sit in one or the other. Irène had never approved of these psychological games, so Camille stopped doing it. The chairs hung around the *brigade* offices for a while, and people used them to play pranks on rookies. But it wasn't as funny as they expected. Then one day the chairs just disappeared. Camille is convinced that Armand took them. He can picture Armand having dinner with his wife, one perched on the high chair, the other sitting on the low chair . . .

When he sees Mme. Bruneau, he's reminded of the chairs, because he used to use them to elicit sympathy, something he wishes he could do now. And quickly. Camille focuses on the interview because if he allows himself to think about the girl in the cage, it conjures a confusion of images, images that muddle his thoughts, stir up memories, and he can feel himself go to pieces.

Unfortunately, he and Roseline Bruneau are not on the same wavelength. She is a small, slim woman who, under normal circumstances, is probably full of life, but right now she's nervous and reticent. She jerks her head this way and that, alert. She is convinced at any moment she'll be told her son is dead. A feeling that's been nagging at her ever since the policeman came to collect her at the driving school where she works.

"Your ex-husband took his own life yesterday afternoon, Madame Bruneau."

Though they've been divorced for more than twenty years, the news seems to give her quite a turn. She looks Camille in the eye, the expression on her face flickering between bitterness (I hope he suffered) and sarcasm (it's no great loss), but most of all, anxiety. At first, she says nothing. To Camille she looks like a little bird. A small, beaklike nose, sharp eyes, angular shoulders, pointed breasts. He knows exactly how he would draw her.

"How did he die?" she says at length.

From what he's seen of the divorce papers, thinks Camille, she's not exactly going to grieve for her ex-husband, and under normal circumstances he'd have expected her to ask about her son. If she hasn't, there must be some reason.

"An accident," Camille says. "He was involved in a police chase."

Though Mme. Bruneau is under no illusions about what her husband was like and remembers how violent he could be, she wasn't married to a gangland criminal. The phrase "involved in a police chase" should come as a shock, but she doesn't bat an eyelid.

"Madame Bruneau . . ." Camille is being patient precisely because there's no time to lose. "We believe Pascal's disappearance and his father's death are connected. In fact, we're convinced they are. The more quickly you can answer our questions, the better our chances of finding your son."

You could trawl the dictionary for hours looking for alternatives, but *dishonest* is the only word to describe Camille's approach. Because as far as he is concerned, there's no doubt Pascal is dead. Using the son as emotional blackmail may be morally wrong, but he's not ashamed, since it might help him find someone else alive.

"Some days ago, your husband kidnapped a girl, a young woman. He has been holding her somewhere, but he died before he could tell us where. Right now this woman is locked up somewhere. If we don't find her, Madame Bruneau, she'll die."

He allows this information to sink in. Roseline's eyes dart right and left like a pigeon's; she is overwhelmed by conflicting ideas. What matters is what she decides to do next. *What has this kidnapping got to do with my son's disappearance?* This is the question she should ask. If she doesn't ask it, it's because she already knows the answer.

"I need you to tell me everything you know . . . No, no, hang on, Madame Bruneau! You're about to tell me you don't know anything, but that would be a very bad move—take my word for it, the worst possible thing you could do. Take your time; think about it for a minute. Your husband abducted a woman who is connected in some way to the disappearance of your son. And that woman will die."

She glances left, right, jerking her whole head now. Camille should put a photograph of the woman on the desk in front of her, try to shock her, but something stops him.

"Jean-Pierre called me . . ."

Camille takes a breath. It's not exactly a victory, but it's an achievement. At least he's got things moving.

"When was this?"

"I can't remember, about a month ago."

"And . . . ?"

Mme. Bruneau stares at the floor. Slowly, she tells him. Trarieux gets the official letter informing him of the unsuccessful search; he's furious—this means the police think Pascal ran away, that they're not prepared to investigate; it's over. Since the police aren't prepared to do anything, Trarieux tells her he will deal with it. He has an idea.

"It's that whore—"

"Whore?"

"That's what he called Pascal's girlfriend."

"He didn't think much of her, then."

Mme. Bruneau sighs. In order to explain, she has to start at the beginning.

"You have to understand that Pascal was always a bit . . . a bit slow, do you know what I'm saying?"

"I think so."

"There was no badness in him; he was just a bit simple. I never wanted him to live with his father. Jean-Pierre had him drinking and getting into fights, but Pascal loved his dad—I never understood what he saw in him, but he loved his dad. Then one day this girl shows up, and it doesn't take long before she's got him wrapped around her little finger. Pascal's crazy about her . . . that's no surprise. Never could handle girls . . . Not that there were many before her, and it had always ended badly. So, anyway, this girl shows up, and she pays him a lot of attention. So obviously he falls head over heels."

"What was the girl's name? Did you meet her?"

"Nathalie? No, never clapped eyes on her. All I ever knew was her first name. When Pascal called me, it was always 'Nathalie this' and 'Nathalie that' . . ."

"He didn't introduce her to you? Or to his father?"

"No. He was always telling me he was going to bring her down to meet me, telling me I'd love her . . ."

It's a whirlwind romance. Mme. Bruneau tells him Pascal met Nathalie in June—she doesn't know where or how—then in July he disappears with her.

"At first I wasn't worried," she says. "I thought: when she dumps the poor kid, he'll go back to his father's and that'll be that. But his father was furious. Tell the truth, I think he was jealous. Pascal had always been the apple of his eye. He was a terrible husband, but he was a good father."

She glances up at Camille, clearly shocked by this assessment of her husband. She has just said something that she's always believed but never realized. She stares at the floor again.

"When I found out Pascal had cleaned out his father's bank account and disappeared, I was like him, I thought this girl, well, you know . . . It wasn't like Pascal, to steal from his father."

She shakes her head. This is something she knows for certain.

Camille remembers the photograph of Pascal Trarieux found in the father's apartment, and his heart bleeds. As a draftsman, Camille has an excellent visual memory. He can see the boy standing, one hand on the bulldozer, looking awkward and ill at ease. His trousers are far too short; he looks pathetic. What do you do when you have a simpleton for a son, when you come to terms with that fact?

"So, eventually, your husband tracked down this girl?"

Her reaction is instant.

"How would I know? All he told me was that he was looking for her, that sooner or later she'd tell him where Pascal was . . . what she did to him."

"What she did to him?"

Mme. Bruneau stares out of the window; this is her way of holding back her tears.

"Pascal would never run away, he's not . . . How can I put it? He's not intelligent enough to disappear for long."

She turned to Camille as she spoke, her words like a slap in the face. In fact, she's clearly sorry for what she has said.

"Like I said, he's a simple boy. He doesn't know many people; he's devoted to his father. He wouldn't go for weeks, for months, without getting in touch; he wouldn't be capable. So something must have happened to him."

"What exactly did your husband say to you? Did he tell you what he was planning to do? About . . ."

"No, he didn't stay on the line for long. He'd been drinking, as usual, and when he's on the bottle he can turn nasty, thinks the whole world is against him. He wanted to find this girl, he wanted her to tell him where his son was—that's what he called to tell me."

"And how did you react?"

In ordinary circumstances, it takes considerable talent to lie convincingly; it requires a great deal of energy, creativity, self-control, and a good memory—it's harder than people think. Lying to an authority figure is even more difficult because it requires all these qualities at a much higher level. And Mme. Bruneau is not cut out for such things. Though she's tried, now that she's let her guard down, Camille can read her like a book. And it's exhausting. He draws a hand over his eyes.

"What exactly did you call him? I'm guessing by that stage you didn't mince your words; I'm guessing you told him exactly what you thought of him—am I wrong?"

It's a convoluted question. "Yes" and "no" lead in different directions, but neither seems to offer her a way out.

"I don't know . . ."

"Oh, but you do know, Madame Bruneau, you know exactly what I'm saying. That night, you finally told him what you thought of him. You told him he hadn't a hope in hell of succeeding where the police had failed. In fact you went further. I don't know the precise words you used, but I know you really laid into him. 'You're an asshole, Jean-Pierre, you're a pathetic, dickless moron,' or something like that."

She opens her mouth, but Camille doesn't give her time to speak. He's jumped up from his chair, and he's shouting now, because he's been pussyfooting around for long enough.

"What exactly would I find if I checked the messages on your cell phone, Madame Bruneau?"

She doesn't move a muscle, but her eyes bore into the ground as though she wants it to open up and swallow her.

"I'll tell you what I'd find—photographs sent to you by your ex-husband. Don't even imagine that you can get out of this; it's right there in his call log. I can even tell you what's in these photos: a girl in a wooden crate. You questioned his manhood—you were hoping it would force him to do something. And when you received those pictures, you were scared. Scared that you might be charged as an accessory."

Camille has a sudden doubt.

"Unless . . ."

He stops, goes over to her, crouches down low, and looks up into her face. She doesn't move.

"Oh, shit," Camille says, getting to his feet again.

Some moments for a policeman are particularly tough.

"That's not why you didn't get in touch with the police, is it? You weren't afraid we might think you were an accessory. You did it because, like your husband, you blame this girl for your son's disappearance. You didn't say anything because you thought she was getting what she deserved, isn't that it?"

Camille takes a deep breath. He feels shattered.

"You'd better hope we find her soon, Madame Bruneau, and not just for her sake. For yours. Because if we don't, I'll be charging you as an accessory to torture and aggravated murder. And any other charges I can find that might stick."

As he leaves his office, Camille is under enormous pressure; precious, vital time is ticking away.

And what exactly do we have? he thinks.

Nothing. It's driving him mad.

21

The greediest one is not the piebald—it's a large gray rat. It loves blood. It fights off the other rats so it can be first. It's reckless and vicious.

For Alex, for the past few hours, every minute has been a battle. She had to kill two of them. To get the others angry, to get them excited, to show them she was something to be feared.

She skewered the first rat with the sliver of wood, her only weapon, then crushed it under her bare foot while it writhed like a soul in pain and squealed like a stuck pig, trying to bite her. Alex drowned it out with her screams; the rat's body started twitching and wriggling like a large fish—they've got a lot of strength, these fuckers, when they're dying. The last moments were excruciating; the rat had stopped moving, blood gushing from it as it moaned and whimpered, eyes bulging from their sockets, mouth quivering, teeth bared, still ready to bite. When it was over, Alex kicked it onto the floor.

After that, the rats realized this was open war.

With the second rat, she had to wait until it came very close. It could smell blood, its whiskers twitching frantically; it was certainly very excited, but it was cautious, too. Alex let it come—she even called to it: "Come on, come on, you little fucker, come to Mama . . ." And as soon as it was within reach, she managed to trap it against the board and plunge the shard of wood into its throat. It staggered backwards as though about to perform a dangerous jump; she kicked it smartly between the slats, and it hit the floor, where it lay whimpering for an hour, the shard still sticking out of its neck.

Alex has no weapons now, but they don't know that, and they are afraid.

And she feeds them.

Using what was left of the water, she diluted the blood coursing from her injured hand, then reached above her head and saturated the rope holding up the cage. Now that there's no water left, she keeps it wet with her blood. This, obviously, makes the rats even happier. When she stops bleeding, she stabs herself somewhere else using another splinter—this one is smaller, much too small to kill a rat—but it's sharp enough to pierce a vein in her calf, in her arm, sharp enough to make her bleed—and that's all she needs.

When the blood starts flowing, she collects it in her palm, reaches up between the planks and smears it onto the rope.

All around the rats are watching, not knowing whether to attack her. Then she pulls her hand back, and they fight over the fresh blood, gnawing into the rope for a taste of it; they can't get enough.

But now they've had a taste of blood, now that she's given them her own blood to taste, nothing will stop them.

Blood drives them into a frenzy.

22

Champigny-sur-Marne.

A large red-brick house by the river. One of the last calls Trarieux made before abducting the girl.

Her name is Sandrine Bontemps.

When Louis arrived, she had just finished breakfast and was setting off for work; she had to call to say she'd be late. The young officer took the telephone and calmly explained to her boss that she was helping with an "urgent police matter." He would have a colleague bring her to her office as soon as possible. For Sandrine Bontemps, all this is moving very fast.

She is prim, a little prissy, twenty-five, maybe twenty-six, and clearly out of her depth. As she sits with one buttock perched on the edge of the IKEA sofa, Camille can already see what she will look like in twenty, in thirty years: it's a little depressing.

"This man . . . Trarieux. He was very insistent on the phone . . . very insistent. And then he came to see me. He scared me."

Now, it's the police who scare her. Especially the little bald guy, the dwarf—he's obviously in charge. His younger colleague was the one who called her, then hurried over; he was there within twenty minutes. Now he looks as if he's not even listening, wandering from room to room, firing off questions from the kitchen. He goes upstairs, comes back down, seems edgy, as though sniffing for something. He told her right at the start, "We've got no time to lose," but every time she hesitates he interrupts. She doesn't even know what all this is about. She tries to get things straight in her mind, but she's being bombarded with questions.

"Is this her?"

The dwarf holds out a sketch toward her, a girl's face, like the sort of E-FIT you see in the movies or in the papers. She recognizes the woman immediately—it's Nathalie, but not as she knew her. In the drawing, she looks prettier than she does in real life, more sophisticated and—above all—not as fat. She looks cleaner. Her hair is different. Even her eyes are not quite the same. When Sandrine saw her they were blue, and though it's difficult to tell what color they're supposed to be in the pencil sketch, they seem much lighter. As a result the E-FIT looks like her . . . and it doesn't look like her. The police officers are waiting for a response, a yes or a no, nothing in between. In any case, despite any misgivings, Sandrine is positive: it's her.

Nathalie Granger.

The officers glance at each other. "Granger," says the dwarf dubiously. The younger one takes out his cell phone and goes out to the garden to make a call. When he comes back, he simply shakes his head, and the dwarf gives him a look as if to say *I'd have put money on it.*

Sandrine talks about the laboratory where Nathalie worked on rue de Planay in the center of Neuilly-sur-Marne. The younger policeman leaves immediately.

Sandrine guesses he's the one who calls half an hour later. Not that she can really tell. The dwarf just keeps repeating, "I see, I see." Sandrine finds this guy infuriating. It's as if he knows he irritates her but doesn't give a damn. On the telephone he sounds disappointed. In the young inspector's absence, the dwarf pesters her with questions about Nathalie.

"Her hair was always lank, dirty."

There are some things you can't tell a man, even a policeman, but sometimes Nathalie could really be messy. The place was never tidy, the table never cleared, not to mention the tampons floating in the toilet—*ugh*. They weren't housemates for long, but they did meet up once or twice afterward.

"I don't really think it would have worked out, Nathalie and me living together."

Sandrine had placed an advertisement looking for a roommate, and Nathalie had got in touch, came around to meet her; she seemed nice. She hadn't looked slovenly that day—she had been very presentable. What she had liked about the place was the garden and the attic room that she thought looked romantic. Sandrine had not pointed out that at the height of summer, it was like a sauna.

"There's no insulation, you see . . ."

The dwarf is looking at her abstractedly, his face like a statue's. As though he's thinking about something else.

Nathalie always paid in advance, always in cash.

"This was in early June. I urgently needed someone to help with the rent; my boyfriend had left me . . ."

Sandrine's personal life irritates the little man: the boyfriend moves in, big love story, and then walks out without even leaving a note a couple of months later. She never saw him again. She'd obviously been signed up at birth for a lifetime of being dumped: first the boyfriend, then Nathalie. This, she confirms, happened on July 14.

"In the end, she didn't stay long. She met this guy just after she moved in here, so, obviously . . ."

"Obviously what?" he asks, exasperated.

"Well . . . she'd want to move in with him. That's normal, isn't it?"

"Ah."

Skeptical, as though to say *Is that all?* This guy clearly knows nothing about women, you can tell. The younger one has come back from the laboratory; she heard his siren in the distance. He's a fast operator, but he still looks as if he's strolling through life.

It's because he's got style. Just look at the clothes he wears. Sandrine noticed as soon as she saw him: designer labels, top-of-the-line, too. Sandrine could tell at a glance how much his shoes cost: twice her monthly salary. It's a revelation to her to discover policemen make so much money—you'd never know from the ones you see on TV.

The officers had a little confab. All Sandrine overheard was the younger one saying, "never seen . . ." and then, ". . . yeah, he went there too."

"I wasn't here when she moved out. I always spend the summer at my aunt's place in . . ."

The older one is annoyed. Things aren't working out the way he wants them to, but that's not her fault. He sighs and waves his hand as though shooing away a fly. The least he could do is be polite. His colleague gives her a sympathetic smile as though to say *Don't worry, he's always like this, stay focused.* He's the one who shows her the photograph.

"Yeah, that's him, that's Pascal, Nathalie's boyfriend."

She's in no doubt about that. And the other picture, the one at the amusement park—it's a little blurred, but it's obviously them. When Pascal's father turned up a month ago, he was looking for Nathalie, too, not just his son, and he showed her the same picture. Sandrine gave him Nathalie's work address. After that, she never heard from him again.

You only have to see the photograph to realize that Pascal isn't the sharpest knife in the drawer. Not exactly handsome either. And his clothes—sometimes you wondered where on earth he bought them. Okay, Nathalie might have been a bit fat, but she had a beautiful face, and you knew that if she made the effort . . . But Pascal, he looked . . . it's difficult to know how to describe it.

"A bit retarded, to be honest."

Not very clever is what she means. He worshipped Nathalie. She brought him home two or three times, but he never stayed the night. Sandrine even wondered whether they were sleeping together. When he came around, Sandrine could see he was all excited, the way he gawked at Nathalie; he was practically drooling, just waiting for the green light to jump her bones.

"Though there was this one time. Just once, he slept here. I remember now, it was in July, just before I went to my aunt's."

But Sandrine didn't hear anything.

"Which is strange, because my room was right under hers."

She bites her lip, realizing she's just admitted eavesdropping. She blushes but doesn't say any more; they've got the picture. She didn't hear anything, and it wasn't for lack of trying. Nathalie and Pascal must have . . . I don't know . . . maybe they did it standing up. Or maybe there was nothing to hear, maybe Nathalie wasn't up for it. This, Sandrine could easily understand. I mean, Pascal . . .

"If it was me . . . ," she says priggishly.

The little one pieces the story together aloud; he might be small, but he's not stupid, pretty sharp in fact. Nathalie and Pascal disappeared leaving two months' rent on the kitchen table and enough money to cover the bills. Then there were all the things that Nathalie didn't take.

"Things, what things?" he wants to know immediately.

Suddenly he's all ears. Sandrine didn't keep any of the stuff. Nathalie was two sizes bigger than her, and, besides, her taste in clothes was terrible. There is the magnifying mirror in the bathroom, but Sandrine doesn't mention this to the police—she uses it for blackheads and nose hairs; besides, it's none of their business. She tells them about the other stuff: the coffee maker, the teapot shaped like a cow, the rainwater tank, the Marguerite Duras novels, which were all she seemed to read; she had pretty much the complete works.

The younger officer says, "Nathalie Granger . . . that's the name of one of Duras' characters, isn't it?"

"Really?" the other one says. "From which novel?"

"Um . . . it's from a film she directed called *Nathalie Granger*," the young one says, embarrassed.

The dwarf slaps his forehead as if to say *Duh*, but Sandrine thinks it's just for effect.

"For collecting rainwater," she explains as the dwarf points to the large green tank outside. It was environmentally friendly, collecting all that water—the roof of the house was huge. Early on, she'd talked to the rental agent and to the landlord about installing one, but they weren't interested. Talking about environmental issues seems to irritate the policeman as well, making her wonder what exactly he *is* interested in.

"She bought it just before she left. I found it here when I got back from my aunt's. She left a little note, apologizing for leaving so suddenly. I suppose the rainwater tank was sort of to make up for that, a surprise present."

The dwarf finds this funny: "a surprise present."

He's standing in front of the window, the net curtain pulled back. It's true it's pretty ugly, that huge green plastic tank at the side of the house with the drainpipes running into it. You can tell it's cobbled together. But he's not really looking at it. He's not really listening either, because as she's in midsentence, he flips open his cell phone and makes a call.

"Jean?" he says. "I think I've found Trarieux's son."

Time is getting on—she has to call her boss back, and the young one talks to him again. No mention of an investigation this time, just some mention of taking samples. An ambiguous phrase, since Sandrine works in a laboratory, as Nathalie did. They were both biologists, although Nathalie never liked to talk about her job. "When I'm off work, I'm off work!"

Twenty minutes later, it's pandemonium. They've taped off the street; the forensics team in their astronaut suits have overrun the garden with their equipment—cases, spotlights, plastic sheets—trampling all over the flower beds. They measured the rainwater tank and then took ridiculous precautions emptying it. They didn't want the water spilling on the ground.

"I know what they're going to find," the dwarf said. "It's 100 percent certain. I'm going to get some sleep."

He asked Sandrine where Nathalie's old room was. He lay down on the bed fully clothed; she's sure he didn't even take off his shoes.

The younger officer stayed out in the garden.

He really is a good-looking guy, and his clothes, his shoes . . . Even his manners are perfect! Sandrine has tried steering the conversation, making it more personal: this house is so big for a single woman, that kind of thing—but he didn't take the bait.

She's convinced he's gay.

The forensics team emptied the rainwater tank, moved it out of the way, and started digging. They didn't have to dig far before they found the body. Wrapped in the sort of plastic sheeting you buy in hardware shops.

It gave Sandrine a bit of a turn. The police kept her back—"I don't think you want to be out here, mademoiselle"—so she went back into the house and looked out of the window. They couldn't stop her doing that—after all, it is her house. What disturbed her was when they lifted the plastic-wrapped body and laid it on a gurney: she knew at once it was Pascal.

She recognized his sneakers.

Peeling back the layers of plastic, they leaned over, calling others to look at something she couldn't see. She opened the window a crack to listen.

One of the officers said, "Oh no, that wouldn't cause this sort of damage . . ."

It was at this point that the dwarf came back downstairs.

He positively skipped into the garden and immediately went over to look at the body.

He nodded, obviously pretty astonished by what he was seeing.

He said, "I'm with Brichot: the only thing which could cause that kind of damage is acid."

23

It's an old-fashioned rope, not the smooth synthetic kind you get on boats, natural hemp and very thick. It has to be to support a cage like this.

There are a dozen rats. Those Alex already knows, the ones that were there at the start, and the new arrivals—she doesn't know where they've come from, how they knew. Together they've adopted a siege strategy.

Three or four have taken up positions at one end of the crate; two or three others are on the far side. She assumes that when they decide the time is right, they'll attack together, but for now something is holding them back: Alex's energy. She continually screams and swears and taunts them. They know that there is still life in the cage, defiance—they know they will have to fight. Two rats already lie dead on the floor. This gives them pause for thought.

They constantly sniff the blood, rearing onto their hind paws, snouts straining toward the rope. Feverish with excitement, they take turns in gnawing at the rope with their teeth. Alex doesn't know how they decide whose turn it is to feast on the blood.

She doesn't care. She has stabbed herself again, this time low down on her calf, near the ankle. She found a clean, rich vein. The most difficult thing is keeping them away while she wipes more blood onto the rope.

It has already been eaten halfway through. It's a race against time between Alex and the rope, between which of the two will break first.

Alex keeps the cage moving, swinging it from side to side, making it more difficult for the rats if they should decide to come and call her to account; and she hopes it also weakens the rope.

The other reason for her tactic is that she needs the cage to fall at an angle in order for the slats to break. She rocks it as hard as she can, pushes the rats away, and douses the rope again. When one rat comes to gnaw on it, she keeps the others at a distance. Alex is absolutely exhausted, dying of thirst. Since the thunderstorms, which went on for more than a day, there are parts of her body she can no longer feel; they're numb.

The fat gray rat is getting impatient.

For an hour now, it has been allowing the others to gorge themselves on the rope. It no longer takes its turn feeding. The rope no longer interests the gray rat. Instead it stares at Alex, making loud, piercing shrieks. And for the first time it pokes its head between the slats and sniffs, lips drawn back like a snake.

What works for the others no longer works for him. Alex can scream and swear as much as she likes, but the rat doesn't flinch, claws digging into the wood to stop itself from falling as the cage rocks wildly.

It clings to the crate and stares at her.

Alex stares back.

They're like lovers on a merry-go-round, gazing deep into each other's eyes.

"Come on," whispers Alex, smiling. Arching her back, she gives the cage all the momentum she can and smiles up at the fat rat above her head. "Come on, *Papa*, come on, Mama has something for you . . ."

24

It left him with a strange feeling, his little siesta in Nathalie's room. Why had he done it? He doesn't know. The creaking wooden stairs, the landing stripped of its carpet, the porcelain door handle—all the heat in the house seems to rise to this attic room. It feels like a country house, a family home, with guest rooms only aired and opened up at the onset of summer. Closed the rest of the year.

Now it is being used as a junk room. She seemed not to have had much in the way of personality; the place looks like a room in a hotel or a bed and breakfast. A few lopsided pictures on the walls, a chest of drawers with one foot missing, propped up with books. The bed is soft as a marshmallow—you sink into it so deeply, it's amazing. Camille sits up, heaves himself onto the pillows, and leaning against the head of the bed, he fumbles for his notepad and his pencil. While the forensics team are clearing the earth from under the rainwater tank in the garden, he sketches a face. His own. When he was young, preparing to study at the École des Beaux-Arts, he did hundreds of self-portraits; his mother always claimed it was the only real exercise, the only one that allowed one to find "the appropriate detachment." She herself had painted dozens of self-portraits. Only one of them remains, in oils, magnificent; he doesn't like to think about it. And Maud was right: Camille's problem has always been finding the appropriate detachment. He's always either too close or too detached. Either he plunges in and disappears, thrashing about, almost drowning, or he remains at a careful distance and is doomed to understand nothing. "What's missing then is the grain of things," Camille says. On the notepad, the face that emerges is emaciated, the eyes stare vacantly, a man beaten down by adversity.

The ceiling of the room is sloping—for most people living here it would mean bending in order to move. But not for him. Camille goes on sketching, but his heart isn't in it; he feels queasy. His heart is heavy. Sandrine Bontemps, his irritation, his impatience—he can be impossible sometimes. He just wants this case over and done with.

Things aren't right with him, and he knows why. He needs to find the grain.

A while ago, he found it in the portrait of Nathalie Granger. Before that, in the pictures on Trarieux's cell phone; she had simply looked like a victim. One more case. This is what he had relegated her to, this girl: a kidnapping case. But in the E-FIT put together by the forensic art team, she became a real person. A photograph is realism. But a drawing is reality, your reality, fleshed out by your imagination, your fantasies, your education, your life. When he held out the picture to show Sandrine Bontemps, when he saw the face upside down like a swimmer, it struck him as entirely different. Had she killed this dimwit Pascal Trarieux? More than likely, but it didn't matter. In the upside-down drawing, he found her touching; she was locked up somewhere, and her survival was his responsibility. He felt the dread of failure grip his entrails. He had been unable to save Irène. What would he do now? Would he let her die, too?

From the first step, the first moment of this case, he has been trying to block out the emotions building up behind the wall; now the wall is crumbling, one by one cracks are opening up, and sooner or later it will collapse, floor him, overwhelm him, and it'll be straight back to the morgue, straight back to the square marked "psychiatric clinic." He looks at what he has been sketching on his pad: a huge rock, a boulder. Portrait of Camille as Sisyphus.

25

The postmortem takes place first thing Wednesday morning. Camille is there. As is Louis.

Le Guen is late, as usual, and by the time he gets to the mortuary, they already know everything they're going to know. In all probability, the body is that of Pascal Trarieux. Everything fits: age, height, hair color, likely date of death, not to mention the fact that Sandrine Bontemps swore she recognized his sneakers, despite the fact that there are half a million pairs in circulation. A DNA test will be done to confirm definitively that the body is that of the missing boy, but for now they can assume that it is him and that Nathalie Granger killed him with a blow to the back of the head with something like a pickax (all the garden tools found at the house have been brought back for examination) before smashing his head in with a shovel.

"Which proves she really had a score to settle with the guy," Camille says.

"Oh yes, thirty separate blows at least," the pathologist says. "I'll be able to give you an exact figure later. A number of the blows were with the edge of the shovel, which is why it looks as though he was attacked with a blunt hatchet."

Camille is satisfied. Not happy, but satisfied. The big picture matches up pretty well to what he suspected. If the asshole magistrate were here, he might make a sarcastic comment, but with his old friend Le Guen, he just winks and says in a low voice:

"I told you there was something not right about her."

"We'll have to run tests, but it's definitely acid," the pathologist says.

The guy had been hit over the head thirty times, and then his killer, Nathalie Granger, had poured at least a quart of acid down his throat. From the damage caused, the pathologist speculates that it was concentrated sulfuric acid.

"Highly concentrated."

It's certainly true that such products cause serious damage. Flesh bubbles and dissolves at a speed directly proportional to the concentration of the acid.

Camille asks the question that's been nagging at everyone since they found the body the day before:

"Was Trarieux still alive when it happened, or was he already dead?"

He knows the routine answer: we'll have to wait for the results. But this time the pathologist is forthcoming.

"To judge by the marks on the remaining tissue, particularly the forearms, the victim appears to have been tied up."

A brief moment of contemplation.

"You want my opinion?" the pathologist says.

No one wants his opinion, which only serves to encourage him.

"In my opinion, he was struck several times with the shovel, tied up, and then awakened with a couple of pints of acid . . . Which doesn't mean he wasn't finished off with the shovel—when you've found the right tool for the job . . . Anyway, in my humble opinion, the poor bastard really suffered."

It's almost impossible to imagine, but right now, as far as the detectives are concerned, the details of the MO make no difference.

But if the pathologist is right, for the victim, whether the acid came pre- or postmortem makes a hell of a difference.

"It'll matter to the jury, too," Camille says.

The problem with Camille is that he never backs down. Never. When he's got a theory in his head . . . One day Le Guen said to him: "God, you're a stubborn fucker! Even a fox terrier knows when to back off!"

"A neat comparison," Camille retorted. "Maybe you'd be better off comparing me to a basset hound. Or, hey, how about a toy poodle?"

Had it been anyone else, it would have ended in a duel.

So right now Camille is living up to his reputation for never backing down. Since yesterday, Le Guen thinks he seems anxious, though at other times he seems to be gloating to himself. When they run into each other in the corridors, Camille barely says hello, then two hours later he's hanging around the divisionnaire's office as though he can't bear to leave, as though he has something to say but can't bring himself to say it; then eventually he does leave, almost reluctantly, giving Le Guen a resentful stare. Le Guen is a patient man. They were coming out of the toilets together (the sight of them standing next to each other at the urinals is priceless), and Le Guen simply said: "Whenever you're ready," which translates as "I've steeled myself, I can take it."

And now comes the moment, out on the terrace just before lunch. Camille has turned off his cell phone to indicate that he wants everyone's undivided attention. All four of them are there: Camille, Le Guen, Armand, and Louis. Now that the storm has cleared the skies, the weather is mild again. Armand knocks back his beer almost in a single gulp and, for good measure, quickly orders a packet of crisps and some olives on the tab someone else will wind up paying.

"This girl is a murderer, Jean," Camille says.

"Maybe she is a murderer," Le Guen says. "We'll know for sure when the test results come back. For the moment, you know as well as I do that's just pure speculation."

"As speculation goes, it's pretty watertight."

"Okay, so maybe you're right . . . what does it change?"

Le Guen looks to Louis for support. It's an embarrassing situation, but Louis is a nice boy from a good family. He was educated at the best schools; one of his uncles is an archbishop, and another is a far-right member of Parliament, so he's long since learned to distinguish between the ethical and the practical. Besides, he was taught by Jesuits. He knows everything there is to know about duplicity.

"The divisionnaire's question seems pertinent," he says in a measured tone. "What does that change?"

"Louis, I thought you were smart," Camille says. "It changes the approach."

Everyone is staggered. Even Armand, who is busy scrounging a cigarette from someone at the next table, whips around in surprise.

"The approach?" Le Guen says. "What the fuck are you on about, Camille?"

"You really don't get it, any of you," Camille says.

Usually they joke and piss around, but this time there's something in Camille's voice.

"You don't get it."

He takes out his notepad, the one in which he's constantly sketching. To take notes (he rarely takes notes, trusting everything to memory), he turns it around to write on the back of the pages he's drawn on. A bit like Armand. Except that Armand would write on the spine, too, if he could. Louis catches a glimpse of a drawing of some rats. Camille really is one hell of an artist.

"I'm finding this girl really interesting," Camille explains calmly. "Honestly. This thing with the sulfuric acid, too, that's interesting. Don't you think?"

And when the question elicits no response:

"So I did a little bit of research. It needs some refining, but I think I've got the essentials."

"Come on," Le Guen says, exasperated. "Spit it out."

Then he picks up his glass of beer, drains it in one gulp, and gestures to the waiter to bring another. Armand gestures *Me, too.*

"March 13 last year," Camille says, "a certain Bernard Gattegno, forty-nine, is found dead in a cheap motel near Étampes. Death caused by the ingestion of sulfuric acid, 80 percent concentration."

"Oh, shit," Le Guen says, horrified.

"Given the state of his marriage, it was put down to suicide."

"Let it go, Camille."

"No, no, it's funny, you'll see. Eight months later, on November 28, Stefan Maciak, a café owner from Faignoy-lès-Reims, is found murdered. The body was found in the café the following morning when they opened up. Postmortem findings: he was beaten and tortured using sulfuric acid, same concentration. Poured down his throat. Proceeds of the theft, about two thousand euros."

"Can you really imagine a girl doing something like that?" Le Guen says.

"And can you really imagine committing suicide by drinking sulfuric acid?"

"But what the fuck has any of this got to do with our case?" roars Le Guen, slamming his fist down on the table.

Camille holds up his hands in surrender.

"Okay, Jean, okay."

In the sepulchral silence, the waiter comes back with a beer for Le Guen and one for Armand, wipes down the table, and clears away the empty glasses.

Louis knows exactly what is going to happen; like a music hall magician, he could write it down, put it in an envelope, and hide it somewhere in the café. Camille will return to the attack. Armand finishes his cigarette with relish—he's never bought a pack of cigarettes in his life.

"One little thing, Jean . . ."

Le Guen closes his eyes. Louis smiles to himself. In the presence of the divisionnaire, Louis only ever smiles inwardly; that's the rule. Armand goes with the flow; whatever the situation, he'd offer thirty-to-one on Camille.

"If you could just clear something up for me," Camille says. "Guess how long it's been since we had a murder involving sulfuric acid. Go on . . . guess."

Right now the divisionnaire is in no mood for guessing games.

"Eleven years—I'm talking unsolved cases, obviously. From time to time we've had villains use acid as part of their MO, but it's secondary, an artistic touch, you might say. But we catch them, we arrest them, and we lock them up—the decent, upstanding vengeful public won't stand for it. No, in the last eleven years, when it comes to sulfuric acid, the police have been remorseless and unbeatable."

"Know what you are, Camille?" Le Guen sighs. "You're a pain in the ass."

"A good point, divisionnaire. I fully understand your reservations. But the thing is, as Danton used to say, 'facts are stubborn things,' and those are the facts."

"Lenin," Louis says.

Camille turns, irritated.

"What about Lenin?"

Louis pushes back his hair with his right hand.

"Facts are stubborn things," says Louis, embarrassed, "It wasn't Danton who said it; it was Lenin. Quoting John Adams."

"So what?"

Louis blushes. He's about to say something, but Le Guen gets in before he can.

"Exactly, Camille, so what? So what if there hasn't been a murder involving sulfuric acid in ten years?"

He's furious, his voice thunders across the terrace, but Le Guen's Shakespearean outbursts of rage alarm only the other customers. Camille, for his part, stares modestly at his shoes, which dangle six inches off the ground.

"Eleven years, sir, not ten."

This is one of the many failings Camille might be accused of: when he practices modesty and restraint he can be a little theatrical, a little too Racine.

"And now," he goes on, "there've been two cases in the space of eight months. Both victims were men. In fact, including Trarieux, there have been three."

"But . . ."

Louis would say that the divisionnaire "eructs"—he's got a way with words, that boy. Only this time his eructation peters out. Because he can't think of anything to say.

"How is this connected to the girl, Camille?" Armand says.

Camille smiles.

"At last, an intelligent question."

Le Guen simply mutters, "A total pain in the ass."

To show how disheartened he is, he gets up, makes a weary gesture as if to say *Fine, maybe you're right, but we'll talk about it later, later.* Anyone who didn't know Le Guen would think he was genuinely depressed. He tosses a handful of coins onto the table and, as he leaves, raises one hand like a jury member taking the oath. From behind he's wide as a truck; he trudges heavily away.

Camille sighs. It's always wrong to be right too soon. "But I'm not wrong." As he says this, he taps his nose with his finger, as though he needs to remind Armand and Louis that, in general, he's got a nose for things. It's just that he gets the timing wrong. Right now, the girl is a victim, nothing more. And not finding her, when that's what you're paid to do, would be a fuck-up, and claiming the woman is a multiple murderer would not be much of an excuse.

They all get to their feet and head back to the station. Armand has cadged a small cigar—the guy at the next table didn't have anything else. They leave the café and walk toward the *métro*.

"I've got the teams together," Louis says. "The first one—"

Camille abruptly places a warning hand on his forearm as though he has just spotted a cobra at his feet. Louis looks up, listening intently. Armand is listening too, ear cocked. Camille is right. It's like a jungle—the three men look at each other, feel the ground tremble under their feet to some deep, rumbling rhythm. As one, they turn, prepared for anything. Twenty yards away a colossal hulk is bearing down on them at a terrifying speed. Le Guen is thundering toward them, the flying tails of his jacket making him seem even more huge, his raised hand clutching a cell phone. Camille fumbles for his own cell, remembers he had turned it off. He doesn't have time to move, to get out of the way; Le Guen is already upon them. It takes him several paces to come to a halt, but he's calculated his trajectory with care and stops right in front of Camille. Strangely, he's not out of breath. He jabs at his cell.

"They've found the girl. She's in Pantin. Get your ass in gear!"

The divisionnaire heads back to the *brigade criminelle*, a thousand things to do on the way; he's the one who calls the investigating magistrate.

Louis drives at breakneck speed. Within minutes, they're at the scene.

The abandoned warehouse is perched on the bank of the canal, a decrepit industrial blockhouse, half ship, half factory. It's a square, yellowish building with—on the ship side—broad gangways running down from each floor along the side of the building, and on the factory side, serried ranks of tall windows. A masterpiece of 1930s concrete architecture. A monument whose lettering, all but obliterated now, reads FONDERIES GÉNÉRALES.

Everything around it has already been demolished. This is the one building still standing and probably about to be redeveloped. Decorated from top to bottom with large white, blue, and orange graffiti tags, it sits enthroned above the canal like one of those Indian elephants adorned from head to foot that lumber mysteriously behind the streamers and the banners. The previous night, a couple of teenage street artists managed to clamber onto the first-floor gangway, something everyone assumed was impossible now that all the doorways have been bricked up, but a piece of cake for kids like that. They were just putting the finishing touches to their work at dawn when one of them happened to look down through the buckled glass roof and clearly saw a wooden cage dangling with a body inside. They spent the whole morning weighing up the risks before eventually putting in an anonymous call to the police. It took less than two hours to track them down to question them about their nocturnal activities.

The fire brigade and the *brigade criminelle* were called. The building has been sealed up for years—the company that bought it had everything bricked up. While one team tried to raise a ladder to the gangway, another attacked the bricked-up doorway with sledgehammers.

Besides the firefighters, there's quite a crowd milling around outside: uniformed officers, plainclothes officers, squad cars with lights still flashing, and the general public—no one knows how they got here—all watching what's going on as the police begin to seal off the area with construction barriers found on the site.

Camille scrambles out of the car—he doesn't even need to flash his police ID—trips and almost falls on the gravel and the broken bricks but regains his balance just in time, watches the firefighters doing their work for a minute, then yells, "Wait!"

He walks over. The watch commandant heads over to block his path. Camille doesn't give him time to block anything—there's a gap in the wall just right for a man of his size; he slips inside the building. It will take a lot more sledgehammering for anyone else to get in.

The interior is completely empty, vast rooms bathed in a diffuse, greenish light that falls like dust from the skylights and the shattered windows. He can hear water trickling, the rattle of loose slates somewhere above that echoes through the cavernous space. Rivulets of water snake past his feet. It's the sort of place that would give anyone the creeps. It's impressive, though, like a derelict cathedral, the mournful atmosphere of the end of the industrial age, but the background and the light are exactly those in the photos of the girl. Behind Camille, the sledgehammers continue to pound at the bricks; it sounds like a military tattoo.

Camille immediately shouts, "Anyone here?"

He waits for a second, then starts to run. The first room is cavernous—forty-five, maybe fifty yards long with a ceiling at least twelve or fifteen feet high. The floor is soaking wet, water seeping from the walls—the whole place is dank and cold. These were clearly storerooms, but before he even gets to the far end of the first room, he knows he is in the right place.

"Anyone here?"

He can hear it himself—his voice is different; it's something that happens at a crime scene, a sort of tension—you can feel it in your belly, hear it in your voice. And what has triggered this is a smell, almost drowned out by the whirling drafts of cold air. The stench of rotting flesh, of piss and shit.

"Anyone here?"

He runs. He hears quick footsteps behind him; the team have come through the wall. Camille rushes into the second room and stops dead, arms dangling, staring at the scene.

Louis has just arrived next to him. The first words he hears from Camille are:

"Fucking hell . . ."

The wooden cage has crashed to the ground, two of the slats ripped away. Maybe they broke during the fall and the girl finished the job. The stink of putrefaction is coming from three dead rats, two of them crushed by the crate. Swarms of flies are everywhere. There is half-dried excrement in bags a few feet from the crate. Camille and Louis look up; the rope has been eaten through by something— one end is still hanging from the pulley fixed to the ceiling.

But there's blood everywhere, too.

And no sign of the girl.

The officers who have just arrived set off to look for her. Camille nods doubtfully; he doesn't think there's any point.

Disappeared.

In the state she was in.

How did she manage to escape? Forensics will tell them. How did she go, and which way? Forensics will find out. The fact remains that the girl they were trying to save has done the job herself.

Camille and Louis are at a loss for words, and as the vast rooms ring with shouted orders and instructions and echoing footsteps, they stare, frozen, at this strange turn of events.

The girl escaped, but she didn't go to the police as any kidnap victim might.

Some months ago, she killed a man with a shovel and melted off half his face with sulfuric acid before burying him in a suburban garden.

Only by pure chance was his body discovered, which makes you wonder whether there are others.

And how many.

Especially since two similar deaths have been reported and Camille would stake his life on them being connected to the death of Pascal Trarieux.

The fact that she managed to escape from this horrifying situation tells you she's no ordinary girl.

They have to find her.

And they have no idea where she might be.

"I suspect," Camille says solemnly, "that Divisionnaire Le Guen might perhaps now have a better grasp of the scope of our problem."

II

26

Half-conscious from exhaustion, Alex can barely take in what is happening.

Using her last shreds of strength, she manages to set the cage swinging so fast, so high, that the petrified rats have to dig their claws into the wood to hang on. She lets out a loud continuous howl. Dangling at the end of the rope, the crate rocks wildly in the icy breeze whipping through the room, like a car on a Ferris wheel before some terrible accident.

The stroke of luck that saves Alex's life is that the rope breaks when the cage is angled downward. Eyes fixed on the fraying rope, Alex watches as the last threads snap one by one; the cable seems to writhe in pain, and suddenly the crate plummets. Given the weight, the drop is lightning fast, a fraction of a second, barely enough time for Alex to tense against the impact. The jolt is brutal, one corner of the cage attempting to drive through the concrete floor; the crate quavers for a moment, then topples heavily in a deafening groan of relief. Alex is pressed against the lid. In an instant, the rats scatter. Two of the planks of wood have split, but none is altogether broken.

Stunned by the force of the fall, it takes Alex a moment to surface, to regain consciousness, but the crucial information reaches her brain: it worked. One of the slats has split almost in two, a space nearly large enough to squeeze through. Alex is suffering from hypothermia; she wonders where she will find the strength. And yet she lashes out with her feet, scrabbles with her hands, and suddenly the crate comes apart. The plank above her gives way. It is as though the sky has suddenly parted, like the Red Sea in the Bible.

This triumph almost makes her mad. She is so overwhelmed by emotion, by relief, by the success of her insane plan, that rather than struggling to her feet and getting out, she stays in the cage, prostrate, sobbing. She can't stop herself.

Her brain sends out a new signal: get out of here. The rats won't dare attack again so soon, but what about Trarieux? He hasn't come for some time—what if he were to turn up now?

She has to get out, get dressed, get out of here.

She begins to uncoil her body. She had hoped for deliverance; this is torture. Her whole body is rigid. She cannot get to her feet, cannot extend her legs or push with her arms, cannot get into a normal position. A hard ball of tetanized muscle. She has no strength left.

It takes a full minute, two minutes, for her to get onto her knees. The effort is so excruciating it seems impossible—she howls helplessly, screams as she forces her muscles, pounds on the cage with her fists. Overcome by tiredness, she collapses again, curled into a ball, exhausted. Paralyzed.

It takes every ounce of courage, of sheer willpower to try again, the unimaginable effort required to stretch her limbs, cursing the heavens, to straighten her pelvis, turn her neck . . . A struggle between the dying Alex and the living Alex. Slowly, her body revives. Painfully, but it revives. Eventually, chilled to the marrow, Alex succeeds in getting into a squatting position, to slide first one leg, then the other, inch by inch over the top of the crate and tumble onto the other side. The fall is painful, but she presses her face joyfully against the damp, cold concrete and starts to sob again.

A few minutes later, she manages to crawl on all fours and fetch an old rag to drape around her shoulders. She gets as far as the water bottles, snatches one up, and drains it. She catches her breath, finally manages to lie on her back. Days and days—how many days exactly?—she has been waiting for this moment, days when she resigned herself to the thought that it might never come. She could stay here until the end of time, feeling her circulation pick up, the searing blood, her joints recovering, her muscles coming back to life. Her whole body aches. This is how frostbitten mountaineers must feel when they're found alive.

Her brain, running in the background, sends out another message: what if he comes? She has to get out of here, quickly.

Alex checks: all her clothes are here. All her stuff, her bag, her papers, her money, even the wig she was wearing that night, is in the pile with Trarieux's things. He took nothing. All he wanted was her life—well, her death. Alex gropes around, picks up her clothes, her hands shaking and weak. She keeps glancing around anxiously. The first thing she needs to do is find something she can use to defend herself in case he should come back. She rummages feebly through the tools strewn around and finds a crowbar. It was obviously used to open crates. When had he been planning to use it? When she was dead? So he could bury her? Alex puts it down next to her. She doesn't even realize how ridiculous the situation is: were Trarieux to arrive, she wouldn't have the strength to pick it up.

As she gets dressed, she suddenly becomes aware of her own smell: it's sickening—she reeks of piss, of shit, of vomit and dog's breath. She opens a bottle of water, then another, rubs herself hard, but her hands are slow. She washes as best she can, dries herself off, her limbs gradually returning to normal. She warms herself, rubbing herself down with a blanket she finds and some filthy rags. Obviously, there's no mirror so she can't see what she looks like. She probably has a mirror in her handbag; as she thinks this, her brains sounds the alarm. Last warning: get the fuck out of here now; clear off. Right now.

The clothes immediately make her feel warmer. Her feet are swollen; her shoes pinch. It takes two attempts before she can stand, and then only barely. She picks up her bag, decides to leave the crowbar, and stumbles out thinking that there are some things she will never be able to do again—fully extend her legs, turn her head, stand up straight. She shuffles forward, half-stooped, like an old woman.

Trarieux left footprints; she has only to follow them from one room to the next. She looks around, trying to find the exit he's been using. That first day, when she tried to escape, when he caught her at the bricked-up doorway, this is what she didn't notice: there, in the corner, the metal trapdoor in the floor. The handle is a loop of wire. Alex tries to lift it. She panics. She heaves with all her strength, but it doesn't budge an inch. She feels tears well up again, and a muffled groan comes from deep in her belly; she tries again, but it's impossible. She already knows there will be no other way out; this was why he didn't rush to try and catch her the other day. He knew that even if she found the trapdoor, she would never be able to lift it.

And now she feels angry, a brutal, murderous anger, a terrible rage. Alex screams and starts to run. She runs awkwardly, as though crippled. She retraces her steps. In the distance, the rats that dared to come back see her charging toward them and scatter. Alex picks up the crowbar and three of the broken planks, and she manages to carry them because she does not stop to ask herself whether she has the strength—her mind is on other things. She needs to get out of here and nothing, absolutely nothing is going to stop her. She'll get out of here even if it kills her. She slides one end of the crowbar into the gap between the trapdoor and the floor and puts her whole weight on the other end. When it grudgingly lifts a few inches, she slides one of the planks under it with her foot and starts again, inserts a second plank, runs to get more wood, comes back, and eventually manages to wedge the crowbar vertically under the trapdoor. The gap can't be more than fifteen inches, scarcely enough to squeeze her body through, and she knows there is a risk that the whole rickety construction will collapse, bringing the heavy manhole cover crashing down and crushing her.

Alex pauses, cocks her head, listens. This time her brain sends no message, no advice. The slightest slip, the slightest hesitation, and her body might nudge the crowbar, and the trapdoor will collapse. In a split second she has tossed her bag through the gap, hears the muffled sound as it lands—the hole doesn't seem too deep. As she thinks this, Alex lies flat on her stomach and, inch by inch, she slides backwards under the trapdoor. It's cold, but she's sweating by the time the tip of her shoe finds a foothold, a step. She slides the rest of her body through the gap, hanging on to the edge with her finger-tips; then, as she turns her head, what she most dreaded happens: she accidentally nudges the crowbar: with a metallic shriek it slips and the trapdoor slams shut with a deafening clang. She just has time to jerk her fingers away, a reflex action, a matter of nanoseconds. Alex stands, frozen, on the step in pitch darkness. She is unscathed. When her eyes adjust to the light, she picks up her bag, which is a couple of steps below. She holds her breath—she is getting out of here, she's going to make it, she can't believe it . . . A few more steps and she comes to a steel door held shut by a breeze block that takes an age to shift since she has no strength left. Then she finds herself in a corridor that smells of piss, a second stairwell, which she negoti-ates, feeling her way with both hands like a blind woman, guided by a dim glow. This is the stairwell where she hit her head and passed out when he first brought her here. At the top of the steps there are three rungs, which Alex climbs, then a short tunnel, a sort of utility shaft that runs to a small metal plate set into the wall. Only a flicker of light comes through from outside, and Alex has to feel around the edge of the plate to work out how it opens. It is simply wedged into place. Alex pulls it toward her and finds it's not very heavy. She care-fully removes it and sets it down next to her.

She is outside.

Immediately, she feels the cold night air—it tastes sweet, the cool damp of evening—and smells canal water somewhere. Life return-ing, a faint glimmer of life. The panel was hidden in an alcove in the wall at ground level. Alex crawls out then turns back to see whether she can put it back into place but gives up; there's no need to take precautions now. As long as she leaves now, fast. As fast as her stiff, aching limbs will allow. She creeps out of the alcove.

Some thirty yards away is a deserted wharf. Farther off, a scattering of small houses with almost every window lit up. There are muffled sounds from the boulevard that can't be far away.

Alex starts to walk.

She comes to the boulevard. Exhausted as she is, she won't be able to walk very far. Suddenly she has a dizzy spell and has to cling to a streetlight to stop herself from falling.

It feels too late to be able to find any form of transport. But there, in the distance, a taxi stand. It's deserted, the few neurons still working whisper, and besides it's much too risky. She is bound to be noticed.

But her neurons have no better solution to offer.

27

When you've got a lot of irons in the fire, as he has this morning, and it's difficult to prioritize, Camille claims "the most urgent thing is to do nothing." It's a variation on his approach to dealing with cases with as much perspective as possible. When he used to teach at the police academy, he referred to this as the "aerial technique." From a man who is four foot eleven in his socks, it's a term that might have raised a laugh, but no one ever dared.

It's six in the morning. Camille is up and showered, he's had breakfast, his briefcase is by the door, and he is standing, cradling Doudouche. He scratches the cat's belly; they both stare out of the window.

His gaze falls on the envelope from the auctioneers that he finally opened last night. This auction is the last act in dealing with his father's estate. Camille had been shocked, upset, had grieved a little, but his father's death had not been devastating. It had caused limited damage. Where his father was concerned, everything had always been predictable; his death had been no exception. If Camille has been unable to open the envelope until yesterday, it is because it marks the end of a whole era in his life. He will be fifty soon. Around him, everyone is dead: first his mother, then his wife, now his father; he will never have children. He never imagined he would be the last living soul in his own life. This is what bothers him; his father's death brings to a close a story, but the story is not yet over. Camille is still here—he may be dead tired, but he's still standing. The problem is his life now belongs entirely to him; he is sole owner and sole beneficiary. When you become the main character in your own life, it's no longer interesting. What troubles Camille is not simply survivor's guilt, but that he feels overwhelmed by such a cliché.

His father's apartment has been sold. All that remains is a dozen or so paintings by Maud Verhœven that her husband had hung on to.

Not to mention the studio. Camille can't bring himself to set foot there—it is the meeting point of all his griefs, for his mother, for Irène . . . No, he simply cannot, he would not even be able to climb the four steps, push open the door, and step inside. Never.

As for the paintings, he has summoned up all his strength. He contacted a friend of his mother's—they were at the Beaux-Arts together; the man agreed to make an inventory of the works. The auction will take place on October 7; it's all arranged. Opening the envelope, Camille sees the titles of the paintings on offer, the date and time; the entire evening is devoted to Maud's work, with speeches and reminiscences.

At first, he made a big deal of the fact that he didn't plan to keep any of the paintings, devised a whole string of theories. The most impressive was the theory that selling off all her works was a tribute to her. "If I wanted to see one of her paintings myself, I would have to go to a gallery," he explained with a mixture of satisfaction and solemnity. Of course, that's bullshit. The truth is he worshipped his mother above everything, and since he has been alone he has been shaken by the ambivalence of this love mingled with admiration, rancor, bitterness, and resentment. This love tinged with anger is as old as he is, but if he is to be at peace with himself he has to cut it loose. Painting was his mother's great cause—she sacrificed her life to it and with it Camille's life. Not entirely, but the part she sacrificed became her son's destiny. As though she had a child without ever imagining he would be a person. Camille will not be relieving himself of a burden, simply ridding himself of baggage.

Eight canvases, mostly from the last decade of Maud Verhœven's life, are to be sold. Mostly abstract works. Looking at some of them, Camille has the same impression he has looking at Rothko's work: the colors seem to vibrate, to throb—it's something you have to feel to know truly what it is to see living painting. Two paintings have already been preempted; they'll go to museums— works from her last days, howls of agony painted in the terminal stage of Maud's cancer and the apogee of her work. The one Camille might have kept is a self-portrait she painted when she was about thirty. It depicts a childlike face, anxious, almost solemn. The subject is looking past the viewer; there is something vacant about the expression, a sophisticated mixture of adult femininity and childlike innocence, the sort of expression one might find in a face once young and tender and now ravaged by alcohol. Irène loved this painting. She took a photograph of it once, a six-by-four-inch snapshot that still sits on his desk next to a blown-glass pot for his pencils, which Irène also gave him, the only truly personal item Camille keeps at work. Armand has always had a fondness for the picture; being figurative, it's one of the few paintings by Maud Verhœven he understands. Camille always meant to give him the photograph one day, but he never has. But even this painting is included in the sale. When his mother's works are finally scattered, perhaps he'll have some peace, perhaps he'll finally be able to sell the last link in the chain that will no longer connect to anything: the studio in Montfort.

Sleep came and with it other images, more urgent and more topical, images of the young girl who was imprisoned and managed to escape. All images of death, but these are images of future deaths. Because he doesn't know how he knows, but from the moment he saw the disemboweled cage, the dead rats, the signs of flight, he has been convinced that all this obscures something else, that there is death still to come.

Downstairs, the street is still humming. For someone like Camille, who sleeps little, it doesn't matter, but Irène would never have been able to live here. For Doudouche, on the other hand, it's entertainment; she can sit staring out of the window for hours at the barges, the opening and closing of the lock. When the weather is fine, she's even allowed to sit out on the windowsill.

Camille won't leave until he has got things clear in his mind. And right now there are too many questions.

The warehouse in Pantin. How did Trarieux find it? Is it important? Though derelict for years, the place has never been squatted; the homeless haven't taken it over. The fact that it was unfit for human habitation would have put them off, but the main reason was that the only possible way in was through a long narrow tunnel just below ground level, making it nearly impossible to bring in everything you would need. Maybe this was why Trarieux built such a small cage—he was limited by the length of the planks he could bring in. And it must have been difficult to bring the girl in. He had to be pretty determined. He was prepared to leave the girl for as long as it took to get her to confess to where she had buried his son.

Nathalie Granger. They know it's not her real name, but since they've got nothing better, that's what they still call her. Camille prefers "the girl," but even he slips up from time to time. Between a false name and no name, how can you choose?

The magistrate has agreed to initiate a manhunt. Though, pending evidence to the contrary, the girl who bumped off Pascal Trarieux with a pickax before almost taking his head off with sulfuric acid is being sought simply as a witness. Her housemate in Champigny formally identified her from the E-FIT, but the public prosecutor's office needs hard evidence.

Samples of blood and hair together with other organic matter have been collected from the warehouse in Pantin, which will quickly confirm a match to the traces of the girl found in the back of Trarieux's van. That, at least, will be something. But it's not much, Camille thinks.

The only way to pursue this lead is to reopen the two recent cold cases involving sulfuric acid and see whether they are connected to the same killer. Despite the divisionnaire's doubts, Camille is absolutely persuaded that the same person—the same woman—is responsible for all three murders. The case files are due to arrive this morning; they should be there by the time he gets to the station.

Camille thinks for a moment about Nathalie Granger and Pascal Trarieux. A crime of passion? If it were, he would have expected things to be the other way around: Pascal Trarieux murdering Nathalie in a jealous rage, or because he could not stand the idea of being dumped, a sudden impulse, a moment of madness, but the reverse . . . ? An accident? Difficult to believe, when you consider how it played out. Camille finds it hard to focus on these theories— another thought is running through his head while Doudouche claws at the sleeve of his jacket. It's the way the girl managed to escape from the warehouse. How exactly did she do it?

Forensic tests will confirm how she managed to snap the rope holding up the cage, but once she was outside, what then?

Camille tries to picture the scene. And in his movie version, there's a sequence missing.

They know the girl retrieved her clothes, and they have her shoe-prints leading to the shaft. These must be the shoes she was wearing when Trarieux abducted her—it's hardly likely her kidnapper would have brought her a new pair. The thing is he beat this girl, she struggled, he tossed her into the back of his van, tied her up. What sort of state would her clothes be in? Rumpled, dirty, torn? They certainly wouldn't be clean, of that Camille is sure. Once outside, a girl like that would be conspicuous, wouldn't she?

Camille finds it hard to imagine Trarieux being at all careful with the girl's things, but leave that to one side. Forget the clothes and focus on the girl.

We know she was filthy. She'd spent a whole week, stark naked, locked up in a crate six feet off the ground. In the pictures she looks half dead. They found dry pet food, kibble for pet mice and rats—this is clearly what Trarieux fed her. For the whole week, she's been forced to relieve herself while huddled in the cage.

"She's shattered," Camille says aloud, "and absolutely filthy."

Doudouche looks up as though she realizes better than her master that he has started talking to himself again.

There were puddles of water on the floor, damp rags, and her prints were found on several water bottles, so before she left she obviously had a perfunctory wash.

"Even so . . . when you've been shitting yourself for a week, what kind of a wash can you do with three quarts of cold water and a couple of grubby rags?"

This brings him back to the crucial question: How did she get home without being noticed?

"Who's to say no one noticed her?" Armand says.

7:45 a.m. The offices of the *brigade criminelle*. Even when you're not altogether with it, seeing Louis and Armand standing next to each other is a trip. Louis in his gray Kiton suit, Stefano Ricci tie, Weston brogues; Armand dressed from a clearance sale at a goodwill store. Good grief, Camille thinks, staring at him. He looks as though he buys his clothes a size too small to save that much more.

He takes another sip of coffee. Armand's right: Who's to say she wasn't noticed?

"Let's look into it," Camille says.

The girl attracted no attention to herself; she got out of the warehouse and disappeared into thin air. It's hard to credit.

"Maybe she got a lift?" Louis suggests, though even he does not believe this. A girl of twenty-five or thirty hitchhiking at two o'clock in the morning? Unless a car pulls up straightaway, she's hardly going to stand there with her thumb out. And she can't exactly stand on the curb flagging down cars like a hooker.

"The bus?"

Possible. Though at night they don't run very often on that route; she would have had to be lucky. Otherwise she'd find herself standing at a bus stop for half an hour or more, shattered, dressed in rags. Not very likely. Could she even stand up?

Louis makes a note to check the bus timetables, question the drivers.

"A taxi?"

Louis adds this to his list of things to check, but there again . . . Did she have money for the fare? And was she presentable enough for a taxi driver to take her? Maybe someone spotted her walking along the street?

The only thing they know for sure is that she would have been heading back into Paris. Whether she caught a bus or a taxi, they should know within a few hours.

At noon, Louis and Armand set out. Camille watches them go: what a pair. He steps behind his desk and flicks through the two files waiting for him: Bernard Gattegno, Stefan Maciak.

28

Alex steps into her apartment building slowly, nervously, suspiciously. Will Trarieux be waiting for her? Does he know she has escaped? No, there's no one in the lobby. Her mailbox isn't overflowing. There's no one in the stairwell, no one on the landing; it's like a dream.

She opens the door to her apartment and closes it behind her.

Exactly like a dream.

Home. Safe. Only two hours ago she was terrified she might be devoured by rats. She falters, almost falls, and has to cling to the walls for support.

She needs to eat something, now.

But first, she needs to look at herself.

My God, she looks at least fifteen years older. Ugly, filthy. Ancient. Bags under her eyes, wrinkles, yellow blotches on her skin, her eyes wild.

She takes everything out of the fridge—yogurt, cheese, bread, bananas—and stuffs her face as she runs a bath. And, unsurprisingly, she barely makes it to the toilet before she throws up.

She catches her breath, drinks a pint of milk.

She takes some rubbing alcohol and cleans the cuts and scratches on her arms, her legs, her hands, her knees, her face; then, after her bath, she treats them with antiseptic cream. She is so tired she can barely stand. Her face is a mess. Though the bruises from the abduction have begun to fade, the cuts on her arms and her legs look nasty, and two are obviously infected. She'll keep an eye on them; it's all she can do. When she's working, she always makes the most of her last day to stock up from the medicine cabinet. It's amazing what she's managed to pick up: penicillin, barbiturates, tranquilizers, diuretics, antibiotics, beta-blockers . . .

Finally, she lay down. Went straight to sleep.

Thirteen hours straight.

Waking up is like emerging from a coma.

It takes more than half an hour for her to work out where she is, to piece together how she got here. Tears well up again, and she curls up on the bed like a baby and cries herself to sleep.

She wakes five hours later; it's 6:00 p.m. Today, her radio tells her, is Thursday.

Groggy with sleep, she stretches her body; every limb aches. She takes her time, careful not to do herself an injury. Very slowly, she does some stretching exercises; though parts of her body are still stiff, she is making good progress. She gets unsteadily out of bed. Walks a little way, then her head starts to spin, she feels weak, and she takes hold of a shelf so as not to fall. She is starving. She looks at herself in the mirror. She needs to dress her wounds, but her brain's first whispered reflex is self-protection. First and foremost, make sure you're safe.

She escaped; Trarieux will come after her, try to capture her again. He must know where she lives, since he abducted her on her way home. He must know by now. She glances out of the window—the street seems quiet. As quiet as the night she was kidnapped.

She reaches out, picks up her laptop, and sets it on the sofa next to her. She opens a browser, types "Trarieux"—she doesn't know his first name, only the son's name, Pascal. It's the father she's looking for. Because she remembers exactly what she did to his fuckwit of a son, that retard. And where she buried him.

The third search engine result mentions an article about "Jean-Pierre Trarieux" on paris.news.fr. She clicks. It's him.

POLICE BLUNDER IN HIGH-SPEED PÉRIPHÉRIQUE CHASE?

Last night Jean-Pierre Trarieux, a man of about fifty involved in a high-speed police chase, suddenly stopped his van on the Périphérique overpass at Porte de la Villette, jumped out of the vehicle, dashed to the railing, and threw himself off. Trarieux was hit by an articulated truck and killed instantly.

According to the *police judiciaire*, the man was a suspect in a kidnapping some days earlier on the rue Falguière in Paris, a news story suppressed, according to a police source, "for security reasons." The fact remains however that the victim of the abduction has not yet been identified, and the location where she was held, "identified" by police, proved, to the police's surprise to be empty. In the absence of a victim to press charges, the death of the suspect—which police have termed "suicide"—remains mysterious and questionable. Magistrate Vidard, leading the investigation, has promised to get to the bottom of the case, which is being handled by Commandant Verhœven of the *brigade criminelle*.

Alex's mind struggles to keep up. When faced with a miracle, it is best to be skeptical.

This is why he hadn't come back. When he was a bloody pulp on the Périphérique he could hardly come back and check on her. Or bring food for the rats. The bastard had been prepared to kill himself rather than have the police come and free her. Let him rot in hell with his fuckwit son.

The other crucial fact: the police don't know who she is. They know nothing about her. Or at least they didn't know anything when the article was published at the beginning of the week.

She types her own name into the search engine. *Alex Prévost* comes up with a bunch of people with the same name, but nothing, absolutely nothing about her.

It's an enormous relief.

She checks her cell phone. Eight missed calls. And the battery's about to die. She gets up to look for the charger but moves too quickly—her body isn't ready for such bursts of speed; she falls back onto the sofa as though gravity is suddenly much stronger. She feels a dizziness, lights flash in front of her eyes, everything is spinning wildly, her heart lurches. Alex grits her teeth. A few more seconds and the dizzy spell passes. Cautiously she gets to her feet, tracks the phone charger down, plugs it in, then sits down again. Eight missed calls. Alex checks them and begins to breathe more easily. All work related: temp agencies—some of them have called twice. There's work. Alex doesn't bother listening to her voice mail; she'll deal with that later.

"Oh, it's you. I was wondering when I'd hear from you."

That voice . . . Her mother and her constant criticism. Every time she hears it, it has the same effect, a lump in her throat. Alex makes her excuses. Her mother always asks a lot of questions; when it comes to her daughter, she's a suspicious woman.

"A temp job? In Orléans? So is that where you're calling from?"

Alex always hears a note of disbelief in her tone. She says, "Yes, but I can't talk long." The response is instant.

"Not much point calling then, was there?"

Her mother rarely calls, and if Alex calls her, it's always like this. Her mother doesn't live; she reigns. Think of something. Talking to her mother is like taking an exam—you have to prepare, revise, focus.

Alex doesn't think.

"I'm going away for a bit, to the country; it's a temporary position. I mean another one . . ."

"Oh, really? Where exactly?"

"It's a short-term contract," Alex says again.

"So you said, a short-term contract, to the country. I'm assuming it's got a name, this place in the country?"

"I got it through an agency, but they haven't got the details yet. It's . . . complicated—we won't know until the last minute."

"Oh," her mother says.

She's clearly not buying this story. A moment's hesitation, then, "So you've got a short-term contract, you don't know where, covering for someone, but you don't know who: is that it?"

There's nothing unusual about the conversation—in fact it's typical. The only difference is that today Alex is weak, much less thick-skinned than usual.

"No, it's n— not like that . . ."

When it comes to her mother, it doesn't matter whether or not she's tired; sooner or later she ends up stuttering.

"Then what is it like?"

"Listen, my b— b— battery's almost dead . . ."

"Really . . . And I don't suppose you know how long it's for, this temporary contract? You'll just cover for this person, and one day they'll tell you that's it, you can go home, is that it?"

She needs something, "a few well-chosen words," as her mother would put it. But Alex can never think of any. Or rather she can, but always after the fact, when it's too late, after she's hung up, on the stairs, in the *métro*. When eventually she thinks of something, she'll kick herself. Repeat the useless quip over and over, replay the conversation in her head for days—it's as pointless as it is destructive, but she can't help herself. Embellish the facts until, over time, it becomes a completely different story, a sparring match in which Alex wins every round, but then, the next time she calls her mother, she's KO'd at the first word.

On the other end of the line her mother is waiting, silent, incredulous. Finally, Alex chucks in the towel.

"I really have to go now."

"Okay. Oh, Alex . . ."

"Yes."

"I'm fine, by the way. It was nice of you to ask."

She hangs up.

Alex's heart sinks.

She shakes herself, shrugs off all thoughts of her mother, focuses on what she needs to do. Trarieux, case closed. The police, out of the loop. Her mother, dealt with. Last: Text her brother.

Heading off to

(she thinks for a moment, weighs up possible destinations)

Toulouse: temping. let the queen mother know, i don't have time—Alex

It'll take him at least a week to pass on the message. If he does at all.

Alex takes a deep breath, closes her eyes. She's getting there. Slowly, she's managing to do what she needs to do in spite of her tiredness.

She changes the dressings on her wounds as her stomach howls with hunger. She goes and checks herself in the full-length bathroom mirror. She looks fully ten years older.

She takes a shower, turns it to cold for the last few minutes, shivers—God, it's good to be alive—a head-to-foot rubdown with a towel, she feels life rushing back—God, it's good when it hurts like this—she pulls on a rough sweater over her bare skin—it's a feeling she used to hate, but now she longs to feel the prickling itch of the coarse wool, to be intensely aware of her whole body, even her skin prickling with life. A pair of linen trousers, baggy and shapeless; they're hideous, but they're soft, loose fitting, like a caress. She picks up her bank card, her keys, says hello to Mme. Guénaude in passing. "Yes, just got back. Yes, I've been away. The weather? Magnificent. Well, in the south of France, what do you expect? Tired? Well, it was a tough job, didn't get much sleep the past few nights. Oh nothing, just a stiff neck, nothing serious. Oh, that?" She touches her forehead. "Completely stupid. I slipped and fell." Mme. Guénaude: "Not too steady on your pins?" A laugh. "Yes, you too, have a lovely evening."

Out on the street, the bluish haze of early evening is so beautiful she could weep. Alex suddenly laughs hysterically to herself. Life is wonderful. There's the Arab grocer, a handsome man—she's never given him a second look before, but he really is very handsome—if she could hear herself—she wants to stroke his cheek, gaze deep into his eyes; she laughs to feel so full of life. Everything she needs to eschew, all the things she's usually so careful about and which now seem like a reward: crisps, chocolate pudding, goat's cheese, a nice bottle of Saint-Émilion, and even a bottle of Baileys. She goes back to her apartment. The slightest effort tires her, almost making her cry. Suddenly she has a dizzy spell. She concentrates, waits, manages to overcome it. Carrying all the heavy shopping, she takes the elevator. She's so in love with life. Why can't life always be the way it is at this moment?

Alex, naked, wearing only an old, baggy bathrobe, stands in front of the full-length mirror. Five years older—okay then, maybe six. She'll recover quickly, she knows that; she can feel it. Take away the cuts and bruises, the bags and the wrinkles, the ordeal and the pain, and what are you left with: Alex looking gorgeous. She holds the bathrobe wide open, stares at her naked body, her breasts, her belly . . . and inevitably she starts to cry, standing, staring at her life.

She laughs to hear herself crying because she's no longer sure whether she's happy that she's still alive or unhappy because she's still Alex.

She knows how to deal with this danger that looms up from the depths. She sniffs, blows her nose, closes the bathrobe, pours herself a large glass of Saint-Émilion, an obscene, ridiculous meal of chocolate, rabbit pâté, biscuits.

She eats and eats and eats. Then slumps back on the sofa. She leans over, pours herself a half tumbler of Baileys, and with her last scrap of energy, goes to fetch some ice. She can feel exhaustion closing in, but the happiness is still there, like a background noise.

She glances at the alarm clock. She's completely out of sync; it's 10:00 p.m.

29

Engine oil, ink, gasoline—difficult to list all the smells that come together here, not to mention Mme. Gattegno's vanilla perfume. Fifty-something, when she saw the police arriving at the garage, she immediately rushed out of her glass-fronted office, and the apprentice who had been hurrying to meet them scampered off again like a puppy surprised by the sudden appearance of his master.

"It's about your husband, Madame."

"What husband?"

This kind of response sets the tone.

Camille jerks his chin out as though his shirt collar is too tight—he scratches his neck distractedly, stares up at the sky. Wonders how he's going to handle this, as he sees the woman fold her arms across her print dress, ready to be a human shield if necessary. He wonders what it is she's got to protect.

"Bernard Gattegno."

This obviously catches her off guard. The arms go slack; her mouth drops open. She wasn't expecting this, wasn't thinking about that particular husband. Admittedly, she remarried last year, a five-star slacker, younger than her, the best mechanic in the garage; she's Mme. Joris these days. It was a disaster. The minute he was married, her husband decides he didn't want to do a thing, reckons he can spend all his time at the bar. She shakes her head—a fucking waste.

"You have to understand, I did it for the sake of the garage," she explains.

Camille understands. It's a big garage, three or four mechanics, two apprentices, seven or eight cars, hoods open, engines turning over; on the hydraulic ramp, an Elvis Presley–style pink-and-white convertible, a strange car to find in Étampes. One of the mechanics, a youngish, tall, broad-shouldered guy, wipes his hands on a dirty rag and comes over, jaw clenched menacingly, and asks if he can help. He looks at his boss. If M. Joris succumbs to liver failure, there clearly won't be any problem finding a replacement. His biceps scream that he's not the type to be intimidated by the police. Camille nods.

"And for the kids," Mme. Joris says.

She harps on about her marriage—maybe this is what she's been trying to do from the start, to justify remarrying so quickly, so disastrously.

Camille wanders off, leaving Louis to deal with her. He looks around. Three secondhand cars, prices on the windshields in white paint. He goes over to the office; the walls are glass, the better to keep an eye on the mechanics while you're balancing the books. It always works, this little ruse, one of them asking the question, the other ferreting about. And today is no exception.

"You looking for something?"

The guy with the biceps has a strangely high-pitched voice, his tone educated but aggressive, defending his turf, even if it's not his. At least not yet. Camille turns around—his face just about comes up to the muscular mechanic's sternum. The guy's easily three heads taller. Consequently, Camille has a privileged view of the man's forearms as he mindlessly goes on wiping his hands on the rag like a bartender. Camille looks up.

"Fleury-Mérogis?"

The rag stops moving. Camille points at the tattoo on his forearm. "This one is from the nineties, isn't it? How long were you inside?"

"I've done my time," the mechanic says.

Camille nods to show he understands.

"Lucky for you, you've learned patience"—he nods toward Mme. Joris, who's still talking to Louis—"because you missed out last time, and it's going to be a while before you get another chance."

Louis is showing her the E-FIT of Nathalie Granger. Camille comes over. Mme. Joris stares, wide-eyed, shocked to see her ex-husband's fancy woman. Léa. "It's a whore's name, don't you think?" Camille is puzzled by the question; Louis nods prudently. Léa what? No one knows. Just Léa. She only ever met the girl twice, but she remembers it "like it was yesterday." "A fat girl." In the E-FIT, she looks like the very portrait of sweetness, but she was a bitch. "Though she did have big tits." To Camille, "big tits" is a relative term, especially given how flat chested Mme. Joris is. She's obsessed with the girl's tits as though they alone were responsible for the collapse of her marriage.

They piece together the story, the details of which are worryingly scant. Where did Gattegno meet Nathalie Granger? No one knows. Not even the mechanics Louis talks to, the ones working there two years ago. "She was a looker," one of them says—he met her one day while she was waiting on the corner in her car. Only ever saw her once, couldn't say whether it's the girl in the E-FIT. On the other hand, he can remember the make, the model number, and the year of the car (he's a garage mechanic), not that that will be much use to them. "Hazel eyes," chips in a man nearing retirement age—he's obviously stopped checking out women's asses, and big tits don't do much for him anymore, so he looks at their eyes. But when it comes to the E-FIT, he couldn't swear to it.

What's the point of being observant, Camille wonders, *when your memory's shot to fuck?*

No, no one knows how they met. But they're all agreed it was a whirlwind romance. Totally besotted, "from one day to the next" the boss was a changed man.

"She obviously knew a thing or two," says a guy who clearly thinks it's funny to talk dirty about his former boss.

Gattegno started ducking out of the garage. Mme. Joris admits that she followed him once—she was going out of her mind on account of the children; they managed to give her the slip, the husband didn't come home that night, showed up all sheepish the next morning, but Léa came looking for him. "She showed up at our house!" wails Mme. Joris. Two years later it still chokes her up. She saw Léa through the window. On the one hand there was his wife—the children were away ("a pity, because that might have stopped him"); on the other, standing at the garden gate, "that slut" (Nathalie Granger, aka Léa, clearly has a reputation). Anyway, the husband hesitates, though not for long, then grabs his wallet and his jacket and is gone. He was found dead in a room in a *Formule 1* motel the following Monday; the chambermaids discovered the body. In a *Formule 1*, there's no lobby, no receptionist, no visible staff. To get your room key you put a credit card in a machine— they used the husband's card. There was no sign of the girl. At the morgue, they wouldn't let her see the lower part of her husband's face—it can't have been a pretty sight. The postmortem was conclusive: no signs of a struggle, the guy lay on the bed fully clothed "shoes and all" and swallowed a pint of acid: "the kind used in car batteries."

Back at the *brigade*, while Louis is typing up the report (he types quickly, using all his fingers, carefully, regularly, as though he's practicing scales on a piano), Camille checks the autopsy report, but it says nothing about the concentration of the acid. A brutal, barbarous suicide—the guy must really have been at the end of his rope. The girl just left him there. Nor was there any sign of the four thousand euros the garage owner had withdrawn the night before—using three separate cards, "including the company credit card."

There can be no doubt: Gattegno and Trarieux had the same fatal encounter with Nathalie-Léa; the amounts stolen in both cases were grotesquely modest. They start combing through Trarieux's past, Gattegno's past, searching for common ground.

30

Her body starts to come back to life, tired and battered but intact. The infections have cleared up, most of the cuts have healed, the bruises are fading.

She's been to see Mme. Guénaude to explain things: "a family emergency." She had carefully chosen makeup that said *I might be young, but I've got a sense of duty.*

"I don't know, we'll have to see . . ."

All this struck Mme. Guénaude as a little sudden, but Mme. Guénaude knows the value of money. She used to be a shopkeeper. And since Alex was offering to pay two months' rent cash up front, she said she understood. She even said, "Obviously if I find another tenant before that, I'll pay you back . . ."

You lying cow, Alex thought, but said simply, "That's very kind," and smiled gratefully, careful not to overdo it—after all, the reason for her sudden departure is supposed to be grave.

She paid the rent, left a fake forwarding address. If worse comes to worst and Mme. Guénaude does write to her, she's hardly going to put herself out when the letter and the check are returned unopened; after all, it would be to her advantage.

"About the inventory."

"Don't worry about that," says the landlady, knowing she's got a good deal. "I'm sure everything's in order."

Alex says she will leave the keys in the mailbox.

There's no problem about the car; she pays for the parking space on the rue des Morillons by direct debit, so she doesn't have to worry about it. It's a six-year-old Renault Clio she bought secondhand.

She brought up the cardboard boxes from the basement, twelve of them, dismantled the furniture that belongs to her: the pine table, the three bookcases, the bed. She doesn't know why she's bothering to hang on to all this stuff—apart from the bed: she loves her bed; it's almost sacred. When it's all disassembled, she looks at it doubtfully; a whole life takes up less room than you might think. At least hers does. Seventy cubic feet. One hundred ten, according to the moving man. Alex just agreed with him—she knows what moving men are like. A white van. No point sending two guys; one will be enough. She also agrees to the price of storage, and the extra charge for next-day service. When Alex decides to leave, she wants to leave straightaway. Her mother is always saying: "With you, everything always has to be done yesterday—it's no wonder it never gets done properly." Sometimes, when she's in particularly good form, her mother adds, "Your brother, now that's a different matter." These days, the areas where her brother outshines her are few and far between. But for Alex's mother, there will always be enough; it's a matter of principle.

Despite the pain and the tiredness, within a few hours Alex has finished packing. She has even managed to throw out a lot of things. She regularly empties her bookshelves of all but a handful of classics. When she moved out of Porte de Clignancourt, she tossed out everything by Karen Blixen and E.M. Forster; when she left her place on the rue de Commerce, it was Stefan Zweig and Pirandello. When she left Champigny, it was Duras. She gets these crazes: when she likes an author, she reads everything (her mother claims she has no sense of proportion), but then when she wants to move, the books weigh a ton.

The rest of the time she lives out of boxes, sleeps on a mattress on the floor. There are two small boxes marked PERSONAL, containing the few things that are really precious to her. Most of the stuff is silly, insignificant: exercise books from school, report cards, letters, postcards, a diary she's been keeping on and off—never for very long—since she was twelve or thirteen, notes from old friends, trinkets that, thinking about it, she could have thrown out years ago and will do one of these days. She knows how childish they are. There's costume jewelry, too, dried-up old fountain pens, hair clips she used to like, vacation photographs, snapshots with her mother and brother when she was little. It all needs to be chucked out; it's worse than useless: it's dangerous to hang on to it—old movie tickets, pages torn from novels . . . One day she'll throw it all out. Right now, the two boxes marked PERSONAL have pride of place in this hasty move.

When it was all done, Alex went out to a movie, to dinner at Chartier, and to buy some battery acid. She has a mask and a pair of protective goggles she wears when she's doing prep work; she turns on the fan and the fan over the oven and keeps the window wide open to get rid of the fumes. To distill the acid to an 80 percent concentration, it has to be heated slowly until it begins to give off fumes. She prepares twelve pints. She stores it in bottles made of corrosion-resistant plastic she bought in a hardware shop near République. She keeps two of them and places the others carefully in a compartmented bag.

At night, her legs spasm, and she wakes with a jolt. It could be nightmares—she has a lot of those, dreams where rats are eating her alive, where Trarieux is boring steel rods into her head with his electric drill. She's also haunted by the face of Trarieux's son. She can picture his moronic face, rats pouring out of his mouth. Sometimes the scenes are real: Pascal Trarieux sitting in the deck chair in the garden in Champigny as she comes up behind him, raising the shovel over her head, hampered by her blouse, which is too tight at the sleeves.

At the time she weighed twenty-eight pounds more than she does now. God did she have tits! The fuckwit was obsessed with them. She'd let him get under her blouse, never for long, and when he was really horny, when his hands started to squeeze her breasts excitedly, she'd give him a sharp slap, just like a schoolteacher. Though on a very different scale, it's not so different from the rap she gave him on the back of his skull, swinging the shovel with every ounce of her strength.

In her dream, the shovel blow is terribly loud, and as she did in real life, she feels the vibrations travel up her arms to her shoulders. Pascal Trarieux, half-unconscious, turns to her with difficulty, reels, gives her a look of astonishment, of disbelief, a strangely serene look in which there is no room for doubt. So with her shovel Alex makes room for doubt: seven blows, eight, Trarieux's head has slumped onto the garden table, which makes the work easier. After that, the dream skips the part about tying him up and jumps straight to the part when she pours the first dose of acid into Pascal's mouth. The stupid fucker screams so loudly he'll wake the whole neighborhood, so she's forced to stand up and whack him in the face with the flat of the shovel. It's amazing the noise those things make.

There are the dreams, the nightmares, the aches, the cramps, the painful spasms, but slowly her body is recovering. Alex knows that it will never entirely go away—it's impossible to survive a week in a tiny cage with a colony of frenzied rats without owing a debt to life. She does lots of exercises, stretching exercises she learned long ago, and she's started jogging again, too. She goes out early in the morning and does several laps of the parc George-Brassens, but she has to stop regularly because she tires easily.

Finally the moving man comes and takes everything away. He's a big guy and a bit of a braggart; he tries to flirt with her—she's seen it all before.

Alex goes and buys a train ticket to Toulouse, puts her suitcase in the baggage room, and checks her watch as she leaves the Gare Montparnasse: 8:30 p.m. She could go back to the Restaurant

Mont-Tonnerre; maybe he'll be there, him and his friends, telling stories and living it up . . . From what she overheard, they go on a boys' night out every week. Though maybe they don't always go to the same restaurant.

But it turns out that they do, because here he is with his friends— there are more than there were before; it's become a little club. Tonight there are seven of them. Alex has the impression the owner is serving them a little disapprovingly—he's clearly not convinced that this little club is to his liking: too much noise, and other diners turn to stare. The pretty red-haired woman . . . All the staff wait on her hand and foot. The table where they've seated Alex makes it more difficult to see him than it was last time—she has to lean, and, unluckily, he notices, his eyes meet hers, and it's obvious he was the one she was looking at. *Oh well*, she thinks, smiling. She has a glass of chilled Riesling, scallops with steamed vegetables al dente followed by crème brûlée and an espresso, then another coffee, the second one compliments of the owner, who apologizes for the noise. He even offers her a glass of chartreuse—he thinks of it as a girl's drink. Alex says, "No, thank you, but I'd love a Baileys on the rocks." The owner smiles; he finds the girl charming. She takes her time leaving, "forgets" her book and comes back for it. The guy is no longer with his friends; he's on his feet, slipping on his coat, his friends making crude jokes about his sudden departure. He is right behind her as she emerges from the restaurant, and she can feel his eyes on her ass; Alex has a fine ass, as sensitive as a satellite dish. Hardly has she walked thirty feet than he's there beside her. He says, "Hi," and something about his face stirs conflicting feelings in her.

Félix. He doesn't tell her his surname. She immediately notices he's not wearing a wedding ring, but there's a white band around his finger—he's probably just taken it off.

"What about you, what's your name?"

"Julia," Alex says.

"Pretty name."

He would have said this regardless. Alex finds it funny.

He jerks his thumb back toward the restaurant.

"We were a bit rowdy . . ."

"A bit," Alex says, smiling.

"It's a boys' night out, so . . ."

Alex doesn't respond. If he carries on, he'll just dig himself in deeper, and he realizes this. He suggests a drink at a bar he knows. She says no thank you. They stroll a little way together. Alex walks slowly, takes a better look at him. He's wearing cheap chain store clothes, and though he's just had dinner, that's not the only reason his shirt buttons are straining; he has no one to tell him he needs to buy the next size up. Or go on a diet and take up a sport.

"No, honestly," he says, "it's just twenty minutes from here."

He's just mentioned that his place is not far; they could have a drink there. Alex says she's tired, not really in the mood. They've reached his car, an Audi piled with junk.

"So what do you do for a living?" she says.

"Technical maintenance operative."

Alex translates: repair man.

"Scanners, printers, hard drives . . . ," he explains, as though somehow this makes him seem more important. Then he adds, "I've got a team of—"

Suddenly he realizes it's stupid to try and big himself up. Worse, it's counterproductive.

He waves his hand. Difficult to tell if he's brushing away the end of the sentence as though it's unimportant, or the beginning as though he regrets saying it.

He opens the car door; there's a cold blast of stale cigarette smoke.

"Do you smoke?"

This is Alex's technique—she blows hot and cold. She's a past master.

"A little," says the guy, embarrassed.

He's about six feet, quite broad shouldered with light-brown hair and dark, almost black eyes. Walking next to her, she notices he's got stubby legs. He's not very well proportioned.

"I only smoke when I'm around smokers," he says, ever the gentleman.

She is convinced that right now he would give anything for a cigarette. He finds her really attractive; he's being very formal, but he can't bring himself to look her in the eyes because he's so turned on. It's intensely sexual, animal; it makes him completely blind. He would be incapable of telling what she's wearing. He gives the impression that if Alex doesn't sleep with him right now, he'll go home and murder his whole family with a hunting rifle.

"Are you married?"

"No . . . divorced. Well, separated."

Simply from the tone of his voice, Alex translates: "I don't know what to say—I'm getting ripped apart here."

"What about you?"

"Single."

This is the good thing about the truth; it rings true. He looks down, not out of embarrassment or modesty—he's staring at her breasts. Whatever Alex wears, the first thing everyone notices is her beautiful, voluptuous breasts.

She smiles and, as she leaves, she says, "Some other time, maybe . . ."

He jumps at this: when, when? He fumbles in his pockets. A taxi passes. Alex hails it. The taxi pulls up. Alex opens the door. When she turns to say good-bye, he's holding out his business card. It's a little crumpled; it looks shoddy. She takes it all the same and, just to show how little it matters, slips it absentmindedly into her pocket. In the rearview mirror, she sees him, standing in the middle of the street, watching the taxi drive away.

31

The *gendarme* asked whether his presence was required.

"I'd rather you stayed," Camille said. "Assuming you can spare the time, obviously."

In general, collaboration between the national police force and the local police of the *gendarmerie* can be a little fractious, but Camille has a lot of time for regional officers. He feels he has a lot in common with them. They tend to be opinionated, pugnacious, the sort who never give up on a lead, even a cold one. The local officer is clearly flattered by Camille's suggestion—he's a chief sergeant, but Camille refers to him as "*chef*" because he knows the form; the officer feels respected, and he's right. He's forty years old and has a pencil-thin mustache, like a nineteenth-century musketeer. There's a lot about him that's old-fashioned—a self-conscious elegance, a stiff formality, but Camille quickly recognizes that the man is really intelligent. He has a high regard for his position. His shoes are polished mirrors.

The weather is gray, maritime.

Faignoy-lès-Reims, population eight hundred, two streets, a square with a vast war memorial; the place is as gloomy as a wet

Sunday in paradise. They head for the bistro—this is why they've
come here. Chief Langlois parks the squad car right outside.

As they go in, the smell of soup, cheap wine, and detergent hits
you in the back of the throat. Camille starts to wonder if he's becoming hypersensitive to smell. Back at the garage, Mme. Joris and her
vanilla perfume . . .

Stefan Maciak died in November 2005. The new owner arrived
shortly afterwards.

"Actually, I took over the place in January."

All he knows is what he's been told, what everyone knows. It even
meant he dithered about whether to take the place over, because the
story was big news in the area. You get burglaries, holdups, that
kind of thing around here—even murders from time to time (the
bar owner tries in vain to get Chief Langlois to back him up), but
something like this . . . Actually, Camille hasn't come here to listen, he's come to see the crime scene, to get a feel for the story, to
clarify his thoughts. At the time, Maciak is fifty-seven, he's of Polish descent, single. He's a big man, about as alcoholic as you can
be when you've been managing bars for thirty years with no self-
discipline. Not much is known about his life outside his workplace.
As for sex, he paid regular visits to the local brothel—Germaine
Malignier and her daughter, known to regulars as "the four cheeks."
Otherwise he seemed a decent enough sort of guy.

"The accounts were all in order."

For the new proprietor, closing his eyes solemnly, this is a blank
check for life.

"Then, one night in November . . ." Chief Langlois takes up the
story. By now he and Camille have left the bar, having refused a
drink, and they're walking toward the war memorial, a pedestal on
which stands a World War I soldier leaning into the wind, about to
skewer some invisible Kraut with his bayonet. "November 28, to be
exact. Maciak is closing up as usual at about ten o'clock—he's pulled
down the metal shutters, and he's started cooking himself something in the kitchen at the back of the café. He's probably planning
to eat in front of the TV, which has been on since 7:00 a.m. But he

didn't get to eat that night; he never had time—we think he went to open the back door. When he comes back, he's not alone. No one knows what transpired exactly; the only thing we know for sure is that some time later, he's hit on the back of the head with a hammer. He's stunned, he's badly injured, but he's not dead—the postmortem was very clear. At this point he's tied up using bar towels, which means this wasn't premeditated. He's laid out on the floor of the café, someone obviously tries to get him to tell them where his savings are, he refuses. They must have gone out through the back kitchen to the garage to get the sulfuric acid he used to refill the battery in his van. They come back and pour a pint of it down his throat, which quickly puts an end to the conversation. They pocket the day's takings—thirty-seven euros—go upstairs and turn the place upside down, rip open the mattresses, empty out the drawers, and find his savings—two thousand euros—hidden in the toilet. Then they just disappear, without being seen by a single soul, taking the container of acid, presumably because it had fingerprints."

Camille is unthinkingly reading the list of names of those who fell in the Great War. Finds three men called Malignier: the name the chief mentioned earlier—Gaston, Eugène, and Raymond. He's trying to find a connection to the "four cheeks."

"Any mention of a woman?"

"We know there was a woman, but we don't know if she is connected to the case."

Camille feels a little shudder down his spine.

"Okay, how do you think it happened? Maciak is closing up, it's ten o'clock—"

"Nine forty-five," corrects Chief Langlois.

"That doesn't change much."

Chief Langlois grimaces: to his mind, it changes everything.

"Surely you understand, Commandant," he says. "A bar owner is more likely to stay open a little later than his license permits. For him to close up fifteen minutes early is very unusual."

A "tryst"—this is Chief Langlois's word, his theory. The regulars had mentioned a woman coming into the bar that evening, but they'd been there since midafternoon and had blood alcohol levels to prove it, so unsurprisingly some reported that she was young, others said old, some claimed she was short, others said fat; a few thought there was someone with her, mentioned a foreign accent, but even those who claimed to have heard it couldn't say where it was from. All in all, none of them knew anything beyond the fact that she chatted for a while to Maciak, who seemed all excited, that this was at nine o'clock and forty-five minutes later he closed up early, telling the regulars he was tired. We know the rest. No record of any woman—young, old, short, or fat—staying at any of the hotels in the area. A call for witnesses was put out, but nothing came of it.

"We should have widened the search area," the chief says, dispensing with the usual litany about lack of resources.

For the moment, all that can be said with certainty is that there was a woman in the area. Beyond that . . .

Chief Langlois permanently looks as though he's standing to attention. He is stiff, wooden.

"Something bothering you, *chef*?" Camille says, still looking down the names of those who fell in the Great War.

"Well . . ."

Camille turns toward Langlois, and without waiting for a response, he carries on. "The thing I find surprising is the idea of trying to get someone to talk by pouring acid down his throat. If they were trying to shut him up, it would make more sense, but to get him to talk . . ."

For Langlois, this is a relief. His rigid posture relaxes a little, as though for a moment he's forgotten he's on parade—he even clicks his tongue—a mannerism hardly in accordance with police regulations. Camille is tempted to call him to order, but he suspects that in his career path, Chief Langlois never checked the box marked "humor."

"I thought that, too," he says at length. "It's curious . . . At first glance, the crime looks like the work of a prowler. The fact that Maciak opened the back door hardly proves that he knew the person; at best, all it proves is that the person was persuasive enough to get him to open up—it would hardly be difficult. So, it could be a prowler. The café is deserted, no one saw him enter, he picks up the hammer—Maciak had a small toolbox under the bar—he stuns Maciak, ties him up; that is compatible with the report."

"But since you don't believe the acid was used to try and make him tell where he'd hidden his savings, you presumably favor a different theory . . ."

They leave the war memorial and walk back to the car. The wind has come up a little and with it the late-season cold. Camille pushes down his hat and buttons his coat.

"Let's just say I've found a more logical one. I don't know why acid was poured into his mouth and down his throat, but to my mind it has nothing whatever to do with the burglary. As a rule, when thieves are inclined to murder, they favor the direct route: first they kill, then they search, then they leave. Vicious thugs torture their victims using orthodox means, which though they may be excruciating, are standard techniques. But this . . ."

"So, what do you think the acid was for?"

Langlois looks dubious for a moment, then comes to a decision.

"I believe it was a sort of ritual. What I mean is . . ."

Camille knows exactly what he means.

"What kind of ritual?"

"Sexual?" Langlois ventures.

Smart guy, the chief.

Sitting next to each other, the two men stare through the windshield at the rain streaming down the war memorial. Camille explains the sequence of events they've established: Bernard Gattegno, March 13, 2005; Maciak later that year, on November 28; Pascal Trarieux, July 14, 2006.

Chief Langlois nods.

"What links them is that the victims are all men."

This is what Camille thinks, too. The ritual is sexual. This girl, if it is her, despises men. She seduces men she meets, perhaps she even chooses her victims, and, at the first opportunity, she bumps them off. As for the sulfuric acid, they'll understand that once they've arrested her.

"That's one murder every eight months," Chief Langlois says. "But geographically it's one hell of a hunting ground."

Camille agrees. The chief doesn't simply put forward very plausible hypotheses, he also asks the right questions. But as far as Camille knows, there's nothing to connect the victims: Gattegno, a garage owner in Étampes; Maciak, a café owner in Reims; Trarieux, unemployed in Paris. Apart from the fact that they were killed in very much the same way and apparently by the same hand.

"We don't know who this girl is," Camille says, as Langlois starts the car to drive back to the train station. "All we know is that, if you're a man, you're better off not crossing her path."

32

When she arrived, Alex checked in to the first hotel she found. It's opposite the station. She didn't get a wink of sleep. When it wasn't the racket of the trains, the rats were still haunting her dreams, something that would happen no matter what hotel she was in. In the last dream, the fat black rat was at least three feet long, and it poked its snout, its whiskers into Alex's face, its black beady eyes piercing her; she could see the slavering jaws, the razor-sharp teeth.

The following morning, she found exactly the place she was looking for in the telephone directory. The Hôtel du Pré Hardy. Luckily, they had a number of rooms available, and the prices were reasonable. It proved to be a nice hotel, very clean, if a little far from the center. Alex likes the city; the light is agreeable, and she has been going for walks, as though this is a vacation.

When she first checked in to the Hôtel du Pré Hardy, she almost turned on her heel and left again. Because of the owner, Mme. Zanetti—"but everyone calls me Jacqueline." It rankled a little with Alex, this pretending to be friends straight off.

"And what's your name, dear?"

She had to say something, so, "Laura."

"Laura?" repeated the owner, surprised. "That's my niece's name."

Alex couldn't see what was so strange about this. Everyone has a first name—hotel owners, nieces, nurses, everyone—but Mme. Zanetti finds it particularly startling. This is why Alex took an instant dislike to the woman—the horribly manipulative way she pretends to be connected to everyone. She's a "people person," and now that she's getting older, she consolidates her communication skills with an aura of protectiveness. Alex is infuriated by this need in her to be best friends with half the planet and mother to the other half.

Physically, she was once a beautiful woman, but her attempt to cling to her beauty ruined everything. Plastic surgery doesn't always age well. With Mme. Zanetti, it's difficult to put a finger on exactly what is wrong; it looks as though everything has shifted and that her face, while still trying to look like a face, is out of all proportion. It's a tightly stretched mask with snake eyes sunk into deep hollows, a network of fine lines around lips that have been ridiculously inflated; the forehead is so taut the eyebrows are permanently arched, the jowls pulled back so far they dangle like sideburns. Her staggering mane of hair is dyed jet black. When she first appeared behind the reception desk, Alex had to fight back the urge to recoil; the woman looks like a witch. Having a monstrosity like this to welcome you every night makes for quick decisions. Mentally, Alex decided to get Toulouse out of the way quickly and head back to Paris. But on her first night, Mme. Zanetti invited her into the back room for a drink.

"Come on, dear, won't you have a little chat with me?"

The whisky is excellent, and her private sitting room is pleasant, all done out in a fifties style, with a big black Bakelite telephone, an old Teppaz gramophone with a Platters L.P. When all's said and done, Mme. Zanetti is pretty okay—she tells funny stories about previous guests. And after a while you get used to the face. You forget about it. Just as she has probably forgotten about it. It's the nature of a handicap; there comes a time when only other people notice.

After the whisky, Mme. Zanetti opened a bottle of Bordeaux. "I don't know what I've got in the fridge, but if you'd like to stay for dinner . . ." Alex accepted, because it was easier. The evening is a long and pleasant one; Alex is subjected to a barrage of questions, and she lies reasonably well. The good thing about casual conversations is that you're not expected to tell the truth—what you say is of no importance. When Alex got up from the sofa to go to bed, it was past 1:00 a.m. They kiss each other spontaneously on both cheeks, tell each other it's been a marvelous evening, something that is both true and false. In any case, the time passed without Alex noticing. She's getting to bed much later than she had planned, utterly exhausted—she has an appointment with her nightmares.

The following morning, she visits the bookstores, has a little nap, and sleeps so deeply it is almost painful.

The hotel "comprising twenty-four guest rooms, was entirely renovated four years ago," according to Jacqueline Zanetti, "call me Jacqueline—no, honestly, I insist." Alex's room is on the second floor. She doesn't encounter many other guests but hears them rattling around: clearly the renovation did not extend to soundproofing. That evening, as Alex attempts to slip out discreetly, Jacqueline suddenly appears behind the reception desk. It's impossible to turn down the offer of a drink. Jacqueline is in even better form. She tries hard to be scintillating: laughing and joking and making faces; she's laid out prepared snacks, and at about 10:00 p.m., she reveals her plans. "Why don't we go dancing?" The proposal is offered with a delighted impulsiveness designed to win Alex over, but Alex does not much like dancing . . . Besides, she finds such places mystifying. "Not at all," tuts Jacqueline, pretending to take offense, "people just go to dance, honestly." Persuasive. As though she really believes what she's saying.

At her mother's insistence, Alex trained to be a nurse, but deep down she is also a nurse at heart. She likes to do good. The reason she finally accepts is that Jacqueline has put so much effort into presenting her proposal. She made supper, talks about someplace where they have dancing twice a week—"You'll see, it's priceless!"—Jacqueline has always been crazy about dance halls. "Well," she confesses, simperingly, "I suppose you also get to meet people there."

Alex sips her claret. She barely even noticed that they sat down to eat, but now it's half-past ten, time to go.

33

As far as they know, Pascal Trarieux's path never crossed that of Stefan Maciak, who as far as they know never met Gattegno. Camille summarizes the police records.

"Gattegno, born in Saint-Fiacre, went to technical college in Pithiviers, where he also did his apprenticeship. Six years later he opens up his own workshop in Étampes, and later (he's twenty-eight by this time) he takes over his former mentor's garage, also in Étampes."

The offices of the *brigade criminelle*.

The magistrate came by for what he insists on calling "a debriefing." He says the word with a pronounced English accent somewhere between affectation and ridiculousness. Today, he's wearing a sky-blue tie; this is as outrageous as his dress sense gets. He is sitting, expressionless, hands splayed on the desk in front of him, like a starfish. He is determined to make an impression.

"From the day he was born to the day he died, this guy didn't go beyond an eighteen-mile radius," Camille continues. "Three kids and suddenly, at the age of forty-nine, a midlife crisis. It drives him crazy, and eventually, it does for him. No known connection to Trarieux."

The magistrate says nothing. Le Guen says nothing. They're keeping their powder dry; with Camille Verhœven, you never know which way things will go.

"Stefan Maciak, born 1949 to a Polish family, a family of modest means, a hardworking family, a model of French social integration."

Everybody already knows all this. Reviewing the details of a case for just one person is tiresome, and it's obvious from Camille's voice that he's losing patience. At times like this, Le Guen closes his eyes as though trying to communicate serenity using thought waves. Louis also does this to try to calm his boss. Camille is not a hothead, but from time to time, he can be a little impetuous.

"This Maciak was so socially integrated he became an alcoholic. He drinks like a Pole, which makes him a good Frenchman. The kind that wants to preserve the French national heritage. So he goes to work in a bistro. He washes dishes, waits tables, he's promoted to head waiter—we're witnessing a miracle of upward mobility through the downward application of alcohol. In a meritocratic country like ours, hard work always pays off. Maciak is managing his first café by the age of thirty-two, a place in Épinay-sur-Orge. He's there for eight years and then comes the peak of his social climb, the bistro in Reims, where he died in circumstances we're already familiar with. Never married. Which might possibly explain him falling head over heels when a passing traveler takes an interest in him. It costs him 2,037 euros (traders like to be precise) and his life. His career may have been a long hard slog, but his passion was a blinding flash."

Silence. Impossible to tell whether this signals annoyance (the magistrate), consternation (Le Guen), forbearance (Louis), or joy (Armand), but no one says a word.

At length the magistrate says: "According to you, there is nothing to connect the victims. Our murderer is killing people at random. You think the murders are not premeditated."

"Whether or not she plans them, I can't say. I'm simply making plain that the victims did not know each other, so there's no point pursuing that line of inquiry."

"So why does the murderer change her identity, if not *so she can* kill?"

"It's not so she can kill, it's because she *has* killed."

The magistrate only has to voice an idea for Camille to start backpedaling. He explains.

"She doesn't really change her identity; she simply changes her name. It's not the same thing. Someone asks her name, and she says 'Nathalie,' or she says 'Léa'—it's not as if they're going to ask to see her ID card. She changes her name because she has killed a number of men, three as far as we're aware, though we have no idea of the true figure. She's covering her tracks as best she can."

"She's doing a pretty good job," snaps the magistrate.

"I concede that . . . ," Camille says.

He says this distractedly because he is looking at something else. All eyes turn toward the window. The weather has changed. Late September. It's 9:00 a.m., but the sky has gone dark. The thunderstorm lashing the windows has suddenly whipped itself up into a raging fury; for two hours now it's been wreaking havoc. It doesn't look like anything will stop it. Camille surveys the damage worriedly. Though the clouds don't quite have the brooding savagery of Géricault's *The Flood*, there is danger in the air. *We need to be careful as we lead our little lives,* Camille thinks; *the end of the world will not be some momentous calamity—it could start out just like this.*

"What's the motive?" the magistrate says. "Money doesn't seem likely."

"We're agreed on that point. The sums involved are pretty paltry; if she was in this for the money, she'd plan her moves more carefully, choose richer victims. Trarieux's father was robbed of 623 euros; with Maciak she got a day's takings; with Gattegno, she spends the balance on his credit cards."

"So the cash is just a perk?"

"Possibly. I think it's a diversion. She's trying to throw us off the scent by making it look like a robbery gone wrong."

"What then? A sociopath?"

"Maybe. It's definitely sexual."

The fatal word has been said. Now it's anybody's game. The magistrate has his own ideas on the subject. Camille wouldn't put much money on his sexual experience, but he's been to university, and he's not afraid to theorize on the subject.

"She . . . if indeed it is a she . . ."

This has been the magistrate's approach right from the start. It's probably something he does in all his cases: harping on rules, the presumption of innocence, the necessity of relying on hard facts; he positively revels in playing the pedant. When he makes an insinuation like this, reminding them that nothing is proven, he invariably contrives to have a moment of silence so that everyone understands the significance of the subtext. Le Guen nods. Later, he'll say: "At least we get to deal with him as an adult. Can you imagine what an irritating asshole he must have been at school?"

"She pours the acid down the victim's throat," the magistrate goes on. "If this were sexual, as you maintain, it seems to me she might have other uses for it. Don't you agree?"

An innuendo. A roundabout phrase. Theorizing keeps reality at a distance. Never one to miss an opportunity, Camille says, "Would you care to be more precise?"

"Well . . ."

The magistrate hesitates a second too long. Camille pounces: "Yes?"

"Well, the acid . . . surely she would be more likely to pour it—"

"On his prick?" interrupts Camille.

"Um . . ."

"Or his balls maybe? Or both?"

"Yes, I'm inclined to think so."

Le Guen stares up at the ceiling. When he hears the magistrate begin to speak again, he thinks, *Round two*, and already he feels tired.

"You're still of the opinion that this girl was raped, Commandant Verhœven; is that your point?"

"Raped, yes. I think she kills because she was raped. I think she's avenging herself on men."

"And her pouring the sulfuric acid down her victims' throats . . ."

"I'm inclined to think it's related to unpleasant experiences of being forced to give fellatio. Such things do happen, you know."

"Absolutely," the magistrate agrees. "In fact, more often than one might think. Luckily, not all women who are shocked by the practice become serial killers. Or at least, not like this."

Astonishingly, the magistrate is smiling; Camille is a little disconcerted. The man seems always to smile at inopportune moments. It's difficult to interpret.

"In any case, whatever her reasons," Camille goes on, "it's what she does. Yeah, yeah, I know, if it *is* a she."

As he says this, Camille twirls a finger in the air: the same old song.

The magistrate, still smiling, nods and gets to his feet.

"In any case, whether or not it's that, there's been something this girl's found hard to swallow."

Everyone is surprised. Especially Camille.

34

Alex made one last attempt to duck out.

"I'm not dressed for it. I can't go out like this—I've brought nothing with me."

"You look perfect."

And suddenly they're face-to-face in the living room. Jacqueline is staring at her, gazing deep into Alex's green eyes, and nods in a mixture of admiration and regret, as though she is seeing a part of her own life, as though she is saying how marvelous it is to be beautiful, to be young, and when she says, "You look perfect," she really means it, and there's nothing Alex can say. They take a taxi, and before she realizes it, they're there. The dance hall is enormous. Alex finds this in itself depressing—it's like the circus or the zoo, the sort of place that immediately makes you feel unaccountably sad, but to make things worse it would take 800 people to fill the place and there are barely 150. There's a band with an accordion and an electric piano—the musicians are fifty if they're a day. The bandleader's toupee is slipping from the sweat and looks as though it will wind up down his back. There are a hundred chairs set around the walls; in the center, on a dance floor gleaming like a new penny, some thirty couples sway to and fro, dressed up as bolero dancers, as wedding guests, as trashy Spaniards, as twenties Charleston babes. It looks like a broken hearts convention.

Jacqueline doesn't see it like that—she's completely in her element. Just looking at her, you can tell she loves the place. She knows a lot of the regulars, introduces Alex: "This is Laura . . ." She gives Alex a wink. "My niece." They're all in their forties or fifties. Here, any girl in her thirties looks like an orphan, and any man looks slightly suspicious. There are about a dozen bubbly, vivacious women like Jacqueline, in their glad rags, their hair and makeup perfect, on the arms of gentle, patient husbands wearing trousers with razor-sharp creases. Loud, jolly women usually described as "up for anything." They hug Alex as though they've been dying to meet her for ages; after that, she is quickly forgotten since they are here to dance.

In fact, the dancing is merely a pretext; the real reason is Mario: this is why Jacqueline is here. She should have told Alex—it would have been easier. Mario is about thirty with a body like a builder's laborer, a little tongue-tied but undeniably manly. So, on the one hand there's Mario, the builder, and on the other there's Michel, in his jacket and tie, who looks like a former company director, the kind of man who tugs his shirt cuffs and wears monogrammed cuff links. He's wearing a pale-green suit with a narrow strip of braid down the outside leg; you can't help wondering where he could wear such a thing other than here. It's obvious that he's stuck on Jacqueline, but the problem is that, compared with Mario, he looks very old for fifty. Jacqueline couldn't care less about Michel. Alex watches this transparent charade. Here, a little knowledge of animal behavior is enough to understand every relationship.

To one side of the room, there's a bar—more of a refreshment room, really—where everybody congregates during less popular numbers. This is where people make small talk, and it is here, too, that the men make overtures to the women. At certain moments, there will be a whole crowd in the corner of the room, making the few couples dancing look even more forlorn, like figures on top of a wedding cake. The bandleader whips up the tempo to get the song over and try his luck with a different number.

It's past two in the morning by the time the place starts to empty out. A handful of men cling feverishly to women in the middle of the dance floor because there's not much time left to seal the deal.

Mario disappears, Michel offers to take them home, but Jacqueline says no, they'll take a taxi, but before that, everyone kisses everyone goodnight, says how much they've enjoyed their evening, promises the moon.

In the taxi, Alex dares to bring up the subject of Michel with a tipsy Jacqueline, who confides something that is surely no secret: "I've always had a thing for younger men." As she says this, she gives a little pout, as though admitting that she can't resist chocolate. Both can be bought, thinks Alex, because sooner or later Jacqueline will get her Mario, but one way or the other it will cost her.

"You were bored, weren't you?"

Jacqueline takes Alex's hand in hers and squeezes. Strangely, they're cold, these long, wizened hands with their ridiculously long nails. Into this gesture Jacqueline pours all the affection that the late hour and her inebriated state permit.

"Not at all," Alex says with conviction. "It was fun."

But she has already decided she will leave tomorrow. Early. She doesn't have a reservation, but it doesn't matter. She'll get a train.

They get back to the hotel. Jacqueline totters on her high heels. Come on, it's late. They kiss each other goodnight in the hall, making no noise so as not to wake the guests. "See you tomorrow?" Alex agrees to everything. She goes up to her room, fetches her suitcase, comes downstairs again and sets it near the reception desk. Now she has only her handbag. She slips behind the desk and pushes the door into the private sitting room.

Jacqueline has taken off her shoes and just poured herself a large whiskey. Now that she's alone, left to herself, she looks a hundred years older.

When she sees Alex appear, she smiles. *Did you forget something?* She doesn't have time to say the words before Alex snatches up the telephone receiver and smashes it full force into her right temple. Jacqueline reels from the shock and collapses. Her glass flies across the room. When she looks up, Alex slams the huge Bakelite telephone down on her head, using both hands this time. This is how she kills people—a blow to the head first. Besides, it's the fastest way when you don't have a weapon. This time, three, four, five massive blows, swinging her arm as high as possible and she's done. The old woman's face is already badly battered, but she's not dead—this is the second advantage of hitting them across the head: it stuns them but leaves them awake for dessert. Two more blows to the face and Alex realizes that Jacqueline is wearing dentures. They're hanging crookedly half out of her mouth, made of acrylic resin, most of the front teeth broken—there's not much left. Blood is streaming from her nose; Alex prudently takes a step back. She uses the telephone wire to tie her wrists and ankles so that if the old bitch struggles a bit, it doesn't matter.

Alex is always careful to protect her nose and her face—she works at arm's length, grabbing a fistful of hair. It's just as well, because when the acrylic resin comes into contact with the sulfuric acid it bubbles dramatically.

As her tongue, her throat, and her neck fuse, the hotelier lets out a raucous, animal cry, and her stomach distends like a helium-filled balloon. The cry is probably just a reflex—it's difficult to tell. But, even so, Alex hopes it's pain.

She opens the window onto the courtyard and half-opens the door to create a through breeze; then, once the air is breathable again, she closes the door, leaving the window open. She looks for a bottle of Baileys, doesn't find one, tastes the vodka, which isn't bad, then settles on the sofa. One eye on the old woman. Dead, she looks completely dislocated, and that's nothing compared with the face—or what's left of it. The flesh melted away by the acid has released a torrent of Botox to create a revolting pulp.

Ugh.

Alex is exhausted.

She picks up a magazine and starts on the crossword.

35

They're getting nowhere. The magistrate, the weather, the investigation: nothing's going right. Even Le Guen is in a state. And then there's the girl, about whom they still know nothing. Camille has finished up his reports; he's hanging around. He never really feels like going home. If it weren't for Doudouche waiting for him . . .

They're working ten-hour days, they've taken dozens of witness statements, reread dozens of reports and charge sheets, correlated information, checked details, times, questioned people. And come up with nothing. It makes you wonder.

Louis pops his head around the door, then comes in. Seeing the papers scattered on the desk, he gestures *May I?* to the commandant. Camille nods. Louis turns the papers around; they're portraits of the girl. The E-FIT created by *l'identité judiciaire* is good enough for witnesses to be able to identify her, but it's lifeless, while here, from memory, Camille has transformed her, brought her completely to life. This girl may have no name, but in these sketches she has a soul. Camille has drawn her ten, twenty, maybe thirty times as though he knew her intimately. Here she is sitting at a table, probably in a restaurant, hands clasped under her chin as though listening to someone telling a story, her eyes bright, laughing. Here she's crying, looking up at the viewer—it's heartbreaking: it looks as though she's lost for words: her lips seem to tremble. Here she is walking down the street, arching her back as she turns around—she's just seen something in a shop window, and the glass reflects her expression of surprise. In Camille's sketches, she is startlingly alive.

Louis feels like saying how good he thinks they are, but he says nothing, because he remembers that Camille used to sketch Irène like this. There were always new drawings on his desk—he would doodle them while he talked on the telephone; it was like an unwitting product of his thinking process.

So Louis says nothing. They chat for a bit. Louis says he's going to stay late, not too late—he's got some things to finish up. Camille understands, gets to his feet, slips on his coat, takes his hat, and leaves.

On the way, he runs into Armand. Camille is surprised to see him in the office at this hour. Armand has got two cigarettes tucked behind each ear, and the top of a four-color pen is sticking out of the pocket of his threadbare jacket. This is a clear sign that there's someone new working on the floor. A situation Armand unfailingly turns to his advantage. A rookie can't take two steps in this building without running into the nicest old colleague you could meet, ready to show him around the maze of corridors, to fill him in on the stories and the rumors, a guy who wears his heart on his sleeve, who *really gets* young people. Camille loves it. It's like a music hall act where the hapless audience member who goes up onto the stage is relieved of his watch and his wallet without noticing. In the course of the conversation, the rookie will find himself relieved of cigarettes, pen, notepad, street guide to Paris, *métro* tickets, luncheon vouchers, parking permit, small change, newspaper, and crossword magazine. Because afterwards, it's too late.

Camille and Armand leave the *brigade* together. Camille greets Louis with a handshake every morning, but never in the evening. He and Armand shake hands in the evening, but never say anything.

Though everyone knows, no one ever mentions that Camille is a creature of habit and constantly accrues new habits that he imposes on everyone.

In fact they're more than habits, they're rituals. Rituals that make it possible for them to recognize each other. With Camille, life is a perpetual celebration, except nobody knows what they're celebrating. And it's a language. With Camille, even the simple act of putting on his glasses is far from simple: it can mean *I need to think*, *Leave me alone*, *I feel old*, or *Bring on the next ten years!* The manner in which Camille puts on his glasses is the equivalent of the way Louis brushes back his hair, a system of coded signs. Maybe Camille is this way because he's short; he needs to feel rooted in the world.

Armand shakes hands with Camille and dashes for the *métro*, leaving him standing there, at loose ends. Though Doudouche is very sweet, and does everything she can to be companionable, when that's all there is to go home to in the evening . . .

Camille once read somewhere that it's just when you've given up hope that the signal comes that may save you. It happens now, in this very moment. The thunderstorm, which a moment before seemed to have abated, now whips up worse than ever. Pressing his hat to his head against the driving wind, Camille heads for the taxi stand. There are two men ahead of him, clutching black umbrellas, irritated. They stare into the distance, leaning out into the street like passengers impatiently waiting for a delayed train. Camille checks his watch. The *métro*. He does a U-turn, takes a few steps, turns back again. He stops and watches the scene playing out at the taxi stand. A car passes slowly outside the reserved lane, in fact, it's moving so slowly that it looks like a proposal, a discreet, unobtrusive invitation; the window is rolled down . . . And suddenly, Camille is convinced he's found the answer. Don't ask him why. Maybe because he's exhausted all other possibilities. It couldn't have been a bus because of the time, the *métro* would have been too risky—too many closed-circuit TV cameras everywhere and too much chance of being noticed, given it would have been deserted. Same problem with a taxi: no better way of making sure someone remembers you.

So.

So, this is how it happened. He doesn't think it through any further; he slaps his hat on his head and, muttering an apology, steps in front of the man just moving forward, leans into the open window of the car.

"How much to the Quai de Valmy?"

"Fifteen euros?" suggests the driver.

Eastern European, but which country . . . ? Camille has never been good with accents. He opens the back door and gets in. The car pulls away, the driver winding up the window. He's wearing a wool cardigan with a zipper that looks hand knitted. Camille hasn't seen one in ten years, not since he threw out his own. Minutes tick by, and Camille closes his eyes, relieved.

"Actually, I've changed my mind. Could you take me back to the Quai des Orfèvres?"

The driver looks in the rearview mirror and sees Commandant Camille Verhœven's police identity card.

Louis is just leaving, pulling on his Alexander McQueen coat, when Camille reappears with his prey. *Surprise, Louis.*

"Got a second?" Camille says, but doesn't wait for an answer. He puts the cab driver into an interrogation room and perches on a chair facing him. This isn't going to take long, a fact Camille points out to the guy.

"Like-minded people always end up getting along, don't you think?"

The concept of "like-minded people" proves a little complex for a fifty-year-old Lithuanian. So Camille resorts to more tried and trusted methods, to cruder and consequently more effective explanations:

"We—the police—can make your lives hell. I can get a squad together to seal off every train station, the Gare du Nord, the Gare de l'Est, Montparnasse, Saint-Lazare, even Les Invalides for the cabs running to Charles de Gaulle. We'll pick up two-thirds of the gypsy cab drivers in Paris within an hour, and the rest of them won't be working for at least two months. The ones we pick up, we'll bring here, go through the drivers with no papers, forged papers, expired papers, and slap them with a fine equal to the price of their car—but obviously we'll impound the car. Yeah, sorry about that, it's the law, nothing else we can do, you get it? When we're done, we'll put half of you on planes back to Belgrade, Tallinn, Vilnius (don't worry, we'll pick up the tab!) and toss the others in the slammer for two years. So, what d'you think?"

The Lithuanian driver doesn't have much French, but he's understood the basics. He's scared shitless, staring down at the desk at his passport, which Camille is carefully rubbing with the edge of his hand as though trying to clean it.

"And I'm going to keep this, if you don't mind, as a souvenir of our little encounter. But you can have this back."

He holds out the driver's cell phone. Commandant Verhœven's face suddenly changes; he's not joking now. He slams the cell down on the metal table.

"Now you're going to start making calls. You're going to stir up a shitstorm with the gypsy cab drivers. I need to track down a girl, about thirty-five, good looking, but she would have been filthy and in pretty bad shape. She was picked up by a driver around eleven o'clock Tuesday night, somewhere between the church and the Porte de Pantin. I need to know where he dropped her. I'm giving you twenty-four hours."

36

Alex knows she has been badly shaken by her ordeal in the cage, that she's experiencing posttraumatic stress. Just thinking that she might have died there, with the rats . . . it makes her tremble so hard she can't get her bearings. Can't recover her balance, can't even stand up straight. Her body is hunched; excruciating muscle spasms wake her in the night, like the imprint of a pain that refuses to go away. In the train, in the middle of the night, she lets out a scream. People say that, in order to survive, the brain suppresses bad memories, preserves only the good, and that may be true, but it must take time, because the moment Alex closes her eyes, she feels the dread twisting her entrails, those fucking rats . . .

By the time she emerges from the train station, it's almost noon. On the train, she finally managed to sleep. Now she wakes to find herself on a street in the middle of Paris—it's like coming out of a muddled dream. She's still half-asleep.

She drags her rolling suitcase beneath the leaden sky. Rue Monge, a hotel: the only available room has a window on the courtyard and a faint smell of stale tobacco. She quickly jumps into the shower,

runs it scalding at first, then lukewarm, then cold; she steps out into
the inevitable white terrycloth bathrobe that transforms third-rate
hotels into palaces for the poor. Hair wet, limbs stiff, starving, she
stares at herself in the full-length mirror. The only thing about her
body she really likes is her breasts. She looks at them as she dries
her hair. She was a late bloomer. By the time they came, she'd given
up waiting, then suddenly they sprouted when she was thirteen,
no, later, fourteen. Before that she was "flat as a pancake"—that's
what the girls at school said. Her friends had been wearing low-cut
tops and tight sweaters for years—some had nipples that looked like
they were made of titanium; she had nothing.

The rest came later—she was in secondary school by then. At
fifteen, everything suddenly fell perfectly into place: the breasts, the
smile, the ass, the eyes, her figure. The sway of her hips. Before that
Alex was ugly; she had what was politely called "an unprepossessing
physique," a body that couldn't seem to make up its mind, androgy-
nous, graceless, featureless. You could just about tell that she was a
girl, but that was all. In fact her mother called her "my poor little
girl"—she sounded heartbroken, but actually Alex's unprepossessing figure confirmed everything she thought about her daughter. A
botched job. The first time Alex put on makeup, her mother burst
out laughing; she didn't say a word, she just laughed. Alex ran to
the bathroom, scrubbed her face, and looked at herself in the mirror; she felt ashamed. When she came back downstairs, her mother
didn't say anything. She just gave a discreet little smile, but it spoke
volumes. Then, when Alex finally did begin to change, her mother
pretended not to notice.

All that is in the past now.

She slips on a bra and panties and rummages in the suitcase. She
can't think what she could have done with it. She can't have lost it—she
has to find it. She tips the contents of her suitcase out onto the bed,
checks the side pockets, racks her brains. She pictures herself standing
in the street: what was she wearing that night? Suddenly she remembers, fumbles through the pile of clothes searching for a pocket.

"There we go!"

It is a small victory.

"You're a free woman."

The business card was already crumpled and dog-eared when he gave it to her—there's a big crease down the middle. She dials the number. Staring at the card, she says, "Hello, Félix Manière?"

"Who's speaking, please?"

"Hi, this is . . ."

Her mind goes blank. What name did she give him?

"Is that Julia? Hello, is that Julia?"

He almost shouts it. Alex smiles, lets out her breath.

"Yes, it's Julia."

His voice sounds very far away.

"You sound like you're driving," she says. "Is this not a good time?"

"No, yes, I mean no . . ."

He's so thrilled to hear from her; he's getting confused.

"So is that a yes or a no?" Alex says, laughing.

He's beaten, but he's a good loser.

"For you, it's always yes."

She pauses for a second or two, long enough to appreciate the rejoinder, to savor what he said, what he said to her.

"You're so sweet."

"Where are you? At home?"

Alex sits down on the bed, swinging her legs in front of her.

"Yeah . . . you?"

"At work."

The silence that follows is like a little dance, each waiting for the other to show their hand. Alex is supremely confident. It never fails.

"I'm glad you called, Julia," Félix says eventually. "Really glad."

No shit. Of course he's glad. Now that she hears his voice, Alex can picture him more clearly: a guy who's been battered and bruised by life and started to put on weight, those stubby legs and that face . . . It upsets her to think about it, that poignant face, the sad, faraway look in his eyes.

"So what are you up to at work?"

As she says this, Alex lies down on the bed facing the window.

"Just checking the figures for the week because I'm off on vacation tomorrow, and if I don't check everything myself, when I get back in a week, well, you know . . ."

He stops dead. Alex is still smiling. It's funny . . . she can turn him on or off simply by batting an eyelid or going silent. If she were sitting opposite him, all she would have to do is smile a certain way, give him a sidelong glance, for him to stop in midsentence or change the subject. She fell silent, and he immediately shut up—he sensed it wasn't the right thing to say.

"Hey," he says. "It's not important. What about you? What are you up to?"

The first time, as they were leaving the restaurant, she played him the way she knows how to play men. It's a recipe she knows by heart—the slightly forlorn walk, the stooped shoulders, the look: head down, eyes wide, almost naive, the lips melting beneath his gaze . . . That night, on the street, Félix had been oozing sexual frustration from every pore, almost desperate at the idea of bedding her. So it isn't much of a challenge:

"I'm lying down," Alex says, "on my bed."

She doesn't go overboard. There's no husky voice, no unnecessary razzmatazz, just enough to sow doubt, confusion. Silence. She thinks she can hear the neuronal overload triggered in Félix's brain as he struggles for words. He laughs idiotically, and when she doesn't react, when she invests her silence with all the tension she can muster, Félix's laugh chokes and dies.

"On your bed . . ."

Félix has left his body. Right now, he has become his cell phone, he has fused with the signal as it moves across the city between him and her. He is the air she breathes, slowly swelling her firm belly crowned with those little white panties; he is the very air in the room, the tiny particles of dust that swirl around her; he cannot say another word—he is incapable. Alex smiles gently; he can hear it.

"Why are you smiling?"

"Because you make me laugh, Félix."

Is this the first time she's used his name?

"Oh."

He doesn't quite know how to take this.

"What are you doing tonight?" Alex says.

He swallows hard, twice.

"Nothing."

"How about inviting me to dinner?"

"Tonight?"

"Okay," Alex says coldly. "Obviously I called at a bad time, I'm sorry . . ."

And her smile widens as she listens to the torrent of excuses, rationalizations, promises, explanations, details, reasons. She checks her watch: it's 7:30 p.m. She interrupts him in midflow:

"Eight o'clock?"

"Sure, eight o'clock!"

"Where?"

Alex closes her eyes, crosses her legs on the bed: this really is too easy. Félix takes more than a minute to come up with a restaurant. She leans over to the nightstand and jots down the address.

"It's really nice," he promises her. "Well, it's nice . . . You'll see for yourself. And if you don't like it, we can always go somewhere else."

"If it's really nice, why would we go somewhere else?"

"It's . . . I don't know, it's a matter of taste . . ."

"Exactly, Félix, and I'm very interested to find out your taste."

Alex hangs up and stretches like a cat.

37

The magistrate has insisted that every last member of the team be present. Le Guen, Camille, Louis, Armand. Because finally they've come up with something. Something big, something major, something new, which is why the magistrate has insisted that Le Guen assemble all his troops. Hardly has Camille stepped into the office of the *brigade* than Le Guen tries to calm him with a forceful stare. Camille can already feel tension welling up in his belly. Behind his back he is rubbing his hands frantically as though about to undertake a major surgical procedure. He watches the magistrate arrive. From the way he's behaved since the start of the investigation, it's clear he believes that the proof of intelligence is having the last word. And today, he has no intention of being beaten.

The magistrate is immaculately dressed: sober gray suit, sober gray tie—the efficient elegance that distinguishes shrewd justice. Seeing this Chekhovian costume, Camille assumes Vidard is planning on being theatrical. He might just as well save his breath. His part has already been written for him: the play might be called

"Chronicle of a Breath Foretold," because the whole team already know what's going on. The plot goes something like this: "You're all a bunch of halfwits." Because Camille's theory has just taken a serious body blow.

The news came through two hours earlier. The murder of one Jacqueline Zanetti, a hotel owner in Toulouse. Severely beaten about the head, then tied up and bumped off using concentrated sulfuric acid.

Camille immediately put in a call to Delavigne. They knew each other when they were starting out—he was the *brigade* commissioner in Toulouse. They called each other eight times in the space of four hours; Delavigne is straight-up, loyal, and seriously embarrassed for his friend Verhœven. Camille has spent the whole morning in his office listening in on witness statements and interrogations: he might as well be there.

"There can be no doubt," the magistrate says, "that we are dealing with the same killer. The methodology has been almost identical in each murder. According to the case file, Mme. Zanetti was murdered in the early hours of Friday morning."

"The name of the hotel is on file," Delavigne told Camille earlier. "It operated as a brothel—very 'discreet,' as they say in English."

Delavigne is fond of peppering his conversation with English words. It's his shtick. It pisses Camille off.

"The girl arrived in Toulouse on Tuesday, checked in to a hotel near the station under the name Astrid Berma. The following day, Wednesday, she changes hotels and checks into Zanetti's place, the Hotel du Pré Hardy, under the name Laura Bloch. On Thursday, in the middle of the night, she beats the woman with a telephone. Right in the face. Then, she finishes her off with sulfuric acid, clears out the hotel cash register— some two thousand euros—and disappears."

"She's not short of identities, I'll give her that."

"No, obviously not."

"We don't know whether she's traveling by car, by train, by plane. We'll check out the train station, the car rental companies and the taxis, but it'll take time."

"Her fingerprints were found everywhere," the judge emphasizes. "In the hotel room, in Madame Zanetti's private sitting room—obviously she doesn't care about being caught. She knows she's not on file, so she's got no reason to worry. It's as though she's taunting us."

The fact that there's an investigating magistrate and a division-naire in the room doesn't stop the other officers from following Camille's rule: at briefings, everybody stands. Leaning in the door-way, Camille says nothing. He waits to see what's coming.

"What else?" Delavigne says. "Well, Thursday evening she went with Zanetti to a dance hall called Le Central, very 'picturesque' as they say in English . . ."

"In what sense?"

"It's a dance hall for lonely old people. Spinsters, ballroom dancing fanatics. White linen suits, cravats, dresses with frills and flounces . . . Personally, I find it 'amusing,' as they say in English, but I suspect you'd find it depressing."

"I get the picture."

"No, no I really don't think you do . . ."

"It's that bad?"

"You can't begin to imagine. Le Central should be on the Japa-nese tourist circuit as the 'pinnacle of achievement' as they say in—"

"Albert!"

"What?"

"Could you ease up on the English? It really pisses me off."

"Okay, boy."

"Good. So their night out—is it connected to the murder?"

"A priori, no. At least none of the witness statements corroborate the theory. The evening was 'marvelous,' it was 'delightful,' some-one even referred to it as 'sublime,' so it was obviously deadly dull, but there were no problems, no arguments, apart from the obvious romantic tiffs, which the girl took no part in. Very withdrawn, according to the witnesses. It was as if she was only there as a favor to Zanetti."

"Did they know each other?"

"Zanetti introduced her as her niece. It took less than an hour to find out she had no brothers or sisters. A niece in her family is about as likely as a virgin in a brothel."

"What would you know about virgins?"

"Oh, that's where you're wrong! The pimps in Toulouse know all about virgins."

"I realize you know all this already from your colleagues in Toulouse," the magistrate says. "But that's not the interesting part . . ."

Go on, Camille thinks, *out with it.*

"What's interesting is that up until now, she killed only men older than her; consequently the murder of a woman over fifty rather jeopardizes your hypothesis. I'm referring to Commandant Verhœven's theory that the murders are sexual in nature."

"It was your theory too, *monsieur le juge.*"

This from Le Guen, who is also beginning to feel a bit irritated.

"I don't dispute that," the magistrate says. He smiles, almost contentedly. "We all made the same mistake."

"It's not a mistake," Camille says.

Everyone turns to look at him.

"So," says Delavigne, "they go to the dance hall. We're up to our eyes in witness statements from friends and relatives of the victim. They describe the girl as very charming; they all recognized her from the E-FIT you sent me. Pretty, slim, green eyes, auburn hair. Though two of the women swear the hair was a wig."

"I think they may be right."

"So they spend the evening dancing at Le Central, then back to the hotel at about three in the morning. The murder must have occurred shortly afterwards because—this is an estimate, we'll have to wait for the postmortem results to be sure—the coroner puts time of death at about three thirty."

"An argument?"

"It's possible, but it would have to be one hell of a disagreement to resort to sulfuric acid."

"And no one heard anything?"

"No, sorry . . . Then again, what do you expect? At that hour everyone was asleep. In any case, a couple of blows with a Bakelite telephone—it's not going to make that much noise."

"Did she live alone, this Zanetti woman?"

"From what we've been told, she had her moments, but recently, yeah, she was living alone."

"The theory doesn't matter, commandant. Cling to it all you want; it won't move this investigation forward an inch, and unfortunately it won't affect the outcome. We're dealing with a murderer who moves quickly and often, kills indiscriminately, a murderer who is free to come and go as she pleases because she's not in the system. So my question is simple: just how exactly are you planning to catch her, divisionnaire?"

38

"Okay, I'll come back if it's just for half an hour . . . but you'll give me a lift back?"

At this moment, Félix would promise anything. It's strange because he got the impression things hadn't gone so well with Julia, that she hadn't found his conversation fascinating. In fact, the first time he'd met her, outside the restaurant, he'd felt she was out of his league, and on the telephone earlier this evening, he didn't exactly put in a brilliant performance. In his defense, it threw him, having her call him; he couldn't believe it. And now tonight . . . The restaurant—what had he been thinking? He'd been caught off guard; he had to come up with somewhere . . .

At first, she took pleasure in turning him on. There was the dress she was wearing. She knows the effect it has on men. It didn't fail—the moment he saw it she thought his jaw was about to hit the pavement. Then Alex said, "Hi, Félix," and laid a hand on his shoulder, brushing his cheek with her fingers, very briefly, a gesture of familiarity. Félix almost melted on the spot; it unnerved him, too, because it could as easily mean "we're on for tonight" as "let's just be friends," as though they were colleagues. It's something Alex does to perfection.

She let him talk about his work, about scanners and printers, the opportunities for promotion, the colleagues who were no match for him, the latest monthly figures; Alex even managed an occasional approving "Oh!" Félix was pleased with himself, reckoned he was back in the game.

No, what kept Alex distracted was the man's face, which stirred up powerful, disturbing feelings, especially seeing the ferocity of his desire. This is why she is here. He wants her in his bed; it oozes from his every pore. It would only take the slightest spark for his manhood to explode. Every time she smiles at him, he looks so horny he might lift the restaurant table into the air. He was like that the first time, too. Premature ejaculator? Alex wonders.

Now, here they are in his car. Alex has hiked her skirt a little higher than she should, and he can't stand it. They've been driving for about ten minutes when he places a hand high up on her thigh. Alex says nothing, closes her eyes, smiling to herself. When she opens them again, she can see she's driving him crazy; if he could, he'd fuck her right now, right here on the Périphérique. Ah, the Périphérique . . . they pass the Porte de la Villette—this is where Trarieux was squished by an articulated truck. Alex is in seventh heaven. Félix slips his hand higher; she stops him. The gesture—calm, affectionate—feels more like a promise than a prohibition. The way she holds his wrist . . . If his dick gets any harder, he's going to explode midjourney. The atmosphere in the car is warm, tangible, silence hovering over them like a flame above a detonator. Félix drives fast; Alex isn't worried. And after the Périphérique, a vast housing development, a bleak, depressing tower block . . . He screeches into a parking space, turns toward her, but already she is out of the car, smoothing her dress with the palm of her hand. He walks toward the building with a bulge in his trousers she pretends not to notice. She looks up; the tower block must be at least twenty stories.

"Twelve," he tells her.

It's pretty decrepit; the walls are filthy and scrawled with obscenities. There are a few ripped-open mailboxes. He feels embarrassed, as though it's only just occurred to him that the least he could have done would be to take her to a hotel. But mentioning the word *hotel* as they were coming out of the restaurant would be tantamount to saying *I want to fuck you*; he couldn't bring himself to do it. So now he's ashamed. She smiles at him to let him know it doesn't matter, and it's true, it doesn't matter in the least to Alex. To reassure him, she lays her hand on his shoulder again, and as he fumbles for his key, she plants a quick, warm kiss right in the crook of his neck, where it will make him shudder. He stops dead, tries again, opens the door, turns on the light, and says, "Go on in. I'll be right back."

It's an apartment that could only belong to a single man. A divorced man. He's dashed into the bedroom. Alex slips off her jacket, puts it on the sofa, and comes back to watch. The bed isn't made; in fact the whole place is a pigsty, and he's hurriedly tidying up. When he spots her in the doorway he smiles awkwardly, apologizes, tries to work faster, desperate to tidy everything away, to be finished. A room with no soul—the bedroom of a man with no woman. An old computer, clothes scattered everywhere, an antiquated briefcase, an old soccer trophy, a picture frame with a mass-produced reproduction of a watercolor, the kind you get in hotel rooms; the ashtrays are overflowing. Félix is on his knees next to the bed, leaning over to straighten the sheets. Alex comes over just behind him, lifts the soccer cup over her head in both hands and brings it down on his skull; with the first blow, the corner of the marble pedestal sinks in at least two inches. It makes a muffled sound, like a vibration in the air. The force of the blow throws Alex off balance. She staggers sideways, comes back to the bed looking for a better angle, raises her arms above her head again, and, aiming carefully, brings the trophy down again with all her strength. The edge of the base smashes the occipital bone; Félix is sprawled on his stomach, his body wracked by spasms. As far as she's concerned, he's had it. Might as well save energy.

Perhaps he's dead, and the convulsions are simply his autonomic nervous system.

She comes closer, leans down, checking, lifts him by the shoulder: no, he looks as though he's just unconscious. He's moaning, but he's breathing. His eyelids are flickering; it's a reflex action. His skull is so staved in that clinically, he's already half-dead. Let's say two-thirds.

So, not completely dead.

So much the better.

In any case, with all the damage to his head, he represents no real threat.

She turns him onto his back; he's heavy, but he offers no resistance. There are ties and belts, everything she needs to tie his ankles and his wrists; it only takes a minute or two.

Alex goes into the kitchen, grabbing her bag on the way, then comes back into the bedroom. She takes out her little bottle, straddles his chest, breaks a couple of teeth as she forces his jaws apart with the base of a lamp, bends a plastic fork in half and sticks it into his mouth to prop it open. She steps back, forces the neck of the bottle down his throat and calmly pours a pint of concentrated sulfuric acid down his throat.

This, unsurprisingly, rouses Félix from his stupor.

But not for long.

She could have sworn buildings like this were noisy. In fact, at night, they're very peaceful, and the city spread out all around is rather beautiful seen from the twelfth floor. She looks for landmarks, but it's difficult to find her bearings in this nocturnal landscape. She hadn't noticed that the Périphérique was so close—it must be the road they took coming here; maybe Paris is on the other side. Alex has a good sense of direction.

If the flat is a shambles and he neglected the housework, Félix clearly took good care of his laptop: it's in a nice, neat case with separate compartments for files, pens, and power cables. Alex opens it up, logs in, and opens a browser. She has fun looking through the browser history: porn sites, online gaming; she turns back toward the room—"Naughty, naughty, Félix." Then she types her own name into a search engine. Nothing. The police still don't know who she is. She smiles, about to close the laptop, then changes her mind and types: *police—wanted persons—murder*, skips down the first few results and finds what she's looking for. A woman is being sought in connection with a number of killings; there's been a call for witnesses. Alex is considered "dangerous." Given the state of Félix next door, the adjective is hardly unwarranted. And the E-FIT is pretty good. They must have used the picture Trarieux took to mock it up. They clearly know what they're doing. That vacant stare always makes the face look a little dead. Change the hair and the color of the eyes and you've got someone altogether different. Which is exactly what she is planning to do. Alex snaps the laptop shut.

Before leaving, she glances into the bedroom. The soccer trophy is lying on the bed. The corner of the plinth is matted with blood and hair. The statuette is of a forward scoring what's obviously a winning goal. Lying on the bed, the winner looks rather less triumphant. The acid has dissolved away his whole throat, which is nothing but a liquefied pulp of pink-and-white flesh. It looks as though if you jerked hard, you could pull the head right off. His eyes are still wide open, but a shadow has passed over them, a veil has snuffed them out: they look like the glass eyes of a teddy bear. Alex used to have one.

Without turning away, Alex rummages in his jacket pocket for his keys. Suddenly she's out in the hallway, then down in the parking garage. She triggers the car lock at the last moment, just as she's ready to get into the car. Five seconds later, she pulls away. She winds the window down—the smell of stale cigarette smoke is disgusting. It occurs to Alex that Félix has just given up smoking: good news for him.

Just before she gets back to Paris, she takes a little detour and stops the car by the canal opposite the Fonderies Générales warehouse. Swathed in darkness, the huge building looks like a prehistoric animal. Alex feels a shiver down her back simply at the thought of what she went through in there. She opens the car door, takes a few steps, tosses Félix's laptop into the canal, and gets back into the car.

At this time of night, it takes less than twenty minutes to get to the Cité de la Musique. She parks on Level 2 of the underground garage, throws the keys down a drain, and heads for the *métro*.

39

Thirty-six hours to track down the gypsy cab that picked up the girl in Pantin. It's twelve hours more than they planned, but at least they got a result.

Three unmarked cars are following behind, and they're making for the rue Falguière. Not far from where she was kidnapped. This worries Camille. The night of the abduction, they spent hours questioning neighbors without coming up with anything.

"Did we miss something that night?"

"Not necessarily."

But still . . .

This time the taxi driver is Slovakian. A tall guy with a face like a knife blade and feverish eyes. He's about thirty, prematurely balding, mostly on top, like a monk. He recognized the girl from the E-FIT. Except the eyes, he said. Hardly surprising—here her eyes are given as green, elsewhere they've been described as blue—she obviously uses colored contact lenses. But it's definitely her.

The taxi driver is driving ridiculously carefully. Louis thinks about saying something, but Camille gets in ahead of him. He lurches forward toward the front seat, his feet finally touching the floor—in this car, some sort of four-by-four, he can almost stand up, which simply irritates him more. He lays a hand on the driver's shoulder.

"Go for it, my friend—no one's going to bust you for speeding."

The Slovak doesn't need to be told twice. He brutally floors the accelerator, and Camille finds himself sprawled on the back seat with his legs in the air: not really a good idea, the driver realizes immediately. He slows down, mumbling apologies—he would give a month's salary, give his car and his wife for the commandant to forget this incident. Camille sees red; Louis turns to him, puts a steadying hand on his arm: *Do we really have time for this shit?* Not that his look says this, it says something more like *We're a little strapped for time to be indulging in tantrums, however transitory, don't you think?*

Rue Falguière, rue Labrouste.

En route, the driver gives them his account. The fare agreed was twenty-five euros. When he approached her at the deserted taxi stand near Pantin and suggested it, the girl hadn't quibbled, simply opened the car door and slumped onto the back seat. She was exhausted, and she smelled: sweat, dirt, who knows. She said nothing during the journey, her head bobbing as though she was trying to ward off sleep; it had all seemed suspicious to the Slovak. Was she on drugs? When they got to her neighborhood, he turned to her, but she didn't look at him, just stared out the window. When he turned toward her she turned away, as though she was looking for something or had lost her bearings, and she pointed to a space on the right and said:

"We'll wait for a bit . . . Pull over here."

This wasn't what they'd agreed. The driver got on his high horse. As he tells the story, it's possible to imagine them: the girl sitting silently in the back seat, the driver furious—he's been ripped off once too often and is not about to be pushed around by a girl. But the girl doesn't look at him; she simply says: "Don't fuck around. Either we wait, or I'm getting out."

No need for her to add "without paying." She could have said "or I'll call the police," but no, they both know she won't; they're both in a tricky position. They're on equal terms. He doesn't know what she's waiting for. She wanted him to park facing the street; she stared at a particular spot (he points up ahead, they look, but they don't know what they're looking at beyond something up ahead). Was she waiting for someone to arrive? Was she meeting someone? The driver didn't think so. She didn't seem dangerous, more anxious. Camille listens as the driver talks about the wait. He can guess that, having nothing better to do, the driver's imagination will have started to dream up stories about the girl, stories of jealousy, of a love affair gone wrong, wondering if she is watching for a man, or maybe a woman—the other woman, or maybe the ex has got another family; it happens more often than you'd think. He glances in the rearview mirror. Not bad looking, this girl, or she would be if she cleaned herself up. But she's so shattered, you have to wonder where she's been.

They spent a long time there waiting. She was on the alert. Nothing happened. Camille knows she was watching to see whether Trarieux had realized she'd escaped, whether he was lying in wait for her.

After a while, she took out three ten-euro notes and got out of the car without a word. The driver saw her walking away, but he didn't bother to watch where she was going. He didn't want to hang around here in the middle of the night, so he cleared off. Camille climbs out of the car. On the night of the abduction, they combed the area as far as here—what happened?

The other officers get out of their cars. Camille points to the buildings in front of him.

"The doorway of the building where she lived is visible from here. Louis, call in for two teams of backup now. The rest of you . . ."

Camille allocates their roles. Everyone's already bustling around. Camille leans on the door of the taxi, thinking.

"Can I go now?" the driver says in a whisper, as though he's afraid of being overheard.

"Huh? No, you're staying with me."

Camille looks at the guy, with that face like a wet weekend. He gives the driver a smile.

"You've been promoted. You're the personal chauffeur of a police commandant. This country offers great opportunities for social mobility, or didn't you know?"

40

"Very nice girl," according to the Arab grocer.

Armand dealt with the Arab grocer. He's always happy to deal with shopkeepers, especially grocers, which is a bonus that doesn't come along every day. He's a little intimidating when he conducts the interview, because he looks like a homeless person. He wanders up and down the aisles, he's quick to make ominous implications, and in the meantime he helps himself: a pack of chewing gum, a can of Coke, another can, all the while rattling off questions. The shopkeeper can see he's stuffing his pockets with bars of chocolate, bags of sweets, biscuits, snack bars: Armand has a sweet tooth. He's not finding out much about the girl, but he carries on—What was her name? So she always paid cash, no credit cards, no checks? Did she come in often? How did she dress? And the other night, what exactly did she buy?—and once his pockets are full, he says, "Well, thank you for your cooperation," and goes to dump the loot in the squad car, where he keeps a supply of plastic bags for such occasions.

Camille was the one who found Mme. Guénaude. About sixty, overweight, with a hair band. She's plump and flushed as a butcher's wife, but she won't look him in the eye. And she's in a state, she's in a real state, fidgeting like a schoolgirl who's just been hit on. The sort of woman police commandants find infuriating; and precisely the sort to call the police out on the slimmest pretext, ever the self-righteous homeowner. No, she tells him, she wasn't just the girl's neighbor, she was . . . how can she put it? Did she know the girl, yes or no? It's impossibly frustrating trying to understand her answers, which are anything but.

Within four minutes, Camille is all for having old mother Guénaude strip-searched. Gabrielle. She reeks of lies, dishonesty, and hypocrisy. Of spite. She and her husband had a bakery. On January 1, 2002, God himself appeared on earth in the form of the change-over to the euro. And when He is made flesh, He doesn't stint on miracles. Having multiplied the loaves and fishes, He now multiplies money. By seven. From one day to the next. God is a great simplifier.

After she was widowed, Mme. Guénaude started renting out all her property cash-only—she only did it to be obliging, she insists. "If it was just me . . ." She wasn't here the day the police flooded the area questioning witnesses. "I was staying at my sister's." Still, when she got back and found out that the girl the police were looking for looked astonishingly like her former tenant, she didn't call them. "I couldn't be completely sure that it was her. I mean obviously, if I'd known . . ."

"I'm going to have you locked up," Camille says.

Mme. Guénaude turns pale; the threat has clearly had its effect. To set her mind at rest, Camille adds, "With all the money you've got put away, you'll be able to buy all those little extras from the prison canteen."

While she was living here, the girl called herself Emma. Why not? After Nathalie, Léa, Laura, Camille is ready for anything. Mme. Guénaude needs to sit down to look at the E-FIT. She doesn't sit down; she collapses. "Yes, that's her, that's definitely her. . . . Oh I'm feeling quite light-headed . . ." She clutches her chest, and Camille thinks she might be about to join her husband in the kingdom of the wicked. This Emma only stayed for three months, never had anyone around, and she was often away, in fact just last week she'd had to leave urgently; she'd just come back from a temporary job in the provinces—she had a crick in her neck, she'd taken a tumble—she said she was going to the south of France, paid two months' rent, a family emergency, she'd said; she was very put out at having to leave so quickly. The former baker rattles off her story—she doesn't know what else to do to satisfy Commandant Verhœven. Had she the nerve, she'd offer him money. Looking at the little policeman with his cold eyes, she vaguely senses that this isn't relevant. In spite of the jumble of information, Camille manages to piece together the story. Mme. Guénaude points to the sideboard; there's a scrap of blue paper in the drawer with her forwarding address. Camille is in no rush—he has no illusions, but he opens the drawer just the same as he extracts his cell phone from his pocket.

"Is this her handwriting?"

"No, it's mine."

"I expected as much."

He dictates the address over the phone and waits. In front of him, above the sideboard, is a framed picture of a stag standing in a woodland glade.

"He looks completely stupid, that stag of yours . . ."

"My daughter painted it," Mme. Guénaude says.

"You're a menace, the whole lot of you."

Mme. Guénaude racks her brains. Emma worked for a bank—she can't remember which one . . . a foreign bank. No surprise there. Camille continues with his questions though he already knows the answers: in return for keeping her curiosity to herself, Guénaude was charging an extortionate rate; this is the unspoken rule when you rent on the black market.

The address is phony; Camille hangs up.

Louis arrives with two forensics officers. The landlady feels so weak she can't go upstairs with them. She hasn't managed to find a new tenant. They already know what they'll find in Emma's apartment: Léa's fingerprints, Laura's DNA, traces of Nathalie.

"Oh, I forgot," Camille says on his way out of the door. "You'll also be charged as an accessory to murder. That's murders, plural."

Though she's already sitting down, Gabrielle Guénaude steadies herself with a hand on the coffee table. She is sweating, almost in agony.

"There is something!" she suddenly shouts after them. "The moving man, I know him."

Camille hurries back.

"Just boxes and flat-pack furniture—she didn't have much, you understand," Mme. Guénaude says, pursing her lips. They immediately get in touch with the moving company; the secretary isn't very helpful: no, she simply can't give out such information without knowing who she's dealing with.

"Okay," Camille says, "I'll come and pick up the information in person. But I should warn you, if I have to put myself out, I'll close the place down for a year, I'll slap you with a tax inspection that goes back to your first year in kindergarten, and you I personally will throw into prison for obstruction of justice, and if you've got kids, they'll be taken into care by social services."

Though it's a ridiculous bluff, it works: the secretary becomes flustered, gives the address of the storage unit where the girl left her stuff and her name: Emma Szekely.

Camille has her spell it.

"Beginning S, Z, right? Okay, I want no one opening that storage unit, you got me? No one. Is that clear?"

The place is ten minutes away. Camille hangs up and screams upstairs:

"I need a team, right now!"

He runs into the stairwell.

41

As a precaution, Alex takes the stairwell down to the garage. Her Clio starts first time. The car is cold. She looks at herself in the rearview mirror. She looks seriously tired; she runs her finger under each eye, gives herself a smile that turns into a grimace. She pokes out her tongue, then drives to the exit.

But she's not out of the woods quite yet. At the top of the ramp, she inserts her swipe card, the red-and-white barrier rises, and she slams on the brakes. Standing in front of her is a policeman. He raises one arm, signaling her to stop, then he turns around, holding his arm out horizontally to stress that there's no exit. Outside, a succession of unmarked cars drive past, sirens wailing.

In the second car, a bald guy who can barely see out of the side window. It's like a presidential cortège. Once they're gone, the officer waves her on. She turns right. She moves off a little abruptly, and in the trunk, the two small boxes labeled PERSONAL rattle, but Alex is not alarmed—the bottles of acid are safely stowed. There is no risk.

42

Almost 10:00 p.m. It's a fiasco. It's been a struggle, but Camille is calm again. As long as he doesn't think about the laughing face of the caretaker at the storage company, an anemic idiot in grubby Coke-bottle glasses who can't see the blindingly obvious.

As for communication: the girl—what girl? The car—what car? The boxes—what boxes? They open the unit she rented, and their hearts skip a beat: it's all still there, ten taped-up boxes, the girl's things, her personal belongings. They pounce on them. Camille wants to tear everything open right now. But they have to follow procedure—everything has to be inventoried, which is speeded up by a call to the magistrate. They carry everything away: the boxes, the flat-pack furniture. When all's said and done, it's not much, but they're hopeful they'll find personal effects, an indication of her true identity. For the investigation, this is the moment of truth.

The faint hope of getting something from the closed-circuit TV cameras placed on every level doesn't last long. It's not a matter of how long they keep the tapes; they're dummy cameras.

"You could say they're just for decoration," the supervisor says, laughing.

It takes all night to draw up the inventory and for forensics to take essential samples and prints. First they deal with the furniture, run-of-the-mill stuff you could buy anywhere: bookshelves, a kitchen table, a bed, a mattress—the techs went to town on it with their cotton swabs and tweezers. After that, the contents of the boxes are catalogued. Sportswear, beachwear, summer clothes, winter clothes.

"This is all chain store stuff you could buy anywhere in the world," Louis says.

Books, almost two boxes full, all paperbacks: Céline, Proust, Gide, Dostoyevsky, Rimbaud. Camille scans the titles: *Journey to the End of the Night, Swann in Love, The Counterfeiters*. Louis meanwhile looks pensive.

"What is it?" Camille says.

Louis doesn't answer straightaway. *Les Liaisons dangereuses, The Lily of the Valley, The Red and the Black, The Great Gatsby, L'Étranger.*

"It's like a schoolgirl's reading list."

He's right. The choices seem studied, representative. All the books have obviously been read and reread—some are literally falling to pieces. Whole passages are underlined, sometimes right up to the last page. In the margins there are exclamation marks, question marks, large crosses, small crosses, mostly in blue ballpoint; in some places the ink has almost bled through.

"She reads what she's supposed to read—she wants to be a good girl; she's diligent." Camille raises the stakes. "Emotionally immature?"

"I don't know. Regression, maybe."

Camille doesn't always understand what Louis says, but he gets the nub of it. The girl's not all there.

"She seems to have a little Italian and a little English. There's a handful of foreign classics that she's started but hasn't finished."

Camille spotted this too. The copies of *I promessi sposi, L'amante senza fissa dimora, Il nome della rosa,* and *Alice in Wonderland, The*

Portrait of Dorian Gray, *Portrait of a Lady*, and *Emma* are all in the original language.

"The girl in the Maciak case . . . someone mentioned a foreign accent, didn't they?"

A sheaf of tourist brochures confirm their theory.

"She's not dumb, our girl—she has studied, and she speaks a couple of languages—not fluently, certainly, but it implies she went abroad on language courses . . . can you see her with Pascal Trarieux?"

"Or seducing Stefan Maciak?"

"Or murdering Jacqueline Zanetti?"

Louis makes rapid notes. From the printouts they've got, he might be able to reconstruct the girl's itinerary, in part at least—some of the travel agency brochures have got dates; it should be possible to piece things together, but they're still no closer to a name. There are no formal documents. Not a single identifiable trace. In what kind of life does a girl possess so little?

By the end of the night, the conclusion is staring them in the face.

"She's cleared things out, left nothing personal. Just in case the police found her stuff. There's nothing here that will help us."

Both men get to their feet, Camille slips on his jacket. Louis hesitates—he'd be happy to stay longer, rummage, go through things.

"Let it go, Louis," Camille says. "She's already got a serious rap sheet behind her, and looking at the way she works, I reckon she's got one ahead of her."

This is also Le Guen's opinion.

It's Saturday, early evening, Quai de Valmy.

Le Guen phoned Camille, and now the two men are sitting on the terrace of La Marine. Maybe it's the canal, the water evoking thoughts of fish, but they've ordered two glasses of dry white wine. Le Guen sat down cautiously; he's come across many chairs that wouldn't take his weight. This one is up to the job.

This is the norm when they talk outside the office: they chat about everything and nothing and only get around to talking shop in the last few minutes, never more than a few sentences.

It is plain that what's been preying on Camille's mind all day is the auction. Tomorrow morning.

"You're not keeping anything?"

"No, I'm selling it all," Camille says. "I'm giving it all away."

"I thought you were selling it?"

"I'm selling the paintings. I'm giving away the money. Done and dusted."

Camille doesn't know when he made this decision—he just blurted it out—but he knows it's the result of much thought. Le Guen is about to say something, stops himself, but he can't help it.

"To whom?"

This, on the other hand, Camille has given no thought to. He wants to give away the money, but he has no idea to whom.

43

"Is this thing speeding up, or am I imagining it?"

"No, this is how it usually plays out," Camille says. "You just need to get used to it."

He says it casually, but in fact things have taken a serious turn for the worse. The body of Félix Manière has been discovered in his apartment. A colleague sounded the alarm when he didn't show up for a "crucial meeting" he himself had scheduled. He was found dead as dead, his head hanging off the torso, the whole neck melted away with sulfuric acid. The case was immediately referred to Commandant Verhœven, who, by the end of the day, had been summoned by the magistrate. This is serious.

It's quickly dealt with. The call log on the victim's cell phone reveals that the last call, received on the night of his death, was from a hotel on rue Monge. They check and it turns out this is where the girl stayed when she got back from Toulouse. She arranged to have dinner with him that evening. This is what he told one of his colleagues when he left work.

Though the hair and the eyes are different, the receptionist at the hotel on the rue Monge positively identifies her as the girl in the E-FIT. The girl was gone the following morning. Checked in under a false name. Paid in cash.

"The kid, this Félix—who is he?" Le Guen says and, without waiting for an answer, flicks through Camille's report. "Forty-four . . ."

"That's right," Camille confirms. "IT support for a computer company. Separated, divorce in the works. Definitely alcoholic."

Le Guen says nothing—he's rapidly skimming through the report, making an occasional *hmm* that sounds like a whimper. People have whimpered over less.

"So what's the story with the laptop?"

"Vanished. But I can assure you stealing the laptop wasn't the reason she hit him over the head with a statuette and poured a pint of acid down his gullet."

"The girl?"

"Unquestionably. Maybe they'd been in touch via e-mail. Or maybe she used his computer and didn't want us to see what she'd been up to."

"Okay. So?"

Le Guen is angry—something that's not his style. The national media, which scarcely turned a hair at the death of Jacqueline Zanetti (the murder of a hotelier in Toulouse is a bit, well, provincial), has finally been roused to indignation. The crime scene in Saint-Denis is a little downmarket, but the extra touch of using acid to finish off the victim is interesting. It's just another murder, but the technique is original, exotic almost. Right now, there are two victims. Practically a serial killer, but not quite. So, in the meantime, it makes the news, but no one's terribly excited. A third victim and the media would be celebrating. The case would be the lead item on the eight o'clock news, Le Guen would be summoned to the top floor of *ministère de l'Intérieur*, Vidard the magistrate to the *ministère de la Justice*, and it would all kick off like the Battle of Gravelotte. No one dares contemplate what would happen if the murders in Reims and Étampes were leaked to the press. The media would mock up a map of France (more or less like the one in Camille's office) scattered with little colored pins, with deeply moving biographies of the victims and the promise of a murderous road movie "*à la française*." Joy. Jubilation.

For the moment, Le Guen has only had to deal with "serious downward pressure"—it could be worse, but it's a headache. Le Guen is a good boss when it comes to dealing with his superiors; he keeps all that to himself. They only get to see the overflow; but today, it seems to be overflowing everywhere.

"You getting shit from upstairs?"

Le Guen is thunderstruck by the question.

"Camille, what could possibly make you think that?"

This is the problem with couples: the scenes are a little repetitive.

"I mean, we've got a girl who's abducted and locked up with a pack of rats, a kidnapper who kills himself and brings a section of the Périphérique to a standstill for half the night . . ."

This scene, for example, is one that Camille and Le Guen have played out at least fifty times.

"The abducted girl escapes before we can find her, we discover she's already bumped off three guys using sulfuric acid . . ."

Camille always thinks it smacks of a cheap farce—he's about to say as much, but Le Guen plows on.

"By the time we've got a case file together, she's dispatched some old biddy in Toulouse to hoteliers' heaven, come back to Paris . . ."

Camille waits for the predictable conclusion.

"Where she's whacked some guy who probably just wanted to get laid, and you're asking me whether . . ."

"They're giving you shit upstairs?" Camille concludes for him, firmly put in his place.

Camille is already on his feet, already at the door. He opens it wearily.

"Where are you off to?" Le Guen bellows.

"If I'm going to have someone read me the riot act, I'd rather it was Vidard."

"Honestly, you've got no taste."

44

Alex let the first two trucks drive past, and the third. From where she's parked, she can clearly watch the movements of the articulated trucks lined up next to the loading bay. For the past two hours the forklift operators have been loading them with pallets high as houses.

She came here the night before to check the place out. She had to scale the wall. It wasn't easy; it meant climbing on the roof of her car. If she'd been spotted, it would have all been over. But no, she was able to perch on top of the wall for a few minutes. Every vehicle has a sign with the order number stenciled next to the top right of the destination. They're all heading for Germany: Cologne, Frankfurt, Hanover, Bremen, Dortmund. She needs the one that's going to Munich. She jotted down the license plate, the order number, but it hardly matters: seen from the front, the truck is unmissable. Across the top of the windshield is a sticker reading BOBBY. She hopped down from the wall when she heard the guard dog, which had obviously caught her scent.

Half an hour ago, she spotted the driver climb into his cab to stash his stuff, pick up his paperwork. He's a tall, lean guy in blue overalls with cropped hair and a mustache like a scrubbing brush.

It doesn't matter what he looks like—what matters is that he picks her up. She slept in her car until the place opened at about 4:00 a.m. The hustle and bustle started about half an hour ago, and it hasn't stopped since. Alex is nervous; she can't afford to miss her cue, because if she does, she's got no plan. Her only option is—what? To sit in a hotel room and wait for the police to arrive?

Eventually, just before 6:00 a.m. the guy goes over to his truck, which has been idling for at least fifteen minutes, checks his paperwork. Alex watches him joking with a forklift operator and a couple of other drivers; then, at last, he climbs into his cab. This is when she gets out of her car, walks around the back, opens the trunk, takes out her knapsack, checks from behind the open trunk that no other truck pulls out in front of the one she needs, and when she's sure, she runs to the vehicle exit.

"I never hitchhike on the road. Too dangerous."

Bobby nods. For a girl, it wouldn't be a good idea. He admires her resourcefulness; waiting at the gate of a trucking company rather than sticking her thumb out on the side of the road.

"But with all the trucks you guys have got, there's bound to be someone who'll take you."

Bobby is astonished by the shrewdness of Alex's technique. But she's not Alex. To him, she's Chloë.

"I'm Robert," he says, reaching across the seat to shake her hand. "But everyone calls me Bobby," he points to the sticker.

Still, he's surprised that she's hitchhiking at all.

"Plane tickets are so cheap these days. Apparently you can get flights on the net for forty euros. Sure, it's always at some ungodly hour, but if your time's your own . . ."

"I'd rather hang on to my money and spend it when I get there. Besides, traveling is about meeting people, isn't it?"

The guy is simple, friendly—the moment he saw her, he had no hesitation in picking her up. Alex was not watching for his reaction, only the nature of his reaction. What she most dreaded seeing was a look of lust. She has no desire to spend hours fighting off a gasoline-pump Lothario. Bobby has a statue of the Virgin Mary hanging from his rearview mirror, and a little gadget attached to the dashboard, a digital photo frame that displays images with various transition effects: dissolve, venetian blind, page turn. The images loop endlessly—it's exhausting to watch. He bought the gadget in Munich. Thirty euros. Bobby likes to mention how much things cost, not so much because he expects to be admired for it as because he likes to be precise, meticulous in his descriptions. And he likes to describe things. He spends almost half an hour talking about the slide show, his family, his house, his dog; most of the photographs are of his three kids.

"Two boys, one girl: Guillaume, Romain, Marion, ages nine, seven, and four."

He likes precision. But he knows how to behave; he never shifts the conversation away from stories about his family.

"When it comes down to it, people aren't really interested in other people's lives, huh?"

"No, honestly, I am interested . . . ," Alex protests.

"You're very well brought up."

The day slips by quite pleasantly; the cabin is very comfortable.

"If you fancy taking a little nap, it's not a problem." He jerks his thumb at the sleeper berth behind him. "I have to keep moving, but you . . ."

Alex takes up the offer and naps for more than an hour.

"Where are we?" she says, brushing her hair as she clambers back into her seat.

"Oh, there you are. You must have been tired. We're coming in to Sainte-Menehould."

Alex pretends to be impressed that they've made such progress. Her sleep was disturbed. Not just by her habitual anxiety, but also sadness. This ride to the border is a painful turning point, the beginning of the end.

When the conversation dies away, they listen to the radio, to the news, to music. Alex watches out for stops, the obligatory rest

breaks, for the times when Bobby will need to get a coffee. He has a
flask, some food, everything he needs to keep driving, but still they
have to stop; it's maddening. When there's a stop coming up, Alex is
on the alert. If it's a rest area, she pretends to sleep—too few people
and therefore too much risk of her being spotted. If it's a service
station, there's less risk, and she'll get out and walk around for a bit,
buy Bobby a coffee; they're good buddies now. In fact, a little while
ago, as they were having a cup of coffee together, he asked her what
was taking her to Germany.

"Are you a student?"

Even he can't possibly believe she could be a student. She may
look young, but she knows she looks at least thirty, and her exhaustion can't be helping. She decides to laugh it off.

"No, I'm a nurse. I'm planning to work when I get there."

"But why Germany, if you don't mind me asking?"

"Because I don't speak German," Alex says with all the conviction she can muster.

Robert giggles; he's not sure he understands.

"In that case, you could have gone to China. Unless you do speak
Chinese. Do you speak Chinese?"

"No. The real reason is my boyfriend is in Munich."

"Oh . . ."

He gives her a look that says he understands everything. He
shakes his head solemnly, his mustache quivering.

"So what does he do, your boyfriend?"

"He works in IT."

"And he's German?"

Alex nods; she doesn't know where this is going—she's only two
steps ahead of him in this conversation, and she doesn't like the
feeling.

"What about your wife, does she work?"

Bobby tosses his plastic cup in the garbage. The question about
his wife didn't offend him; it saddened him. They're on the road
again now; they flick back through the slide show to the picture of

his wife, a nondescript woman of about forty with straight hair. She looks sickly.

"Multiple sclerosis," Bobby explains. "Can you imagine it? With the kids? We just have to trust to Providence now."

As he says this he nods to the statue of the Virgin Mary swaying gently beneath the rearview mirror.

"You think she's going to do something to help you?"

Alex didn't mean to say this. Bobby turns toward her. There's no bitterness in his voice—he's simply stating the obvious. "The reward for salvation is forgiveness. Don't you think?"

Alex doesn't understand; she's never really understood religion. She hadn't noticed it before, but now she sees a sticker on the dashboard: *He is coming. Are you ready?*

"You don't believe in God," Bobby says, laughing, "I can tell."

There is nothing critical in this observation.

"I tell you, if I didn't have religion . . . ," he says.

"But it's the Good Lord who's got you into this mess," says Alex. "Aren't you bitter?"

"God is testing us."

"Well," Alex says, "I can't disagree with that . . ."

Suddenly the conversation peters out; they stare at the road.

A little later, Bobby says he needs to take a break. It's a service area the size of a small town.

"This is where I always stop off," he explains, smiling. "It'll only take an hour."

They are twelve miles outside Metz.

Bobby climbs down first to stretch his legs, take a breather; he doesn't smoke. Alex watches him strolling up and down the car park. He's swinging his arms; she thinks this is because she's watching him. Does he do it when he's alone? Then he comes back to the cab.

"Excuse me," he says, clambering into the sleeper compartment. "Don't worry, I've got my alarm clock in here." He taps his forehead.

"While you're napping, I think I'll take a little walk," Alex says. "And I need to make a call."

Bobby finds it amusing to say "Give him my love!" as he draws the curtain of the berth.

Alex is in the car park, moving between the countless vans and trucks. She needs to walk. The more time passes, the more her heart sinks. It's the dark, she thinks, but she knows this is not true. It's the journey.

Her very presence on this highway simply serves to highlight the fact that the game is almost over. She pretends she is blasé, but in fact she is terrified of the real end. It will come tomorrow; it will come soon.

Alex starts to weep softly, arms folded across her chest, standing between the hulking trucks lined up like sleeping insects. Life always catches up with us—no one ever escapes.

She repeats these words to herself, snuffles, blows her nose, tries to take a deep breath to relieve the pressure in her chest, restart her weary, heavy heart, but it's difficult. Leave all this behind—this is what she tells herself to buck herself up. Afterwards she won't have to think about it; it will all be dealt with. This is why she is here on this highway, because she is leaving everything behind. As she thinks this, her chest feels lighter. She walks on. The cool air revives her, calms her, invigorates her. A few more deep breaths and things feel better.

A plane passes overhead—she can just make out the triangle of winking lights. She gazes up at it for a long moment as it moves across the sky with hypnotic slowness; actually it is moving quite fast, and soon it has disappeared.

Planes often make you think about things.

The service area straddles the highway. On either side of a pedestrian bridge are snack bars, newsstands, minimarts, and shops of all sorts. On the other side of the bridge is the opposite direction, the road back to Paris. Alex climbs quietly back into the cab of the truck so as not to wake Bobby. Her return disturbed his sleep, but within a few seconds she once again hears the slow, deep breaths, each ending in a hiss.

She pulls her knapsack toward her, slips on her jacket, checks that she hasn't forgotten anything, that nothing has fallen out of her pockets: no, everything's there, everything's fine.

She kneels up on the seat and gently pulls the curtain back.

"Bobby . . . ," she calls in a whisper.

She doesn't want to startle him. But he's a heavy sleeper. She turns around, opens the glove compartment—nothing—closes it again. She fumbles under her seat—nothing. Under the driver's seat she finds a plastic toolbox; she pulls it out.

"Bobby," she says, leaning over him again. She has more success this time.

"What?"

He's not really awake. He asks the question automatically; his mind still hasn't surfaced. Never mind. She grips the screwdriver like a dagger and, with a single thrust, plunges it into his right eye. A very exact strike. Hardly surprising, given that she is a nurse. And since it was a powerful thrust, the screwdriver has traveled deep into his skull—it looks as though it's buried into the brain. Obviously it isn't, but it is certainly deep enough to slow Bobby's reflexes as he tries to sit up, legs flailing. He is screaming. So Alex plunges the second screwdriver into his throat. Again, very precise, though she can hardly claim much credit—she had plenty of time to aim. Just below the Adam's apple. The scream becomes a sort of unintelligible gurgle. In fact, Alex bends down, frowning: *I can't make out what this guy's saying*. But she manages to avoid Bobby's thrashing arms, since the hulk could floor an ox with a single blow.

In spite of the confusion, Alex follows through with her plan. She rips the screwdriver out of his eye socket, shields herself and stabs it into the side of his neck; blood immediately spurts out. Then, taking her time, she goes back to find her knapsack. It's not as if Bobby's going anywhere with a screwdriver embedded in his throat. By the time she comes back to him, he's half dead. There's no point tying him up; he's still breathing, but only just; his muscles seem paralyzed, and she can hear the death rattle. The most difficult part is forcing his mouth open—short of using a hammer it could take all day. So she grabs the hammer. These little toolboxes are great; they've got everything you might ever need. Alex smashes the top and bottom teeth, making just enough space to insert the neck of the sulfuric acid bottle into Bobby's mouth. It's impossible to tell what he can feel, the state he's in, what it must be like to have acid pouring into his mouth, his throat; no one will ever know how he felt, and it doesn't matter. As they say, it's the thought that counts.

Alex gets her things together and she's ready to leave. One last glance at Bobby, who's gone to thank the good Lord for all His bounty. It's a holy sight. A guy sprawled out with a screwdriver buried to the hilt in one eye, he looks like a Cyclops come to earth. Severing the jugular has caused massive blood loss in a few short minutes, and already his face is white as a sheet—the top half, at least, because the bottom half is a bloody pulp; there are no other words for it. The whole sleeping compartment is crimson with blood. When it coagulates, it will be an awesome sight.

It's impossible to kill a man this way without getting dirty. The jugular makes a hell of a spray. Alex rummages in her knapsack, changes her T-shirt. Using what is left of the bottle of mineral water, she swiftly washes her hands and forearms, then dries them on her old T-shirt, which she tosses onto the seat. Then, shouldering her knapsack, Alex sets off across the pedestrian bridge to the far side of the highway, heading back toward Paris.

She chooses a fast car because she doesn't want to waste time. The registration plate is from the Hauts-de-Seine area. She doesn't know a lot about cars, but she can tell that this one is fast. The driver is a slim, dark-haired, elegant woman of about thirty who reeks so much of money it's uncomfortable. All smiles, she immediately agrees to give Alex a lift. Alex dumps her bag on the back seat and gets in. The young woman is already behind the wheel.

"Shall we?"

Alex smiles, holds out her hand.

"Hi, my name's Alex."

45

Back in Paris, Alex collects her car and drives to Charles de Gaulle. She spends a long time staring at the departures board: South America is way beyond her budget, America itself is a police state, which leaves only Europe, and as far as she's concerned, Europe leaves only Switzerland. This is the best possible destination. It's an international hub with people constantly coming and going, a haven of anonymity where anyone can reinvent themselves. In Switzerland they launder drug money, war criminals—it's a country that welcomes murderers. Alex buys a ticket for Zurich leaving the following day at 8:40 a.m. and makes the most of her time at the airport to buy a handsome suitcase. She's never been one to buy herself expensive things. This is a first; there'll never be a better time. She lingers over a suitcase, but in the end plumps for a stylish monogrammed leather travel bag. It costs a fortune. But she loves it. She also buys a bottle of Bowmore from the duty-free shop. She pays for it all by credit card. She does a mental calculation: she's pushing it, but it's fine.

When she's done she heads for Villepinte, miles and miles of industrial parks and a scattering of chain hotels. Aside from one or two deserts, there's no place more anonymous, more forsaken than this. The Hotel Volubilis. An impersonal chain hotel boasting "comfort and privacy." The comfort entails a hundred parking spaces, the privacy, a hundred identical rooms all paid for in advance: trust does not figure in the equation. Alex pays by credit card again. "How long to get to the airport?" she asks. "Twenty-five minutes," the receptionist gives the standard answer. Alex decides to be on the safe side and orders a cab for 7:00 a.m.

She's obviously tired—she barely recognizes herself in the mirrored elevator.

Third floor. The carpet here is tired, too. The room defies description. The number of guests who have passed through here is incalculable, the number of lonely nights, of restless nights, of sleepless nights. How many illicit couples walked into this room all fire and passion, tumbled onto the bed, and left feeling they had ruined their lives? Now Alex dumps her bag near the door and gazes at the repulsive décor, wondering what to do next.

It is exactly 8:00 p.m. She doesn't even need to check her watch—she can hear the news starting on the TV in the room next door. She'll take a shower later; right now, she peels off her blonde wig, takes out her toiletry bag, removes her cobalt-blue contact lenses and flushes them down the toilet. Then she changes into a pair of baggy jeans and a figure-hugging sweater. She empties all her stuff out onto the bed, slings the empty knapsack over her shoulder, and leaves the room, taking the stairs rather than the elevator. As she comes to the bottom steps, she waits for a moment until the receptionist disappears, then darts outside and back to her car. It suddenly feels abominably cold. It's dark already. She has goose bumps. Above the parking lot, the roar of planes is muffled by the heavy clouds scurrying across the sky.

She has bought a roll of plastic garbage bags. She opens the trunk of her car. Her eyes well with tears she refuses to see. She opens the two cardboard boxes marked PERSONAL and, without giving herself time to think, starts grabbing everything in them, racked by sobs she refuses to hear, and stuffing it all into the bags: copybooks, letters, sections of her private diary, Mexican coins. Now and then she wipes her eyes with the back of her sleeve, but she doesn't stop, she can't stop, it's impossible, she has to see it through, put everything behind her—the costume jewelry, the photographs—she has to throw it all away, without thinking or remembering—the novels, the carved black wooden head, the lock of blonde hair tied with red elastic, the heart-shaped key ring inscribed DANIEL, the name of her first great love in primary school, the letters faded now. Alex ties off the third bag, but it's all too much for her, too brutal, and she turns, sits down heavily, collapsing onto the open trunk of the car, and takes her head in her hands. What she really wants to do is scream. If only she could. If only she still had the strength. A car moves slowly down the parking lot aisle. Alex quickly gets to her feet and pretends to be rummaging in the trunk; the car passes and parks farther along, closer to the hotel lobby: it's always better when you don't have so far to walk.

The three garbage bags are on the ground. Alex locks the trunk of the car, picks up the bags, and strides across the parking lot. The sliding gate separating it from the road clearly hasn't been used in years; beneath the paint that was once white it's rusted. Outside, the road is almost deserted: a few lost cars looking for a hotel, a moped, but no pedestrians. Why would anyone want to wander around such a wasteland unless they were Alex? Where is there to go, in these identical streets? The garbage containers are lined up along the side of the road outside the gates of each business; there are dozens of them. Alex walks for several minutes, then suddenly, she decides: this one. She opens the container, tosses the garbage bags inside, slips off her knapsack and throws it in too, then slams down the lid and walks back to the hotel. Here lies the life of Alex, unhappy, murderous, methodical, weak, seductive, lost, no police record. Tonight Alex is a big girl: she dries her tears, takes a deep breath, walks purposefully, arrives back at the hotel, this time strolling straight past the receptionist, who is watching television. Alex goes back up to her room, takes off her clothes and melts beneath a warm shower. She turns the water up to scalding, opens her mouth wide beneath the spray.

46

Decisions can be mysterious. Camille, for example, would be incapable of explaining the decision he has just made.

Earlier this evening, he brooded about this case, about the number of crimes this girl will go on to commit before they put her out of harm's way. But mostly he was thinking about the girl, about the face he has sketched a hundred times, about how she has brought him back to life. This evening, he realizes his mistake. This girl has nothing to do with Irène; he simply confused two people, two situations. Obviously, being kidnapped immediately connected her to Irène, and since that moment, Camille has been unable to dissociate the two because this case evoked similar feelings, similar fears, and stirred in him a similar sense of guilt. This is precisely why a detective is not assigned a case in which he is personally involved. But Camille can see that in this case, he didn't fall into the trap: he created it. His friend Le Guen had simply offered him a way finally to face up to his fears. Camille could have handed the case over, but he didn't. What is happening to him is what he wanted to happen, what he needed.

Camille puts on his shoes, puts on his jacket, picks up his car keys, and an hour later he is slowly driving through the sleepy streets on the outskirts of the forest of Clamart.

A turning on the right, one on the left, and straight ahead, the road running beneath the tall trees. The last time he was here, he had his service revolver wedged between his thighs.

Fifty yards ahead he sees the building. The headlights are reflected in the grimy windows. Tall, narrow windows in serried ranks like the ones you find in factories. Camille stops the car, turns off the engine, leaving the headlights on.

That day, he had a doubt: What if he was wrong?

He turns off the headlights and climbs out of the car. The night is chillier here than it is in Paris, or perhaps he is simply cold. He leaves the car door open and walks toward the house. It must have been about here that the helicopter suddenly came down through the treetops. Camille was nearly knocked over by the roar, the downblast, and he began to run. At least that's how he remembers it. It's so long ago it's difficult to remember anything.

The studio is a single-story outbuilding, once the home of the caretaker of the property, long since dead. From a distance, it looks like a hut, with an open veranda on which you might expect to see a rocking chair. The path Camille is walking on is one he followed hundreds of times as a child, as a teenager, when he came to visit his mother, to watch her work, to work alongside her. As a boy, he had never been drawn to the forest; the most he would do was take a few cautious steps—he always said he preferred to stay indoors. He had been a solitary boy. He made a virtue of necessity, since he found it hard to make friends, given his height. He didn't like being the constant butt of jokes. He preferred not to play with anyone. The fact was, the forest had scared him. Even now, the tall trees . . . Camille is fifty years old, or very nearly, so he's a little old to be scared of the Erl King. But he is no taller now than he was at thirteen, and however much he tries, he still finds the darkness, the forest, this isolated house disturbing. This is where his mother worked, but it is also where Irène died.

47

In the hotel room, Alex has folded her arms across her chest. She will call her brother. When he recognizes her voice, he'll say: "Oh, it's you . . . what do you want this time?" He'll be angry from the start, but it can't be helped. She picks up the hotel telephone, checks the sticker to see what she has to do, dials 0 to get an outside line. She spotted a place where she can meet him—it's very close to the industrial park; she jotted down the address. She rummages for it now, finds it, takes a deep breath, and dials his number. Voice mail. Surprising—he never turns off his cell phone, not even at night; he always says that work is sacred. Maybe he's going through a tunnel, or maybe he left it on the hall table, who knows? It doesn't matter: she leaves a message. "Hi, it's Alex. I need to see you. It's urgent. Meet me at eleven thirty at 137 boulevard Jouvenel in Aulnay. If I'm late, wait for me."

She's about to hang up, then says, "But don't keep me waiting."

Now she is once again caught up in the atmosphere of the room. Alex lies on the bed and daydreams for a while—the time passes slowly, her dreams come naturally, logically following on one from another. From the next room she hears the muffled sound of the TV; people don't realize how loud their television is, how annoying it can be. She could have it silenced if she wanted. She could get up, go next door, and knock, a man would open, surprised; he would be an ordinary man like those she's killed—how many? five, six, more? She would smile sweetly, the way she does, say, "Hi, I'm next door," nodding toward her room. "I'm all alone, can I come in?" The astonished man would stand aside to let her in, and she would immediately say, "Would you like me naked?" in the same tone as one might say, "Could you pull the curtains?" The man's jaw would drop in amazement. He'd be in his thirties, with a bit of a paunch, obviously—they're all the same; all the men she killed had a bit of a belly, even Pascal Trarieux—may the Devil in His Infinite Cruelty torture him—with him it was the beer. She would open her bathrobe and ask: "So what do you think?" It would be wonderful to do that for once, just for once. To open her bathrobe, stand naked, and ask, "So what do you think?" and be sure of the reaction, be certain that the man would open his arms wide and she could melt into his arms. In real life, what she would say is: "Would you mind turning off your TV?" The man would stammer an apology and fumble clumsily for the Off button, flustered by this miraculous apparition. He is bent over, his back is to her—if she wanted she could grab the aluminum bedside lamp and bring it down with both hands just behind his right ear; nothing could be simpler. Once he's dazed, it would be child's play; she knows where to strike to stun him and line up the next blow; tie him up using the sheets, tip a pint of concentrated acid down his throat, and that's that, there's no more noise from the TV, the guy's not likely to turn up the sound now, and she can have a peaceful night.

This is the sort of thing Alex daydreams about as she lies on the bed, hands behind her head. She lets herself drift. Memories of her life flood back. She has no regrets: one way or another, she had to kill these men; she needed to make them suffer, needed to watch them die. No, she doesn't regret any of them. In fact, there could easily have been more, many more. This is simply how the story took its course.

Time for a little drink now. She considers pouring a small Bowmore in the plastic toothbrush glass but changes her mind and swigs straight from the bottle. Alex is sorry she didn't buy a pack of cigarettes, too. After all, she is celebrating. It's been fifteen years since she gave up cigarettes. She doesn't know why she wishes she had bought some tonight; she never really enjoyed smoking. She did it to fit in. She was following every young girl's dream: to be like everybody else. She has no head for whisky—even a little makes her tipsy. She hums songs to which she doesn't know the lyrics, and as she hums she packs away her things again, folds her clothes one item at a time and carefully packs them into her new travel bag. She likes things to be neat—her apartment was something to behold, all her apartments, in fact, always spotless. In the bathroom, on the little cream-colored plastic shelf marked with cigarette burns, she arranges her toiletries: toothpaste, toothbrush. From the toiletries bag, she takes out her bottle of happy pills. There's a stray hair caught under the lid. She opens the bottle, takes the hair and lets it drop like a leaf; she wishes there were a handful of them so she could create a shower of rain, of snow; she used to do that with a friend when she was little, sit on the lawn and spray each other with a hose. This is the whisky talking, because as she does her little chores, she's still drinking from the bottle, and though she's been drinking slowly, she's quite tipsy.

The tidying up now done, she finds she's reeling slightly. She hasn't eaten anything in a long time; a little drink and she's all over the place. She didn't think. This makes her laugh, a tense, nervous laugh, a worried laugh; this is how she always is: worry is second nature to her; that and cruelty. As a girl she would never have imagined she was capable of such cruelty, she thinks now as she puts her nice new travel bag into the closet. She was such a gentle child—everyone always said so: "Alex is so sweet, she's absolutely adorable."

Admittedly, she was small and ugly, so they always rushed to compliment her on her personality.

And so the evening passes, the hours pass.

And Alex sips and sips, and in the end she cries a lot, too. She wouldn't have thought she had so many tears left in her.

Because tonight is a time of great loneliness.

48

Like a gunshot in the darkness, the wooden step cracks the moment he puts his weight on it. Camille almost topples over, steadies himself, manages to stay upright, one foot trapped by the broken floorboard. He's hurt himself. He struggles to pull free, has to sit down. Now here he is, with his back to the studio, staring at the car, its headlights still glaring, exactly where he had been when he saw the emergency services arrive. He hadn't been himself—they'd found him, distraught, in much the same place he's sitting now. Or maybe he'd been standing against the railing a little farther along.

Camille gets to his feet, walks carefully across the boards of the veranda, which also creaks and threatens to give way. He can't remember where exactly he was that night.

What's the point of trying to remember? It kills time.

Camille turns toward the door. It was hastily boarded up, but he doesn't need to worry, since both the gabled windows have been smashed, not a single pane of glass left. He climbs over the windowsill, hops down on the other side. The old red floor tiles still gleam beneath his feet; his eyes begin to adjust to the darkness.

His heart is hammering; his legs can barely hold him up. He takes a few steps.

The whitewashed walls are covered with graffiti. People have been here, have squatted here; there's an old mattress on the floor, ripped open now, and here and there are burned-out candles, empty cans, and bottles. The wind whips through the room. Part of the roof has caved in; through it you can see the forest.

All this is terribly sad, because there's nothing left now on which to hang his grief. Even his grief is different. Suddenly, unexpectedly, a brutal image comes back to him.

The body of Irène and the baby.

Camille falls to his knees and bursts into tears.

49

Alex slowly rolls over and over on the hotel bed; naked, silent, eyes closed; she holds her T-shirt at arm's length, waving it like a gymnast's ribbon, and lets the images rise to the surface: she sees her dead victims again, watches as the images flit past in a strange, random order as the T-shirt—her pennant—whirls, whipping against the walls of the room. She remembers the bloated face, the bulging eyes of the café owner in Reims, whose name she can't recall. Other memories flood back; Alex dances, she twirls and twirls, and her pennant has become a weapon. Now she sees the terrified rictus of Bobby, the truck driver. At least she remembers his name. She winds her T-shirt around her fist, stabs and thrusts at the hotel room door as though planting a screwdriver in an imaginary eye. She twists her hand as though grinding it deeper. The door handle shrieks under the pressure, Alex twists savagely, and her weapon plunges in and disappears. Alex is happy—she swings the weapon around her balled fist. Laughing, she skips and dances across the room; over and over she kills, over and over she sees the faces of her victims. Then finally the dance palls, the dancer tires. Did all those men truly desire her? Sitting on the bed, gripping the whisky bottle between her knees, Alex pictures what a man's desire looks like: Félix, for example—she can see his feverish eyes. He was hot for her. If he was sitting opposite her, she'd stare deep into his eyes; lips parted slightly she'd reach out with her T-shirt in her hands and stroke him gently, skillfully, the whisky bottle between her knees like a giant phallus, and Félix would explode, in fact that's exactly what he did, explode in midair, the warhead decoupling from the rocket and flying across the room.

Alex tosses her T-shirt into the air, imagining it drenched in blood, and it lands gently like a seagull on the broken sofa next to the door.

Later—it is completely dark now—her neighbor has turned off his TV and gone to sleep, without knowing what a miracle it is still to be alive in a room next to Alex.

Standing in front of the bathroom sink, as far back as possible so she can see herself full-length in the mirror, naked, serious, a little solemn, Alex gazes at herself. Nothing more, just gazes at herself.

So this is Alex; this is all there is to her.

It's impossible not to cry when you are face-to-face with yourself.

Something inside her snaps. She feels a crack open up, feels herself sucked inside.

This image of her in the mirror is so powerful.

Suddenly she turns away, her back to the mirror; she gets down on her knees, and without a second's hesitation, she brutally slams her head back against the edge of the sink, one, two, three, four, five times, each time harder than the last, each time exactly the same part of her skull. It makes a terrible clanging noise, like a gong, because Alex does it with all her strength. The last blow leaves her dazed, disoriented, in tears. There are cracked and broken things inside her head, and not just today. They've been broken for a long time. She staggers to her feet, totters to the bed, and collapses. Her head is incredibly sore; the pain comes in steady waves; she squeezes her eyes shut, wonders whether she's bleeding into the pillow. Using her left hand, she reaches out as precisely as she can, grabs the bottle of barbiturates, and lays it on her belly; with infinite care (her head is agony), she pours the contents into her hand and swallows all the pills at once. She props herself awkwardly on her elbow, turns toward the nightstand, reeling, picks up the whisky, gripping it tightly; she drinks straight from the bottle, she drinks and drinks for as long as her breathing will allow. In a few short seconds, she downs half the bottle; then she lets it go and hears it roll away across the carpet.

Alex falls back in a heap on the bed.

With great difficulty she suppresses a wave of nausea.

She dissolves into tears, though she doesn't realize that.

Her body is here, but her mind is already elsewhere.

It curls into a ball. Everything coils around her life; what remains turns in on itself.

Suddenly her brain is seized by panic, but it's purely neuronal.

What will happen now concerns only this mortal coil; these last moments, the moments from which there is no way back. Alex's mind is already elsewhere.

If there is an elsewhere.

50

The place has been turned upside down. All the exits have been blocked, the parking lot cordoned off; there are police cars, flashing lights, uniforms. To the hotel guests it almost looks like a TV series, except that it's not night. In crime series, scenes like this almost always happen at night. It's 7:00 a.m., the time when it's all go, when everyone's racing to catch a flight. For more than an hour the manager has been apologizing profusely to the guests, giving all sorts of assurances. One wonders what he's promising them.

The hotel owner is standing in the doorway when Camille and Louis arrive. As soon as he understands the situation, Louis steps in front. He's used to such situations—he wants to talk to the hotelier first; if he lets Camille do it, within half an hour there'll be civil war.

So Louis, looking compassionate and sympathetic, takes the owner aside, leaving a passage open. Camille follows a local officer, the man who was first on the scene.

"I saw at once it was the girl from the missing persons appeal."

He's waiting for congratulations, but they don't come; the little man isn't friendly, he walks quickly, and he looks as if he's self-sufficient, completely withdrawn. He refuses to take the elevator, so they take the concrete stairwell no one uses, and it echoes like a cathedral.

In spite of everything, the officer adds, "We didn't let anyone in. We waited for you to get here."

Things play out curiously. Since the room is still sealed off waiting for forensics and Louis is downstairs distracting the owner, Camille is alone as he steps into the room, as if he is a family member visiting someone on their deathbed, and—out of respect for his privacy—he is being left alone with the deceased for a moment.

In places with no grandeur, death is always rather mundane. This young woman is no exception. She'd rolled herself up in a sheet, and later the convulsions wound it tighter, such that she looks like an Egyptian corpse about to be mummified. One hand hangs languidly over the edge of the bed, terribly feminine and human. Her face is bruised. Her eyes are open, staring fixedly at the ceiling. At the corners of her lips, there are traces of vomit, most of which is probably still in the mouth. The whole scene is unutterably painful.

As with any death, the room seems to be pervaded by a sense of mystery. Camille remains on the threshold, though he is well used to bodies; he's seen a lot in his time—hardly surprising since he's been on the force twenty-five years—one day he'll have to work out the figures, but it must be the equivalent of a village. There are some that have an effect on him and some that have none. The subconscious decides. This one is painful. It hurts. He doesn't know why.

His first thought was that he always arrives too late. This is why Irène died; his instinct had been wrong, he'd been too pigheaded, he got there too late, and by then she was dead. But no, now that he's here, he knows that's not it, that history doesn't mindlessly repeat itself, that no dead girl can take the place of Irène. First and foremost, because Irène was innocent; this is not something he can believe about this girl.

And yet he's troubled, and he can't explain why.

He senses, he knows, that there's something he hasn't understood. Maybe even right from the start. And this girl has taken her secrets with her. Camille would like to go over, to take a closer look, lean over her, to understand.

He hunted her while she was alive; now here she is lying dead, and still he knows nothing about her. How old is she? Where is she from?

And, incidentally, what was her real name?

Beside him on a chair is her handbag. He takes a pair of latex gloves from his pocket and snaps them on. He picks up the bag, opens it—it's amazing all the stuff women keep in their handbags—he finds her ID card, opens it.

Thirty years old. The dead never resemble the living they once were. He looks at the official photograph, then back at the dead girl on the bed. Neither of these faces is anything like the countless sketches he did in the past few weeks based on the E-FIT. And so the girl's face remains elusive. Which is her real face? The stamped image of her on the ID card? She could be about twenty in the picture; the hairstyle is dated, and she is not smiling, simply staring ahead vacantly. Or is it the E-FIT of the serial killer, cold, hard, fraught with menace, printed out a thousand times? Or is it the lifeless face of the dead girl lying on the bed whose body, as though disconnected from her, is haunted by unspeakable pain?

Camille finds her eerily like a painting by Fernand Pelez, *The Victim*: the staggering effect of death when it strikes.

Fascinated by her face, Camille forgets that he still does not know her name. He peers at the ID card again.

Alex Prévost.

Camille repeats the name to himself.

Alex.

Laura is gone and with her Nathalie, Léa, Emma.

She is Alex.

Or rather she was . . . She was.

III

51

Vidard the magistrate is delighted. The suicide is the logical outcome of his astuteness, his skill, and his single-mindedness. As with
all vain men, what he owes to chance and circumstance he attributes
to his talent. Unlike Camille, he is jubilant. Discreetly so. The more
reserved he is, the more triumphant he obviously feels. Camille can
see it in the set of his mouth, the shoulders, in the purposeful way
he slips on his protective gear. It's bizarre, seeing Vidard in a sur-
geon's mask and blue overboots.

He could simply have viewed the scene from the corridor, given
that the forensics team are already at work, but no—a thirty-year-old
multiple murderer, especially a dead one, like a hunting scene, is something that demands to be seen up close. He's satisfied. He steps into the
room like a Roman emperor. Leaning over the bed, his lips twitch as
though to say *Good, good*, and as he leaves his expression reads *Case
closed*. For Camille's benefit, he points to the crime scene investigators.

"I want the result as soon as possible, understood?"

Which means he wants to hold a press conference. Quickly.
Camille agrees. Quickly.

"Of course," Camille says. "We'll get to the bottom of this."

The magistrate is about to leave. Camille hears the cartridge enter the barrel.

"We need this to be over and done with," says the magistrate. "For everyone's sake."

"You mean for me?"

"If you want me to be frank, then yes."

He peels off his protective gear as he says this. The cap and the overboots are ill suited to the dignity of his words.

"You have demonstrated a singular lack of clear-sightedness in this case, Commandant Verhœven," he says at length. "You were constantly overtaken by events. Even the identity of this girl we owe not to you but to her. You were saved by the bell, but you were lucky; had it not been for this . . . fortunate 'incident,'" he nods toward the room, "I'm not at all sure you'd still be on the case. I strongly feel you simply don't have . . ."

"The stature?" Camille supplies. "Say it, sir, it's on the tip of your tongue."

Exasperated, the magistrate takes several steps down the corridor.

"That's you all over," Camille says. "You don't have the bottle to say what you think, or the honesty to think what you say."

"Very well then, I'll tell you exactly what I think . . ."

"I'm shaking in my boots."

"I think that you're no longer fit to handle serious cases."

He takes a moment to make it clear that he's thinking, that being an intelligent man, aware of his importance, he never says anything lightly.

"Your return to work has been less than stellar. You might perhaps wish to take a step back."

52

First, everything was shipped off to the forensics lab, and when they were done, the stuff was left in Camille's office. It might not seem like it, but it takes up a lot of space. Armand had them bring in a couple of tables and cover them with a sheet, push back the desk, the coat rack, the chairs, the sofa, and then lay everything out carefully. It feels strange, looking at all these childish things and realizing they belonged to a woman of thirty. As though she never grew up. Why would anyone want to keep a cheap pink barrette with a paste diamond, or a movie ticket?

All of these things were picked up at the hotel four days earlier.

After leaving the dead woman's hotel room, Camille went back down to the lobby, where Armand was taking a statement from the receptionist, a young man with his hair gelled into a side flip as though he'd just been slapped. For ostensibly practical reasons, Armand has set himself up in the dining room, where hotel guests are having breakfast.

"You don't mind, do you?" he said and, without waiting for a response, helped himself to a pot of coffee, four croissants, a glass of orange juice, a bowl of cereal, a boiled egg, two slices of ham, and a couple of portions of cheese. As he eats, he questions the reception-ist, and he's clearly listening carefully since, even with his mouth full, he's capable of correcting the man.

"Earlier you told me it was eight thirty yesterday evening."

"Yes," the receptionist says, astonished by this scrawny man's appetite, "but five minutes either way, it's hard to say . . ."

Armand nods that he understands. When he's finished the inter-view, he says, "I don't suppose you'd have a cardboard box or some-thing?" He doesn't wait for an answer; instead he lays out three paper napkins, tips out a whole basket of bread and croissants onto them, and ties them up in a bow; it looks like a gift. To the worried receptionist, he says, "For later . . . what with all the work we've got on, we won't get to break for lunch."

It is 7:30 a.m.

Camille goes into the conference room, which Louis has requi-sitioned to take witness statements. He's questioning the chamber-maid who found Alex's body, a woman of about fifty with a pale, careworn face. Usually she does the evening shift, cleaning up after dinner, then goes home, but sometimes, when they're short staffed, she has to come back at 6:00 a.m. to do the bedrooms. She is a heavyset woman and suffers from lumbago.

Her instructions are to leave the bedrooms until late morning, and even then, knocking loudly and waiting, because the things she has walked in on . . . She could tell some stories, but the pres-ence of the officer who's just come into the room and is watch-ing them intimidates her. He doesn't say anything, he just stands there, hands in the pockets of the coat he hasn't taken off since he arrived; the man is obviously either sick or sensitive to the cold. But this morning, she made a mistake. Room 317 was on her list—the guest had already checked out, which meant she could clean the room.

"It wasn't properly written," she explains. "I thought it said 314."

She is quite vehement; she doesn't want to be blamed for all this. It's not her fault.

"If the room number had been properly written, none of this would have happened."

To calm her, reassure her, Louis places a neatly manicured hand on her arm and closes his eyes; sometimes he looks just like a cardinal. For the first time since she went into room 314 by mistake, the chambermaid realizes that above and beyond the confusion with the numbers, which she keeps harping on about, there is a thirty-year-old woman who committed suicide.

"I realized at once that she was dead."

She falls silent, struggles to find the right words; she's seen a lot of dead bodies in her time. But still, it's unexpected every time. It knocks the wind out of you.

"It gave me such a shock."

She claps her hand over her mouth at the thought. Louis silently sympathizes. Camille says nothing; he watches, waits.

"A beautiful young girl like that. She seemed so alive . . ."

"You thought she seemed alive?"

It is Camille who asks this.

"Well no, not there in the room . . . That's not what I meant . . ."

And when the two men don't respond, she carries on; she wants to do the right thing, wants to help. Because of the mix-up with the room numbers, she's convinced they're going to try to blame her for something. She has to stand up for herself.

"When I saw her the night before, she seemed so alive—that's what I meant to say. It was the way she walked; she seemed so gutsy. I don't know how to explain it." She becomes irritated.

Louis says calmly, "Where did you see her walking the night before?"

"On the road there outside the hotel. She was taking out garbage bags and . . ."

She doesn't get a chance to finish the sentence; the two men have already disappeared. She watches them run for the exit.

On the way, Camille nabs Armand and three officers, and they all rush outside. To the right and left, on either side of the street, about fifty yards away, a garbage truck is emptying containers hurriedly loaded by the operators; the policemen all shout, but at that distance, they can't hear. Camille and Armand run up the road, waving their arms; Louis runs the other way, all three of them brandishing their warrant cards; the other officers blow their whistles as hard as they can; the effect is to completely paralyze the garbagemen: they all stop in midaction. The policemen keep running, panting and out of breath. It's not often a garbage collector gets to see the police trying to arrest a garbage can.

The dazed chambermaid is led outside, like a celebrity surrounded by fans and paparazzi. She points to the spot where she was standing when she saw the girl the night before.

"I was on my moped, over there, and she was here—well, more or less here; I can't say exactly."

Some twenty containers are wheeled as far as the hotel parking lot. The manager immediately panics.

"But you can't—"

"What *exactly* can't we do?" Camille interrupts him.

The manager gives up; this is not going to be a good day: garbage containers emptied all over the car park, as if a suicide wasn't enough.

Armand is the one who finds the three garbage bags.

He's got flair. Experience.

53

On Sunday morning, Camille opens the window for Doudouche because she loves to watch the market. After he finishes breakfast—it is not yet 8:00 a.m., and he slept very badly—he goes into one of the long periods of indecision that he has always suffered from, where all the possible solutions balance each other out, where to do or not to do something seems equally valid. The difficult thing about these periods of uncertainty is that deep down he knows which solution he will choose. Pretending to deliberate is simply a means of masking a dubious decision with a semblance of rationality.

Today is the day his mother's paintings are being auctioned. He told himself he wouldn't go. Now he knows he won't.

Camille projects himself into the future; it's almost as though the auction is over. His thoughts turn to the proceeds and this idea of not keeping the money, of giving it away. Until now, he has refused to guess how much there will be. Though he does not want to do the calculations, his brain has already worked out the figures; he can't help it. He will never be as rich as Louis, but even so. According to his calculations, it should raise about

150,000 euros. Maybe more, maybe 200,000 euros. He's angry at himself for doing the math, but who wouldn't? When Irène died, the insurance paid off the apartment they had bought together. He immediately sold it. With the proceeds, he bought this apartment, took out a small mortgage that the money from the auction would comfortably repay. This kind of thought is the first flaw in his good intentions. He'd tell himself, I could just pay off the mortgage and give away the rest. Then it would be, pay off the mortgage, upgrade the car and give away the rest. It's a vicious circle. Until there is no "rest." He'd end up donating two hundred euros to cancer research.

Come on, Camille thinks, shaking himself. Just concentrate on what's essential.

Toward 10:00 a.m., he abandons Doudouche, walks through the market, and—the day is bright and mild—resolves to walk to the *brigade* offices. It'll take as long as it takes. Camille walks as fast as his stubby legs will allow. Unsurprisingly, his determination and his resolution fade, and he catches the *métro*.

Though it's Sunday, Louis has said he'll join him at the office around 1:00 p.m.

Ever since he got there, Camille has been in silent communion with the objects laid out on the big table. It looks like a little girl's stall at a garage sale.

The night after Alex was found dead, after her brother came to the morgue to identify the body, her mother, Mme. Prévost, was asked if she recognized anything among the effects.

Mme. Prévost is a small, spirited woman whose angular face is of a piece with her gray hair and her threadbare clothes. Everything about her transmits the same message: *we come from a modest background*. She didn't want to take off her coat or put down her handbag; she was eager to be out of there.

"It's a lot for her to take in all at once," Armand said. He was the first to speak to her. "Your daughter committed suicide last night after murdering at least six people—it's a little disconcerting, to say the least."

Camille talked to her at length in the corridor to prepare her for the ordeal; she will be confronted by so many personal things that belonged to her daughter as a toddler, as a girl, as a teenager, the things of no great value that become utterly heartbreaking the day your daughter dies. Mme. Prévost steels herself, she doesn't cry, she says she understands, but as soon as she is faced with the table full of memories, she breaks down. Someone brings her a chair. As an onlooker, such moments are painful; you shift your weight from one foot to the other, forced to be patient, to do nothing. Mme. Prévost is still clutching her handbag, as though she is visiting; she sits in the chair, points to the objects: there are many that she has never seen or doesn't remember. She often seems puzzled or uncertain, as though faced with an image of her daughter she doesn't recognize. To her, these are like spare parts. To reduce her dead daughter to this catalogue of junk seems monstrous. Her grief turns to indignation; she turns this way and that.

"What possessed her to keep all this rubbish? Are you even sure it's hers?"

Camille spreads his hands. Her reaction is familiar—it's a way of defending oneself against the brutality of the situation, a reaction common to people in shock, this aggressiveness.

"Then again, this here, this is definitely hers."

She points to the carved black wooden head. She seems about to tell a story but changes her mind. Then points to the pages torn from various novels.

"She used to read a lot. All the time."

By the time Louis arrives, it's almost 2:00 p.m. He starts out with the tattered pages. *Tomorrow in the Battle Think on Me, Anna Karenina*. There are passages underlined in purple ink. *Middlemarch, Doctor Zhivago*. Louis has read them all. *Aurélien, Buddenbrooks*. One of the witnesses mentioned her having the complete works of

Duras, but here there are only a couple of pages from *War: A Memoir*. Louis can find no connection between the titles; there's an element of romanticism, which is hardly surprising—young girls and mass murderers are tenderhearted creatures.

They go to lunch. As they're eating, Camille gets a call from the friend of his mother who organized this morning's auction. There's not much to say. Camille thanks him again—he doesn't know what else to do, so he discreetly offers money. Louis can tell the friend is saying that they'll talk about it later, that what he did, he did for Maud. Camille falls silent, they agree to meet up soon, knowing that they never will. Camille hangs up. The auction raised much more than expected: 280,000 euros. The small self-portrait alone, a minor work, sold for 18,000 euros.

Louis is not surprised. He's familiar with prices and valuations; he has experience in such things.

Two hundred and eighty thousand. Camille can't believe it. He tries to calculate how many years' salary this comes to. A good many. The idea that he's well off now makes him uncomfortable; it's a weight on his shoulders. He stretches himself a little.

"Was it a stupid thing to do, selling everything?"

"Not necessarily," Louis says cautiously.

Still, Camille wonders.

54

Freshly shaved, square-jawed, determined, eyes bright, lips thick, voluptuous, expressive. He stands ramrod straight; he would have a military air were it not for the mane of curly brown hair tied back in a ponytail. The belt with its silver buckle emphasizes a bulging waistline intended to be proportional to his social standing, the product of business lunches, of his marriage, of stress, or perhaps all three. He looks as though he's forty plus. He is thirty-seven. He's six feet tall and broad shouldered. Louis isn't fat, but he's tall—next to this man he looks like a teenage boy.

Camille met him once before, at the morgue when he came to identify the body. He leaned over the aluminum autopsy table, his expression formal, pained. He said nothing, merely nodded to indicate yes, that's her, and the sheet was pulled up again.

That day at the morgue, they didn't speak to each other. It's tricky, offering your condolences when the deceased is a serial killer who has destroyed the lives of half a dozen families. It's hard to find the words; fortunately, this is not something that police officers are expected to do.

In the corridor on their way back in, Camille is silent. Louis says:
"He seemed a lot more shifty when I met him . . ."

Camille remembered that Louis first met him during the investigation into the death of Pascal Trarieux.

It's Monday, 5:00 p.m., the *brigade criminelle* headquarters.

Louis (Brioni suit, Ralph Lauren shirt, Forzieri brogues) is sitting at his desk. Armand is sitting next to him, his socks down around his ankles. Camille is sitting in a chair at the far end of the room, legs swinging, poring over a sketch pad as though this has nothing to do with him. Right now he's drawing from memory a portrait of Guadalupe Victoria he once saw on a Mexican coin.

"When will the body be released?"

"Soon," Louis says. "Very soon."

"It's been four days already . . ."

"I know, these things always seem to take a long time."

Objectively, this is something Louis does to perfection. This consummate look of commiseration is something he must have learned early, a legacy of family, of class. Right now, Camille would paint him as Saint Mark presenting the doge of Venice.

Louis picks up his notepad, his case file, as though he wants to get the painful formalities out of the way as quickly as possible.

"Okay, then. Thomas Vasseur, born December 16, 1969."

"I think that's in the file."

Not aggressive, but spiky. Irritated.

"Oh, yes, yes," Louis says effusively. "We just need to check everything is in order. To put this to bed. From what we know, your sister killed six people, five men and one woman. Her death makes it impossible to piece together these events. We have to have something to tell the families—I'm sure you understand. Not to mention the magistrate."

Ah, yes, the magistrate, Camille thinks. He was dying to give a press conference. It didn't take him long to get the backing of his superiors; everyone wanted a press conference. It's hardly a triumph, a serial killer who commits suicide—it's not as good as an arrest—but it's worth it from the point of view of security, public safety, civil peace, and all that shit. The murderer is dead. It's like a medieval town crier announcing the wolf is dead; everyone knows it's not going to change the fate of the world, but it affords relief, reinforces the impression that some higher power is watching over us. And the higher power in this case is reveling in it. Vidard appeared before the assembled journalists as though this was the last thing he wanted to do. To listen to him talk, you'd think that the police had the murderer cornered, and she had to choose between surrender and suicide. Camille and Louis watched it on the TV in the local bistro. Louis was resigned about it. Camille was laughing to himself. After that moment of glory, the magistrate calmed down. In front of the cameras, he talked the talk, but now it comes to closing the investigation, it's the *brigade criminelle* who have to walk the walk.

So this is about what they're going to tell the families. Thomas Vasseur understands; he nods, still fractious.

Louis becomes engrossed for a moment in the case file, then he looks up, brushes his hair from his face with his left hand.

"So, date of birth: December 16, 1969."

"Yes."

"And you're a sales director with a games hire company."

"That's right. We work with casinos, bars, nightclubs; we rent slot machines. All over France."

"You're married with three children."

"Yeah, and now you know everything."

Louis meticulously makes a note, then looks up again.

"So you were . . . seven years older than Alex?"

This time Thomas Vasseur simply nods.

"Alex never knew her father," Louis says.

"No, my own father died young. My mother got pregnant with Alex much later, but she didn't want to be in a relationship with the guy. He disappeared."

"So, we might say that you were the only father she ever had?"

"I looked after her, yeah. I took charge of her; she needed it."

Louis says nothing, allows the silence to drag on. Vasseur continues.

"Even back then Alex was . . . what I mean is, Alex was unstable."

"Yes," Louis says. "Unstable . . . that's what your mother said."

He knits his brows slightly.

"We have no record of a psychiatric episode; she doesn't seem to have been hospitalized or committed."

"Alex wasn't crazy, she was unstable!"

"Because she never had a father . . ."

"Mostly it was her personality. Even as a kid, she didn't make friends, she was withdrawn, isolated, didn't talk much. And she was undisciplined."

Louis gives a look that says he understands, and when Vasseur says nothing, he ventures, "She needed a strong hand . . ."

Difficult to know whether this is a question, a statement, or a comment. Vasseur decides that it's a question.

"Exactly."

"Your mother wasn't enough."

"It's no substitute for a father."

"Did Alex ever talk about her father? I mean, did she ask questions? Ask to see him?"

"No, she had everything she needed at home."

"You and your mother."

"My mother and me."

"Love and discipline."

"If you want to put it like that."

Divisionnaire Le Guen deals with Vidard. He acts as a screen between him and Camille. He has all the necessary attributes: the stature, the forbearance, the patience. Whatever one may think of the magistrate, and he can certainly be unpleasant, Camille really is a liability. For several days now, since the girl's suicide, there have been rumors. Verhœven isn't the man he used to be; he's impossible to work with; he can't handle large-scale investigations. Everyone is talking about him, the story of a girl who wasted six people in two years can't help but attract attention—even leaving aside how she went about it—and it's true that it looks as though throughout the investigation Camille was a step behind the curve. Right to the end.

Le Guen rereads the conclusions in Camille's final report. They had a meeting an hour ago.

"Are you sure about this, Camille?" Le Guen says.

"Absolutely."

Le Guen nods.

"If you say so . . ."

"Listen, if you prefer, I can—"

"No, no, no," Le Guen cuts him short, "I'll take care of it. I'll see the magistrate myself and explain. I'll keep you posted."

Camille throws up his hands in surrender.

"Come on, Camille. What the hell is the deal with you and magistrates? You're always at loggerheads with them from the start—it's as though you can't help it."

"You'd need to ask the magistrates."

Behind the divisionnaire's question is an awkward implication: is it Camille's height that means he constantly has to challenge authority?

"So this Pascal Trarieux, you knew him at school?"

Thomas Vasseur throws his head back and puffs impatiently as though blowing out a candle on the ceiling. He makes it clear he's finding it hard to keep a grip; he mutters a firm, curt "yes," the sort of yes usually designed to deter someone from asking any more questions.

This time, Louis doesn't hide behind the case file. He has an advantage, since he is the one who interviewed Vasseur a month ago.

"When I first interviewed you, you said, and I quote: 'Pascal was always busting our balls about this girlfriend of his, Nathalie . . . Though I suppose at least he had one for once.'"

"So?"

"And we now know that this Nathalie was in fact your sister, Alex."

"You might know that now, but I had no idea at the time."

When Louis says nothing, Vasseur feels obliged to elaborate a little.

"You have to realize, Pascal was a complicated guy. He never really had girlfriends. Actually, I thought he was just bragging. He talked about this Nathalie girl all the time, but none of us ever got to meet her. We laughed about it, to tell you the truth. I for one never took it terribly seriously."

"But you're the one who introduced Alex to your friend Pascal."

"No I didn't, and he wasn't a friend."

"Really? So what was he then?"

"Listen, I'm going to come clean with you. Pascal was a fucking moron; the guy had the IQ of a sea urchin. Okay, so I knew him at school; he was a childhood friend, if you prefer—I used to run into him now and again. But he wasn't what you call 'my friend.'"

Here, he laughs quite loudly to emphasize how ridiculous the idea is.

"You ran into him now and again . . ."

"From time to time I'd see him in the bar when I stopped in to say hi. I still know a lot of people in Clichy. I was born there, he was born there, we went to school together."

"In Clichy."

"Exactly. You might say we were friends back in Clichy. Will that do you?"

"That'll do nicely, thank you."

Louis worriedly buries himself in the case file again.

"So were Pascal and Alex also 'friends back in Clichy,' as you put it?"

"No, they weren't 'friends back in Clichy,' and you're starting to piss me off with this whole thing about Clichy. If you—"

"Calm down."

Camille says this. He doesn't raise his voice. Like a kid with his crayons in the corner, they had forgotten he was there.

"We ask the questions. You answer them."

Vasseur turns toward him, but Camille does not look up; he goes on sketching. He simply adds:

"That's how things work around here."

Finally, he looks up, holds the drawing critically at arm's length, tilting it slightly, and then, just as he peers over the sketch pad, adds, "And if you talk out of turn again I'll charge you with Contempt of Cop."

Camille sets the sketch pad down on the table and, just before leaning over it again, he says, "I hope I've been sufficiently clear."

Louis pauses for a beat. Vasseur, caught off guard, glances from Louis to Camille and back again, his mouth hanging open. The atmosphere is like a late summer day when a storm breaks unexpectedly and you suddenly realize you've come out without a coat, the sky is black as thunder, and you're very far from home. Vasseur looks as though he's about to pull up the collar of his jacket.

"So?" Louis says.

"So what?" says a bewildered Vasseur.

"So, were Alex and Pascal Trarieux also 'friends back in Clichy'?"

"No, Alex never lived in Clichy," Vasseur says. "We moved, she would have been, I don't know, four or five at the time."

"So how did she meet Pascal Trarieux?"

"I don't know."

Silence.

"So, your sister meets your quote-unquote friend Pascal Trarieux by pure chance . . ."

"I suppose so."

"And she tells him she's called Nathalie. And she murders him with a shovel in Champigny-sur-Marne. And none of this has anything to do with you."

"What do you want from me? Alex is the one who killed him, not me!"

He's angry now, his voice becoming shrill, then suddenly he breaks off. Very coldly, he says slowly, "Why are you interrogating me anyway? Have you got something against me?"

"No," Louis says quickly. "But you have to understand, after Pascal's disappearance, his father, Jean-Pierre Trarieux, went looking for your sister. We know he tracked her down, that he abducted her

near her home, kept her hostage, tortured her; we believe he was
planning to kill her. Miraculously, she escaped . . . you know the
rest. But this is precisely what interests us. What is surprising is that
she should be going out with his son under an assumed name. What
did she have to hide? But what's even more surprising is, how did
Jean-Pierre Trarieux manage to find her?"

"I wouldn't know."

"Well, we have a little theory."

With a sentence like this, Camille would have a field day; it
would sound like a threat, an accusation—it would be heavy with
subtext. With Louis, it's just a statement. This is the great thing
about Louis—his British officer side. Whatever has been decided is
what he does. He allows nothing to distract him, to stop him.

"You have a theory," Vasseur echoes. "Would you mind telling
me what it is?"

"When he was looking for his son, Jean-Pierre Trarieux visited
everyone he could think of who knew him. He showed them a poor-
quality photograph of Pascal with Nathalie. That is, Alex. But of all
the people he spoke to, you are the only one who must have recognized your sister. And this is precisely what we think happened. We
think you gave him her address."

No reaction.

"However," Louis goes on, "given Monsieur Trarieux's agitated
state and his explicitly hostile attitude, giving him the address was
tantamount to facilitating grievous bodily harm. At the least."

This piece of information slowly percolates around the room.

"Why would I do any such thing?" Vasseur says, seemingly genuinely curious.

"That is precisely what we would like to know, Monsieur Vasseur.
His son, Pascal, had—as you put it—the IQ of a sea urchin. The father
was not much more evolved, and you didn't have to be a genius to
work out what his intentions were. I said that this was tantamount to
getting your sister beaten up, but in fact anyone would have realized
that he might well have killed her. Is that what you wanted, Monsieur
Vasseur? For Jean-Pierre Trarieux to kill your sister? To kill Alex?"

"What proof have you got?"

"Aha!"

This is Camille again. It begins as a roar of joy and ends with an appreciative laugh.

"Ha, ha, ha! I love it!"

Vasseur turns to look at him.

"When a witness asks what proof we have, it means he's not disputing our conclusion," Camille says. "He's just trying to wriggle out of it."

"Right." Thomas Vasseur has just made a decision. He does so calmly, placing his hands flat on the desk in front of him. He leaves them there and stares at them as he says, "Could someone please tell me what I am doing here?"

The voice is powerful; the sentence thundered like an order. Camille gets up, no more sketching, no more cunning, no more proof: he strides over and stands in front of Vasseur.

"How old was Alex when you started raping her?"

Vasseur looks up.

"Oh, so that's it . . ."

He smiles.

"Why didn't you just say?"

As a child Alex kept a diary sporadically. A few lines here and there, then nothing for ages. She doesn't even always write in the same copybook. Among the stuff in the garbage bags, they found all sorts of things. An exercise book with the first six pages filled with spidery writing, a hardback notebook with a picture of a galloping horse against the sunset.

The handwriting is childlike.

Camille reads only one sentence: *Thomas comes into my bedroom. He comes nearly every night. Maman knows.*

Vasseur gets to his feet.

"Okay, gentlemen, if you'll forgive me . . ."

He takes a few steps.

"I don't think that's how it's going to go down," Camille says.

Vasseur turns. "Really? And how is it going to go down, in your opinion?"

"In my opinion, you're going to sit down and answer our questions."

"Questions about what?"

"About you sexually abusing your sister."

Vasseur looks from Louis to Camille and says in mock alarm, "Really? Is she intending to press charges?"

He's clearly amused now.

"You're a bunch of jokers, the lot of you. I'm not going to spill my guts to you; I wouldn't give you the satisfaction."

He folds his arms across his chest, tilts his head like an artist looking for inspiration and says in a sensual voice, "The truth is, I was very fond of Alex. Awfully fond. Enormously fond. She was an adorable little girl, you can't imagine. A little skinny, and her face was a little plain, but she was delicious. And sweet. And, yes, unstable. You have to understand, she needed a lot of discipline. And a lot of love. That's often the way with little girls."

He turns to Louis, spreads his hands, palms up, and he smiles.

"You said it yourself: I was her papa."

Then he folds his arms again, satisfied.

"And now tell me, gentlemen, has Alex pressed charges alleging rape? Might I see a copy?"

55

According to Camille's calculations, having cross-checked the files, when Thomas "comes into her bedroom," Alex was not quite eleven. He was seventeen. To come to this conclusion required a number of hypotheses and deductions. Half-brother. Protector. My God, the savagery in this story, Camille thinks. And people say *I'm* brutal.

He comes back to Alex. They have a few childhood photographs, none of them dated, so they have to rely on the background elements (the clothes, the cars) to approximate the year. That, and Alex's physical appearance. She grows steadily, from one photograph to the next.

Camille has spent a lot of time running through the family saga. The mother, Carole Prévost, a nurse's aide, marries François Vasseur, a printer, in 1969. She is twenty at the time. Thomas is born in the same year. When the father dies in 1974, the boy is barely five and probably has no memory of his father. Alex is born in 1976.

Father unknown.

"He was a useless prick," Mme. Prévost said decisively, oblivious to the pun. She doesn't have much of a sense of humor. Then again, being the mother of a woman who's murdered six people is hardly conducive to joke-making. Camille wanted to spare her having to see the handful of images found among Alex's effects, so he took them off the table. Instead, he asked her if *she* had any pictures. She brought a bundle of them. He and Louis organized them, noted the where and when they were taken, and the names of the people Mme. Prévost had identified. Thomas, for his part, gave them no photographs, claimed that he had none.

The pictures of Alex as a child show a terrifyingly thin little girl, gaunt face, prominent cheekbones, eyes ringed with dark circles, lips thin and pouting. She poses awkwardly, reluctantly. One of them was taken at the seaside: there are beach balls and parasols, and the shot is backlit. It was taken at Le Lavandou, according to Mme. Prévost. Both children are in the picture, Alex, aged ten, and Thomas, seventeen. He stands head and shoulders above her. She is wearing a two-piece swimsuit; she hardly even needs to wear the bikini top—it's just for show. Her wrists are so thin, two fingers would be enough to encircle them; her legs are so skinny that her knees stick out; her feet are turned a little inwards. The fact that she looks sickly and puny might not matter were it not that her face is ugly. Even her shoulders look wrong. It's harrowing when you know what you're looking at.

It was around this time that Thomas Vasseur began to visit her bedroom at night. A little before, a little afterwards, it hardly matters. Because the next set of pictures are not much more encouraging. They show Alex at thirteen. Group and family photographs. Alex stands on the right, her mother in the middle, Thomas on the left. They were taken on the patio of a suburban house. A birthday party. "At my late brother's place," says Mme. Prévost, quickly making the sign of the cross. A simple gesture can sometimes open up new perspectives. The Prévost family are plainly religious, or were religious—or at least they pay lip service. Camille feels this does not bode well for the girl. In the picture, Alex has grown a little, but only in height. She is still skinny, gangling; she looks awkward and uncomfortable in her own skin. She makes you want to protect her. In the groups she is standing slightly behind the others.

On the back of the print, Alex has written: THE QUEEN MOTHER. Mme. Prévost does not look particularly regal, more like a cleaning woman in her Sunday best. She is turned toward her son and smiling.

"Robert Praderie."

Armand has taken over. He notes down the answers with a new ballpoint pen on a brand new notepad. This is a big day at the *criminelle*.

"Never heard of him. This is one of Alex's victims, right?"

"Yes," Armand says. "He was a truck driver. His body was found in the cab of his truck at an service station near the German border. Alex drove a screwdriver into his eye and another into his throat, then poured a pint of sulfuric acid into his mouth."

Vasseur is thinking.

"Alex always was vitriolic . . ."

Armand does not smile. This is his strength; he pretends not to understand or not to care—in fact, he's completely focused.

"Probably so," he says. "She certainly had a temper from what I can tell."

"Women . . ."

Implication: you know what women are like. Vasseur is the kind of guy who says something lewd and looks around for support. It's the sort of thing you expect from aging Lotharios, the dickless wonders, the perverts, but in fact it's all too common among men of all sorts.

"So, this Robert Praderie," Armand goes on. "His name means nothing to you?"

"Nothing—why, should it?"

Armand does not respond; he rummages in the case file.

"What about Bernard Gattegno?"

"Are you planning to go through them one by one?"

"There are only six; it won't take long."

"How is any of this connected to me?"

"It's connected to you because you *did* know Bernard Gattegno."

"I'd be surprised."

"Oh, but you did . . . cast your mind back. Gattegno was a garage owner in Étampes. You bought a motorcycle from him in, let me see . . ." he checks the file, "in 1988."

Vasseur considers for a moment, then nods.

"Maybe. It's a long time ago. I was nineteen in 1988; how do you expect me to remember?"

"And yet . . ."

Armand leafs through the loose pages in the folder.

"Here we go. We have a witness statement from a friend of Monsieur Gattegno who seems to remember you very well. You were both big motorcycle fanatics back then. You used to go out riding together."

"When?"

"In 1988 and '89."

"I suppose you remember all the people you used to know in 1988?"

"No, but I'm not the one answering the questions, you are."

Vasseur gives him a weary look.

"Okay, fine, maybe I did go on bike rides with this guy twenty years ago. So?"

"So, it's a link in a chain. You didn't know Monsieur Praderie, but you knew Monsieur Gattegno, and he *did* know Monsieur Praderie."

"Show me two people who have no connection whatsoever to each other."

Armand tries and fails to come up with a clever retort. He turns to Louis.

"Frigyes Karinthy's six degrees of separation?" Louis says. "Yes, we're familiar with the theory; it's very seductive. But I fear we may be straying from the point of the interview."

Mademoiselle Toubiana is sixty-six and fit as a fiddle. She stresses the word "mademoiselle," proudly asserts her spinsterhood. Camille met her two days ago. She was just coming out of the swimming pool, and they had a chat in a café opposite; her damp hair had a lot of gray. She's the sort of woman who enjoys growing old because it emphasizes her energy. Given her age, she sometimes confuses her former pupils. She laughs. When she runs into parents who talk to her about their children, she pretends to be interested. Not only does she not remember, but she couldn't care less. "I should be ashamed," she comments. But she remembers Alex better than many of the girls she taught—she recognizes her in the photographs, that shocking thinness.

"A charming child, always in and out of my office. She would often come to see me at break time; we got along well together."

Not that Alex talked much, but she did have friends. What was striking about her was her seriousness. "Out of the blue she could suddenly become deathly serious," then a minute later she'd be chatting away again. "It was like she was absent for a moment, as though she fell into a sort of hole—it was most peculiar." When she was in trouble, she would stammer a little. Mlle.. Toubiana refers to it as "fumbling her words."

"I didn't notice it at first. It's rare, because usually I have an eye for these things."

"Maybe it only started in the middle of the school year."

This is what Mlle. Toubiana thinks; she nods. Camille tells her she'll catch flu sitting around with damp hair. She tells him that it doesn't matter, that she catches a cold every autumn. "It's like a vaccine—it keeps me healthy the rest of the year."

"So what do you think might have happened during the year to cause it?"

She doesn't know. She shakes her head, staring at the enigma in the picture; she has no words, no idea—the little girl who until then she had felt was so close has drifted away.

"Did you ever mention the stammer to her mother? Suggest a speech therapist?"

"I thought she'd grow out of it."

Camille observes this aging woman intently. She's got character. Not the kind to have no answer to suggest to such a question. Something rings false, but he doesn't know what.

"The brother, Thomas, did he pick her up from school?"

"Oh yes, all the time."

This tallies with what the mother said: "Her brother always looked out for Alex." A tall boy—"a handsome boy"; Mlle. Toubiana remembers him well. Camille doesn't smile. Thomas was studying at the local vocational school.

"Was she happy that he came to collect her?"

"No, of course not. What do you expect? Little girls always want to be grown-up; she wanted to walk to school and walk home on her own, or with her friends. Her brother was an adult, you understand . . ."

Camille takes the plunge:

"Alex was raped by her brother; it started the year she was in your class."

He lets the words sink in. There is no explosion. Mlle. Toubiana is looking elsewhere, at the café counter, the terrace, the street, as though she's waiting for someone.

"Did Alex try to talk to you about it?"

Mlle. Toubiana sweeps the question aside with the back of her hand.

"Yes, maybe, but if we listened to everything the kids tell us . . . Besides, it was a family matter; it was no concern of mine."

"So Trarieux, Gattegno, Praderie . . ."

Armand seems satisfied.

"Good."

He shuffles some papers.

"Ah, Stefan Maciak. I suppose you didn't know him either?"

Vasseur says nothing. He's clearly waiting to see how things pan out.

"A café over in Reims . . . ," Armand prompts.

"Never set foot in Reims."

"Before that, he had a café in Épinay-sur-Orge. According to the records of your employer, Distrifair, he was on your route between 1987 and 1990; you leased him two pinball machines."

"It's possible."

"It's certain, Monsieur Vasseur, absolutely certain."

Vasseur changes tack. He checks his watch, seems to make a quick calculation, then leans back in his chair and folds his arms across his stomach, ready to wait things out for hours if need be.

"If you want to tell me what you're getting at, maybe I can help you."

1989. The photograph is of a house in Normandy, between Étretat and Saint-Valery, a mansion of brick and stone with a slate roof and a sweeping front lawn with a hammock and an orchard; here the whole family are gathered—the Leroy family. The father would say to people: "Leroy, all one word," as though there might be any doubt. He had extravagant tastes. He'd made his fortune from a chain of DIY shops; he had bought the house from a family engaged in a bitter inheritance dispute and thereafter considered himself lord of the manor. He held great barbecues, sent out invitations to staff that had the air of a summons. He had his eye on a seat on the town council, dreamed of getting into politics because it would look good on his business card.

He called his daughter Reinette—"little queen"—a truly idiotic name to inflict on a girl; the man was capable of anything. Indeed Reinette speaks harshly of her father. She is the one who tells Camille the story; he hadn't asked her anything.

She is in the photograph with Alex, the two girls hugging and laughing. The picture was taken by Reinette's father at some point during a sunny weekend. The day is hot. Behind the girls, the spray from a lawn sprinkler traces a fan shape in the sunlight. The shot is badly framed. M. Leroy clearly was not a gifted photographer. His only talent was for business.

The interview takes place at the Paris offices of R. L. Productions just off the avenue Montaigne. These days, she calls herself "Reine" rather than "Reinette," oblivious to the fact that this makes her even more like her father. She's a TV producer. When her father died, she sold the Normandy house and used the money to set up her own production company. She receives Camille in a living room that is also used as a conference room. Busy bright young people dash around clearly convinced of the importance of their work.

One look at the deep plush sofas and Camille decides not to sit down. He stands for the interview. He says nothing, simply shows her the photograph. On the back, Alex wrote: "*My beloved Reinette, the queen of my heart.*" It's written in a child's hand in purple ink with lots of curlicues. The fountain pen they discovered among Alex's effects had an empty purple ink cartridge inside, and they found a cheap purple ballpoint—it was clearly a fashionable color at the time, or perhaps, like many of Alex's effects, an attempt at being quirky.

At the time of the picture, the girls were in middle school. Reinette had been held back a year, so though they were in the same class, Reinette was almost fifteen, two years older than Alex. In the photograph, she could be a Ukrainian girl, her hair in fine, tight braids pulled back on her head. Looking at it now, she sighs.

"My God, we looked crazy . . ."

Reinette and Alex had been great friends, the way girls can be at that age.

"We were inseparable. We'd be together all day, and when we got home in the evening we spent hours on the telephone. Our parents used to forbid us to use it."

Camille asks questions. Reinette is good at banter. She's not the type to be intimidated.

"What about Thomas?"

Camille is sick and tired of this whole story. The longer it goes on, the more wearisome it feels.

"He started raping his sister in 1986," he says.

Reinette lights a cigarette.

"You were friends at the time; did she say anything to you about it?"

"Yes."

The response is definite. As if to say *I know what you're getting at, let's not take all day about it.*

"Yes . . . what?"

"Yes, nothing. What were you expecting? You think I should have reported it to the police for her? At fifteen?"

Camille says nothing. There are many things he could say if he weren't so exhausted, but what he needs now is information.

"What exactly did she tell you?"

"That he hurt her. Every time, he hurt her."

"How close were you exactly?"

She smiles.

"You want to know if we were sleeping together? At thirteen?"

"Alex was thirteen, you were fifteen."

"That's true. Okay, yes. I initiated her, as they say."

"How long did the relationship last?"

"I don't remember, not long. Alex wasn't exactly . . . committed, if you know what I mean."

"No, I don't know."

"To her it was just a distraction."

"A distraction?"

"What I mean is, she wasn't really interested in a relationship."

"But you managed to persuade her?"

Reine Leroy doesn't like the tone of this sentence.

"Alex made her own decisions! She was perfectly capable of making up her own mind."

"At thirteen? With a brother like hers?"

"Absolutely," Louis takes over again, "I absolutely think that would help us, Monsieur Vasseur."

He seems a little preoccupied.

"There's just one small detail I'd like to clear up first. You say you don't remember Monsieur Maciak, the café owner in Épinay-sur-Orge, and yet according to Distrifair's records you visited him at least seven times in the space of four years."

"Sure, I visited lots of clients . . ."

Reine Leroy stubs out her cigarette.

"I don't know exactly what happened. One day, Alex just disappeared. She was gone for days. And when she came back, it was over. She never spoke to me again. Then later, we moved, and I never saw her again."

"When was this?"

"I couldn't tell you, it's all so long ago. It was late in the year. 1989, maybe . . . I honestly couldn't say."

56

From the far end of the office, Camille is still listening. And drawing. From memory, as always. It is a sketch of Alex at about thirteen, on the lawn of the house in Normandy, posing with her best friend, their arms around each other's waists, clutching plastic cups. Camille is trying to capture her smile in that photograph. Her face. This is what he can't quite catch. In the hotel room, her eyes were lifeless. He can't capture her expression.

"Okay," Louis says. "Let's move on now to Jacqueline Zanetti. Did you know her any better?"

No answer. The net is closing. Louis is like the epitome of a country solicitor, scrupulous, considerate, meticulous, organized. A pain in the ass.

"So, tell me, Monsieur Vasseur, how long have you been working for Distrifair?"

"I started in 1987, as you know very well. I'm warning you, if you've been to see my employer—"

"What?" Camille interrupts him from the far end of the room.

Vasseur wheels around, livid.

"'If we've been to see your employer' . . . ," Camille repeats the phrase. "That sounds like a threat to me. But please, carry on, I'm fascinated."

Vasseur doesn't have time to answer.

"How old were you when you started at Distrifair?" Louis says.

"Eighteen."

"Tell me something . . . ," Camille interrupts once more.

Vasseur is constantly being forced to turn from Louis and Armand to Camille and back again, so he gets up, angrily turns his chair so it's at an angle and he can see all three of them without having to turn this way and that.

"Yes?"

"Were things good between you and Alex at the time?" says Camille.

Vasseur smiles. "My relations with Alex were always good, commissioner."

"Commandant," Camille corrects him.

"Commandant, commissioner, captain . . . I don't give a shit."

"You were sent on a training course by the company," Louis picks up again. "This would have been in 1988, and . . ."

"Okay, all right, fine. I know Zanetti. I fucked her once—let's not make a big deal out of it."

"You were in Toulouse on three separate occasions, each time for a week . . ."

Vasseur makes a face as if to say *What do I know, you think I remember all that?*

"Oh yes, I assure you, we checked. You stayed three times, each time for one week, from the seventeenth to the—"

"Okay, fine, I was there three times!"

"Keep your temper." This is Camille again.

"This routine you three have got going, it's like some old comedy sketch," Vasseur says. "The golden boy leafing through the file, the tramp asking the questions, and the dwarf at the back of the class-room with his coloring book."

Camille sees red. He leaps from his chair and charges. Louis is already on his feet; he puts a restraining hand on his boss's chest, closes his eyes as if to say *I'll handle it.* This is how he often deals with Camille: he mimes the appropriate behavior, hoping that the commandant with fall into line, but this time it does no good.

"And you, you fat bastard, what's your shtick? 'Yeah, I fucked her when she was ten and it was great'—where exactly do you think that's going to get you?"

"I . . . I said no such thing. You're putting words in my mouth." Vasseur sounds hurt. He is very calm, but seems very anxious. "I never said such terrible things. No, what I said was . . ."

Even sitting down he's taller than Camille; it's comical. He takes his time, stressing every word.

"What I said was that I loved my little sister. A lot. There's no harm in that, I assume. It's not against the law, is it?" In an offended tone he adds, "Or is brotherly love a crime these days?"

His words are those of disgust, of revulsion. But his smile says something very different altogether.

For this picture, they have a date. A birthday. On the back, Mme. Prévost has written *Thomas, December 16, 1989.* The day he turned twenty. The photograph was taken outside their house.

"A SEAT Malaga." Mme. Prévost proudly points out the car. "Secondhand, obviously, otherwise I'd never have been able to afford it."

Thomas is leaning on the car door, which is wide open, probably so you can see the faux-leather interior. Alex is standing next to him. For the photograph, he put an arm protectively around his sister's shoulders. When you know, you see things differently. Since the print is small, Camille had to use a magnifying glass to see Alex's face. Unable to sleep the night before, he had drawn this face from memory—he had trouble trying to capture her expression. She is not smiling in the photograph. It being winter, she is wearing a thick coat, but she's obviously still very thin; she is thirteen.

"So how were things between Thomas and his sister?" Camille asks.

"Good, very good," Mme. Prévost says. "He always looked after his sister."

*Thomas comes into my bedroom. He comes nearly every night.
Maman knows.*

Vasseur looks at his watch, not happy.

"You have three children," Camille says.

Vasseur can feel the wind shifting. He's tight lipped.

"Yes. Three."

"And you've got daughters? Two, isn't it?"

Camille leans over and peers at the file open in front of Louis.

"That's right, one called Camille—well, well, just like me—and
Élodie . . . and just how old are they now, the little treasures?"

Vasseur clenches his teeth, says nothing. Louis decides to move
the conversation on, to change the subject.

"So, Jacqueline Zanetti—" he begins, but he doesn't have time to
finish the sentence.

"Nine and eleven!" Camille says.

His plants his finger triumphantly on the case file. His smile van-
ishes in an instant. He turns toward Vasseur.

"And your daughters, Monsieur Vasseur, do you love them very
much? And in case you were worried, no, fatherly love is not against
the law."

Vasseur clenches his teeth harder, his jaw muscles visibly
contracting.

"Are they unstable? Do they need discipline? Though of course
in little girls a need for discipline is often the need for love. Every
father knows that . . ."

Vasseur glares at Camille for a long moment, then suddenly the
pressure seems to ease; he smiles up at the ceiling and gives a big
sigh.

"You're really unsubtle, commandant. It's surprising in a man of
your height. Do you really think I'm going to rise to the bait? To
punch you in the face and give you an opportunity to—"

He looks around at all of them.

"You're not just inept, gentlemen, you're mediocre."

With this, he stands up.

"You set one foot outside this office . . . ," Camille says.

No one knows what's going on. Things have become heated. They're all on their feet, even Louis; it's a standoff. Louis tries to find a way out.

"When you stayed at her hotel, Jacqueline Zanetti was seeing a man named Félix Manière, who was a good deal younger—there was at least twelve years between them. And at the time you would have been nineteen, twenty?"

"You don't have to beat around the bush. Jacqueline was an old slut! The only thing she cared about was fucking younger men. She probably screwed half the guests in the hotel. She pounced on me the minute I walked through the door."

"So," Louis concludes, "Madame Zanetti knew Félix Manière. It's a bit like the chain we had earlier: Gattegno, whom you knew, was friends with Praderie, whom you didn't know, and Madame Zanetti, whom you knew, was acquainted with Monsieur Manière, whom you didn't know."

Louis turns to Camille worriedly. "I'm not sure I'm being clear."

"No, I'm afraid it doesn't sound very clear at all," Camille says.

"I thought as much. Let me just clarify things."

He turns to Vasseur.

"Directly or indirectly, you knew all the people your sister murdered." He turns back to his boss. "Is that better?"

Camille does not seem especially enthusiastic. "Sorry, Louis, I don't mean to be rude, but you're still not being completely clear."

"You think?"

"Yes, I think."

Vasseur's head whips backwards and forwards; these fucking assholes . . .

"Would you mind?"

With a chivalrous flourish, Louis steps aside.

"So, Monsieur Vasseur," Camille says. "Your sister Alex . . ."

"Yes?"

"Exactly how many times did you sell her?"

Silence.

"Let's see: Gattegno, Praderie, Manière... You see, we're not sure we've got the whole list. That's why we need your help, because since you ran the show, you must know how many people you invited around to abuse Alex."

Vasseur is outraged.

"Are you calling my sister a whore? Have you no respect for the dead?"

A smile begins to play on his lips.

"So tell me, gentlemen, how exactly are you planning to prove all this? I repeat, are you going to get Alex to testify?"

He gives the policemen a taste of his wit.

"Are you going to put the customers on the witness stand? It won't be easy. They're not in terribly good health, these alleged clients, are they?"

Whether she's writing in a copybook or a notepad, Alex never gives the date. What she writes is vague—she is afraid of words, even when she's alone with her diary; she can't seem to bring herself to say it. It's as though she can't find the words. She writes:

Thursday, Thomas came with a friend of his, Pascal. They were at school together. Pascal seems really stupid. Thomas made me stand in front of him, he gave me that look he has. His friend giggled. When we went into the bedroom, he was still giggling, he giggles all the time. Thomas said: you be a good girl for my friend here. Afterwards, it was just him and me in the bedroom, he was on top of me laughing, even when he hurt me, it was as if he couldn't stop. I didn't want to cry in front of him.

Camille can well imagine the moron pounding away at the girl and giggling. It would have been easy to convince him of anything: maybe even that she was enjoying it. But whatever it says about Pascal Trarieux, about Thomas Vasseur it speaks volumes.

"This is all very well," Vasseur says, slapping his thighs, "but it's getting late. Are we done, gentlemen?"

"Just one or two minor points, if you don't mind."

Vasseur ostentatiously checks his watch, hesitates for a moment, and then accedes to Louis's request.

"Okay, then, but be quick about it; they'll be starting to worry at home."

He folds his arms, as if to say *I'm listening.*

"I'd like, if I may, to outline our theories to you," Louis says.

"Good. Personally I like things to be very clear, especially when it comes to theories."

He seems genuinely happy.

"When you started sleeping with your sister, Alex was ten years old and you were seventeen."

Vasseur worriedly looks from Camille to Louis.

"We are agreed, gentlemen, that you are simply continuing with what are pure speculations."

"Absolutely, Monsieur Vasseur," Louis says at once. "I am simply outlining our theories, and I merely ask that you point out any internal inconsistencies . . . things that could not be true, that sort of thing."

Louis may sound as though he's going overboard, but in fact this is his usual style.

"Fine," Vasseur says. "So, these hypotheses of yours . . ."

"The first is that you sexually abused your sister when she was barely ten years old. An offense, according to article 222 of the penal code, punishable by twenty years' imprisonment."

Vasseur raises his finger, his voice professorial.

"If charges were brought, if the case were proven, if . . ."

"Of course," Louis interrupts him, no longer smiling. "It's merely a supposition."

Vasseur is satisfied; he's the kind of guy who wants everything done by the book.

"Our second hypothesis is that, after you had abused her, you loaned her out and probably even rented her to other men. Pimping, contrary to article 225 of the penal code, is punishable by up to ten years' imprisonment."

"Hang on, hang on! You said 'loaned' a minute ago. The other officer . . . ," he nods toward Camille at the far end of the office, "said 'sold.'"

"I'd like to propose 'rented,'" Louis says.

"Sold! Just joking . . . Okay, let's go with 'rented.'"

"Rented out to others. First Pascal Trarieux, an old school friend, then Monsieur Gattegno, a customer (in both senses since you were also renting him pinball machines). Monsieur Gattegno clearly recommended your services to his friend Monsieur Praderie. As for Madame Zanetti, a woman you knew intimately, having stayed in her hotel, she did not hesitate to suggest your services to her young lover Monsieur Félix Manière, probably as a way to keep him sweet. Maybe to make sure he didn't leave her."

"This isn't just a theory, it's a whole library."

"And it has no basis in fact?"

"None at all, to my knowledge. But I admire your logic. And your imagination. Alex herself would probably be impressed."

"Impressed by what?"

"By all the effort you're making for a dead girl."

He glances from one officer to the other.

"It's not as if she would care anymore."

"Do you think your mother would care? Your wife? Your children?"

"Oh, no!"

He looks first Louis, then Camille, straight in the eyes.

"I'm afraid, gentlemen, that to make such an accusation with no proof and no witnesses would be libel, pure and simple. You do know that's a crime?"

Thomas says I'll like him because he's called Félix, same as the cat. His mother paid for him to come. He doesn't look anything like a cat. The whole time, he just stared at me, he didn't say anything. But he had this weird smile, he looks as if he wants to eat my head. For a long time afterwards, I could still see his head, his eyes.

There is no other mention of Félix in the notebook, but there is one later, in one of the copybooks. It's very brief.

The cat came back. He stared at me for a long time again and smiled like he did the first time. Afterwards, he told me to get in a different position and he hurt me a lot. He and Thomas weren't happy because I was crying too loud.

Alex is twelve, Félix twenty-six.

The awkward silence drags on for a long time.

"In this 'library' of theories," Louis says finally, "there remains only one point that we need to clear up."

"Let's have done with it, then."

"How did Alex manage to track down all these people? Because, after all, the original events took place almost twenty years ago. Alex had changed a lot; we know that she went under various aliases, that she took her time, had a strategy. In each of her encounters, she was very methodical. With each of them, the role she played was convincing. A fat, rather slovenly girl for Pascal Trarieux, a classic beauty for Félix Manière . . . But the question remains: how did Alex track all these people down?"

Vasseur looks at Camille, back at Louis, then back at Camille as though he doesn't know which way to turn.

"You're not telling me . . . ," he says in mock horror, "that you don't have a theory?"

Camille turns around. Sometimes in this job you have to make sacrifices.

"Actually, we do," Louis says modestly. "We have a theory."

"Aaaah . . . Come on then, I'm all ears."

"Just as we suspect that you gave Jean-Pierre Trarieux the name and address of your sister, we suspect that you also helped your sister trace these people."

"But before Alex bumped off all 'these people' . . . And assuming that I knew them," he waggles a peremptory finger, "how would I know how to find them twenty years later?"

"In the first place, many of them still lived where they did twenty years ago. In the second, I suspect you only had to give her the names and Alex made her own inquiries."

Vasseur gives a slow hand clap, then suddenly stops.

"And why exactly would I do such a thing?"

57

Mme. Prévost wants the world to know she's not afraid of poverty. She's a woman of the people, she wasn't born with a silver spoon, she dragged up two kids on her own, she's not beholden to anyone . . . all these platitudes are obvious from the way she sits bolt upright on her chair. She's not about to let herself be taken in.

Monday, 4:00 p.m.

Her son has been summoned to arrive at 5:00 p.m.; Camille has coordinated the visits to make sure they don't see each other, don't have an opportunity to talk.

The first time, the day the body was identified at the mortuary, she was invited to come in. This time, it is a very different matter: she's been summoned, not that she seems to care—the woman has built her life around her like a fortress. She is determined to be impregnable. What she is protecting is inside her. It's an uphill struggle. She didn't come to the morgue to identify her daughter; she told Camille it was too much for her to bear. Seeing her now, sitting opposite him, Camille doubts she has any such weaknesses. But the fact remains that for all her prim propriety, her uncompromising stare, her defiant silence, she is intimidated by the headquarters of the *brigade criminelle*, and by this little man next to her, feet dangling off the ground, who stares at her intently as he asks: "What exactly do you know about the relationship between Thomas and Alex?"

She looks surprised, as though to say what "exactly" is there to know about the relationship between a brother and sister? That said, her eyes flutter briefly. Camille lets the seconds tick by, but it's a zero-sum game. He knows, and she knows that he knows. It's tedious. Camille is out of patience.

"At what age precisely did your son begin raping Alex?"

She makes a terrible fuss. No surprise there.

"Madame Prévost," Camille says, smiling, "don't take me for a fool. In fact, I advise you to do everything you can to help me because otherwise I'm going to make sure your son's locked up for the rest of his natural life."

Threatening her son has the desired effect. She doesn't care what happens to her, but no one touches her son. Even so, she sticks to her guns.

"Thomas loved his sister; he would never have touched a hair on her head."

"We're not discussing her hair."

Mme. Prévost is impervious to Camille's humor. She shakes her head; it's hard to know whether this means that she doesn't know or that she refuses to say.

"If you were aware of what was happening and you allowed it to continue, you are guilty of accessory to aggravated rape."

"Thomas never touched his sister!"

"How do you know?"

"I know my son."

They're going around in circles. This is impossible: there's no charge, no witnesses, no crime, no victim, no executioner.

Camille sighs and nods.

Thomas comes into my bedroom. He comes nearly every night. Maman knows.

"What about your daughter? Did you know her well?"

"As well as any mother knows her daughter."

"That sounds promising."

"I beg your pardon—"

"No, nothing."

Camille takes out the slim case file.

"The autopsy report. Since you knew your daughter, I assume you know what's in here."

Camille puts on his glasses. Meaning *I'm dead on my feet, but here goes.*

"It's a little technical. I'll translate."

Mme. Prévost hasn't batted an eyelid since she got here. She sits ramrod straight, her very bones stiff, her every muscle tensed, her whole body an act of resistance.

"She was in a terrible state, your daughter, wasn't she?"

She stares ahead at the partition wall. It looks as if she's holding her breath.

"According to the pathologist," he goes on, leafing through the report, "your daughter's genital area showed signs of acid burns. I'm guessing sulfuric acid. What people used to call vitriol . . . These were deep and extensive burns. The clitoris was entirely destroyed—it seems to have been a form of female circumcision—the acid melted the labia majora and the labia minora and penetrated deep into the vagina. The acid was poured directly into the vagina in sufficient quantities that it mutilated everything. The mucous membranes were almost entirely destroyed, the flesh literally dissolved, leaving the whole genital area looking like magma."

Camille looks up at Mme. Prévost, stares hard at her.

"That's the phrase the pathologist used: 'a magma of flesh.' All this would have happened long ago; Alex would have been a young girl. Does it ring any bells?"

Mme. Prévost looks at Camille; she is deathly pale, and her head shakes like a robot.

"Your daughter never spoke to you about it?"

"Never!"

The word bursts out like a gust of wind, the sudden crack of the family banner.

"I see. Your daughter didn't want to bother you with her little problems. It probably just happened: someone poured a pint of acid into her vagina, and she just came home as usual as if nothing had happened. A model of discretion."

"I don't know."

Nothing about her has changed: not the expression, not the posture, but her voice is solemn.

"The pathologists pointed out something else that's curious," Camille goes on. "The whole genital area was profoundly affected, nerve endings destroyed, the natural orifices permanently fused and disfigured. Your daughter would never have been able to have normal sexual relations. To say nothing of any other hopes she might have had. But, as I was saying, the curious thing . . ."

Camille stops, drops the report, takes off his glasses, and sets them down in front of him, folds his arms and stares hard at Alex's mother.

"Is that the urinary tract was crudely 'patched up.' Because obviously this was a life-threatening condition. With the flesh fused together, she would have died within hours. According to our pathologist, it was botched, brutal: a cannula forced through the meatus to open up the urinary tract."

Silence.

"According to him, the result is nothing short of miraculous. And an act of butchery. That's not how he puts it in his report, but that's the gist."

Mme. Prévost tries to swallow, but her throat is dry; she seems about to choke, to cough, but no, nothing.

"Now obviously he's a doctor. I'm a police officer. He makes observations; my job is to draw conclusions. And my theory is that this had to be done quickly. To make sure Alex didn't have to go to the hospital. Because they would have asked a lot of awkward questions, like the name of the man who had done this—I'm assuming it was a man—because the extent of the injuries was such that it could not have been an accident, it had to have been deliberate. Alex, brave little girl that she was, didn't want to make a fuss; you knew her, it wasn't her style, she was discreet . . ."

Mme. Prévost finally manages to swallow.

"Tell me, Mme. Prévost, how long have you worked as a nursing assistant?"

Thomas Vasseur bows his head. He has listened to the conclusions of the autopsy report in complete silence. He is now staring at Louis, who has been reading the report aloud, and when Vasseur does not react, he asks:

"Anything you'd like to say?"

Vasseur spreads his hands.

"It's all very sad."

"So you know about it?"

"Alex had no secrets from her big brother," Vasseur says with a smile.

"In that case, you'll be able to explain exactly how it happened, won't you?"

"I'm afraid not. Alex mentioned it in passing, that's all. I mean it was very private . . . She was very evasive."

"So there's nothing you can tell us about it?"

"I'm sorry."

"You have no particulars?"

"None."

"No details?"

"No."

"No theory?"

"Well, I suppose . . . maybe someone got a little annoyed. Very annoyed."

"Someone . . . you don't know who?"

Vasseur smiles again.

"No idea."

"So you think 'someone' got angry . . . About what?"

"I couldn't say. That's just what I gathered."

It's almost as though, until now, he'd been testing the water and has finally decided that he likes it. They aren't being aggressive, these policemen, they've got nothing on him, no hard evidence—all this is written on his face. Besides, provocation is in his nature.

"You know . . . Alex could be a pain in the neck sometimes."

"How so?"

"Well, she could be stubborn. She threw tantrums . . . you get the idea."

And since no one reacts, Vasseur can't be sure he's made his point.

"What I mean is, with a girl like that you're bound to get angry. Maybe it was not having a father, but there was a side to her that was . . . defiant. Deep down, I think she had issues with authority. So sometimes, when the mood took her, she'd say no, and you couldn't get a thing out of her."

It almost feels as though Vasseur is reliving the scene rather than recounting it.

"That's what she was like. Out of the blue, for no reason, she'd start up. I swear she could really get on your nerves."

"Is that what happened?" Louis asks in a faint, almost inaudible voice.

"I don't know," Vasseur says carefully, "I wasn't there."

He smiles at the officers.

"All I'm saying is that Alex was the kind of girl this sort of thing eventually happens to. She'd be pigheaded, stubborn . . . Eventually you run out of patience."

Armand, who hasn't uttered a word in the past hour, is rooted to the spot.

Louis is white as a sheet; he's beginning to lose his composure. With him, this takes the form of an exaggerated formality.

"But . . . we are not talking about a garden variety spanking here, Monsieur Vasseur! We are talking about committing cruel, barbaric acts on a child who was not yet fifteen and who had been pimped out to adult men!"

He stresses every word, articulates every syllable. Camille can see how upset he is. Once again Vasseur, who is still perfectly composed, has got the better of him, and he's determined to rub his nose in it.

"If your theory about prostitution is correct, I'd say it was an occupational hazard."

This time, Louis is flummoxed. He glances around for Camille. Camille smiles at him; he has seen it all and come through it. He nods as though he understands, as though he agrees with Vasseur's conclusion.

"And did your mother know?" he says.

"About what? Oh, that—no . . . Alex didn't want to worry her with her little problems. My mother had her fair share of problems. No, our mother never knew."

"That's a pity," Camille says. "She would have been able to offer advice. Being a nurse, I mean. She would have been able to take emergency action."

Vasseur simply nods, adopts a hurt expression. "What can you do?" he says resignedly. "We can't rewrite history."

"So when you found out this had happened, you didn't want to press charges?"

Vasseur looks at Camille in surprise.

"But . . . against whom?"

What Camille hears is "But, why?"

58

It is 7:00 p.m. Night drew in so stealthily that no one has realized that for some time now the interview has been taking place in a half-light that makes everything seem unreal.

Thomas Vasseur is tired. He struggles to his feet, as though he's just spent the night playing cards, puts his hands on his hips, arches his back, and heaves a sigh of relief, stretching his stiff legs. The officers remain seated. Armand looks at the case file to give an impression of calm. Louis cautiously brushes the desk with the back of his hand. Camille also stands up; he walks to the door, then turns back and says wearily:

"Your half sister, Alex, was blackmailing you. Why don't we pick up from there, if it's all right with you."

"No, sorry," Vasseur yawns. His expression is apologetic: he'd like to help, would be happy to oblige, but it's not possible. He rolls down his shirtsleeves.

"I really have to get home now."

"You could just call . . ."

Vasseur waves his hand as though refusing to stay for one last round.

"Honestly . . ."

"You have two options, Monsieur Vasseur. Either you sit down and answer our questions, which should only take an hour or two . . ."

"Or . . . ?" Vasseur puts his hands flat on the table.

Head bowed, he looks up, the heavy-browed stare of a movie hero about to pull a gun, but here it falls flat.

"Or I arrest you, which allows me to keep you in custody for at least twenty-four hours. We'd probably be allowed to hold you for forty-eight hours—the magistrate is a big fan of victims; he wouldn't have any problem letting us keep you a little longer."

Vasseur stares, wide eyed.

"Arrest me . . . on what charge?"

"It doesn't matter—aggravated rape, torture, procuring, murder, acts of barbarism, whatever you like; personally, I don't give a shit. But do say if you've got a preference . . ."

"But you've got no proof! Of anything!"

He explodes. He's been patient, very patient, but that's all over now. The police are abusing their authority.

"Fuck you! I'm out of here."

At this point, everything happens very quickly.

Vasseur says something that no one catches, grabs his jacket, and before anyone can move he has dashed to the door, flung it open, and has one foot outside. The two uniformed officers standing guard in the corridor immediately intervene. Vasseur stops, turns back.

"I think," Camille says, "that perhaps it would be best to arrest you. Let's say for murder. All right with you?"

"You've got nothing on me. You're just busting my balls—that's it, isn't it?"

He closes his eyes, prepared once more to tough it out, shuffles back into the office. He has realized he's fighting a losing battle.

"You have the right to make one telephone call to a relative," Camille advises him, "and to see a doctor."

"No, I want to see a lawyer."

59

Le Guen informs the magistrate about the arrest and Armand takes care of the formalities. It's always a race against time, since police custody is limited to twenty-four hours.

Vasseur does not object to anything; he wants this over and done with. He needs to square things with his wife, blame everything on these assholes. He agrees to remove his shoelaces, his belt, lets them take his fingerprints, his DNA—let them take what they want—all he cares about is that this is handled quickly. He refuses to speak while he waits for his lawyer. He will respond to administrative questions, but otherwise he's not saying anything; he is waiting.

And he calls his wife.

"It's work—nothing serious, but I can't get away right now. Don't worry. I've been unavoidably detained."

In the circumstances, the choice of words seems unfortunate; he tries to think of something, but he's not prepared, he's not used to having to justify himself. So having no excuses, he adopts an overbearing tone that clearly says: stop bugging me with these trivial questions. On the other end of the line there is embarrassed silence, a refusal to understand.

"I already told you, I can't get away right now!" Vasseur shouts. He can't help himself. "You'll just have to go on your own."

Camille wonders whether he hits his wife.

"I'll be home tomorrow."

He doesn't say what time.

"Right, I have to go now . . . Yeah, me too. Yeah, I'll call you later."

It is 8:15 p.m. Vasseur's lawyer arrives at 11:00 p.m., a forceful, energetic young man none of them has met before, but he clearly knows his stuff. He has half an hour in which to confer with his client, tell him how to behave, advise prudence, prudence at all costs, and wish him luck—because without seeing the case file, in thirty minutes there's not much more he can do.

Camille decides to go home, shower, change. A few minutes later, the taxi drops him outside his place. He takes the elevator; Camille has to be utterly exhausted to decide not to take the stairs.

The parcel is waiting outside his door, wrapped in brown paper, tied up with string. Camille knows what it is at once. He grabs it and goes into his apartment. Doudouche gets only the most perfunctory pat on the head.

It gives him an odd feeling, seeing Maud Verhœven's self-portrait. Eighteen thousand euros.

It has to be Louis. He was out of the office this morning, didn't get in until 2:00 p.m. To Louis, spending eighteen thousand euros on a painting is nothing. Still, Camille feels uncomfortable. In situations like this it's difficult to know what's implicitly owed to the other person, what's expected, what to do. Accept, refuse, say something? What? Gifts always imply some form of quid pro quo—what is Louis expecting to get in return? As he undresses and gets into the shower, Camille reluctantly returns to his worries about what to do with the proceeds of the auction. The idea of donating it all to good causes is terrible—it's a gesture that says to his mother *I want nothing more to do with you.*

He's a little old to be thinking like this, but when it comes to parents, you're never done—look at Alex. He towels himself off, reaffirms his decision. He'll do it calmly. Giving up the money is hardly disowning his mother. It's just a means of closure.

Am I really going to do this, give everything away?

The self-portrait, on the other hand, he plans to keep. He looks at it as he gets dressed again; he has propped it up on the sofa opposite him. He's happy to have it back. It's a magnificent work. He's not angry with his mother—surely this is what wanting to keep the painting means. For the first time, this man who has always been told he takes after his father sees in the painting a resemblance he himself has to his mother. It comforts him. He is sorting his life out. He doesn't know where this is heading.

Just before setting off again to the *brigade*, Camille remembers Doudouche and opens a can of cat food.

As Camille arrives back at the office, he runs into the lawyer, who's just finishing up. Armand called time on the client briefing. Thomas Vasseur is still in the main office. Armand has opened the windows to let some air in. The place feels rather chilly now.

When Louis appears, Camille gives him a nod of complicity, but Louis looks at him puzzled; Camille signals to him that they'll talk about it later.

Vasseur looks to be rather ill at ease; his five o'clock shadow seems to be developing at an alarming rate, like some ad for fertilizer, but there's still the flicker of a smile on his face that says *You want to send me down, but you've got nothing on me and you'll get nothing. You want war? Bring it on. You must think I'm a complete idiot.* His lawyer advised him to wait and see—always the best tactic—to weigh his words, do nothing rash. For Vasseur, the race against time works the other way: he needs to stall, to drag things out. The lawyer said in order to prolong the detention period, they'll have to go back to the magistrate with something new, and they won't have anything. Camille can see it all in the way Vasseur's mouth opens and closes, the way he puffs out his chest; he's doing breathing exercises.

People say that the first minutes of any encounter encompass the whole relationship in miniature. Camille remembers that the first time he met Vasseur, he hated him on sight. This has had a significant bearing on how he has conducted this case. And Vidard knows this.

Deep down, Camille and the magistrate are not so different. This is a depressing realization.

Le Guen told Camille that Vidard approved of his strategy. Wonders will never cease. Right now, Camille's feelings are complicated. Now that the magistrate has come down firmly on his side, Camille needs to rethink how he's going to play this. It's irritating.

Armand begins by noting aloud the date and time, the names and ranks of those present, like the chorus in a Greek tragedy.

Camille takes the lead.

"Before we get started, we'll have no more of your crap about 'theories.'"

Change of tactics. As he says this, Camille marshals his thoughts, checks his watch.

"So, Alex was blackmailing you."

There's a tension in his voice. It is as if he is worried about something else.

"Talk me through that," Vasseur says.

Camille turns to Armand, who, caught off guard, flicks his way through the case file, which seems to take an age. Post-it notes and loose sheets of paper flutter everywhere; you have to wonder whether the French Republic has put its faith in the right men. But he finds it: Armand always finds what he's looking for.

"A loan from your employer Distrifair for twenty thousand euros on February 15, 2005. Your house was already mortgaged to the hilt, you couldn't go to the bank, so you asked your boss. You're paying the loan back monthly as a percentage of your earnings."

Vasseur looks doubtful.

"So what?"

Camille gestures to Armand, the loyal dogged detective, who takes over.

"Your bank confirms that you deposited a check from your employer to the value of twenty thousand euros on February 15, 2005, and drew out the same sum in cash on February 18."

Camille closes his eyes, silently cheering. He opens them again.

"And why exactly might you need twenty thousand euros in cash, Monsieur Vasseur?"

A moment's hesitation. Even when you're expecting it, the worst can still come back and bite you on the ass; this is what's written on Vasseur's face. They've been to see his boss. He's been in custody for five hours, and there are nineteen hours to go; having spent a career in sales, Vasseur isn't trained to withstand shocks. He's taking a hammering here.

"Gambling debts."

"You gambled with your sister and you lost, that it?"

"No, it's nothing to do with Alex . . . it was someone else."

"Who?"

Vasseur is having difficulty breathing.

"Let's save time, shall we?" Camille says. "The twenty thousand euros was clearly intended for Alex. When we found her body in the hotel room, she still had a little less than twelve thousand euros. We recovered your fingerprints from several of the plastic security strips."

They've gone this far. Just how far back have they gone? What do they know? What do they want now?

Camille can see these questions in the wrinkles on Vasseur's forehead, in his eyes, in the tremor of his hands. It's deeply unprofessional, and Camille would never admit it to anyone, but he loathes Vasseur. He despises him. He wants to kill him. He wants to kill him. He had that same thought about the magistrate a couple of weeks ago. You're not in this job by accident, he thinks; you're a potential killer.

"Okay, fine," Vasseur concedes. "I lent the money to my sister. Is that illegal?"

Camille relaxes, as though he's just chalked a cross on the wall. He smiles, but it is not a nice smile.

"You know perfectly well that it's not illegal, so why did you lie?"

"It's none of your business."

Precisely the words not to say.

"In the situation you're in, what precisely is none of the police's business?"

Le Guen calls. Camille steps out of the office. The divisionnaire wants to know where they're at. Difficult to say. Camille opts for being reassuring.

"Not bad. We're getting there."

Le Guen doesn't respond.

"What about your end?"

"The custody extension: it's going to be tough, but we'll make it happen."

"Then we'd better get our act together."

"Your sister was n—"

"Half sister," Vasseur corrects him.

"Your half sister, then. Does it make a difference?"

"Of course. It's not remotely the same—you could at least be accurate."

Camille glances from Louis to Armand as though to say: "See, he can handle himself."

"In that case, let's just call her Alex. You see, we're not at all convinced that Alex was planning to kill herself."

"Well, that's what she did."

"Indeed. But you knew her better than anyone; maybe you can explain it to us. If she wanted to die, why was she planning to leave the country?"

Vasseur raises an eyebrow; he doesn't understand the question.

Camille simply nods at Louis.

"Your sister . . . Excuse me, Alex bought a plane ticket in her own name the night she died, a flight to Zurich leaving the following morning, October 5, at 8:40 a.m. In fact, while she was at the airport, she bought a travel bag, which we found in her hotel room neatly packed and ready to go."

"That's news to me . . . Maybe she changed her mind. As I told you, she was unstable."

"She checked in to a hotel near the airport; she even ordered a taxi, although her car was in the hotel parking lot. She obviously didn't want to have the hassle of trying to find somewhere to park and maybe missing her flight. She wanted to make a quick getaway. She also dumped a lot of her personal effects—she was planning to leave nothing behind, not even the bottles of acid. We had forensics test it, by the way: it's the same stuff she used in the murders, sulfuric acid at 80 percent concentration. She was running away, leaving France. She was absconding."

"What do you want me to say? I can't answer for her. No one can answer for her now."

Vasseur glances from Armand to Louis, looking for confirmation, but his heart isn't in it.

"Granted, you can't answer for Alex," Camille says, "but you *are* able to answer for your own actions."

"By all means, if I can . . ."

"Of course you can. On the night of Alex's death, October 4, where were you, let's say between 8:00 p.m. and midnight?"

Vasseur hesitates. Camille rushes in.

"We'll help you out . . . Armand?"

Curiously, perhaps to emphasize the drama of the moment, Armand gets to his feet, like a schoolboy asked to stand up and recite. Diligently, he reads his notes aloud.

"You received a call at 8:34 p.m. on your cell phone; you were at home at the time. As your wife says: 'Thomas got a voice mail from work, some sort of emergency.' A call from work at that hour was very unusual. 'He was very annoyed,' she told us. In her statement, your wife said you left home at around 10:00 p.m., and you didn't get back until after midnight. She can't be more precise—she was asleep so didn't notice the time, but it could not have been before midnight since that was when she went to bed."

Vasseur has a lot of information to digest. His wife has been questioned. He wondered about that earlier. What else?

"However," Armand goes on, "we know that this was not true."

"Why do you say that, Armand?" Camille says.

"Because the call that Monsieur Vasseur received at 8:34 p.m. was from Alex. The call was logged because she made it from the telephone in her hotel room. We will, of course, check with Monsieur Vasseur's phone provider, but his boss has confirmed that there was no such emergency. In fact he said, 'In our business, we don't get callouts in the middle of the night. We're not the ambulance services.'"

"A very astute point . . . ," Camille says, turning back to Vasseur. But he doesn't have time to press his advantage.

"Alex left me a message," Vasseur blurts out. "She wanted to see me, told me to meet her at half past eleven at Aulnay-sous-Bois."

"Aulnay . . . that would be very near Villepinte. where she died. Okay, it's eight thirty; your darling sister calls. What did you do?"

"I went."

"Were they a regular occurrence, these meetings?"

"Not really."

"What did she want?"

"She asked me to meet her, gave me an address—it was only supposed to be for an hour."

Vasseur continues to weigh his words, but in the heat of the discussion, Camille can tell he wants to get it all out; the sentences rattle off like machine gun fire. Vasseur is desperately trying to keep his composure, to stick to his strategy.

"So what did you think she wanted?"

"I didn't know."

"Really? You didn't know?"

"She didn't tell me."

"To recapitulate: Last year, she extorted twenty thousand euros from you. In our opinion, she did so by threatening to wreak havoc in your little domestic arrangements, to tell your wife and kids that you raped her when she was ten, that you prostituted her . . ."

"You've got no proof!" Vasseur is on his feet, screaming.

Camille smiles. Vasseur losing his cool is a bonus.

"Sit down," Camille says calmly. "I said *in our opinion*—it's a theory. I know how much you love theories."

He lets the seconds tick by.

"Actually, on the subject of proof, Alex had conclusive proof that her childhood had not been a happy one. She had only to go and see your wife. Women can tell each other these things, even show them . . . If Alex had shown your wife the injuries to her private parts, I am willing to wager that it would have created a bit of a stir in the Vasseur house. So, to go back to what I was saying . . . *In our opinion*, since she planned to leave the country the following day, she had almost nothing in her bank account and only twelve thousand euros in cash . . . she called you to ask for more money."

"She didn't say anything about money in her message. Anyway, where would I get money in the middle of the night?"

"We think that Alex was letting you know that you'd have to come up with the money soon, by the time she got herself settled abroad. And that you were going to have to get yourself organized, because she was going to need more money . . . It's expensive, being on the run. But I'm sure we'll get back to that. For the moment, we've got you leaving your house in the middle of the night . . . What did you do?"

"I went to the address she gave me."

"What address?"

"137 boulevard Jouvenel."

"And what exactly is at 137 boulevard Jouvenel?"

"That's the weird thing. Nothing."

"What do you mean, nothing?"

"I don't know, nothing."

Louis doesn't even need Camille to glance over at him; he's already typing the address into an online mapping site. A few seconds later, he beckons Camille over.

"Well, well, you're right, there's nothing. Offices at 135, a dry cleaner at 139, and in between, number 137, a shop for sale. Boarded up. Do you think she was planning to buy a shop?"

Louis moves the mouse to explore the map onscreen; it's obvious from his expression he's come up with nothing.

"Obviously not," Vasseur says, "but I don't know what she did want since she didn't show up."

"Didn't you try to call her?"

"The number was disconnected."

"That's true, we checked. Alex canceled her cell phone contract three days earlier. In preparation for her departure, probably. So how long did you stand in front of this shop for sale?"

"Until midnight."

"You're a patient man. That's good. Love is patient, everyone knows that. Did anyone see you?"

"I don't think so."

"That's unfortunate."

"For you, maybe: you're the ones who have something to prove, not me."

"It's not unfortunate for you or for me, it's just unfortunate; it leaves a gray area, creates doubt, makes your story sound like a fabrication. But never mind. I'm assuming that that's all there is, that when your sister failed to show up, you simply went home."

Vasseur doesn't answer. An MRI scan would reveal his neurons scrabbling to come up with a solution.

"Well?" Camille says. "Did you go home?"

Despite marshaling all its resources, Vasseur's brain cannot come up with a satisfactory solution.

"No. I went to the hotel."

He's taken the plunge.

"Well, well," Camille says, astonished. "So you knew which hotel she was staying in?"

"No. Alex had called me, so I just dialed the last incoming number."

"Very ingenious! And . . . ?"

"There was no answer. I got an answering machine."

"Ah, what a pity. So you drove off home."

This time the two hemispheres of the brain all but collide. Vasseur closes his eyes. Something tells him this is not the right strategy, but he doesn't know what else to do.

"No," he says finally, "As I said, I went to the hotel. It was closed. There was no receptionist on duty."

"Louis?" Camille turns to his colleague.

"The reception desk is open until half past ten. After that, there's a key code you need to enter to get in. It's given to hotel guests when they arrive."

"So." Camille turns back to Vasseur. "Then you drove back home."

"Yes."

Camille turns toward his fellow officers.

"Well, what an adventure! Armand . . . you look dubious . . ."

Armand does not stand up this time.

"Witness statement from one Monsieur Leboulanger and one Madame Farida."

"Are you sure of that?"

Armand glances at his notes again.

"No, sorry, you're right. Farida is her first name. Madame Farida Sartaoui."

"You'll have to excuse my colleague—he's always had problems with foreign names. So these people were . . . ?"

"Staying at the hotel," Armand goes on. "They got back at fifteen minutes past twelve."

"Okay, okay!" Vasseur roars. "Okay, fine!"

60

Le Guen picks up on the first ring.

"We're about to call it a night."

"What have you got?"

"Where are you?" Camille says.

Le Guen hesitates, which means he's with a woman, which means he's in love—Le Guen doesn't do casual flings, it's not his thing—and that means . . .

"Jean, I told you last time, I will not act as your witness at another wedding. It's out of the question!"

"Yeah, I know, don't sweat it. I'm not planning to fall in love here."

"Can I quote you on that?"

"You certainly can."

"Now you really are starting to worry me!"

"How are things with you?"

Camille checks his watch.

"Lent money to the sister, got a call from the sister, went into the hotel where the sister was staying."

"Good. Will it hold up?"

"It'll be enough; we have to be patient. I just hope the magistrate—"

"Don't worry. As far as this goes, he's on our side."

"Good. Well, in that case the best thing to do now is get some sleep."

And it's night.

3:00 a.m. He couldn't stop himself, and, for once, he managed to deal with it by himself. Five blows, no more, no less. The neighbors are very fond of Camille, but even so, banging nails into the wall at that hour . . . The first hammer blow surprises, the second wakes, the third astonishes, the fourth shocks, the fifth has neighbors thumping on the walls. There is no sixth: silence returns. Camille can hang Maud Verhœven's self-portrait on the living room wall; the nail holds firm. As does Camille.

He had intended to catch up with Louis as they were leaving the *brigade* offices, but Louis had already left, disappeared. He'll see him tomorrow. What will he say? Camille trusts to his intuition, to the situation; he plans to keep the painting, to thank Louis—a lovely gesture—and to reimburse him. Or maybe not. This thing about the 280,000 euros is still going around in his head.

Ever since he's lived alone, he's slept with the curtains open; he likes to be awakened by the dawn. Doudouche has crept up beside him. He can't get to sleep. He spends the night on the sofa, staring up at the painting.

Obviously the interrogation of Vasseur has been an ordeal, but that's not the only thing.

What was kindled in him some nights ago in the studio in Montfort, what assailed him in the hotel room when he came face-to-face with the corpse of Alex Prévost is now before him.

This case has allowed him to exorcize the death of Irène, to make his peace with his mother.

The image of Alex, the plain-faced little girl, makes him want to weep.

The childlike handwriting in her diary, the pathetic collection of objects she kept; this whole story breaks his heart.

He feels as though, deep down, he is just like everyone else.

Even for him, Alex is just a means to an end.

He has used her.

In the course of the next seventeen hours, Vasseur is taken from his cell on three occasions and led back to the offices of the *brigade*. Twice, Armand is there to meet him; the last time it is Louis. They go over details, and Armand gets him to confirm the exact dates of his stays in Toulouse.

"It was twenty years ago—what fucking difference does it make?" Vasseur explodes.

Armand gives him a look that says *Hey, don't have a go at me, I'm just following orders.*

Vasseur is prepared to sign anything, prepared to acknowledge anything.

"You've got nothing on me, absolutely nothing."

"In that case," says Louis, who is now leading the interview, "you've got nothing to be afraid of, Monsieur Vasseur."

Time drags on, the hours pass; Vasseur is convinced this is a good sign. He was taken from his cell again and asked to sign something confirming the dates on which he met with Stefan Maciak as a sales rep.

"I don't give a fuck," he says and signs.

He glances at the clock on the wall. No one can accuse him of anything.

He's unshaven and has scarcely washed.

He is led out again. This time it is Camille's turn. The moment he walks into the room, he looks up at the wall clock. 8:00 p.m. It has been a long day. Vasseur is triumphant, prepares to claim his victory.

"How are things, captain?" he says, all smiles. "Sadly we'll be parting company soon. No hard feelings, okay?"

"Soon? Why do you say 'soon'?"

Vasseur is no fool—he has a warped sensibility; he's sharp; he has a sixth sense. He immediately knows what is coming. The proof being that he says nothing, simply goes pale, crosses his legs nervously. He waits. For a long moment Camille stares at him wordlessly. It's like a staring match where the first to look away loses. The telephone rings. Armand comes over, lifts the receiver, says, "Hello," listens, says, "Thank you," and hangs up again.

Camille, who has still not taken his eyes off Vasseur, says simply: "The magistrate has just granted our request to extend police detention by twenty-four hours, Monsieur Vasseur."

"I demand to see this magistrate!"

"I'm terribly sorry, Monsieur Vasseur, terribly sorry. Monsieur Vidard sends his regrets, but his workload means he cannot be with us. We'll just have to carry on together for a little while longer. No hard feelings, okay?"

Vasseur looks around wildly, determined to make an impression. He stifles a laugh; they're the ones he feels sorry for.

"And what are you going to do after that?" he says. "I don't know what you said to the magistrate to get this extension, what lies you told him, but whether it's now or twenty-four hours from now, you're going to have to let me go. You're . . ."

He gropes for a word.

"Pathetic."

He is taken back to the cell. They hardly question him anymore. They could try to wear him down, but Camille thinks it's better this way. Skeleton service. It'll be more effective. But doing nothing, or almost nothing, is very difficult. They all do their best to focus. They imagine the release, imagine Vasseur slipping on his jacket, knotting his tie; they picture the smile he'll give, the words he'll find, the farewell he's already rehearsing.

Armand manages to track down two new rookies, one on the second floor, one on the fourth. He stocks up on cigarettes and pens. It takes quite some time. But it keeps him busy.

Sometime in midmorning, there is a strange series of to-ings and fro-ings in which Camille tries to take Louis to one side to talk about the painting, but nothing seems to go as planned. Louis keeps being called away; Camille can feel the atmosphere between them become awkward. As he types up his reports, half an eye on the clock, he realizes that what Louis has done has royally screwed up their working relationship. Camille could say thank you, but so? He can pay Louis back, and then what? There is something paternalistic about Louis's gesture. The longer this drags on, the more Camille feels that this whole thing about the painting is Louis trying to teach him a lesson.

At about 3:00 p.m., they finally find themselves alone in the office. Camille doesn't stop to think. He says, "Thanks"—this is his first word.

"Thanks, Louis."

He needs to say something more; he can't just leave it at that.

"It—"

But he stops. From Louis's quizzical expression he realizes the enormity of his mistake. This whole deal with the painting—Louis has got nothing to do with it.

"Thanks for what?"

Camille ad-libs, "For everything, Louis. For your help . . . with all this."

"Sure," Louis says, astonished; they're not in the habit of saying things like this to each other.

Camille had hoped to come up with the right words, and he just did; he himself is surprised by this unexpected confession.

"This case, it's kind of my comeback. And I know I can be a difficult bastard to get along with, so . . ."

The presence of Louis, this mysterious young man he knows so well yet hardly knows at all, is suddenly powerfully moving, perhaps more so than the reappearance of the painting.

Vasseur has been brought up from his cell once more to corroborate a few details.

Camille goes to Le Guen's office, knocks, and goes straight in. It's clear from his expression that the divisionnaire is expecting bad news. Camille immediately raises a hand to reassure him. They discuss the case. They've each done what they needed to do. All they can do now is wait. Camille talks about the auction of his mother's paintings.

"How much did you say?" says a thunderstruck Le Guen.

Camille repeats the figure, one that he finds increasingly abstract. Le Guen looks impressed.

Camille doesn't mention the self-portrait. He's had time to think now, and he's worked it out. He'll call his mother's friend, the man who organized the auction: he must have made a tidy profit from the sale and clearly decided to thank Camille by giving him the painting. It's no big deal. Camille feels relieved.

He telephones, leaves a message, and heads down to his office.

The hours tick by.

Camille had decided to do it at 7:00 p.m., and the moment has come: it is seven o'clock. Vasseur shambles into the office, sits down, and stares fixedly at the clock on the wall. He is obviously exhausted; he has hardly slept in the past forty-eight hours, a fact that is starkly etched on his face.

61

"This thing is . . . ," Camille begins, "we have a number of little niggles about the death of your sister. Your half sister. Sorry."

Vasseur doesn't react. He struggles to work out what this means, but makes little headway—scarcely surprising given his exhaustion. He considers the possible meanings, the questions that might follow from it. He feels calmer. As far as Alex's death is concerned, he's got nothing to reproach himself for. His whole face says as much. He takes a deep breath, relaxes, silently folds his arms, glances again at the wall clock, and when he finally says something, it is completely unrelated.

"The detention period ends at eight o'clock, does it not?"

"I can see that you're not much bothered by Alex's death."

Vasseur stares at the ceiling as though searching for inspiration, as though in a restaurant someone had asked him to choose between two desserts. Embarrassed, he puckers his lips.

"I'm upset by it," he says at length. "Very upset, actually. You know how it is with families: blood is thicker than water. But what can you do? This is the thing with depressives."

"I'm not talking about the fact of her death, but the way she died."

Vasseur understands, he nods.

"Barbiturates, yeah, it's terrible. She told me she was having trouble sleeping, said without them she wouldn't sleep at all."

He hears the words as he says them; exhausted as he is, he has to struggle not to make some crude joke about her closed eyes. Eventually, he opts for an exaggeratedly concerned tone.

"That's the thing about medicines—they should be more tightly controlled, don't you think? Though I suppose she was a nurse, so she could get her hands on whatever she wanted."

Vasseur becomes suddenly thoughtful.

"I don't know what death from a barbiturate overdose is like . . . I assume it causes convulsions."

"Unless quickly intubated, victims slip into a coma," Camille says. "Protective respiratory reflexes are lost; they inhale vomit into the lungs and choke to death."

Vasseur gives a disgusted look. Ugh. He plainly thinks it lacks dignity.

Camille gives him an understanding look. Were it not that his fingers are trembling slightly, one might think he shares Vasseur's opinion. He leans back in his chair, takes a breath.

"If you don't mind, I'd like to go back to your visit to the hotel on the night of Alex's death. This was shortly after midnight, yes?"

"You've got witnesses—why don't you ask them?"

"We did ask them."

"And . . . ?"

"Twenty past twelve."

"Okay, then, let's say twelve twenty; it's all the same to me."

Vasseur settles himself in his chair. His frequent glances at the clock on the wall are plain to see.

"So," Camille goes on, "you slipped in behind our two witnesses, and they thought nothing odd about this. Just coincidence . . . another hotel guest who happened to arrive back at the same time. The witnesses say they last saw you waiting for the elevator. After that, they don't know what happened. Their room was on the ground floor. So, you take the elevator . . ."

"No."

"Really? But . . . ?"

"Where would I have been going?"

"That's precisely the question we've been asking ourselves, Monsieur Vasseur. Where exactly *were* you going?"

Vasseur frowns.

"Listen, Alex calls me, asks me to meet her, doesn't say why, and then she stands me up! I go to the hotel, but there's no one on reception—what am I supposed to do? Knock on two hundred doors and say, 'Excuse me, have you seen my sister?'"

"Your half sister!"

Vasseur grits his teeth, takes a breath, pretends he hasn't heard.

"So anyway, I'd been sitting waiting in my car for ages, and the hotel she called me from is two hundred yards away—anyone would have done what I did. I went there because I assumed there would be a list at reception, that I'd see her name marked somewhere. I don't know, do I? But when I got there, there was nothing. The reception area was locked up. I saw there was nothing I could do, so I went home. And that's it."

"You're saying you didn't think it through."

"Exactly, I didn't think it through properly."

Camille is uneasy; he shakes his head from left to right.

"What?" Vasseur says indignantly. "What difference does that make?"

The police officers do not move; they stare at him calmly.

His eyes drift back to the clock. Time is ticking. He smiles, at ease again.

"No difference," he says, sure of himself. "It makes no difference, does it? Except . . ."

"Yes?"

"Except that if I had found her, none of this would have happened."

"Meaning?"

He entwines his fingers as though hoping he's getting this right.

"I think I would have been able to save her."

"But unfortunately you didn't. And she died."

Vasseur spreads his hands, resigned. He smiles.

Camille focuses.

"Monsieur Vasseur," he says slowly, "I have to tell you that the pathologist has his doubts about Alex's suicide."

"Doubts?"

"Yes."

Camille allows this information to sink in.

"In fact, we believe that your sister was murdered and the murder made to look like suicide. Rather ham-handedly, in my opinion."

"What is this bullshit?" His whole body conveys surprise.

"First," Camille says, "Alex's behavior was not that of someone contemplating suicide."

"Her behavior . . . ?" Vasseur echoes, frowning.

"The ticket to Zurich, the suitcase neatly packed, the taxi ordered for the following morning. On their own these things wouldn't mean much, but we have other reasons to doubt that this was suicide. For example, her head was violently struck against the washbasin in the en-suite bathroom. Several times. The autopsy notes several injuries to the skull that clearly indicate several violent blows. We believe there was someone else with her. Someone who brutally beat her . . ."

"But . . . but who?"

"Well, to be frank, Monsieur Vasseur, we believe it was you."

Vasseur is on his feet, screaming, "*What?*"

"I would advise you to sit down."

It takes some time, but Vasseur sits down again, perches on the edge of his chair, ready to spring up again.

"This concerns your sister, Monsieur Vasseur, and I know how painful this is for you. But, without wishing to offend you by seeming to be overly pragmatic, I have to say that suicide victims choose a particular method. They throw themselves out of the window; they slit their wrists. Sometimes they mutilate themselves; sometimes they swallow pills. But they rarely do both."

"What has any of this got to do with me?"

It's obvious from the urgency of his voice that this has nothing to do with Alex anymore. His attitude veers from incredulity to indignation.

"How do you mean?"

"I said, what has this got to do with me?"

Camille looks over at Louis and Armand with the hopeless expression of someone who can't seem to make themselves understood, then he turns back to Vasseur.

"It has everything to do with you, because of your prints."

"Prints? What prints? What fu—"

The telephone rings, cutting him off, but he doesn't stop. As Camille answers, Vasseur turns to Armand and Louis.

"What fucking prints?"

In response, Louis gives him a puzzled look that says he doesn't know either; Armand doesn't even look up—he's otherwise occupied crumbling tobacco from three cigarette butts onto a flimsy scrap of paper to make a homemade cigarette.

Vasseur turns back to Camille, who is on the telephone, staring out of the window, listening intently to whoever is on the other end. Vasseur drinks in Camille's silence; the moment seems interminable. Eventually, Camille puts down the receiver, looks up at Vasseur—where were we again?

"What prints?" Vasseur says.

"Oh, yes . . . well, Alex's fingerprints, obviously," Camille says.

Vasseur gives a start.

"What about her fingerprints?"

It must be said that Camille can be difficult to follow.

"It was her room," Vasseur says, and laughs a little too loudly. "Finding her fingerprints there would be completely normal."

Camille applauds, clearly agreeing.

"Well, that's the thing." He stops clapping. "Her prints are largely missing."

Vasseur can tell that there's a question in here somewhere, but he doesn't know what it is. Camille, in a kindly tone, comes to his rescue.

"We found very few fingerprints from Alex in the room, you see . . . We believe that someone was trying to eliminate their own prints and, in doing so, wiped away Alex's. Not all, but most of them. Some are particularly significant. The door handle, for example. The handle someone who was there with Alex would have had to use . . ."

The penny drops. Vasseur doesn't know which way to turn.

"What I'm saying, Monsieur Vasseur, is that a person who commits suicide doesn't go around wiping away her own fingerprints; it makes no sense!"

Vasseur swallows hard, his mind a jumble of images and ideas.

"Consequently," Camille says, "we believe that there was someone in the room with Alex when she died."

He gives Vasseur time to digest this information; from the look on his face, it could be a while. Camille adopts a pedantic tone.

"From the point of view of fingerprints, the whisky bottle is another problem. Alex drank almost a pint of whisky. Alcohol potentiates the effects of barbiturates; it makes death a virtual certainty. The thing is, the bottle was carefully wiped clean of prints— there are fibers on it from a T-shirt we found on the sofa near the door. Even more curiously, what fingerprints of Alex's we did find are flattened as though someone forcibly pressed her fingers against the glass. Post mortem, probably. To make us think that she was holding the bottle. What do you have to say about that?"

"Wha . . . I don't have anything to say about it. I don't know anything about it."

"Oh, but you must know something about it, Monsieur Vasseur," Camille says, affronted, "given that you were in the room."

"Absolutely not. I was never in her room. I told you already, I went home."

Camille allows a brief moment of silence. As much as his height allows, he leans over Vasseur.

"If you weren't there," he says calmly, "how do you explain the fact that we found your fingerprints in Alex's room, Monsieur Vasseur?"

Vasseur is speechless. Camille sits back in his chair.

"It is because we found your prints in the room at the time of her death that we believe you murdered Alex."

A sound lodges somewhere between Vasseur's belly and his throat, a sound like a strangled yelp.

"That's impossible! I never set foot in that room! Where were these fingerprints?"

"On the bottle of barbiturates that killed your sister. You probably forgot to wipe it. Too panicked, I shouldn't wonder."

Vasseur's head waggles like a chicken's—he can't get his words out. Suddenly, he roars, "I've got it. I saw that bottle! Pink pills! I handled it! With Alex!"

The meaning is unclear. Camille knits his brows. Vasseur swallows, tries to explain things calmly, but the pressure, the fear is getting to him. He squeezes his eyes shut, balls his fists, takes a long, deep breath, and tries to focus.

Camille nods encouragingly, as though trying to help him to explain.

"When I saw Alex . . ."

"Yes."

". . . the last time . . ."

"When was that?"

"I don't remember. Three weeks ago, a month maybe."

"Okay."

"She showed me that bottle."

"Really? Where was this?"

"In a café near my work. Le Moderne."

"Very good, Monsieur Vasseur, why don't you tell us about it?"

He's breathing more easily now. A window has finally opened. Everything will be fine now. He'll explain; it's a perfectly simple explanation—they'll have to accept it. It's stupid, this whole thing about the medicine bottle. You can't build a case on something like that. He tries to take his time, but his throat closes up. He articulates every word.

"About a month ago. Alex asked to meet me."

"Did she want money?"

"No."

"Then what did she want?"

Vasseur doesn't know. In fact, she never told him why she wanted to see him—their meeting had ended abruptly. Alex had ordered a coffee, and he'd had a beer. And that was when she took out the bottle of pills. Vasseur had asked her what they were. Okay, he'll admit he was a little tetchy.

"Seeing her taking shit like that . . ."

"You obviously worried about your little sister's health."

Vasseur pretends not to hear the insinuation—he struggles to explain, wants this over with.

"I grabbed the bottle off her, held it in my hand. That's why it's got my fingerprints on it!"

What's surprising is that the detectives seem not to be convinced. They wait, hanging on his words, as though there must be something more, as though he hasn't finished.

"What was the name of the medication, Monsieur Vasseur?"

"I didn't look at the name! I opened the bottle, I saw some pink pills. I asked her what they were, that's all."

The detectives relax. This sheds a whole new light on the case.

"I see . . . ," Camille says. "I think I understand. It wasn't the same bottle. The pills Alex took were blue. Not pink."

"What does that matter?"

"It matters because it means it's probably not the same bottle."

"No, no, no!" Vasseur is agitated again, waving his finger in the air, stumbling over his words.

"It won't hold up, this thing, it won't hold up."

Camille gets to his feet.

"Let's recap, if you don't mind." He counts the points off on his fingers. "You have a strong motive. Alex was blackmailing you; she had already extorted twenty thousand euros and was probably planning to ask for a lot more so she could survive abroad. You have no alibi: you lied to your wife about the call you received. You claimed you went to an address where no one saw you. Later you admitted that you went to see Alex at her hotel, something that can be confirmed by two witnesses."

Camille lets Vasseur grasp the scale of the problem.

"None of that is evidence!"

"It already gives us motive, no alibi, your presence at the scene of the crime. If we add to that the fact that Alex suffered serious blows to the head, that her fingerprints were wiped away while yours were found at the scene, it begins to sound like rather a lot—"

"No, no, no . . . it won't be enough!"

But however much he shakes his finger, there's clearly a question lurking behind this statement. This is perhaps what prompts Camille to add: "We also found your DNA at the scene, Monsieur Vasseur."

Vasseur is utterly dumbfounded.

"A hair found on the floor next to Alex's bed. You tried to get rid of all traces of your presence, but the cleanup wasn't good enough."

Camille stands in front of the man.

"So, Monsieur Vasseur, now that we've got your DNA, do you think that will be enough?"

Until now, Thomas Vasseur has been very impulsive. This statement by Commandant Verhœven should have him bounding to his feet. But he doesn't move. The men stare at him, unsure how to react since Vasseur is totally withdrawn; he's thinking hard, oblivious to the interview—he's no longer in the room. Elbows propped on his knees, he keeps touching his fingertips together in a jerky movement, as though faintly applauding. He is staring at the floor, his foot tapping nervously. They are almost concerned about his mental state. Then suddenly he jumps up, stares at Camille, stands stock still.

"She did it on purpose . . ."

He sounds as though he's talking to himself, but in fact he is addressing them.

"She set the whole thing up to frame me . . . That's it, isn't it?"

He has come down to earth with a bump. His voice quavers with emotion. Under normal circumstances, the police should seem surprised by such an allegation, but not these ones. Louis is methodically reorganizing the case file; Armand is meticulously cleaning his nails with a paperclip. Only Camille is still party to the conversation, but having nothing to contribute, he folds his arms and waits.

"I hit Alex . . . ," Vasseur says.

His voice is toneless. He is staring at Camille, but it's as though he's talking to himself.

"In the café. When I saw she was taking pills, I was angry. She tried to calm me down, she ran her fingers through my hair, but her ring got snagged . . . When she pulled it away, it hurt. There were hairs stuck in it. I slapped her—it was a knee-jerk reaction. My hair . . ."

Vasseur emerges from his daze.

"She had it all planned from the start, didn't she?"

He looks around for help, finds none: Armand, Louis, Camille simply stare at him.

"The whole thing is a frame-up, pure and simple, and you know it! Everything—the ticket for Zurich, the new suitcase, the taxi she ordered . . . it was all to make you think she was making her get-away. That she had no intention of killing herself. She arranges to meet up with me somewhere I won't be seen, she bangs her head against the washbasin, she wipes away her fingerprints, leaves the pill bottle with my prints, drops one of my hairs on the floor . . ."

"I'm afraid that might be rather hard to prove. As far as we're concerned, you were there, you wanted to get rid of Alex, you hit her, you forced her to drink the whisky and swallow the pills. Your fingerprints and your DNA support our case."

There is silence for a moment.

"I've got good news and bad news. The good news is that the custody period is over. The bad news is you're under arrest for murder."

Camille smiles. Vasseur, slumped in his chair, manages to raise his head.

"It wasn't me! You know she did this, don't you? You know that!"

This time he is speaking directly to Camille.

"You know it wasn't me."

"You've displayed quite a fondness for black humor, Monsieur Vasseur." Camille is still smiling. "So I feel I can allow myself a little witticism of my own. I'd say this time it was Alex who screwed you."

At the far end of the office, Armand, who's just tucked his hand-rolled cigarette behind his ear, is just going out of the door as two uniformed officers are coming in.

"I'm sorry to have kept you in custody for so long, Monsieur Vasseur," Camille says apologetically. "I realize two days is a long time. But we needed the DNA tests, and the forensics lab is snowed under. These days, two days is the minimum."

62

For some inexplicable reason, what triggers the epiphany is Armand's cigarette. Maybe because of the hardship implied by a cigarette rolled from old butts. Camille is so dumbfounded by the realization, he stops dead. He does not for a moment doubt it—something that is also impossible to explain—he simply knows.

Louis walks down the corridor; behind him is Armand, shoulders permanently hunched, dragging his heels, wearing the same clean but shabby worn-out shoes.

Camille pops back into his office and scribbles a check for eighteen thousand euros. His hand is shaking. Then he picks up his files and darts back out into the corridor. He feels overcome, but there will be time later to consider what this gesture means. He is soon standing in front of Armand's desk. He sets the check down in front of him.

"It was a kind gesture, Armand. I'm really touched."

Armand's mouth forms an O, dropping the toothpick he's been chewing.

"No, please, Camille." He sounds almost offended. "A present, it's a present."

Camille smiles. Nods, hopping from one foot to the other. He rummages in his briefcase, takes out the framed photograph of the painting and proffers it. Armand takes it.

"Oh, that's so sweet, Camille. That's really kind."

He is genuinely happy.

Le Guen is standing on the flight of steps, two steps below Camille. The weather has turned cold again, and it's late; it's like a winter night come early.

"Good work, gentlemen," the magistrate says, shaking the divisionnaire's hand. He takes a step down and holds his hand out to Camille.

"Commandant . . ."

Camille shakes his hand.

"Vasseur will probably claim this is a conspiracy, a frame-up, Your Honor. He insists he's going to 'demand the truth.'"

"Yes, I heard something of the sort," Vidard says.

For a moment he seems preoccupied by this thought, then he shakes it off.

"Oh, the truth, the truth . . . Who's to say what's true and what isn't, commandant? As far as we're concerned, what's important is not truth, it's justice—right?"

Camille smiles and gives him a nod.

A NOTE ON THE TRANSLATION

The judicial system in France is fundamentally different from that of the United States. Rather than the adversarial system, where police investigate and the role of the courts is to act as an impartial referee between prosecution and defense, in the French inquisitorial system, the judiciary works with the police on the investigation, appointing an independent *juge d'instruction* (investigating judge, or magistrate) entitled to question witnesses, interrogate suspects, and manage all aspects of the police investigation. If there is sufficient evidence, the case is referred to the *procureur*, the public prosecutor, who decides whether to bring charges. The *juge d'instruction* plays no role in the eventual trial and is prohibited from adjudicating future cases involving the same defendant.

The French have two national police forces: the *police nationale* (formerly called the *sûreté*), a civilian police force with jurisdiction in cities and large urban areas, and the *gendarmerie nationale*, a branch of the French Armed Forces, responsible both for public safety and for policing towns with populations of fewer than twenty thousand. Since the *gendarmerie* rarely has the resources to conduct complex investigations, the *police nationale* maintains regional criminal investigations services (*police judiciaire*) analogous to American local police crime scene investigation units and also oversees armed response units (RAIDs).

GLOSSARY

BRIGADE CRIMINELLE—combines elements of the American homicide division and major crimes unit, responsible for investigating murders, kidnappings, and assassinations

BRIGADIER (GENDARMERIE)—a rank roughly equivalent to sergeant

COMMANDANT—chief of detectives

COMMISSAIRE DIVISIONNAIRE—police chief; the divisionnaire has both administrative and investigative roles

IDENTITÉ JUDICIARE—forensics department of the *police nationale*

JUGE D'INSTRUCTION—the "investigating judge," sometimes addressed as *monsieur le juge*; responsible for determining if a case should go to trial, a role somewhat similar to that of an American district attorney

MARÉCHAL DES LOGIS CHEF (GENDARMERIE)—a rank roughly equivalent to staff sergeant

LE PARQUET—public prosecutor's office

PÉRIPHÉRIQUE—inner ring road circumscribing central Paris, linking the old city gates, or *portes*—e.g., Porte d'Italie, Porte d'Orléans

PROCUREUR—public prosecutor, sometimes addressed as *magistrat*, as one might say "sir," or "your honor"

RAID (RECHERCHE, ASSISTANCE, INTERVENTION, DISSUASION)—a special operations tactical unit of the French *police nationale*, similar to an American SWAT team

ACKNOWLEDGMENTS

Thanks to Samuel for his unstinting kindness, to Gérald for his invariably knowledgeable rereading, to Joëlle for her advice on medical matters, and to Cathy, my affectionate sponsor. To all the team at Albin Michel.

Last, but not least, to Pascaline.

As ever, I owe much to many other writers.

My sincere thanks to—in alphabetical order—Louis Aragon, Marcel Aymé, Roland Barthes, Pierre Bost, Fyodor Dostoevsky, Cynthia Fleury, John Harvey, Antonio Muñoz Molina, Boris Pasternak, Maurice Pons, Marcel Proust, and others for borrowing slightly here and there.